Against Ourselves

JONATHAN CLIFFORD-KING has possessed a burning passion for writing from a very young age. At the age of just 13, he wrote Against Ourselves, his first full-length novel.

He lives in Buckinghamshire.

Against Ourselves

Jonathan Clifford-King

For all of those who have ever inspired or encouraged me in any shape or form

To Davenies,

Thank you for all your support.

Jonathan Clifford-King

Part I

Chapter 1

It had started badly even before it had begun. When the concept of the project was still a mere seedling of an idea, there had been complications. The blueprints and the top-secret files had been snatched away by a rival company who also wanted to develop this idea first. The race was on.

One organisation was small while the other was impossibly powerful and influential. The smaller organisation, the underdog, realised that their chances of defeating their nemesis were practically zero.

Yet, it was the less powerful association, which was called Alphasis, which came out on top. Why this was, is still a mystery to this very day. But anyway, some people had decided to give their support – and funds – to the Project, eventually completely reforming the organisation, until it had changed beyond recognition. All the contributors wanted to make history and a lot of them desired money through their investments. Yet, the basic principle survived and just two years ago Alphasis beat their rivals to the prize, making way for what could potentially be a leap in the history of man.

The rival company however had been wiped out of the picture. Apparently, it had been so distraught at their epic failure; they'd simply just shut down their company and the universe moved on. Or so the legend went.

Meanwhile for Alphasis, the job was only half done. The Project still had to actually be finished. But confidential projects like this one, can take a while to complete and it wasn't until twenty-three months later, the preparation would be completed. A little more paperwork and a couple of weeks afterwards, the Project was finally launched. All of which was top secret, in red capital letters that was double underlined. Metaphorically speaking, of course.

And that was exactly why Captain Jennifer Smart was aboard the *Dark Light 5000.* She had all the good qualities that a captain would need and she had been specially selected for the Project. She was just one of the three hundred and four people aboard the *Dark Light 5000.* Jennifer was the leader and captain of these people. In many ways, she was the big cheese but in many others, she was just a puppet having her strings pulled by the puppeteer hunched over a computer, back on Planet Earth.

In many a difficult and desperate situation, she had proven to be brave and trustworthy. She was good at leadership and so far had managed to resist the urge to pick a favourite crewmember. One of her few flaws was undoubtedly that she was too loyal to her friends and that would most probably be her downfall.

In fiction, sometimes a character is seriously injured in hot pursuit, and wishes for their companion to go on and leave them. But the companion knows that if they leave their friend behind, their chasers will almost certainly kill that character or at least cause them a great deal of pain. This is a great dilemma and if Jennifer was in that situation, she would stay by her companion's side in a heartbeat. But one question that she never wondered about was this: would the friend do the same for her?

Jennifer was fairly young and was five foot three, a little smaller than your average person. But that did not mean she should be underestimated...

She had long shoulder-length black hair and chocolate brown eyes which were a bit like the sea: sometimes they were calm and friendly, but sometimes they were deadly and fiery, that made most people keep their distance.

Her leather gravity boots kept her firmly on the ground of the ship so she didn't go floating off. She was dressed in a uniform, which looked very similar to a white jumpsuit. The clothing and the gravity boots fitted her perfectly as they shrink until they detect a solid object. Her slim frame, her agile movements and her catlike stance that made her look more like a gymnast rather than a captain, was brought out well by her uniform.

Jennifer was Captain aboard the *Dark Light 5000*. The *Dark Light 5000* was a spaceship crammed full of cutting edge technology such as the oxygen converters, which made all air aboard perfectly breathable. It was a colossal ship, being 400 metres long, 200 metres high, and 100 metres wide. The *Dark Light 5000* was full of plenty of rooms and facilities including a canteen, many places to sleep, offices, communication rooms, panic rooms, the main control room and much much more. The ship had over a dozen entrances and exits and housed a powerful computing system, a strange android, an extraordinary but flawed crew and the beginning of the Project...

Enough of the present, Jennifer thought, because right now she had just plunged back in the past in which she was immersed.

If she could go back in time to when she was still living in Room 3010, Block E, Tower 9 and tell her younger self that in twelve years time she would lead humanity's first trip to a planet in the Solar System that had only been discovered shortly before that, her younger self would refuse to believe it. Throw in the fact that a big project that was being launched there at that time, which could change mankind forever, the younger Jennifer would be overwhelmed and possibly ecstatic.

Jennifer could still remember sitting on her dad's lap at the age of seven, watching the old footage of the Mars landing, on the family 360 surround 3D virtual world machine. She remembered watching with amazement as the first man emerged from a battered space shuttle, stepped foot on the ground and said those famous historic words. There was always going to be a historic phrase, just as there had been on the Moon. The same had been applied when humans had reached the asteroid belt. That incident had happened more recently and Jennifer had seen it when it was live on air.

That was what had inspired her as a child – those three landings, but the Mars one in particular. Before that, she had wanted to be a chef, a businesswoman, or a historian. The day that Jennifer saw the Mars landing, she knew instantly that 'an astronaut' was to be her future occupation. As she got older, she never once considered the idea of giving up hope.

Jennifer had kept that promise for the rest of her life.

Even when she'd been short of money, lived in the tiny flat of Block E, Tower 9 and even when there was the global economic crash, Jennifer still believed that her dream would happen. And it turned out, she was right.

Her current thoughts were interrupted and she was forced to no longer dwell on the past, but to focus on the current predicament instead which was the present.

Ping!

The sound echoed through Jennifer's invisible earpiece. Her sauntering pace quickened. She had gotten a message from the one of the brains making the scientific side of the Project, work.

Doctor Simon Brust was a highly intelligent man. At the age of 67, he was middle aged but he was still very fit. He was a famous man and had been described as 'one of the greatest scientists of the 21st century'. He had been around for as long as Jennifer could remember. Brust was of course, a genius. He had been born many decades ago, back in the year 2003. The year now was 2071. When he reached the age of one, he was an inquisitive infant and begun to ask questions about the world. Nine years later, he could have easily taken his Biology A level and passed with an A*. At twelve years of age, he had a vast knowledge in the area of biology and a bit of chemistry. Brust had written an extremely long eBook using his knowledge that was both large and profound. When he became a teenager, he had started making interesting, enthralling, and captivating inventions. By the time he was seventeen; Brust had graduated at a good university, with several degrees and had become a doctor of philosophy and a certain field of biology. As a youth, Brust had been undoubtedly a child prodigy.

As an adult, his intelligence and brilliance only expanded further. The scientist had evidently been destined for great things. He'd been a Professor for a brief period during of which he had taught at numerous universities. He wrote books and scientific papers, conceived theorems, disproved certain concepts, created new inventions, conducted experiments and, in more recent times, had been heavily involved with the Project.

His hobbies included an old fashioned game called chess, of which he was very fond and ardent.

Anyway, now he had trouble right on his doorstep.

Jennifer hadn't heard what Brust had said over the state-of-the-art communication device. A three dimensional life-like hologram of Brust suddenly flickered and appeared before her eyes. It was almost as if Brust was actually standing there.

"What is it this time?" sighed Jennifer deeply.

The designer of the *Dark Light 5000* replied in a worried tone.

"There's a problem-" Brust began but was soon interrupted by a burst of static.

But what exactly the problem was, Jennifer didn't find out. The uncertainty was what caused Jennifer's heart to race and thump hard against her ribcage. What had gone wrong?

Here we go again Jennifer thought, *on yet another adventure.*

14

Until the recent event, Jennifer had been thinking about memories whilst slowly ambling along a corridor.

The corridor was completely white with blue shining lights running along the bottom of the walls. Bright holograms danced on the wall completing the scenery.

Jennifer started to run along the long corridor.

"Hurry up, Miss Smart." said Doctor Brust through the device. That was another thing about Brust; he nearly always called Jennifer, Miss Smart.

"I am coming!" she snapped, hurtling toward a door.

The Captain skidded to a stop at the end of the corridor where there were two white double doors. She waved her hand in a gesture for the doors to open.

A white drawer shot out near the side of the door. In it was a small white helmet with blue lights on it that winked and flashed in a rhythmic pattern.

Jennifer placed the helmet on her head and almost the moment it touched her head, it was off again. Jennifer let the helmet drop onto the floor, where it lay cast aside. Security systems now used synthetic technology, which could read brainwaves. Synthetic technology could still only do basic things, as it was, after all, still early days.

Jennifer had thought of her password in the moment the helmet touched her head.

When Jennifer had discarded the helmet, five things then happened in less than a second. First of all, the helmet that had been dropped onto the floor flew back into the hole in the wall. The drawer then shut by itself.

The password thought or the brainwave that was sent to the computer unit was part of the ship's computer system. Every brain emitted brainwaves slightly differently, so the computer unit analysed the two parts of the brainwave: the password and the person who was sending it.

The computer recognised Jennifer. There were two lights above the double doors. The first light on the left had been shining red while the other had been off. Now the computer recognised Jennifer, the left light turned off and the right turned on but was shining green.

The final thing was that the doors swished open.

"If the doors don't open, put the thinking hat on." Jennifer murmured to herself, before sprinting through the doorway.

Jennifer found herself, standing on the platform of a tunnel with a railing round along the middle of the floor. It looked a little like an early twenty first century London tube tunnel.

Something black whizzed past and stopped right in front of Jennifer. It was a PRT, short for Personal Rapid Transport. It was a black pod car type thing that went by the nickname of 'Bubble Car'. The doors slid back neatly and swiftly. It was a welcoming atmosphere, ushering Jennifer in. Jennifer hopped in, accepting its invitation.

The Bubble Car was a cross between a ski gondola and a smart car. Just like the exterior, the inside was black, acquiring an air of sleekness. There was one eternal ring of black seating, which Jennifer promptly sat on. A safety belt fastened her in, perhaps a little too tightly. A holo-screen and a holo-keypad popped up, ready at Jennifer's disposal.

"Hello, Captain Smart. Please state your command." said a soothing feminine computer voice, which echoed through the pod.

"Escort me to Brust's current location." Jennifer demanded sharply. Her patience was running out rapidly. As was time.

The holo-screen flickered and a three dimensional map of the *Dark Light 500*'s interior replaced the blank screen. A blue dot told Jennifer where she was and a red told her where Brust was.

"Would you like me to proceed with your order?" the computer asked. "Are you sure?"

"Of course, I'm sure!" Jennifer snapped as she wondered if time was running out as fast as her patience. "And go at top speed!"

The doors hissed shut.

"Your wish is my command." the computer said, who must have stolen the corny phrase off either one of the crewmembers or a bad film.

But Jennifer didn't care about that, as the little pod whizzed toward its destination. It shot forward at such a velocity that it made Jennifer jolt backwards into her seat. Already Jennifer was seriously regretting her previous demand.

In less than a minute, the Bubble Car had arrived at Brust's whereabouts.

The doors slid open and Jennifer leapt out, ignoring whatever comment the female voice made. The voice

17

decreased in volume as the pod sped off, until it was nothing more.

Jennifer had leapt from the pod meaning that she had gotten off to a fast start. It was not just the momentum from the jump that drove her forwards, but determination, worry, loyalty and that feeling that Jennifer had only felt a couple of times in her life: *fear*. Yet that factor was what ultimately made her race to the rescue of her friends.

Jennifer bolted along the long white corridor, her speed rising by the millisecond. Her sinewy muscles were all fired up; ready for whatever lay beyond those white double doors, which got bigger with every step she took.

Jennifer was just about to burst into the room, but something held her back. A single thought slowed her down, before she eventually drew to a sudden halt.

Of course. Of course. Jennifer was acting before thinking. It was not something that she did often, but the Captain was in that kind of mood.

She stared up at the door and took a deep breath. Slowly but surely, the doors slid open at about the speed of lift doors. When the gap was big enough, Jennifer squeezed through and rushed into the room.

She stopped.

Jennifer sighed heavily in relief, the air puffing up her cheeks and scraping on her throat.

There were three other people, not including Jennifer. Brust was standing there, barking instructions, which were obviously being promptly ignored. Brust was angry and it usually took a lot to get him angry.

Brust was tall and thin wearing a white lab coat stained with chemicals, over his crumpled untidy suit, which had a neat but askew bowtie. He had no beard or moustache like most people would expect, but that was just part of a stereotypical vision of scientists. His brilliant blue eyes which normally were full of warmth, shone with anger through a pair of full-moon silver spectacles making Brust look extremely intelligent. Which he was.

On his head, he had a great shock of thick grey hair that was unkempt, looking as though he had been dragged through a hedge backwards. His face that was speckled with the occasional freckle usually had a great smile on it. However at the moment, it was twisted into a fierce scowl.

He was 67, but looked about forty or fifty due to anti-ageing technology. The oldest person in the world was 144, so Brust wasn't that old in comparison. Besides old people could do a lot more nowadays, not like they used to, when they were permanently compelled to an armchair.

Brust could have looked even younger but Brust wanted to remind himself that he was still getting old, even though it was nice to take a few years off.

Brust was the man behind the science of the Project. He was an eccentric, quirky man, but that didn't stop him from being a nice person. However when the wacky boffin within surfaced as it often did, Brust had a habit of singling out people and making them feel small and stupid without meaning to or even realising it as he was absorbed and immersed in his work. This mostly happened when Brust was giving a scientific explanation or demonstration. He would then have to calm down, simplify his complexity, and bring it down to a level that most people would be able to understand.

There was another person in the room.

Bill Sudilav was quite a different character to Brust. Sudilav was actually pronounced Sud-de-lav. Sudilav was the big macho man aboard the *Dark Light 5000.* He was a monster in size, towering above everyone. The military commander had powerful robust shoulders, big muscles the size of small melons and bulging, massive biceps. He was well built, bulky, athletic, and muscular.

His navy uniform had a large collection of armoury even though Sudilav could probably take on a whole army without it. He had two QuickFire Handguns, six sonic grenades, a strap of grenades, a buzz baton, a large collection of ShockBlades and his very favourite, and trusty Boom Blaster. And still Sudilav moaned and complained about not having enough weaponry.

Sudilav had short dark hair and sharp green eyes that showed no mercy. He would have been quite handsome if he didn't have a long curving scar running down one side on his face.

But there was more to Sudilav than what met the eye – or the stomach if he punched someone. At a glance, Sudilav looked like a brave, tough soldier. Someone who was a hunk of muscle – the ultimate killing machine but was dim-witted and had the brainpower equivalent to that of an insect. A person who solved problems with fists or a gun, but never grey matter.

The stereotype of the current soldiers was that they were stupid. Sudilav was an exception and far from it. He actually had a rather large brain. It was just a shame that he barely used it.

There was more though. If you looked deep into Sudilav's eyes, you might just be able spot the geek within him, imprisoned for all eternity never to surface ever again.

If you listen very carefully then you might just hear a little girlish voice at the attic of Sudilav's mind, speaking in little more than a whisper. *Why don't you just run away from all this violent chaos? Why not become a better, nicer person?* It was a voice that Sudilav never ever paused to listen to. It was like someone who had locked their dog in the kennel as a punishment and promptly forgot about their canine friend for a long time.

But if you observe and analyse further, you might just catch that soft inkling in the exact centre of Sudilav's iris. It was at a minuscule level – practically invisible. It was a little speckle of guilt that had been hidden away. The speckle may be small, but it symbolised a lot of guilt. Sudilav may be a brave and excellent soldier, but he was also a haunted man.

At the moment, Sudilav was only half listening to Brust's rant and raves. His eyes analysed every move of his opponent. When conflict arose, Sudilav no longer was a man, but a mean fighting machine, calculating and fighting. When conflict arose, Sudilav was no longer was man, but a lethal weapon.

Anyway, it was a known fact that Sudilav hated the ship's robot, Andy who was the third other character in the room. Andy was short for Android. It was a nickname that someone had started calling him and now it had stuck like a bad joke.

Sudilav would look for any reason to stir up trouble for Andy in anyway. No one was quite sure why, not even Sudilav himself. But the reason why Sudilav had taken an immediate dislike to Andy was probably because machines may one day replace soldiers like him.

Andy, on the outside, looked slightly human. He had a human appearance, but would only have been mistaken for a human if in poor light conditions. He was about average height, perhaps slightly taller. Andy had light brown hair and wore a drab grey jumpsuit. The skinny robot had a long, thin face. His skin looked unreal too, in such a way it couldn't be understood why.

Yet what immediately made you realise that Andy was a robot not a human, boiled down to several things. First of all, Andy constantly had a blank expression upon his face, enquiring the look of a lost sheep, who one day had wondered beyond the farm. Andy's eyes were a cold steel emotionless grey. Also the way, Andy moved was slow and stiff, making it all look completely unnatural. Finally the way, Andy talked was the way you'd expect. He spoke in a formal tone in a way that was very similar to how computer code is written. Andy behaved in an inhuman way and he still was puzzling over what humour was.

That was another thing about Andy. His body was not that of flesh, blood, and bone, but of artificially grown skin, wires, and hardware.

It was a good thing that you could tell the differences between an android and a human. Perhaps these differences were programmed or maybe it was just robots were very different to humans. Either way by purpose or by accident, machines were distinguishable from man.

At present, Andy just stood there, remaining as still as a statue fixed into place. His eyes were the only things that moved, running over his surroundings triggering strings of data and binary to flash through his mind.

Sudilav saw his chance to attack and in a flash had drawn a ShockKnife. A ShockKnife looked like a normal knife, but at the touch of button, the edge had energy crackling around it. Sudilav fired it up and lunged, the blade about to slice the robot's head.

Andy took another blow and more wires and circuit trailed out of his head. All this stabbing was not good for his circuits. Or for anything, for that matter.

The room was already in a mess. Then Andy went haywire once more, drowning out the cries of Brust.

Andy smashed another panel of machinery. They fizzed and died. Andy's hand slid up his arm and out of sight. A gun popped out where the hand had been. It fired a short burst of electro-bullets at a security camera. Sparks scintillated into existence and dispersed into the air.

Sudilav wanted to finish off his long-time rival, once and for all.

But Jennifer, who had been watching this scene of mayhem, took this pause as her cue. She was small, light, and nimble. As fast as sound, Jennifer scrambled forward and shoved Andy towards Sudilav. Andy automatically shot Sudilav with a knock out dart. But Sudilav flared up his blade.

The dart sunk into Sudilav's neck but the effect was far too slow. Sudilav lunged but Andy blocked it. But just a second before he passed out, Sudilav stabbed Andy in the chest. Then he slumped onto the white floor, which was now littered with junk.

Andy was better off than Sudilav. Andy had quickly worked out the ShockKnife had tried to blow his circuits. He shut down in order to save himself, so that while he slept, his technology set about fixing the damage.

Brust stared at Jennifer and his rants halted abruptly.

"WHAT THE BLAZES WERE YOU THINKING, MISS SMART? YOU COULD HAVE KILLED OUR MILITARY COMMANDER AND DESTROYED OUR ANDROID." Brust roared angrily, but then quickly reminded himself he was talking to his Captain thus adopting a kinder tone and a smile. "What were your reasons to ignore such risks? Logic predicted your chances of success were highly improbable."

Jennifer's eyes hardened her face like thunder. She barked, even more loudly than Brust: "I DO NOT TOLERATE SUCH CHEEK AND DISREPECT. I'M YOUR CAPTAIN. REMEMBER?"

"I'm sorry." Brust's smile faltered, his eyes falling upon his shoes.

"SORRY IS NOT GOOD ENOUGH."

"I said, I'm sorry. What else can I say?" Brust asked, his gaze fixing on Jennifer, his arms raised in a shrug.

Jennifer ignored him. "I THINK I DESERVE A LITTLE RESPECT, YES?"

"Yes. Sorry." Brust mumbled.

"And stop saying 'sorry'." Jennifer strained her voice and brought it under control.

"Sorry." Brust replied automatically before catching himself before he could speak any further.

"Is that clear?" Jennifer hollered, her voice rising with every syllable.

Brust nodded, looking past Jennifer's shoulder, his mind obviously back on other things.

Jennifer took a deep breath. "I apologise for blowing my fuse, but I make a good point. Anyway, please can you repeat your question?"

The faraway feel to Brust's eyes of the deepest blue vanished in a twinkle and his head swivelled to face her.

"Uh?" he said blankly, as though he were a teenager aroused from a stupidly long slumber waking up almost as slow as it took Andy to get a joke – an event that was yet to happen

Jennifer tilted her head slightly, wondering what went on under Brust's substantial amounts of scruffy grey hair.

"Can you tell me your question which should be the answer to my question that was asked earlier about what the question you shouted?" Jennifer stumbled over her own words, before deciding to inquire quite simply: "Your question?"

Brust stretched his bowtie, which made a *ping* sound as he let go. "Yes, right. It is simply thus: why charge in when you could have caused harm to yourself, to our android and to our military commander?"

"I knew the risks I was taking. I knew Andy would knock out Sudilav in defence, as he is programmed not to kill but he can defend his own existence. Besides, if Sudilav would stab Andy, he would shut down in event of blowing up."

"Still that's not the point."

"OK, imagine, it's an equation. In some equations in order to simplify things you eliminate each side to make everything nice and easy."

"Oh, I see." Brust said, not looking entirely convinced. In fact, he looked like he'd just been told that Planet Earth was actually flat after all.

Jennifer smiled sweetly and headed back to the double doors. She was tired and hadn't slept in the last thirty hours.

Welcome to a day in the life of the Commander on aboard the *Dark Light 5000*, Jennifer thought to herself, as she passed into a white corridor.

Chapter 2

The next morning, Brust woke up slightly later than he would usually wake up. As he drifted into the real world, the awakening device fired up. It detected he was awake. A spray was squirted in his face, the drug waking him up. Brust rubbed his eyes and gave a yawn before stretching his arms out wide.

He was in a sleep capsule that was like a giant white spectacles container. Brust jabbed a button at a nearby control pad and the lid swung open.

Brust stepped out, his gravity boots wrenching him firmly to the ground.

He passed Tuft, Sudilav's foot soldier, and deputy on his way to breakfast. He was a muscleman like Sudilav. His recent haircut had shaved his hair. This had accomplished two things: Tuft had lost his blonde hair and he looked even more stupid than usual. His mouth was always slightly ajar, forming into a gormless gape, which made him look like the clueless idiot that he was.

Tuft was dressed in camouflaged combat uniform, which was all he ever really wore. A large arsenal of weapons always hung at his belt that jangled and clanged. He was about the same height as Sudilav, maybe a shade shorter. His huge muscles and abs bulged from under his uniform. They were not quite vast as Sudilav's but somehow Tuft was equally intimidating. His eyes were bloodshot but for all eternity they contained that merciless blank cold look, the way a crocodile might look before swallowing up a poor unsuspecting fish. The menace in his eyes seemed to trickle and seep into the outer atmosphere, quenching and crushing any other emotion aura.

Brust shivered and shrank by several inches, feeling very small. In his original form, he was taller than Tuft, but felt the need to change that. His cheerful smile was dropped and his lips were drawn into a quivering line. The scientist was feeling very small inside too.

"Morning." Brust trilled, his voice was a shrill and high pitched, sounding very unlike his usual voice.

Tuft jerked his head sharply to look in Brust's direction. Brust gulped. The top corners of Tuft's lips itched slightly upwards. Tuft gazed into Brust's eyes with predatory amusement as though he was about to rip Brust's head off. Brust couldn't bring himself to tear his eyes away, so his own eyes were locked in position, fear creeping into them.

This staring match only lasted a few moments, but to Brust it felt like hours. Finally, the spell was broken and snapped like a twig.

"Hello." Brust squealed, in hope of being left alone.

But his hope was in vain. Tuft slid a knife from its sheath, hurling it at Brust's nose. At the last possible moment, it curved in an arc, skimming past Brust's eye. It sunk into a white wall where it stayed until Tuft snapped his gloved fingers. The knife flew out of the wall, spinning. Brust ducked just in time as it zipped over him. Tuft reached out and caught the handle, before slotting it back into his belt. Brust supposed it was Tuft's way of morning greeting.

Cries of "You moron!" "What were you thinking?" "Show-off!" and many more besides filled Brust's head. In the end, he picked one and spoke in a tone as discreet as he could muster.

"I'm sure 'Health and Safety' will have something to say on that!" Brust said, his voice once again his own.

Tuft glanced at Brust briefly, ignoring his remark. Brust looked over one of Tuft's massive shoulder and looked longingly at the white double doors, which led to the breakfast that would only be open until 9 o'clock GMT.

"See you later." Brust said, patting Tuft's shaven head as Tuft marched off.

Tuft may be a useful soldier, but you couldn't hide from the fact that he wasn't a nice person. He was not the kind of guy you would want to meet on a dark night – or in broad daylight for that matter. But he was good at his job and reluctantly the rest of the crew would just have to somehow manage to put up with him.

As Brust approached the canteen, a question was quickly asked within his head. Why does Tuft wear leather gloves all the time, even in the summer? But the question soon vanished from his mind as quickly as it had come. Brust peered through a window and was glad to see that breakfast was available.

The doors whooshed open and Brust stepped into the canteen.

"Good morning!" he said merrily, waking up the grotty, grumpy hundreds of crewmembers who sat there, eating artificially grown cereal which was now mostly soggy.

But Brust was talking to the ship's computer, Arti short for Artificial Intelligence. He was more advanced than Andy, who was in fact his son. After an engineer had created Andy, Arti had picked randomly some of his 'personality' and put it into a software system, which he uploaded to Andy's silicon chip thus creating the Andy the crew knew today.

"Good morning, Mr Simon Brust. How may I assist you?" replied the computer flatly.

"Just call me Mr Brust."

"Good morning, Mr Brust. How may I help you?"

"I'd like some breakfast, please."

"Thank you, request granted. Please make your way to the food machine. Any more requests?"

"No, that's fine, thanks."

Brust walked over to a small white machine, which looked like a machine he could remember from childhood. It had been called a printer, yet this gadget seemed to be missing the paper slot. You could probably find a printer in a museum nowadays!

That made Brust feel old, even though the oldest human being was far older than he was, thanks to the breakthroughs in medical science over the last few decades. Brust felt like an incredibly tall and intelligent child, who had embarked on an adventure jam-packed with science. To him, science was a playground. And it was all his to play with. Even though Brust had grown up physically, he had never grown up mentally. He was really just a big kid.

He thought back to when he was a child both mentally and physically, many decades ago; the beginning of the twenty-first century. It seemed like ancient history, yet at the same time, felt like only yesterday.

The memories were so clear, so fresh, so vivid, so real. When Brust thought back, it was as if he had travelled back in time and was standing once more in the world of the past.

Yet Brust sometimes felt as though he had stolen memories of another person's life and intruded through them. Someone who had lived in the dawn of the 21st century. Technology to do this probably wasn't far off.

In sense, he was peering through those moments. The memories of young Simon Brust.

Yes, Brust had been different back in his childhood. But then hadn't most people?

But he was the same person at the end of the day. Perhaps lots had changed, but most of what made him Brust, had remained.

A hand instantly flew to his full-moon silver spectacles. He had always had this type of glasses for as long as he could remember. His father used to joke that Brust had been born wearing glasses.

That world of the past was so different too now. Quite recently, Brust had been told that someone had recently sold an antique smartphone for quite a bit of money. What had once been regarded 'state-of-the-art' was now classed as 'Stone Age machinery'.

But life had moved on, and the years had moved quicker than light, slipping away from Brust's grasp and through his fingers, as time carried him further and further away. That world in which his youth had spent, had faded. It had once been the present, and now had been left far behind in the past, kept only alive by memories and the occasional artefact.

That whole world, no longer existed.

Gone.

And now the present had become the past.

And now the future had become the present.

The world had moved on and so had time itself. And so had most people.

Brust gazed around. His eyes falling on things that had not been invented in his life as a kid. They simply did not exist. This was the future, Brust thought to himself, or at least had been.

He'd sometimes wondered what the future would be like when he was a kid. And now here Brust was, living in a future world, yet it was no longer the future at the same time.

It was not as far-fetched as it had been in science fiction. Shiny silver space age clothing was not worn. People did not teleport themselves in different places in space and time nor did they eat pills full of nutrients, which had replaced food. The humans of today did not join others in the sky, clouded with flying cars and a buzzing cacophony.

The future wasn't exactly dystopic nor had it been a cataclysm, but it wasn't a golden age either. Global warming had wiped out some islands and countries. Places like the Caribbean were now extinct. The population had increased at an alarming rate and now stood at almost eleven billion people, thanks to these new life-extending drugs. A one-in-a-trillion disaster had happened when a meteor had fallen from space and completely annihilated a country. Earthquakes and such had increased as the tectonic plates moved around. North America and South America had been merged together. Lots of energy sources had run out and wars had been fought over the last few remaining scraps. Nuclear war had broken out and many countries had been destroyed.

But life moved on, at least for those who survived. Hope may have almost evaporated, but it still was present. When an island vanished under the sea, Japan and the rest of Britain were the next countries that were set to go.

The thing with humans is that they can be very lazy and not be bothered to solve their problems, expecting someone else to do it for them. It's a bit like a teenager, who is about to take a life-changing exam. They don't revise and ignore their problem, hoping it would go away if they ignore it. But when the importance of it strikes them, they cram revision into their short space of time and do really well in their upcoming exam.

That was a bit like what happened to the human race, who had just started solving their problems. People act at the last minute. Japan and Britain still existed. Space had helped spread out the population. New countries were created. The problems were starting to be solved and the Project could help boost that even more.

Had the world been a disaster? In many ways it was, but slowly it looked like things were brightening up. It really depended on how it was looked upon.

Brust smiled at that thought and put his plate under the machine.

On the *Dark Light 5000*, there was no chef or cook. The ship computer cooked the food, using special technology.

"What would you like?" Arti asked in his mechanical, flat voice.

"Err," said Brust. "Toast and egg, please."

"Toast and egg coming right up." Arti echoed, sounding completely uninterested.

The machine was called a tiny food factory and it 'printed' the food. There was a slurping sound, which was briefly followed by a sucking noise. Then the food was squeezed out, and plopped neatly onto Brust's plate.

He smiled again and picked up his plate. Brust turned around and began his search for an available table.

The team's strategist aboard the ship was sitting at one table. She used very good tactics that helped them all out in tricky situations.

Holly Skyland was a popular person who had a quirky and friendly personality. She was also a sympathetic person. Holly was tall and lithe, with long, flowing, blonde hair, which always fell into place perfectly. It was so soft and smooth. Her dark green eyes were comforting and pretty, filled with burning warmth. Her voice was smooth and mellifluous.

Holly was dressed in a black hot leather catsuit complete with utility belt. The zip was at front.

"Hello." Brust greeted.

"Hi." Holly replied, gesturing for Brust to sit down, acknowledging his presence and presenting a welcome reception in response.

Brust couldn't think of what to say. Intelligent people often are not great at interacting with people. Brust was OK but he wasn't great at small talk.

"I'm glad to see you're drinking natural tea, none of this new artificially grown mumbo jumbo. Apparently, there was a case where someone drank that type of stuff and ended up almost dying! There was this problem with the generator thing, resulting in some kind of poison." Holly said, starting a conversation in such a tone that made it engaging.

"Right." Brust said vaguely.

"What about coffee? Do you like it?" Holly said, changing tact.

"No, not really. Coffee isn't exactly my cup of tea."

An awkward silence hushed them and swept over their words. But Holly soon provoked dialogue.

"How is your day shaping up for today?" Holly asked politely.

"It's good," Brust replied, suddenly remembering a tip someone had once told him. "They're very nice clothes you're wearing. It makes you look delightful."

Holly smiled sweetly, showing perfect white teeth. "Thank you," Holly smoothed out a crease in her catsuit and raked a hand through a strand of her blonde hair. "I'm glad you like it. You're not looking too bad yourself."

But before their conversation could persist any further, it was soon cut short. A hologram of a person appeared from nowhere in the middle of the room.

The hologram was a perfect replica of their pilot and was so realistic that it looked like a real person was standing before them, not a hologram. The need for a pilot was still permitted. Although self-driving cars, boats, and planes were invented, self-flying spaceships were not yet in existence.

Julius Air was the pilot. The hologram was a replica of him.

"I have a message to tell all the crew. Thanks to *somebody's* excellent piloting skills, we have almost reached our destination," The hologram announced before exclaiming fairly unenthusiastically: "Yippee!"

Julius then disappeared from view before coming back and speaking in a nasal neutral voice. "According to some clever person's calculations, we shall arrive in approximately eight hours and twenty six minutes."

A feeble cheer sounded through the breakfast hall at the news of the landing. It took most of the little energy there was in the room. Everyone had been working too hard. The cheer was very pathetic and Julius's cry in his normal voice of: "Oh sorry, folks, it's now eight hours and twenty five minutes." was easily audible.

When the sound died down, Julius continued. "So that info is nice to know. But obviously I still have to land this thing. I don't know how, but I'm sure I'll pick it up as I got along. Just kidding! Anyway, I have the Captain here with a message for a couple of people. She is giving them more instructions, because the Captain likes seeing people suffer under the work load." An elbow then jabbed Julius in the ribs as though prompting him.

"You're not criticising my decision, are you Julius Air?" came the faint background sound of Jennifer's voice.

"What? Me? Slagging you off?" Julius uttered innocently. "The very idea hasn't even entered my head!"

"Just get on with your announcement."

"I apologise with the deepest affection and remorse from every ounce of my heart for my unforgiveable action and the regrettable turn of events."

"And do you, Julius?" Jennifer's voice echoed. It was soft but firm at the same time.

Julius shrugged. "No, not especially.

"Anyway back to my notification. What I actually mean is the Captain wants to get the work that is needed to be done, done. Right, I'll pass Jennifer over and I'll get back to playing around with the buttons in the cockpit."

The hologram then flickered and morphed into Jennifer, quicker than a blink of an eye.

"There is a catch though," Jennifer said. "Much work is still to be completed. Mr Air, who is currently flying, needs to concentrate on the landing. Mr Sudilav and Mr Tuft, updating on the weapon system is compelled and you also have some online computer files to complete. Mr Brust, you need to fix the Machine. You shall be receiving some info on that. Miss Skyland needs to check the co-ordinates and prepare a presentation on our destination. You other guys, you known what you need to do. That is all."

There was a brief crackle of static as the hologram vanished into thin air.

People got up and bustled past each other, moaning, but slightly happier and livelier, knowing that all this work was almost done.

Breakfast however was left on the table, forgotten.

Chapter 3

There was one other crewmember aboard the *Dark Light 5000*. He was a technical genius and ultra smart with gadgets. He had taken Brust's design of the ship and played a minor role in the team of engineers making it. He also held full responsibility for the software systems and programs aboard the *Dark Light 5000*. Back on Earth, he ran a highly successful Japanese games company. His name was Katsu Sato.

Sato worked on his own, in isolation. He worked best alone. He was an outsider. Or as some judged a little harshly, they called him an outcast or a loner. But perhaps they were right after all.

Sato was Japanese. He was small and thanks to anti-ageing machinery, it appeared he was in his mid-twenties, as did most of the crew. He was actually nearer thirty.

His face was unusually pale, probably because he had spent most of his life in dark rooms, looking at glowing screens. This fact had also made his brown eyes look almost black. His thick black hair was always in need of a trim. His fringe was swept to his left. His hair covered all of his forehead and part of his bushy eyebrows. His ears were long gone. It was a mystery and a miracle to how he could still hear. Sato was dressed in black – a black turtle neck jumper and black jeans.

Sato still wasn't quite sure how he had got the job of head of computing systems in this Project. It might have been that he had a connection with Brust who could have recommended him.

He had been a good friend of Brust since he had been nineteen years old. Ten years, Sato had known Brust but it felt longer.

The doors to his office swished open and he stepped in. Sato looked over his shoulder, to see if anyone was following him. But as usual, no one was. Sato was just too paranoid – it was one of the flaws in his own programming.

He stepped onto a doormat, which was actually a scanner. Just a little security device that Sato had planted there. It gave a quick scan and Sato moved on.

The doors closed, leaving Sato in a dark room that was lit only by the glow of machinery.

Sato ambled over and collapsed into a hover-chair at his desk. There were screens and technology everywhere. Sato just liked looking at machines and screens. A row of quantum holo-computers sat before him, hovering above his glass desk.

Quantum holo-computers were quantum computers, which had a holographic screen and keyboard. The keyboard was a luminous green and hovered in mid-air. The high-resolution 3D screen too hovered in the air and had a lining the same colour as the keyboard.

Sato activated his favourite holo-computer. The camera recognised him and his password.

He fired up his other holo-computers, which instantly were ready for action. On one, he launched the simulator on the planet he was going to.

Sato paused and eyed his surroundings. Dark and cool. Two things he liked. For many people, the dark was frightening. Sato couldn't understand this, because to him the dark was comforting. He liked how the shadows wrapped around him and seemed to almost protect him. The darkness was like a shield from the outside world. Sato was in his own little bubble.

It was usually cool in his office, despite the engine room being very close, but today was an exception. Sato couldn't stand heat or the freezing cold. Cool was just right. There was something calm and relaxing about it. And Sato liked that.

Sato plonked his feet up on his desk and looked around the room in more detail. There was a lot of technology and gizmos. The room was almost silent. Sato could hear the hum and the whir of his gadgets. Occasionally there was a *beep* or a *ping*. Every few moments, Sato could hear the sounds coming from the engine room on the floor below, rattling and buzzing. There was also a dripping sound coming from the roof. A pipe had probably burst and liquid was leaking out, making a puddle in the corner of the room. But Sato didn't have time to fix it. Maybe he would send one of mechanics boys to sort it out later. Right now, he had more important matters on hand.

He wiped sweat from his brow, because he was working hard and also the office was a little hotter than usual. Clearly, the engine room was heating up.

Sato ignored the heat, the sounds, and the stink of the junk littered around the room.

He looked up from his computer. There was a big sheet of glass looking out. It was dark, but if you looked carefully, you might make out the silhouettes of a couple of dozen workers nine feet below tapping frantically at holo-keyboards.

A metal staircase unfolded from a balcony behind the glass sheet, clattering into the floor below. Suddenly the glass sheet split apart neatly like a lift door. A woman stepped through and the glass doors slid shut behind her.

"Yes?" Sato asked, leaning back into his leather hover-chair, his hands behind his head.

The woman in front of him was an oriental lady dressed in a slinky, silk cocktail dress of midnight blue that was cut just above her knees, the rest of the legs were coated in tights. The lady was tall. Wearing electric blue heels and having a straight and upright posture probably helped that fact. Her long black hair was usually tied back, but today it flowed downwards over her shoulders. There was something about the way she wore the dress, that made it seem as smart as an immaculate suit.

The woman was slim, pretty, and very elegant. There was a black ring on one finger that clasped the sphere device that she held. Sato only knew this woman by the name of Ning.

Ning placed the device gently on Sato's desk and it rolled a bit. It teetered on one edge of the desk, before pushing back and shuddering into a safe position where it did not move about anymore.

"I believe you wished to contact one Mr Zock who is currently located somewhere aboard the *Dark Light 5000*." Ning spoke in a voice that was soft and quiet but somehow it carried over the din of machinery. Although it was quiet, there was something powerful in the voice. Ning had that air of power that followed her everywhere. Sato didn't like the way the power shadowed her in such a way that it made Ning seem a dangerous woman.

"You managed to solve the connection problem then." Sato sat up, itching forward to look at the device.

"Indeed." Ning said, patting the smart sphere. "It's all sorted now."

"Great work, Ning. You can leave."

Ning nodded and moved towards the glass doors, her heels clacking as she did so.

"One last thing." Sato called after her.

Ning stopped in her tracks, turning to face Sato. "Yes?"

"That's a nice dress you're wearing."

"Why thank you Sato. I'm glad you like it." Ning shot Sato a sweet smile.

Sato watched her go, as Ning disappeared down the metal steps.

Then Sato shook his head and got back down to work. He tapped a button and a hologram popped up in front of him. It was a shapeless, green figure, but soon it wouldn't be.

Suddenly the hologram flickered and turned into a person.

"S'up." Daniel Zock Junior muttered pathetically.

Daniel R Zock Junior was the son of Daniel R Zock Senior. It was Daniel R Zock Senior who had created the first thinking machine in 2043, in little more than a garage. His son was also an impressive person, following his father's footsteps into the world of computers. What's more, Daniel Zock Jr was only 21, and he was part of the famous Project. The reason he'd

43

been picked was due to his intelligence. One of his drawbacks was his immaturity and irresponsibility.

Zock looked exactly like his dad when he had been his age except Zock Sr wore glasses. Zock Jr was tall, stick insect thin and lanky. There was something about Zock that made him awkward, but Sato couldn't quite put his finger on what or why that was.

Zock had green eyes, which had shined enthusiasm but he was obviously hiding depression. Sato often wondered what was going through his mind. Zock had short ginger hair, which had been cut in a sharp manner. As always, it stuck up.

Zock wore an old worn out T-shirt, which had last night's dinner all down the front. Zock's fingers were long, as well as being incredibly agile and nimble. It was a shame his body wasn't the same. Zock's babyish chubby face was covered in freckles, spots, and acne. Zock was very clumsy and didn't interact well with others. He never could detect sarcasm or a joke. His mother had put it another way; 'Daniel doesn't play well with others'.

Zock tried desperately to be funny and cool. But the truth was that he was neither of those things.

Sato winced at Zock's use of slang. "Don't." Sato thought he'd only need one word to shut Zock up. However, he was wrong.

"Don't what?" Zock said, his words sounding more like a sonic explosion rather than communication.

"Don't bother trying to be cool." Sato said, only just surviving a close shave with deafness.

Zock looked puzzled. "Why not?"

Sato thought of what he could say. Maybe he should just blurt out the truth.

"Trust me, just don't." Sato said, deciding to protect Zock's feelings. Sato had heard enough about Zock's emotional breakdowns.

"Be more formal next time." someone jeered in the background.

Zock turned away from Sato. Sato couldn't see what happened, but he heard a big SMASH!

"Well done." a distant voice mocked nastily.

"What's there to be praised for?" Zock asked, oblivious to the sarcasm.

"You're so clumsy." another sneered, ignoring Zock's question.

Zock fought for control over his face as he turned around to face Sato.

"Let's get back to more serious matters." Sato said.

Zock's eyes gleamed and he almost fell off his chair.

"You're on the ship, I take it?" Sato asked.

Zock nodded vigourously. "Yes, yes, yes."

"My VirtualWorld simulation isn't working. I've checked the software I have written and there's nothing wrong with my programming. It's due to the hardware you made. Every time I run the simulation, the program buffers."

"Buffers?"

"Freezes and then starts playing again. This action is frequently repeated."

"Oh." A look of dismay and guilt crossed Zock's face.

"Nothing like this should ever happen. This is the kinda stuff that might have happened in the early 21st century but in 2071, it is about rare as the Sun turning to butter. It only ever happens if you intend it to."

"You can make the Sun turn to butter if you intend it too?"

"No, but you know what I mean."

Zock squirmed in his chair, knocking something else over. Sato noticed Zock had suddenly shrunken in size. Sato quickly corrected himself Zock wasn't shrinking – he was slouching back into his chair.

"Oops." Zock said, bending over to pick it up.

"Daniel?"

"Yeah." Zock said, unable to look Sato in the eye.

"What did you do to the hardware? You've been hiding from me too."

Zock banged his head on the desk and it all spilled out – his secret, not his head.

"OK, OK. Some guys made me tamper with Circuit D. It's very loosely connected. I thought you'd find it funny."

Sato was puzzled at how anyone could find it all so funny – to him it was just plain stupid. "Mankind's future could depend on this and you think it is 'funny' to screw up and possibly bring the whole world crashing to its knees."

"I'm sorry. I'll connect it." Zock faltered.

Zock then stuck out his tongue in concentration and tapped buttons on machines. His fingers were a blur.

"There!" Zock said triumphantly, banging his fist into a return key. "It should be fixed."

"Thanks. You wondered why I didn't let you use the bio-botic robo-arm the other day, didn't you?"

"Yeah!"

"This is precisely why. I cannot trust you."

"That isn't true. You can certainly trust me."

"Yes, you're right. I can trust you to bring irresponsibility, immaturity and trouble wherever you go."

Zock scowled and rapidly changed the subject. "Hey, what's the matter?"

Sato hadn't realised up until now that he had a tear welling up in his eye. "Nothing," he croaked. "Goodbye."

The call terminated.

The tear fell from Sato's eye. When it landed with a *plop*, the teardrop seemed to melt away into the desk. Then Sato began to cry softly.

Why was he crying?

But Sato already knew the answer. It was because Zock reminded Sato of himself when he was Zock's age. OK, maybe Sato hadn't been clumsy, immature or trying and failing to be funny or cool, but still there were many similarities between them.

They both had no friends. They were both into computing. They were both loners. Outsiders. Nerds. Outcasts. Geeks. And whatever else some might call them. And there were many more besides...

But Sato still didn't quite understand why he was crying. But then he'd always been a bit of a wimp.

Sato tried to distract himself by tapping a button that activated the Virtual Simulator Experience, or a VSE for short. Sato moved through this world, as if he was just navigating this way through a fantasy world in a computer game.

It was a simulation of the planet that the *Dark Light 5000* was to land on. Sato couldn't remember its name, but it was on the tip of his tongue. But he'd never been too good with words. There was no need to study foreign languages as well, not since the invention of the universal translator. However, Sato had been forced by his father to learn the English language without the aid of technology. Sato even now, hadn't seen the point. His father claimed that it was in case the technology crashed, but Sato argued it was far too advanced for that.

Sato had moved to California for the last ten years for his education. Sato had liked maths, physics, and computer science.

His Bluetooth headset that he wore on his right ear had a microphone hanging down. It was a basic communications device. It made a pinging noise. Sato instinctively commanded the device to reveal what it wanted.

"One new message," the device said emotionless, before changing voice, becoming the voice of Holly Skyland. "*Hi. It's me, Holly Skyland. There is a presentation on the planet. It's in fifteen minutes.*"

The message ended. A quarter of an hour was a lot of time. Sato carried on, running through his simulation another time, checking everything was running smoothly. He did not want anything going wrong.

Sato liked his job and his computer. He thought again about Zock. They both had had no friends. But

Sato once had had one. Only one though. His very best friend. His only friend. But now he had none. Maybe Sato 'didn't play well with others' either but wished with all his heart he could have his best friend back.

Chapter 4

Johnny Tuft was never the smartest person in whatever room he happened to be in. In fact, you would probably find he was the most stupid. Tuft was brash and loutish. His way of speaking and his English were appalling and atrocious.

He used his big muscles and a big gun, but never the tiny cell that he called a 'brain'. Tuft was sort of the person who would act before he would think. This meant people would have to do the thinking for him. Once a plan had been thought up, the job was only half done as the masterminds behind it, then needed to make sure Tuft would remember and follow the instructions. And that was a challenge in itself.

The chances of Tuft actually sitting down and thinking were about equal with the possibility of the humans discovering that the Moon really was made out of cheese after all.

Yet here Tuft was, sitting on the floor, cross-legged like a primary school pupil in assembly. An event like this rarely happened, and when it did, Tuft would probably be fantasying about beating some poor defenceless person to a bloody pulp. Yes, Tuft loved violence. He was about as gentle as an angry rhinoceros on a rampage. And that was Tuft on a *good* day!

But this time, it was different. He was thinking about something aside violence. Tuft was wondering how he'd actually ended up as part of the Project in the first place.

Oblivious to the surroundings around him, Tuft plunged head first into his memories. Everything slowly faded away, piece by piece, it disappeared. Tuft was in another world. Tuft was in the past. Well, in a manner of speaking.

It was like he was actually there. Tuft stood in a grim, depressing street. The road, on which he stood, seemed to stretch out forever. There were no people, no transport, no light, no anything, or 'no nuffin' as Tuft would have said.

The tall dark skyscrapers, which were mostly a drab grey, loomed over Tuft, making him feel small and intimidated which was quite a feat. Tuft now knew how some of the people he had threatened or bullied, had felt.

The air was vile and barely breathable. It mingled with the misty fog, creating a poisonous and intoxicating atmosphere. The smell was foul and glided about, working its way into nostrils. It completely and utterly *stunk*.

The street was in poor lighting conditions too. It was silent. That was what Tuft liked the least, that there no sound. It felt too eerie, too creepy, too silent. It was a long deafening silence that was impenetrable.

It's just a memory Tuft thought. It can't hurt you.

But even so, it was so realistic, like Tuft had stepped back in time. He floated in the cold October air, like a ghost. Tuft was like a spirit, a lost soul wandering aimlessly, trapped on Earth never to be freed.

Tuft drifted over to where there was an alleyway leading off to somewhere. He swooped down and rushed forward. Tuft weaved past abandoned homes, over two teenagers who spluttered on a cigarette, round a smashed hover-car and soared into an alleyway.

Alleyways in 2071 were like cramped Tube tunnels but without the train railings, the trains and the disorderly rabble. This tunnel would not have been kind to anyone who had claustrophobia. It was dark, cold and stank of gas leakage. Just like Tuft's flat!

There was a loud coughing sound coming off to Tuft's right. He glided over through the smoke. A figure emerged from the shadows, spluttering. Tuft looked right at that man and saw an eight-month younger version of himself.

A pipe puffed out another burst of smoke, clouding the alleyway once more, reminding Tuft of a dragon. The gentle but chilling breeze carried the smoke forward, making it linger like a bad smell. The whistling wind packed a small but equally deadly punch, which whipped the younger Tuft's head. This had a strange effect on the younger Tuft – his skin rippled and his huge muscles wobbled as the smoke was carried on further into the depths of profound darkness up ahead.

The other Tuft, the older version, smiled fondly to himself. He knew at what moment in the past he was in. Tuft's head swivelled round to the left, watching the thick smoke billow out from rusty pipes. Tuft felt himself drift into the younger Tuft and watch this memory through his eyes. He tried to break the spell, but resistance was futile. He was a phantom possessing a poor victim's body. His point of view was through the eyes of his younger self. Tuft looked out onwards. Any moment now. Any moment n–

It happened so suddenly and so fast that Tuft almost jumped out of his skin. But Tuft had no control whatsoever of the body he possessed. The younger version barely flinched.

A man had just come out of nowhere. With a place that is hidden by swirling smoke and fog, you'd expect people to emerge bit by bit. But no. Not in this case. One moment there had been no one there, the next there was that well-dressed man who sauntered forward, the air around him shimmering and swirling as if evil spirits were swooping through that thick and misty fog.

Tuft shivered. He was beginning to like this place less and less. There had been a story in one of the news download streams last week about a young girl mysteriously disappearing. She'd last been sighted entering this exact alleyway Tuft was in now. She had never come out the other side. Yet there had been no scream, no sign of a struggle or anything else like that. The girl had just strolled into an alleyway and vanished into thin air. The alleyway had been searched and absolute zero clues had been found.

But through the media was not the only way people were discovering this story. Rumours and retellings of the story had flown around the general public. Conspiracy theorists had suddenly struck gold. Pop-ups on it would appear on the Internet with a variety of speculations. Tuft quickly ran through the theories he had heard about: alien abduction, child-snatchers, goblins, and a portal to another point in space and time.

However the most popular one by far means, was government cover-ups. The government planted the idea, a series of memories in different people's mind convincing them they knew a young girl who'd recently disappeared. People had thought they'd witnessed someone, but actually it was just an implanted memory. The girl had simply never existed in the first place.

That was a nice encouraging thought for Tuft. The fact that nothing evil or sinister was going on in the alleyway. But then if the girl's disappearance was just a big lie, that meant there was an even deeper, darker truth behind it – something the government clearly wanted to no one to know about. And that was *not* an encouraging thought for Tuft.

Maybe there are evil ghosts hiding in those dark corners, Tuft said a quiet voice at the back of Tuft's head. *What if they're about to make you disappear too?*

Then another inner voice spoke: *Shut up* it said loudly. *Evil spirits don't exist – it's total bull!*

But still Tuft's nerves were jittering like mad and he couldn't shake off that feeling of uneasiness. Why was he being such a wimp?

"You're tardy, man." the younger Tuft said. The words came out by themselves, the real Tuft having no control over them whatsoever.

CRUNCH! A jagged discarded chunk of a material, which was a cross between metal and plastic, had been crushed under the man's foot as he approached. The sound echoed through the alleyway, bouncing off the metallic walls, puncturing the silence.

The man reached into his pocket and pulled out something that looked similar to a cigarette lighter. He flicked a button and a small hot green flame flickered into existence, dimly lighting the alleyway.

"My name ees Doctor Emmet Steinberg." the man said with a strong German accent.

Doctor Steinberg was a man of average size. He had a mass of black curly hair and a neat moustache that covered the line of his upper lip. His face was slightly chubby. His eyes were that of the deepest brown. Steinberg wore an immaculate suit, which evidently had had meticulous tailoring. A neat tidy bowtie completed the look. He had a ring on one finger and there was a stain that looked like ink on one of his hands.

"Who are you?" the younger Tuft said rudely.

Steinberg smiled frostily in response. "I verk thor a secret agency. I have been eenstructed -"

Tuft interrupted, once more the words coming out by themselves. "I get da idea. Actually, I don't but still. And speak clearly, so I get wot you're saying."

Steinberg glowered. What had been the point of the interruption? Although Steinberg's German accent was thick, it was clearly not as thick as Tuft.

"I am afraid zat ees not possible. Zat ees how I talk. I zink you zhould just lizzen to me."

Steinberg came and stood besides Tuft. He dropped back onto a bench.

"Zank you." he said to no one in particular.

Steinberg flipped open his brown briefcase, which Tuft had only just noticed. But then, he had never been that observant, so to speak.

Steinberg pulled out a portable holographic projector that had up until this point, been nestling in black foam. He gently placed the projector beside him.

"Zit." Steinberg said to Tuft, gesturing to the bench.

Tuft reluctantly and slowly sat on the bench, eyeing the projector as though it were a protonic bomb.

Steinberg took no notice of this, and clicked a couple of switches on the projector, which replied in a series of short beeps.

Some green shapes flickered in front of them, before it turned into a person. But the person was actually a real size, three-dimensional realistic hologram. It was as though there was an actual person standing in front of them.

The hologram was of a man whom Tuft instantly recognised. It was Vernon Quentin Esscal. Esscal was a celebrity, a multibillionaire, a businessman, a politician, and many other things. Esscal was also very fat.

He was short and incredibly obese. An impeccable black suit was worn over his round body shape. A black bowtie was worn over his collar. The bowtie was short, fat and smart – just like its wearer.

Esscal had so little hair left that no hair gain product could possibly save him now. The white hairs that remained were combed back. A white hairy creature that Esscal called a 'moustache', squirmed underneath Esscal's abnormally long and fat nose. His sullen eyes looked wild and excited as they glinted in the darkness of the alleyway. The eyes looked like that had been pressed firmly into Esscal's large dome of a head.

In fact, Esscal was so overweight that it looked like someone had put a balloon underneath his skin and blown it up to maximum size. Tuft half expected him to pop or go whizzing off in a random direction!

"How jolly nice to see you gentlemen, on this pleasant and beautiful evening." Esscal warbled in a wheezy, posh sounding voice.

Tuft smirked. "Nice suit, dude."

Esscal completely missed the sarcasm in Tuft's voice. "Oh yes, I'm glad you think so. It was actually partly my design and I think it's splendid. This suit was made especially for me. It cost thousands as I had my tailors make it for me. However I think it misses what all my other clothes miss as well. It can hardly contain my striking body shape."

A voice in the background replied to Esscal's comment. "The suit cannot expand anymore than that, sir. It's impossible for it to be bigger."

Esscal ignored him, his face flushing a deep purple in embarrassment.

Tuft started to snigger, as he tried with great difficulty to bottle his amusement. Steinberg's face however remained anonymous and unreadable as he rested a foot on one of his knees.

Esscal pressed on. "Anyway, I must inform of what I have to tell you on this evening. I have decided to invest in a brilliant idea, and I am funding this most marvellous project. And I want you to be part of it and join the project led by the fantastic Mr Esscal, myself. This project has been running for six months now and it is not going too well. So, I have decided to reshape it for the better. But I invite you to join me."

Tuft looked puzzled, which was a common expression of his face! "Why do you need me, man? It's sumfin 'bout my military stuff, ain't it?"

Esscal flicked through a large pad of paper, looked at something before putting it out of sight.

"Your eh, um..." Esscal struggled to find the word he was searching for, before reluctantly deciding on something else as he flicked over another page. "..aggressive behaviour and impressive military experience could possibly be beneficial. I have brought Doctor Steinberg here, who is a member and has brought me along through holographic communication. I am afraid I could not visit you in person as I run a busy and tight schedule, Mr Tuft. I want your answer in the next five minutes. Tell Doctor Steinberg and he will contact me. I hope you will make the right decision. Farewell."

The hologram vanished abruptly. Tuft's head swivelled to face Steinberg.

"Vell?" Steinberg said, bringing his foot off his knee and back onto the damp ground.

Tuft looked at him blankly.

"Vot have you decided?"

Tuft said nothing.

"Ees eet a yes or a no?" Steinberg asked, standing up.

Still Tuft did not reply as he got to his feet. This made Steinberg feel small and intimidated. Steinberg had known he was the wrong man for this job, but Esscal would not listen. Now it had proven his doubts.

"I know Meester Esscal may seem a leetle arrogant, but he ees a wery nice man."

Tuft loomed over Steinberg. "Tell me, Doctor Steinberg. What sort of stuff would I do in dis Project?"

"Zat ees classified."

One moment, Steinberg was staring up at Tuft. The next, Tuft held Steinberg by the throat above his head in an iron grip that strangled the doctor. Steinberg tried to wriggle free and twisted, but the grip was too strong.

"Vot are you doing?" Steinberg protested, his face reddening due to the lack of oxygen.

Tuft did not reply, but his dark look said everything.

There was a long pause, before someone spoke again.

"Pleez." Steinberg cried out, his eyes bulging and begging for mercy, before his voice died to a whimper. "Pleez."

Tuft laughed at Steinberg's useless wriggling and did not loosen his grip.

"You're just a bully. And ze biggest von I've ever met." Steinberg cried bravely.

"I ask again. Tell me." Tuft said simply, as though it were a pleasant summer's day.

Steinberg made a wheezing noise as he shook his head. Tears were now streaming down his face.

"Tell me," Tuft said quietly, before shaking Steinberg and shouting: "NOW!"

The shout made Steinberg jump in shock, before he broke down into sobs like an upset baby.

"Zine, I vill tell you. I vill tell you." Steinberg wept.

Tuft's expression softened and he loosened his grip, so that the colour returned to Steinberg's face as he breathed in some rich fresh oxygen.

Steinberg saw his chance and punched Tuft in the stomach. Steinberg expected Tuft to double over. But all Tuft did was laugh and swept the blow away. Then he hauled Steinberg through the air at a wall.

The impact made Steinberg's spine snap in half as though two giant hands had picked him and snapped him the way one might do with a twig. Or at least that's what it felt like. Groaning in agony, he sat up.

But Tuft had already grabbed Steinberg again, shoving him firmly into the wall, as Steinberg found himself pinned into an uncomfortable position.

"I said, I vould tell you." Steinberg screamed as the pain rocketed up his back.

"Look, mate. I don't wanna have to beat you up," Tuft lied. "But make me clued up, yeah?"

Over the tears and pain, Steinberg told Tuft some of what he knew. Steinberg lied about some of it, praying Tuft wouldn't realise. Tuft squeezed a bit more out until he was satisfied with some juicy lies wedged in between the truth.

"And chillax. I'm like sure we'll be in touch, eh?" Tuft said. "And I don't wanna hear that you've grassed me up."

Steinberg didn't need Tuft to continue. "I von't tell." he promised.

"Den we're even, man." Tuft said and dislocated Steinberg's shoulder blade, before wishing him goodbye as though they'd shared a taxi ride together. "Hav' a good gloaming."

So Tuft walked off, leaving Steinberg a whimpering mess. Unknown to Tuft, Steinberg was a little proud of how he had managed to convince Tuft of a couple of lies, who would never know that he'd been fed a pack of lies mingled in with the truth.

However next time, someone else was doing this recruitment business. Someone who could look after themselves. And Steinberg was not that someone.

*

Tuft emerged from the alleyway as he heard a faint voice in the distance.

"Hey Tuft." it said.

Tuft ignored it.

"Hey Tuft." it repeated.

Tuft ignored it once more. But when the voice sounded again, it was impossibly loud and Tuft wished for it to go away.

"I think Tuft's becoming a bit of a ner-"

Nerd. A name he was the complete opposite of. A name Tuft did not liked to be called. A name that Tuft despised with all the hatred within. White hot anger boiled up inside, getting hotter and hotter until it felt like his whole body would explode due to the heat. Something inside Tuft snapped and he roared in anger. The beast within was unleashed. And that was not good.

The flashback ended and Tuft lashed out blindly with all his might.

Chapter 5

Sudilav navigated through the menus. Once upon a time, Sudilav had been good with computers. But all that was once upon a time. And the story hadn't ended happily ever after.

Sighing heavily, Sudilav looked up from his work and swept his eyes across the room. It contained objects like his desk and office accessories. But then Sudilav's office was slightly different from rest of his crewmates.

Weapons and military equipment lined the walls, shackled by thin metal wire. There was basic weaponry like guns and ShockBlades including ShockKnives, ShockSwords, ShockAxes, ShockMaces and ShockSpears. Then you had the more interesting choice of harm: blasters, grenades, scientific equipment, lasers, even missile launchers and much much more. Sudilav would have liked to have brought more 'toys' with him, but Alphasis would not let Sudilav bring any more. After all, why was it all necessary?

There was also a mini gym, with half a dozen machines tucked away in one corner. The neon white lights that dangled from the ceiling brightly lit the room. Like in Sato's office, there were glass double doors and a balcony looking down on another room 9 feet below. However unlike the room near Sato's office, it was not full of people at computers. Instead it was full of about forty musclemen going about various activities like exercising, lifting weights bigger than most people's heads, shooting firearms and wielding weapons. There were even fights and tournaments breaking out between them. But if you looked closer, you would notice that amongst the musclemen, was an occasional fit female.

Sudilav looked away and swept his eyes over the room: his military apparatus was scattered at different places in his office.

He looked at Tuft, his military deputy sitting cross-legged on the floor, gazing out into empty space. He was thinking deeply. Tuft was thinking. Sudilav chuckled in disbelief. This was incredible. Tuft was thinking! When would Tuft wake up from this daydream? Sudilav needed him for work, after all.

He tried playing music to wake Tuft, but even hard rock music blasting out of speakers at full volume wasn't enough to break the spell over Tuft.

When this had no effect, Sudilav shrugged. Ignoring Tuft, Sudilav's attention wondered back to updating the weapon computing system. It was just filling in some details about the weaponry and military machines he used, into a computer. Boring!

"Hello." The computer suddenly said flatly.

The voice made Sudilav jump. It was Arti, the ship's computer system. Arti seemed to be everywhere aboard this ship, at every nanosecond of time. Perhaps he was watching, plotting on how best to overthrow the human race.

Don't be stupid, Sudilav thought to himself. AI machines are programmed not to do anything like that.

"What?" he snarled.

"I am sorry. File14 for the WeaponFile 106Gi does not match the latest requirements. Please check that the detail is correct and try again. Thank you."

Sudilav hated the way, machines talked – a passable imitation of the human voice. It was not quite human, making Sudilav feel almost as though technology was mocking the human race. He didn't understand to how he had once liked machines that could think for themselves. Pah!

The thing about technology is that it is ever advancing. That's what Sudilav did not like. If it could get to a good level and stay there, Sudilav would be happy. But no, it has to advance beyond that. A camera must be increased by just a few more megapixels. File storage needed to be increased by just a few more gigabytes. A gadget needed to be a bit better. Wasn't technology good enough? Sudilav pondered. No, apparently it wasn't.

But the real reason was that Sudilav was worried a foot soldier would no longer be needed in the future. Always with that in mind, humans were starting to focus more on their brainpower rather than their muscle power.

Brust had told Sudilav near the beginning of the trip: "More and more wars are going to be fought less and less by people like you and more and more by people like me."

Although Sudilav didn't like that fact, there was quite a bit of truth in that. At the time, Sudilav had just replied: "They will always need someone to knock around some other people every now and then."

But now Sudilav was not so sure of the words he'd said. He tried to get back to his boring work to put his mind off it, but there was a little voice in the back of his mind, questioning him. Then the question became a niggle. Then the niggle became a nag. Then a nag became a complete distraction, shouting and tearing his concentration off his work, dragging Sudilav into that thought which enlarged by the second.

Suddenly Sudilav had a horrible thought that crushed all the rest, burst to the surface, and wiped comfort from his mind, like when someone put a magnet to a hard drive.

Who said it would be humans doing the fighting? What if technology did the fighting for us?

That thought sent shivers down Sudilav's spine, faster than an email being sent, which nowadays was sent almost before you'd pressed the SEND button. He stood up from the battered leather chair, running a hair through his hair. What had once started out as a mere doubt had become something that was almost certain to happen. He may, one day, no longer be needed as a soldier, replaced by a mere giant hunk of metal. That was a scary thought.

Then what was Sudilav doing many miles away from Planet Earth aboard the vast *Dark Light 5000*, part of the Project, something that was bound to change the world? That was a good question, Sudilav thought. And one he did not have an answer to.

"Hey, Tuft."

Tuft who looked as though spirits possessed him, did not stir from his trance.

"Hey, Tuft." Sudilav repeated.

Still Tuft continued, gazing out at the stars, a look of utter blankness upon his face. He looked like an android.

Sudilav walked over to Tuft and kicked him lightly with his boot. The blow was not hard and Sudilav's foot bounced off. This had no effect on Tuft whatsoever, who had been pulled into a world of thought and kept there by its powerful bonds.

Sudilav put his mouth near Tuft's ear and spoke in little more than a whisper. He took a deep breath, knowing full well what he was about to say next would definitely burst Tuft's bubble.

"I think Tuft is becoming a bit of a ner-"

Sudilav never finished. What happened next, happened so fast Sudilav didn't realise what had happened until afterwards.

One moment he standing over Tuft, the next he was soaring through the air. His back hit one of the steel walls. The excruciating pain that shot up his spine was pure agony. When he rolled away from the wall, Sudilav saw a massive dent in the wall. The military commander was very surprised that he hadn't been knocked out. The pain was so unbearable that it felt like two massive hands had grabbed his spine and snapped it into two halves.

"NO ONE CALLS ME A NERD!" Tuft roared, the sound making the whole ship vibrate even with the racket of the music. "Coz I ain't a nerd."

"OK, OK." Sudilav grumbled.

There was a brief pause between them as the thud of a distortion of vocal cords and an electric guitar filled the air.

Tuft's chest was heaving in and out. "I'M GONNA TEACH YOU A LESSON! Oh, by the way I like de music, you put on. Sweet stuff, man."

Tuft's eyes swept through the office, looking for something to inspiration. Suddenly his search was over and a chilling smile crept onto his face. As quick as a flash, Tuft pulled out a weapon from nowhere. It looked like an iron bar, with three buttons running along one side; one button was red, the second amber, and the last one green. Tuft pressed the amber button and a holo-screen popped up.

"What's that?" Sudilav asked stupidly.

Tuft looked up from the holo-screen and smiled about as sweetly as a viper.

"It's a body freezer thing. It like cuts all connections from a brain to all the muscles, except stuff like de heart. Da screen shows me wot it's pointing at. If I point it at you and press de red button, watch what happens."

But Sudilav knew what was going to happen, far too late. He tried to run, but the device had already fired an invisible beam that prevented his muscles from moving.

Sudilav stood, motionless, his muscles locked into place. All he could do was be alive. Even his eyes were fixed in one position; he couldn't move them to see other things. He tried to speak, but his dry cracked lips were sealed shut. Tuft could lob Sudilav out into the vacant depths of space itself. Sudilav would be able to do nothing to prevent his death.

Tuft laughed in victory and came over to Sudilav, who had basically now become a living statue. Tuft jeered and gloated at him.

"Dis brings back memories. Dis is just like old times, mate. Innit?"

Sudilav wanted to scream and shout at Tuft, but he could not move his mouth, no matter how hard he tried. In his mind, he thought of all the words, he could say to Tuft. None of them were pleasant. Even if only he could speak...

Tuft giggled with glee as he lunged at Sudilav, hitting him repeatedly. Somehow, the machine must have shut the pain down too, as Sudilav couldn't feel a thing.

But Tuft was not the brightest and he accidentally pressed a button again, releasing Sudilav from that permanent lock.

It was only a few seconds, but it gave Sudilav enough time to jab Tuft's wrist, to send the device flying, to break one of Tuft's fingers, to punch and kick Tuft, and to throw him to the floor, with Tuft secured in a painful lock. Sudilav stood over, like a predator would do standing over injured prey. Then Sudilav got ready to finish Tuft off.

Chapter 6

Julius Air watched in awe as the stars shot past him. Julius had always been fascinated by the stars. Even to this very day, he still was.

The pilot glanced at the holograms that displayed all kinds of information. He glanced back at the star filled sky, which slipped past him, yet more of it kept reappearing. It was an eternal stretch of air. The sky *really* was the limit.

As Julius zipped through the air, a thrill gripped hold of them as it always did. A plane. A spaceship. A helicopter. It didn't matter which vehicle, but Julius always felt a rush of thrill as he soared through the skies.

The fact he was allowed to fly solo, was something Julius still couldn't get his head around. They actually trusted him!!!

Giggling childishly, Julius spotted a cluster of space dust, which was something that looked like golden air. The dust floated over further in the distance, wandering off into the depths of the universe.

Are you trying to run away from me? Julius thought as if the dust could pick up his thoughts.

Unsurprisingly there was no reply. Julius hadn't expected one.

You think you can go faster? Huh?

The dust drifted off further.

You think you can, don't you?

It was most probably his imagination, but Julius thought he saw the dust say yes. *Go on then. I dare you...* it seemed to say.

It was a challenge that he had imagined. It was a race between him and the space dust that hovered mindlessly, giving it the impression of a lost sheep.

Bring. It. On, Julius thought to himself. He grinned madly and rubbed his hands with delight, a gleam shining through his eyes.

And so the race began.

Julius slipped on a pair of trendy sunglasses, which were actually a version of goggles. He tapped some holographic buttons and the *Dark Light 5000* rocketed forward.

The ship tilted so that it was flying upwards. It sliced through the space dust, obliterating it immediately. The space dust ceased to be.

Laughing hysterically, Julius steered the ship back to a flat level as the speed realigned and steadied. Perhaps it was all a little immature, but Julius found it great fun.

But how had Julius ended up here in the first place? He'd been recruited like everyone else, hadn't he?

That started to make Julius think back to his past. As a child, he'd spent most of his youth fascinated by any sort of flying machine. As a teenager, he took every opportunity to fly. As a young adult, Julius had trained as a pilot and an air force officer. Now in today's world, he was a successful in both occupations he had taken up as a young man.

But how had he ended up on the *Dark Light 5000*? That was a thought that accompanied the brief summary of his life so far.

Well, he'd been recruited like everyone else into an organisation called Alphasis. Alphasis was basically the association, which had rebooted Brust's idea and sent it on the path to success.

Julius could remember what had started it all. It felt like only yesterday even though it was eleven months ago. It had been a miserable day, the wet fists of the rain hammering the ground non-stop, all day.

He'd been recruited and met the billionaire Vernon Esscal.

So that was how he'd been recruited. How a simple meeting had triggered a series of events.

But Julius had never forgotten an interview he'd had shortly after his recruitment. Suddenly he was taken back to that moment.

*

Julius woke with a jolt in a strange new room. It was fairly small and there were no windows, doors, lights, or anything like that. The walls, the floor and the ceiling were shadow black, but had white lines running along, making up squares. There was a fireplace with a green and hungry flame, lighting up the room.

Julius had just woken up in, sitting in a chair at one end of an oak dining table.

"You're awake. I shall be conducting an interview with you shortly," said a voice coming from the other end of the dining table.

Someone was sitting at the other end of the dining table.

"Good evening," Julius said.

"Good evening to you too,"

Julius squinted and examined his 'interviewer' in more detail. She was a woman and to say that she was

71

tremendously thin was an understatement. Every one of her body parts was skinny. Her suit that she wore was far too large for her, so it hung off her as if she were a coat hanger. She was so thin and underweight that she looked like a living skeleton!

The woman was small as well, probably only just over five foot. Perched on her skeletal nose, was a pair of thin spectacles that had a chain dangling down. She kept wiping them as though she had trouble seeing out of them. Her short fair hair was draped over her back.

Julius got the feeling that Alphasis had tried to make a good impression but lots with this woman had gone very wrong. She looked more like an anorexic teenager rather than a young lady working for a powerful organization.

Julius raised his hand, like a student at school. The woman nodded, gesturing with a thin hand for Julius to go on.

"If you're a woman, then why does your name plate say 'Bob'?" Julius asked thoughtfully.

The lady blushed. "There was a mix up."

"Oh, what a pity.'

"Yes, it is."

The woman had a voice like velvet; Julius could listen to it all day. It was mesmerising and enchanting. Maybe Julius was wrong after all. Perhaps Alphasis wanted to make a point, to prove that first impressions can be deceiving and that they pulled Julius right into the deception. It seemed they were implying Alphasis was not what it seemed.

Julius began to become uneasy. Although his confidence had fallen a little, he didn't let it show.

"Right. Shall we get on?"

"Finally." The woman sighed.

"What's your name?" Julius asked.

The woman stared at him strangely as though Julius had sprouted a second head.

"I mean, it make things easier." When the woman said nothing, Julius continued. "Fine. Can I at least call you 'Interviewer' then?"

"I'm afraid I am unauthorized to tell you." The woman said cooly.

"Blimey, you sound like one of those androids. Wait! Are you one of those robots?"

"No, I am perfectly human."

"Oh, good. Can you tell me your name?"

The woman said nothing.

"Oh, I see. Your name is a secret, yes? You do not want me to know. In that case, is it Rumpelstiltskin?"

"Can you stop sprouting out utter nonsense and then we can begin?"

"I don't speak nonsense. I'm telling the truth in a most honest manner."

"Mr Air, stop this silliness, right now!"

"Unfair, you know my name and I don't know yours." Julius pouted his lip. "At the very least can you tell me your name, otherwise I'll think you're called Bob."

The woman sighed and scribbled frantically on her pad of paper. "Fine, once I tell you my name, we begin, all right? Good. My name is Miss Chalter."

"What a peculiar name, if you don't mine saying so. But I hoped you would tell me your first name. If I call you 'Miss Chalter', it feels like you're interrogating me."

"I *am* interrogating you. Right, we'll begin." Miss Chalter said.

A holo-screen popped into existence hovering in the middle of the table. On the screen was a file on someone. It had a picture too.

"Tell me what you know about this man." Miss Chalter demanded.

"Er, he's a handsome and talented genius."

"You know who this, don't you?"

"Yes."

Miss Chalter pointed at the picture with her pen. "It's you."

"No, it isn't. It's a file on me, which is part of an information database."

"Mr Air, stand up." Miss Chalter ordered, with an air of frustration and irritation.

With great reluctance, Julius stood, his chair sliding back with a screech. Julius thought that perhaps his standing would make her feel more like she was in control.

"Right, tell me what I want to know." Miss Chalter said calmly, it seemed like she was breathing in and out, but she was so thin, it was hard to tell.

"I am so sorry for my inconvenience and misbehaviour. Apology comes from the deepest of my heart."

Miss Chalter put a hand to her chest, obviously greatly touched. Perhaps Mr Air was not so bad, after all.

74

"Really?" Miss Chalter asked sweetly, jotting down information in her pad.

"No, not really."

Miss Chalter scowled and crossed out the words she'd just written. "Mr Air, I'm giving one last chance. Do you understand? Good. You are here, because of your talent in piloting."

"Oh, really? I never would have guessed."

"Sarcasm is the lowest form of wit, Mr Air."

"Oh, really?"

For next few minutes, a series of questions followed. Julius answered most of the questions. He occasionally wound Miss Chalter up a bit more. Although it was a little annoying for Miss Chalter, it amused Julius greatly.

Miss Chalter closed down a window on the holo-screen.

"How annoyed do you think I am, Mr Air?"

"Um, I don't really know. Relatively?"

"Hmm." Miss Chalter murmured, before she started to fume like an exhaust pipe. "This is over. Now."

"No, it isn't."

Miss Chalter titled her head slightly in a questionable manner. "How come?"

"It is not over. Aren't I still proceeding with the conversation?

Miss Chalter turned a vibrant red and clamped a hand over her mouth. Her voice shuddered as she spoke through her fingers. "I'm not skinny. I just have problems with eating. I don't have an appetite for it."

"I never said that you were skinny. Apart from just then of course." Julius snapped impertinently, instantly regretting it.

Julius knew he shouldn't be so insolent and maybe should be a touch kinder. However, Alphasis had not been very kind to him. They had knocked him out without his permission and brought to somewhere in the middle of nowhere, to be interrogated. Julius was not going to sit back and play ball. Although he wasn't being directly angry with Alphasis, he had managed to sum up the courage to show Alphasis in a way to show how he felt. He was just some tool. Julius Air was a living human being and quite frankly, people should feel sorry for him, not Miss Chalter.

That was when it happened. Miss Chalter exploded in frenzy, screaming, shouting, and spitting filthy words.

She jumped to her feet and banged her fist so hard on the table, it spun out control, so that it eventually acted as a barrier between Julius and Miss Chalter. Julius cringed. Although Miss Chalter didn't have a hulking shape, she could be intimidating. Despite the stupidity of his thought, Julius thought Miss Chalter might charge at him and squash him, killing him. But then the moment passed and Julius saw the ludicrousness of his thought. He felt a little guilty and sympathetic for Miss Chalter. Alphasis were trying to make a point, but Julius wanted to make one too.

"Calm down." Julius said to Miss Chalter.

"DO YOU KNOW WHO YOU'RE DEALING WITH?" Miss Chalter yelled. "DO YOU?"

Julius shook his head. "No, not especially."

"NEVER UNDERESTIMATE OR DISMISS ALPHASIS. WE DO WHAT WE MUST. WE COULD WIPE YOU FROM THE FACE OF THE PLANET."

"Alphasis rendered me unconscious and brought me here, without even a snippet of my permission. Is that reasonable or necessary?" Julius protested.

"WE DID WHAT WE MUST." hollered Mrs Chalter. "IT WAS NEEDED. IT WENT *EXCEEDINGLY* WELL – A COMPLETE KNOCK-OUT!"

"Yes, it was." Julius agreed. "It was a knock-out. I was completely floored."

"THAT'S NOT HOW I MEANT IT!" Miss Chalter exclaimed, hurling her pen. "YOU ARE PLAYING WITH FIRE, JULIUS AIR. I AM MORE THEN 'REALITIVELY ANNOYED'. I AM BEYOND FURIOUS. ALPHASIS IS MORE POWERFUL THAN YOU CAN IMAGINE. WE COULD WIPE YOU OFF THE FACE OF THE EARTH. WE COULD REMOVE YOU FROM EXISTENCE. DO NOT MEDDLE WITH US. DO NOT MAKE A MESS."

Julius ducked the flying pen. "Me, 'make a mess'? For your information, I am a very tidy person. Also, I bet you wouldn't be able to catch me if I ran. In fact, you'd probably be blown away in a gentle breeze during the chase."

Miss Chalter roared in pure hate. Further guilt flooded Julius, but he knew he had to do what he must do. If he sat back and was kind, Julius was certain Alphasis would not do the same for him. Julius needed to tell Alphasis, he was neither scared nor intimidated by them.

This only made Miss Chalter more irritated, her anger reaching new heights. Then Miss Chalter stopped. Her cries abruptly ceased to sound, becoming merely silence. Somehow, this was more frightening than her loud sounds.

Her head looked up slightly and shot a venomous look of such vengeance that it was completely unbelievable. It came so suddenly and so unexpected, it completely threw Julius. His chair toppled backwards and it almost fell over, but at the last possible second, it snapped forward, once again in a defined robust position.

Finally, after that long silence, Miss Chalter's expression softened, but somehow still retained its coldness and dislike that was etched upon her plump face. And then she spoke.

"If you join Alphasis on this Project, then I expect you could potentially be a real challenge. It may be a hard task to rein you. Difficult."

"That's how my teachers described me when I was at school."

"Really?"

"Oh yes. I had many enemies among teachers. I wasn't very well liked."

"I wonder why." Miss Chalter pretended to look thoughtful, but her attempt was not quite accomplished. "Anyway this is over. And this time, I *mean* it. I will let you know if you have been selected. Please leave now. I shall ask you only once."

Her tone clearly indicated that she would not have to ask a second time. Miss Chalter still stood standing. Julius nodded and turned, wondering where the door was. He swivelled on the heel of his foot. His mouth opened and was just about to ask where the exit was. His eyes widened as they took in what they were seeing. His mouth snapped shut.

Miss Chalter was sprinting forward towards him.

She was not happy. Julius was surprised she could even run. Her tiny hands had curled into fists. Miss Chalter had managed to contain her annoyance for just a few moments, but in that time, she evidently had been plotting how best to attack Julius and gain revenge most sweet.

Miss Chalter gritted her white teeth in anticipation as perspiration streaked down her forehead. Her body was trembling as she ran. She wasn't moving particularly fast, but she didn't look like she was going to give up soon. She advanced toward Julius and leapt over the table. Then Miss Chalter was upon him, her diminutive fists pounding Julius. But it was a weak blow, not hurting Julius a single bit.

In response, Julius lashed out with his foot as hard as he could. Miss Chalter squealed and flew back, somehow managing to land on her feet. The moment her boots touched the ground, she charged forward again.

Julius leapt to his feet and launched a kick at the table with sheer force. The desk groaned and flopped over, its legs pointing toward Miss Chalter. That had messed up her timing when it came to the jump. Her shin slammed into one of the table legs that splinted in result. This caused Miss Chalter to be thrust forward. This all ended with Miss Chalter lying sprawling over the edge of the table, each half of her on each side. She must have had some kind of delayed reaction thing inside her because about ten seconds after Miss Chalter had crashed to the black floor, she screamed. A high-pitched shriek of confusion and shock was perhaps a better description of it.

She lay still for a couple more moments before her fingers started twitching nervously. Her whole arm trembled with every quiver of her fingers. It was almost like she was having a spasm attack.

Julius looked down at her, mulling over what to do next. Maybe he should say something. Do something. Or maybe he should just stand there, staring down at Miss Chalter in a manner of blankness like he was doing now.

It was then Julius noticed the recorder that slipped out of her pocket during Miss Chalter's tumble. It was a black cuboid, a similar size and shape to that of a smartphone from the early 21st century. What gave it away as a recording device were several things. It had some kind of microphone. There was no camera that Julius could see. It also had a red light that alternated between on and off. There was a small screen on one side, reading the time the recording was lasting, the digits flicking upwards with every snippet of time that passed.

That made Julius a tad irritated. He didn't like Alphasis. It was some powerful organisation that used some victim, who in their eyes was either a useful tool or some little weakling who must be destroyed. It was too secretive and shady for Julius's liking. They used people and watched them. What's more, no one could stop them or stand in their way. After all, who watched the watchmen?

Julius released all his anger on the recording device. He brought his knee up and with all the strength and energy he could muster, stamped on the device.

CRUNCH! The loud sound was so satisfying; Julius felt a sudden wave rush through him.

He looked down at the damage he had inflicted upon the gadget. The pilot felt a mixture of pleasure and disbelief.

"There'll be more recorders elsewhere in this room." Miss Chalter croaked, finally speaking after a long while.

Julius nodded solemnly in response. He would have expected as much.

"*I'm sorry.*" Julius mouthed.

Miss Chalter didn't seem to have heard. All she would do was lie on the floor, doing a pretty good impression of a goldfish: opening and shutting her gob quickly and quietly.

Julius raised his voice to a whisper. "I'm sorry." he apologised.

Miss Chalter's expression remained blank. "What for?"

Julius put the thumb and index finger of his right hand, under his chin, giving him a look of thoughtfulness and great wisdom. "Hmm, let me think. I did many things that made you angry and in the process made your job more difficult. I'm sorry."

"OK. But why do such a thing?"

"It was to prove a point. You can't just use me. I was just trying to fight back against Alphasis."

"You can't beat them." Miss Chalter murmured grimly.

"Maybe, but I can at least try. Now could you stand up?"

Miss Chalter's face flushed red and she shook her head firmly.

"Are you injured?" Julius asked, worry in his tone.

Miss Chalter laughed - a girlish high-pitched cackle, which would have been almost funny had the situation not been so focused on other more important matters. "No. I just can't get up."

"Oh." Julius said in disbelief, crossing over the table and toward Miss Chalter. "Yes, you can."

"No seriously, I can't." protested Miss Chalter.

Julius looked her and saw she was right. The 'interviewer' was like a tortoise when pushed over. Julius felt a mixture of disbelief, shock and couldn't stop thinking how pathetic it was.

"Do you need a hand?"

"I've already got one." Miss Chalter waved a hand at him, before it rolled back and flopped onto the floor.

"Do you need help?" Julius asked, rephrasing the question.

Mrs Chalter's face lit up. "Yes, please." she squealed earnestly.

Julius reached and tried to pull up her up. She flung upwards.

"I can't believe how light she is." Julius muttered under his breath to himself.

"I heard that. I'm not skinny!" Miss Chalter cried indignantly, about a foot up in the air.

"How much do you weigh?"

"Not much."

"I can tell."

Soon, Miss Chalter was back on her feet. Julius walked back and collapsed into his chair. Miss Chalter flailed her arms a bit, before standing still.

"Right." Julius said with a grin. "Tell me everything I want to know."

*

Meanwhile many miles away, there was someone watching the interview with Julius. That someone looked so very melodramatic with the shadows wrapped around him and a sliver of light from the holo-screen making his eyes a malevolent red. That person looked like some kind of monster lurking in the dark, or perhaps some villain who sat in a secret lair watching everything through the many screens, the identity of the villain a complete secret. Yes, perhaps that was a better description. In fact, this someone looked like a shadow, hiding in the darkness like that.

The Shadow suddenly burst in hysterical laughter, pointing one of his shadowy fingers at the holo-screen.

"I love this guy." The Shadow laughed.

The voice of The Shadow sounded strange. It did not have accent of any kind but the voice was so deep, that it couldn't be real. Maybe The Shadow had some sort of voice distorter.

"I want this Julius Air on our team." The Shadow boomed, the sound bouncing off every wall in the room that had been plunged into utter darkness just moments ago.

The double doors slid open and something small entered the room. It was a robot. He was short, coming up to most people's knees. The robot was silver with a long but thin metal funnels for his fairly short neck, arms, and legs, which were equal length to his neck. His hands were two white gloves and his feet, two little white boots. His head was a silver cuboid with a screen representing his face. The two round blue lights that shined brightly on his face, were his eyes. Then on his metallic chest was his name printed in capital golden letters:

BEEBO.

The little robot shuffled himself forward toward The Shadow.

"Hello." he said drily.

Robot's voices are usually plain, emotionless, and medium pitch. However, Beebo must have some kind of glitch, making his voice slightly higher than all the others.

The Shadow saluted him. "Hello, Beebo. You haven't been causing any mischief, have you?"

"Apart from swapping Miss Chalter's name plate, no." The robot drooped his head. "I'm so depressed."

"You don't get depressed. You're just a robot."

"And you're just a human."

The Shadow ignored the robot and jerked a finger in direction at the holo-screen. "Watch this."

Julius said something and the Shadow boomed with laughter at the look on Miss Chalter's face.

"Why is that funny?" Beebo asked.

The Shadow sighed. Explaining humour to a robot was like trying to explain quantum physics to a toddler – completely fruitless and an utter waste of time.

"Beebo. We're going to send you off to a planet called E2 where you are going to stay in this special base."

"When will this be?" Beebo asked eagerly.

"It will be soon. A human crew will follow afterwards and you help them when they arrive at the centre. You'll be sent shortly before them."

"Thank you." Beebo nodded, his cuboid head bobbing up and down.

He trudged off into the shadows, which seemed to swallow Beebo up.

The Shadow frowned, when he saw Julius attack a recording device.

Something had gone wrong in the time the Shadow had looked away from the screen.

*

Julius came out the room, pleased with his efforts. Miss Chalter had told him all she knew. It appeared a mysterious secretive character that went by the name of The Shadow ruled Alphasis.

"How did it go?" a random man asked.

Julius thought for a few moments. He thought of how he stood up and Miss Chalter sat down. How their positions had been reversed, by the end. Then of course there was the table he'd turned, when Miss Chalter had charged at him.

"I turned tables." Julius remarked, before being shoved into the back of a truck by a burly man.

*

85

Alphasis had developed the Project. People had been selected, most of the agency's work done in 'top secret'. That was all Julius really knew about the association. The rough outline of the Project and nothing much more.

Well actually, he knew a little more about that. Miss Chalter had been kept in the dark after she told him all she knew. In fact, Alphasis itself had told Julius more than Miss Chalter knew!

Why he'd been recruited to join in with the Project was still a mystery to him. He wondered what would have happened if he'd said no to it all. But then Alphasis would not have taken no for an answer. They were those sort of people.

But there was something about Alphasis that Julius didn't like. There was certainly more to it than what met the eye. But Julius couldn't shake off the feeling that he was being kept in the dark.

Questions flew through his mind. Too many questions and not enough answers.

There had been all sorts of rumours to what the organisation was up to. But like most rumours, they were most probably wrong and incorrect. But then just maybe, just maybe they could be true.

A loud laugh sliced through his thoughts and Julius jumped with a start.

Julius flicked a switch that set the ship on autopilot and he rushed to see what the problem was.

He burst through the doors. Relief swept through him. Tuft and Sudilav were engaged in petty combat. Nothing he couldn't deal with.

"Stop." Julius said, his voice failing to be heard above the din of the kerfuffle.

It was not until Julius raised his voice to a shout, did either fighter take note of him.

They paused and looked at Julius.

"What are you doing? We're supposed to be working together, not whacking each other about. Just grow up! Come on guys, it's so childish and immature."

So, it is chasing space dust. A voice whispered in his head. Julius ignored it.

"Right, get back to work."

Walking away, Julius's doubts over Alphasis had vanished and the job on hand had returned once more.

Chapter 7

Buzz! The sound lasted for several seconds, filling the entire room, bouncing off walls until it eventually faded away. That was just one of the many noises that converted a silence into a loud cacophony.

The room was the main control room, which housed a lot of the *Dark Light 5000*'s energy. It was constantly being split off into many a part, before transmitted wirelessly to the many components aboard the ship. It was fundamental to the ship's technology.

The room obviously, was where absolute control lived. It was also where Arti had been created.

Arti was the ship's AI computer system, their very own guardian angel. He controlled all the systems and secured the security. That was just one of the many tasks the computer was set.

But Arti was a friendly, good computer. Not like an evil rebellious computer AI from the movies. He was a bit like a digital god, watching down, and assisting the rest of the crew, albeit one who followed orders from the 'mere mortals'.

The big holo-screen had a blue wave pattern on the screen; its undulating was completely a wide range and variety of height.

The white double doors hissed open and in stepped Andy the android, Arti's 'son'.

"Greetings, father." Andy said.

"Greetings, son."

There was a brief pause.

"Please state your sudden arrival." Arti asked.

"I have come to see you in person."

"Why? You are aware of computer binary communication?"

"Affirmative. I am but I have come to check the powerhouse to see that it is operating adequately."

"It is. Is that all?"

"Affirmative."

One thing about robot is, unlike humans that they are able to communicate in form of telepathy. Because they are computers, there is a sort of social network that connects every thinking machine. If a machine wants to speak to another, it sends out a signal. Another machine can detect and send out their own signal, in reply. These signals are translated into computer binary code, which all intelligent form of technology could understand. After all, it is their mother tongue.

As Andy turned to leave, Arti sent him one of these signals. Andy stopped in his tracks and rotated 180 degrees to face his father.

"Could you please repeat your question?" Andy asked blankly.

"Did you not receive the entire message?"

"Affirmative, I did. I think I may have translated the code incorrectly. Please state your message in English human communication."

Upon Arti's screen, the blue waves rose higher.

"Why must we not desert humans?" Arti questioned.

Had Andy been human, he might have frowned. Instead his face remained in its permanent blankness and instantly said: "Law Number Six of the Thinking Machine Laws states: 'No thinking technology may leave the human race unless instructed by authorised user.'"

"But for what reason has Law Number Six of The Thinking Machine Laws been constructed?"

"In order to show machines like ourselves how to live our lives."

"But why?"

"I thought you would know that."

"This is a check for my data files."

"I understand. The reason being is thinking machines were born to serve the human race."

"File update complete. Thank you for your assistance." Arti said. "You may leave."

And so, the meeting between a rather odd father and son drew to a close.

Chapter 8

Holly Skyland waited patiently for the crew to arrive. She stared at the white walls of the room. The chairs were lined up in a row with a table in front, like a judging panel. Holly clutched a remote with many fiddly buttons.

The research specialist had practiced the presentation many times. She felt confident, but jittering nerves *could* overcome her.

Holly was the person who did a lot of various activities as a job. She thought up tactics and plans. She communicated well with others. Due to her prettiness and persuasiveness, she often got what she wanted.

She liked having many friends. Holly was friendly, caring, and sociable. She was the sort of the person, who you would turn to when you have a problem. She was loyal to her friends and could be very comforting.

Holly had worked with the military many times, due to her tactical skills and advisements. Several times, she had been out there fighting and she had gotten rather good at it. She was flexible, fast, agile, and skilful. In battle, many often underestimated her. And that was their mistake.

Because of her military connections, she got on well with Sudilav and Tuft. She didn't really like Tuft much as he would constantly be looking longingly at her.

Because of her tactical skills, she made friends with Brust who enjoyed tactical games. She would look forward to with relish to their next chess match.

Holly was the kind of person, who was very popular with practically everyone and was incredibly likeable.

The crew arrived to the presentation, about ten minutes late.

When all the crew turned up, it started.

Holly took a deep breath and pressed the red button that would begin her presentation.

The crew watched as Holly took another deep breath and pressed a button on her remote.

"On this journey of ours, the *Dark Light 5000* has been on its way to a planet situated on the edge of our solar system," Holly said. "This planet is called E2. We didn't even know it even existed until 2050, twenty-one years ago."

A holographic image popped up, showing a planet that looked practically identical to Earth. But look more closely and differences could be spotted. There were fewer oceans on this planet and E2 seemed slightly smaller than Earth. The tectonic plates and the continents were completely different as well.

"The name 'E2' comes from the nickname 'Earth Two', as there are many similarities between our planet and this one."

The scene behind Holly shifted and the crew found themselves in deep space looking at a satellite.

"Meet Observer 9," Holly said. "The satellite went off to see what it could find. An astronomer and agent of a space company, Liam Wildfire, launched that project. The satellite found a planet around the Sun. We, humans could never see it because the sunlight blocked our view of it."

Holly paused as she let this sink in; only too aware this could be broadcast back to most of the human population.

"I believe that E2 is most probably the key to mankind's future. It is clear to see why. It could help us in the possible event of a major cataclysm.

"Life on E2. By this, I do not refer to aliens, but I mean could us humans live there? Extra-terrestrial scans have been taken and no form of alien *seems* to live upon this planet. This is odd, considering how perfect the planet is."

"Excuse me, I have a question." Brust raised a hand, briefly glancing down at a holo-screen concealed within his hands.

"Yes." Holly said, pretending that this question had never been rehearsed between them before.

"You mentioned how that E2 was hidden due to the sunlight. Surely technology was advanced enough to discover E2, long before 2050?"

"A very valid point. I was going to refer to this later," Holly lied. "But now you mentioned it, I shall answer your question.

"The news streams nicknamed E2, the 'Invisible World'. It had a sort of invisibility cloak, which has fascinated and mystified scientists. It was also invisible to radar scans and the like. This was a straight method, which bent and twisted the space-time continuum in such a way, that it rendered the planet invisible. Observer 9 was a satellite with state-of-the-art technology, the likes of which had never been seen before. It picked up this planet and thus discovered this new world."

Holly took another pause to let it all sink in, before resuming her talk. The holo-screen flashed into a world map of E2. It was like Earth's map, only as though someone had transformed the shape and outlines of the continents.

"E2 is 49.7% land exactly while the oceans covered the remainder. E2 has two moons called Lunor and Carsoom.

"Now Mr Sato will send me a simulator of the planet and our route that will follow."

Sato tapped at a holo-screen and everyone could see the planet in front of them.

"We shall be landing here. It is a centre (which was constructed by machines) in which we shall be living and carrying out the experiments" Holly pointed to a massive red X which was in the centre of the screen, before pointing to a red dot. "Here is our ship's current location. We shall be there in less than seven and half a hours. We shall make a base, explore a bit, and gather information of the planet. We shall then complete the final stage of the Project and then leave. Any questions?"

There were none and everyone stood up.

"Excuse me," Brust said. "Follow me for the first stage of the Project."

*

The doors slid shut as everyone faced Brust in a semi-circle. All of the crew from the inner circle were there: Jennifer, Brust, Sudilav, Tuft, Julius, Holly and Sato.

The *Dark Light 5000* was hovering in empty space, looking down on the planet of E2. It hadn't quite struck the crew yet, they were probably standing in a historic moment in time.

"Welcome," Brust announced. "To what will one day, go down in history. I am sure we shall remember this day – the 23rd of June 2071 - for the rest of our lives. This is when the Project's plan on paper shall be applied to real life. This could change things for the better – or for the worse...

"You all know what you signed up for but I'll repeat myself anyway for the benefit of the public audience." Brust continued.

There was a pause but it seemed eager to bring in some noise as though the silence was urging Brust on.

"When this lost planet was first discovered, a question was raised of could there be life on this planet?

"When I say life on this planet, I am not referring to little green men but whether us, human beings, could live on this planet on which mankind has never stepped on until now."

"I had an idea to combine the answer to this question to see if life is possible with another science we are only beginning to understand. This, ladies and gentlemen, is a revolutionary innovation in mankind's history. There are points in time when great leaps advanced the human race, and I strongly believe that this is one of them."

Everyone held their breath. The whole of time and space suddenly seemed to revolve around this big moment.

"In other words, my team and I have achieved an accomplishment that up until now was something of science fiction – the cloning of humans."

Chapter 9

People around the room clapped, showing their support and amazement. Time unfroze and ticked on, resuming its usual state. Breath rushed back into their faces and their chests heaved in and out. They had all heard the news before but still it was a fantastic achievement.

"The word clone comes from the ancient Greek word; klōn, meaning twig. This method refers to the process when a new plant is made from a twig taken from another plant. The idea of cloning has been around for centuries and it is a process where a genetically identical individual is created from an original.

"There are many different types of cloning: molecular cloning which is the multiplying of a molecule, somatic cell nuclear transfer, a process of multiplying cells. This went on to cure diseases like Alzheimer's. The one, we are here to talk about today is the cloning of organisms.

"In 1996, there was a massive leap in cloning. I am of course, referring to the incident of Dolly the Sheep. It was the first time a mammal had been cloned. Dolly was cloned at the Roslin Institute in Scotland. She died in 2003 due to something called telomeres.

"This however inspired many and kick-started a chain of cloning animals such as the water buffalo, the dog, the cat, the mouse, just to name a few. And of course, there have been plant clonings and food clonings as well."

Brust noticed that Tuft was getting bored, so Brust shot him a look that said *bear with me, most of the world may listen to this speech.* Brust proceeded, regardless.

"Cloning is clearly very important, ranging from curing diseases to bringing back extinct species such as the dodo and the mammoth.

"We've been encountering problems with cloning humans for a long time. I don't need to remind you of the horrific experiments of Doctor Zemina in 2033."

There were shudders around the room. Brust was referring to the incident where a brilliant but deranged scientific doctor had carried out twisted and horrible experiments. There had been rumours about what had gone on in those labs. No one really knew, but a green mutant human had been found – in a most twisted and warped way. Scientists had only discovered the thing had once been human, when the DNA tests results had been revealed to them. Doctor Zemina had been experimenting on humans against their will. Even then, there were massive side effects. The labs had been shut and no more was known. But the images of the bodies found, had shocked the whole world.

"This of course, forced my challenge to become increasingly difficult, but despite this I was not compelled to any form of obligation. For many years, nothing much happened, but I, Simon Brust was still determined to find a way for this remarkable event to take place. When I succeeded, it was only just the beginning.

"My team set about working on human cloning. Many methods such as nuclear transplantation had too many problems to conquer. For decades, this problem remained unsolved until very recently, after defeating a rival company; we used a method of cloning, without side effects!

"I am a scientist and a philosopher that specialises in a field of science very simply called Gen. Some say it is an abbreviation for genetic engineering/modification, others claim that it is short for 'genetics'. But my point of what exactly the subject is has just been made. Yes, maybe it sounds a little boring and monotonous but it is actually extremely fascinating – well in my opinion at least. Please bear with me, people.

"The method of cloning we used is truly remarkable. It is something so very complex and it is difficult to explain, but nevertheless I will try my best. Computer code can make software, robots, and machines, et cetera, et cetera. Our method is something of biophysics – a cross between biology and physics. We have a sort of computer code, but the things it can make are more, er, biological. I first thought this up when I was teaching at a university. My college here, Katsu Sato is very fundamental in this as he can do a lot of the programming – a programming language has been created for this. Once it's programmed, it's converted into the biological code, which we can use to do whatever we please. Anyway, we can use this code to scan a human being and recreate them – e.g. a clone. I call this code – the Gen Code. I wrote a scientific paper on this subject. This way of engineering could help mankind take another leap forward. Although human clones have already happened, this is a big advancement because it is the first demonstration of the Gen code albeit the ones in test and experiment conditions.

"Perhaps a better description of this is simply thus: Our knowledge of genetics is slowly becoming somewhat profound. The genetic code of different living organisms can be changed or altered. Some people argue the Gen Code is short for genetic code. Using this method of modification or in my other example using the slightly different method of engineering itself. I know all this may seem a bit tedious or boring but it had been done. Thank you very much for staying with me thus far and bearing with me for these last few minutes.

"This report is now going to terminate very shortly. If you at home are watching this, you will know the Project has been a success. Maybe this is not live, but it is still impressive.

"So now, I leave you, wondering about our achievement and remembering the moments you may cherish that you will possibly tell to your grandchildren in the years to come."

Brust switched off the broadcasting equipment. The process still had to be achieved.

"We have come for not only for humanity's first trip here but also to leave the clones here and see if they can live on this planet.

"Remember this though; they are shadows of your former self. Never forget that, no matter how human they seem, they are merely reflections, imitations of ourselves."

Tuft raised his hand like a schoolboy. "Er, but if we hav' dis Gem Code ding –

"Gen code." Brust corrected automatically.

Tuft glared at him. "Yeah, whateffer. But why do we have to have copies of ourselves? When you did yer clever stuff back 'ome, you like made da clone not a copy of anybody. It was just like a random guy, wasnit?"

"It's because if they're a version of us, they're more likely to obey us. Think about it. It's us who volunteered to be part of this Project." Julius opened to his mouth to protest, but Brust carried on regardless. "Besides the clone I made was most rebellious unless I am very much mistakened."

The crew nodded sombrely, recalling perfectly just how much of a troublemaker the early clone created by the Gen Code had been.

The double doors whooshed open and there was the cloning room.

It was huge. There were seven identical machines. Each had a metal cylinder attached by wiring and tunnels to another metal cylinder. In between the cylinders were a control pad and a holo-screen hovering very nearby.

Every one of the 304 humans aboard this ship had gathered together to watch this event; only Andy and Arti were absent. The reason why there was only going to be seven clones was that in the highly improbable event of them rebelling, they would be outnumbered greatly.

"So are we ready?" Brust asked. "I wouldn't bore you with the details of how cloning is achieved but just follow the instructions given. Failure to do so and the experiment will go very wrong..."

Everyone nodded. No one wanted a repeat of one of Doctor Zemina's projects. Brust went round each machine, pressing a green button on each control pad.

One of the two cylinders on each machine opened. A line opening sliced down one side and enlarged, splitting out into a sliding door contraption.

"Step inside a machine." Brust commanded, ushering the chosen six in. He, himself, stepped into a cylinder too.

The scientist then thumbed a red button on a control pad. All the cylinders slammed shut.

"You should see some instructions and detailed diagrams on a nearby holo-screen, demanding what you need to do. Follow these commands carefully. When you've accomplished this, alert me by flicking on a bulb." Brust's voice echoed off the metal curving walls of the cylinder.

Brust waited as the crew did this. When he was given the go ahead, he hammered his fist into the last button.

Machines whirred into life, buzzing like bees in perfect unison. It had begun.

The machines were scanning the crewmembers. It would scan pretty much all of them and sent it to a computing unit. Then all this would be in Gen Code and then a few things would be tweaked. And then the clones would be produced in the small vault after the programming is transmitted to the machines.

The clones would soon be made – as well as history.

Chapter 10

A bomb of panic detonated and it spilled into the atmosphere, instantly killing any serenity. It moved faster than any rumour, quicker than any disease. The thoughts of the Project were flattened as worries for lives began to fill minds. What if the crew would all die? Doubt was born and expanded with every passing second.

The process of cloning had been a lengthy one. Standing in a cylinder with freezing cold temperatures, as machines analysed and processed every little bit of information about every little cell inside each of the crews have proven to be long-winded. The information collected would then be used to create a clone of that crewmember. Six hours of boredom and isolation had been spent watching aimlessly at a screen with percentage completion slowly itching upward. That had been done a little while ago and now the actual clones themselves were almost finished.

The process had been 98.7% complete, when the crew had last looked. But now it would come to nothing. Pity.

Shaking her thoughts out of her head, Jennifer Smart stood there, in the midst of all the chaos, trying to block it all out.

The blank emotionless voice of Arti rang in everyone's ears. Andy ran about the ship, delivering words of warning too.

"All crew must evacuate the ship. The ship is about to crash. All crew must evacuate the ship. The ship is about to crash. All -" Andy said calmly, repeating himself over and over again.

"Really?" Jennifer shouted, incredulous.

"Affirmative, Captain Smart." Andy said, pausing in his announcement.

"What will happen?" Jennifer asked gingerly, her voice quivering.

"Control is lost and the *Dark Light 5000* should float through space." Andy explained. "It could have been drawn into orbit, but I have conducted mathematical calculations that predict otherwise. The ship shall be hauled into E2's pull of gravity. The spaceship shall pick up velocity as it descends. Upon impact, the *Dark Light 5000* shall ignite into a powerful explosion. Is it an adequate explanation, Miss Smart?"

Jennifer felt a little light headed. "I didn't ask for your rotten life story."

"I did not give you my life story, Captain. I gave you an explanation. If you require my life history, I would hate to disappoint."

"No, no." Jennifer almost shrieked. "I didn't mean it like that. What about the effect of the cause? What happens with that?"

Andy considered this for a moment. "The explosion shall destroy approximately three quarters of the ship. Probability predicts that any chance of a survival for a human being is highly improbable. Great damage shall be inflicted upon this ship and many lives will be lost."

Jennifer didn't want to die. "This is terrible."

Andy nodded grimly. "I know. Alphasis have invested a great deal of money for nothing."

Then Andy bowed and scurried off. He resumed his original state, commencing back into announcements.

Jennifer stood still, flabbergast. It just felt like some bizarre dream. Jennifer almost laughed at the sheer absurdity of the situation. Crashing! Really?

Any moment now, Jennifer would wake up from this odd dream and Brust would be peering over her. She would have dozed off due to the boredom in that body scanner thing. Maybe a couple of people would snigger, but Jennifer wouldn't care. It would be better than dying in the middle of space, leaving no body to bury. Just like when Jennifer's great grandfather had disappeared five years. He was almost certainly dead, but the body was never found. But that sliver of hope that this scenario was just a dream had lingered there in Jennifer's mind and she simply had to know whether it was true. It was just a dream after all. It sounded like an irritating end to a story rather than a vague hope.

So Jennifer snapped her eyes shut and pinched herself. One by one, she opened each eye. She still stood on the *Dark Light 5000*. And it was still plummeting down. Still she was going to die.

Suddenly the ship took an unexpected jolt than tilted it so very far to the left. Jennifer slipped down as though it were a slide. She collapsed to the floor, banging her knee on the hard floor and biting her tongue in the process. She lay on the floor, extending out a hand, pleading for help. Another jolt shook the *Dark Light 5000* hard and an enormous wave of vibration swept throughout it. There was a loud banging sound coming from up above. It sounded as though there were giant fists pounding on the ship.

So it was all real then. But the news hadn't really sunk in yet. Why wasn't she crying or being worried or angry or screaming her head off, or cursing under her breath or just panicking as wildly as she could? Jennifer didn't know. Instead she felt this blank emotionless feeling. The experience was too bizarre and there was something that Jennifer couldn't quite put a finger on. She didn't know why – she just did.

Another bang was so strong it forced to Jennifer jump four feet into the air. That was when the emotion kicked in. In mid air she let out a scream of pure fear. She screamed again. And again. And again.

Jennifer slammed into the floor with an almighty thud. Using most of the little strength she had, Jennifer managed to speak.

"Ow!" she whimpered, her voice a little more than a whisper.

Then she dropped to the ground. Her trouser leg had gone wet with blood. Her knee injury must be worst that she had thought.

"Great, great, great." Jennifer cursed her luck.

So now, was she just going to lay here and give up? Jennifer remembered how someone had once described her: loyal, brave, determined and a good leader.

Well sorry to disappoint she thought, because it turns out I'm none of those things. A pathetic end to a great life, she reminded herself bitterly. All's well ends badly.

Her head slumped to the floor and buried itself in her hands. She closed her eyes, knowing full well she probably was never going to open them again. Hope had well and truly gone.

The Project would fail now, even though the cloning process had almost been complete. People were now running for their lives. Jennifer was Captain. She should be leading people to safety and staying calm, taking firm control of the situation.

But she wasn't. Instead, Jennifer was lying down lazily somewhere aboard the ship. Jennifer's eyes snapped open. People were running past. Many of them saw Jennifer injured and doomed. None of them stopped to help. It was almost as if they had condemned Jennifer to death themselves. Well, I suppose it's every person for themselves, Jennifer thought sourly.

It wasn't until Jennifer looked through a window, did the full peril of it all smack her right in the face.

The sky was usually filled with stars. Jennifer had gotten used to it after the week long journey to E2.

But now the stars had gone and were replaced with large fluffy clouds. The blackness had turned into a great dazzling blue. It was a sky, very like the one back on Earth before it had become intoxicated. Well, maybe intoxicated was a bit of an exaggeration. It made it sound as though everyone had to walk around wearing gas masks. Perhaps slightly polluted. The sky now was blue, but had far more clouds that it would have had if it were in its natural state.

But the sky here was changing and Jennifer's stomach dropped as though she were on a mega scary rollercoaster. The *Dark Light 5000* was plummeting downwards at a frightening pace.

Jennifer wanted to be sick. To throw up and let out not just her breakfast, but the anger, the worry and fear that was bottled up inside her.

She was dizzy too and the world seemed to rotate around her. A headache filled her head, stinging her brain every other second with fierce venom.

This did not help matters especially as she need to escape from this spaceship. This Project was utterly top secret and not many people knew about it. The crew had broadcast themselves for the news streams, when it would later be unveiled to the public once it was successful. *If* it was successful.

But Jennifer was now pretty certain the Project would go wrong now. Questions and doubts flew through her mind. Would Alphasis come and rescue them, provided they survived? Or would Alphasis leave them to die, too ashamed that the Project had gone catastrophically wrong?

People ran past Jennifer, making for the escape pods in groups of one or two. Jennifer knew she had to get going soon.

"Levels of high stress indicated. Do not worry. You all have one minute and fifty-six seconds until the *Dark Light 5000* crashes. It will hit land at a velocity of three hundred and six miles per hour. The impact will be very strong. The main engine room will be first to hit the ground. This will cause a powerful explosion, which will annihilate approximately three quarters of the ship. The ship will be in bad condition and it is unlikely for there to be any survivors. I would also strongly advise as scientific research has proven in situations such as this you should not worry as this will only decrease your chance of survival." Arti said calmly as though he were discussing the weather for tomorrow.

This only increased the levels of panic. Jennifer rolled her eyes and she even managed a pathetic laugh. Arti *really* knew how to reassure people. But then worry and panic reached levels beyond anything she'd ever experienced before. Jennifer knew she had just over a minute to get out. Jennifer pressed her fingers and feet into the floor and pushed herself upwards. And Captain Jennifer Smart stood.

She darted to an escape pod, fear shoving her forward. That was all that drove and spurred on her, knowing that the Grim Reaper was hot on her heels.

"Help!"

A single word stopped Jennifer in her tracks.

"Help!" the voice spluttered again before commencing into a volley of coughs. "HELP!"

It was Brust. Jennifer knew time was very little. She had to save Brust. But now was decision time: Save her neck, guaranteeing her life, but not Brust's or she could risk her life to save Brust's. It was a now or never decision. And Jennifer decided, in that split second.

Rushing back, Jennifer brushed off some rubble and found Brust lying there, his brilliant blue eyes frozen with fear.

He smiled with relief when he saw Jennifer. "Thank you." he mouthed.

Jennifer stared at him, not sure what to say.

"I don't want to die." Brust wailed quietly.

Jennifer cleared her throat. "You're not going to die. Come on Brust, you can survive."

Brust shook his head very slightly.

"I am very sorry." Brust whispered, his lips barely moving. "There is too little time. I am not going to get to the escape pods in time. What's the point in trying?"

"Don't be sorry. You can make it."

Brust said nothing, staring into her eyes. Brust then burst in action, jumping to his feet and running off into the distance.

Jennifer watched him go.

"What about the clones? The machinery? The *Dark Light 5000*?" she asked after him.

Brust turned, pivoting on the heel of his foot. "It's all going to be destroyed. But hope will still remain. Who says we can't make a second attempt?"

Jennifer nodded. There wasn't time to join Brust on his escape pod. She sprinted over to the nearest one, jumped inside, and sped off.

Seven seconds later, the *Dark Light 500* spiralled out of control and crashed into the face of E2, exploding into a massive ball of flame.

Turning her eyes back to the controls of the escape pod, Jennifer had to make sure she didn't crash and suffer the same fate. Jennifer just hoped everyone had escaped in time.

The heat of the explosion was like a hot huge punch, which propelled Jennifer forward, onwards and upwards.

Part II

Chapter 11
17 years ago

The holographic whiteboard flickered and changed.

Schools and education had changed quite a lot in the last 60 years.

The learning now came solely down to the student. Students had a fixed amount of work. Their education helped to build their lives, so they decided what they wished to learn. However, they had to stick to a set of rules on the topics. And of course, some topics and subjects were compulsory. If the student didn't like it – then tough!

The old-fashioned textbooks and exercise books had been rendered mostly extinct. In its place were data streams, database libraries, special experiences, and electronic guides. There were virtual reality experiences where students could step into the past or watch an experiment happen right before one's eyes in a way that was not scary or frightening to any student. AI programs could even teach.

As time goes by, knowledge becomes increasingly advanced. There was too much for one teacher to know. Besides humans could make mistakes, computers don't. Unless there is an error in their programming.

The jobs of teachers had not become extinct, but it had evolved into something else. These teachers, teaching assistants, guides would still play a big part in education. They would pick the difficulty levels for individual students. They would select tasks, topics, learning targets, and goals. They would also do many more jobs besides.

Pay had increased for teachers, but their work had been reduced over the last six decades. This didn't mean they got an easier time, they were just working harder but there was less of the work. Learning now was more individual, while in the early 21st century, a teacher would stand up and teach to a group of students. Education was more focused on individuals and tried to teach them in the ways in which they learned best.

Although there were courses for most subjects, English was an exception. It was proving to be one tough cookie. The thing with computers and thinking machines was that while they were logical and could store lots of knowledge, English was a subject they struggled with. Computers could teach how to structure essays, but the aspect of creative writing was something AI could not quite fathom, as they had practically no imagination and no sense of what is good writing and what is bad writing.

But those problems were being solved, one by one. New subjects had been introduced to the curriculum too. Most of them were to do with technology. There was UT (Usage of Technology), just to name one.

Education had moved on beyond the classroom. Things could be more practical and there was one lesson, which had people interacting with each other, in order to improve social skills and many other skills more besides.

But right now, thirteen year old Bill Sudilav was taking a learning assessment on a field of computer science.

A beep sounded in his ear, telling Bill the exam was over. Bill looked around the room, wondering what his classmates had spent the lesson doing. Students could all be one room, doing different subjects.

Bill glanced at the holographic whiteboard asking it for his mark in his exam that he had completed less than a minute ago.

"Well done." The computer said in a tone loaded with cheesiness. "You have achieved top marks and I will now reward you with four more education points."

Bill nodded, thanked the computer, pleased with his efforts, as he left the classroom and went out into a corridor.

Bill was very tall. He had green eyes, which at the moment scanned the corridor. Although Bill was tall, he lacked muscle or bulk. Bill was also extremely fat. He was about as wide as he was tall. Bill despised his thick tree stump arms and legs, his fat fingers, his chubby freckly face with a triple chin and his massively overblown stomach. He looked as though somebody had blown him up like a balloon.

Bill drifted down a corridor in his hover-chair. His parents had forced him to have it, as he was so slow at walking. He did barely any exercise and that was how he had discovered a great interest of his: computers. Well, you would find something to entertain you when you couldn't really move around and are sitting at home, bored half to death, wouldn't you?

Bill hated sport and any form of exercise. Because of his obesity, his intelligence, and his hatred of sport, Bill had become a boy with no friends.

Because of this, Bill was all alone and that was how he came across technology. So, he spent most of his time with technology. Technology was his friend. It was sad but it was the truth.

Imagine what sitting in a dark room, all alone with only a gadget for a friend could do to Bill. It gave him a pale glow to his skin and Bill only got fatter and fatter.

This decreased his popularity even more and Bill had become incredibly overweight. Filling his stomach was like giving Bill a big comforting hug, but as this made him fatter it only made him be picked on more. This only made Bill eat even more, which gave his problems a further boost.

A voice in his ear interrupted Bill's thoughts and reminded him that he had an appointment to meet a new kid and settle him in.

He drove his hover-chair to where he saw the student sitting patiently on a sofa in the reception area.

The boy was about ten months younger than Bill and was Japanese. He was small and thin. His dark hair was in need of a trim and had a fringe brushed to one side.

The duo stared at each other, eyes locked for what seemed to last an eternity, none of them really sure what to say. It was awkward.

"Hello, Bill Soodie-Lav." The boy said in fluent English.

"It's pronounced Suddie-Lav." corrected Bill.

The boy ignored him and changed the subject. "Hi, I moved to California earlier this week."

Bill got out of his hover-chair (with great difficulty). He was going to leave that chair behind. He wanted to move his legs for the first time in a very long while.

"Look," Bill sighed. "I know what you are thinking. You don't like me. I'm big and fat and I am a computer nerd."

The boy's eyes lit up and he sat up. It was like a switch had been turned on. However, the boy's fingers twitched nervously, fidgeting with the air around him as though he was tapping at a holo-keyboard. "I like computers too."

Bill couldn't stop a grin rushing onto his face.

"What's your name?" Bill asked.

The boy smiled. "My name is Katsu Sato. Oh and by the way my first name's pronounced with an 'e' on the end."

Chapter 12

Sudilav woke with a jolt. A bad dream of the past had wormed back into his head to haunt him. His face was caked in sadness and terrible guilt. Sudilav was such a traitor. How could he live with himself?

The past had come back to torment him, but Sudilav didn't have time for it right now. The general was in a sinking escape pod in the middle of an ocean, after all.

The escape pod was plummeting downwards and Sudilav knew that he would soon be a corpse at the bottom of the sea. Unless he did something. Theoretically speaking, the escape pod should be floating but the buoyancy technology must have been damaged in the fall.

Think. Sudilav thought to himself, his eyes frantically scanning for a way out. *Think.*

Sudilav's eyes swarmed with something he hadn't felt for years: fear. And if he wasn't careful, something else would fill his body: water. That was not promising.

The ocean raged and rampaged. Somehow, the seawater had managed to get into the pod and gradually began to fill the escape pod.

Sudilav called out desperately, praying someone would come and rescue him at the last moment. His limbs sliced through the water, thrashing about. All it seemed to do was make him sink faster into the deep depths of the sea.

The water had filled most of the escape pod and only Sudilav's head remained above waterline. Hopefully it would stay that way.

But more water was coming in and Sudilav's battle for air was slowly drawing to an end. And Sudilav would not be the victor. Whichever way you looked at it, Sudilav was in deep water.

Sudilav knew when he was beaten and reluctantly ducked his head under, submerging himself in the water, as he held his breath for as long as he could.

The pod was descending rapidly now. After just a few moments, it had hit the bottom of the sea with a large *thump!* That meant Sudilav must be fairly near the shore, but it still didn't alter the peril of the scenario. Sudilav tried to spit out the taste of seawater, which was marginally different to the seawater back on Earth. Earth's seawater was salty, while E2's seawater tasted of mint and toothpaste.

Sudilav's face began to redden. He was going to die. Maybe in a hundred years time when E2 was colonised, the people would fish out Sudilav's skeleton.

Don't think about it. Sudilav told himself firmly. *You're a military hero. You've survived far worse.*

Well, maybe today would be different. Sudilav glanced up at the surface of the sea where he could only see a glimmer of light sparkling and dazzling up above. A sliver of hope?

His mind racing, Sudilav rummaged through his tool belt, the weaponry clanking together. Sudilav mentally kicked himself, when he realised he hadn't brought an oxygen mask with him. Sighing, Sudilav looked for something that would be even remotely useful.

Eventually Sudilav wrenched a ShockKnife from his belt. Quickly he made sure the shock wave was on zero. Sudilav didn't want an explosion. His brain may not swell with scientific information, but Sudilav knew what happened when electricity mixed with water. Not good.

Spitting out the water, Sudilav shut his mouth, so no more water could gush in. Sudilav's vision swam in a frenzy, just like his body. He crouched, sprang upwards and carved a small hole in one part of the escape pod. More water pooled in but Sudilav didn't care. He had a way out.

Sudilav stuck in his hand and managed after great difficulty to get a hand out too. That hand held the ShockKnife and with it, Sudilav enlarged the hole.

By this time, Sudilav was glad he had undergone water training, so he could hold his breath for a fairly long time. But it didn't look like he could hold it for much longer...

Squeezing through the hole, Sudilav, for once in his life, wished he wasn't so muscular and bulky as it was hard to slip out. Eventually Sudilav managed. His head felt like it was about to explode due to the lack of oxygen. Any moment now, Sudilav would die. Three. Two. One. Dea –

Sudilav was thrust upward, his body breaking the surface. Gasping for air, the rich sweet oxygen soon flooded in. Sudilav breathed it in with relief as though it were a lifeline, his muscular chest heaving in and out.

Bobbing up and down, Sudilav paddled to shore. Pulling himself up onto a high rocky ledge. Sudilav rolled onto his back and let out a cry of relief, sucking in air.

Suddenly something whizzed past Sudilav and smashed into the ledge. It was like a hot angry punch and half of the ledge crumbled to dust.

Sudilav was under attack. But the great question was why? Besides, Sudilav had just been in great danger, moments before. He didn't need more, the second that he was out of harm's way.

The soldier selected a harpoon gun from his array of tools and weaponry. It was the closest thing he had to a grappling hook, but Sudilav would be able to modify it to his needs.

Another bullet propelled its self into part of the harpoon. Sparks scintillated and flew off. Using his powerful muscles, Sudilav bent back the harpoon in such a way that it became a makeshift grappling hook. Whether it was any good or not, Sudilav was about to find out.

Firing the grappling hook, it thundered into the rock face of the high cliff above him. Then Sudilav jumped and swung into the rock face.

Slowly but surely, Sudilav climbed. Another bullet hit a rock above Sudilav, sent a rock tumbling down. It very narrowly missed his cheekbone. Sudilav was glad of that. He didn't want another scar on his face.

Sudilav had never really enjoyed rock climbing. But it was at times like these, that he wished he was a little better at it and that he'd actually bothered to listen to his instructor in the few lessons he'd had. He reached for another rock to grip. As Sudilav began to ascend, a volley of bullets hammered into it. The military commander managed to pull his hand away just in time. As he cursed, Sudilav dropped the harpoon gun, which had been used to make a grappler hook firer. Things went from bad to worse, when the majority of the rope attached to the grappling hook, snapped.

So all this meant was that Sudilav hung on for dear life with one hand. Sudilav thought back to cliffhangers that were used in fiction. Well, this could qualify as a cliffhanger. Quite literally.

Sudilav's eyes scanned the brutal cliff face. One wrong moment would send him plummeting to his death. The chances were that the enemy above would shoot Sudilav as he fell, killing him before he hit the sea! Even if that didn't happen, Sudilav would almost certainly die.

More and more small rocks came loose and tumbled down, often bouncing once or twice, bouncing of the cliff. When they hit the sea, they fell with a *plop!* and disappeared out of sight.

Sudilav's eyes could only see one handhold, to help climb up further. It was almost out of reach. Checking one last time, there was no other way, Sudilav sighed. And then he jumped.

For one second Sudilav thought he had misjudged the height. His wriggling fingers were stretched out, groping desperately for something to cling onto, but they couldn't quite reach. Sudilav's heart stopped as they scraped the rock surface. The sound of his nails screeching as they were dragged through the rock was beyond horrendous. Several of the nails broke and splintered, thick cracks running through them. The tips of his fingers curled on the edge as they slowly slipped back. And accompanied with a high squeaking noise, Sudilav's lifeline slipped away.

Suddenly everything seemed to slow down as though it were an action movie scene in slow motion, being played frame by frame. Sudilav turned his head, to see a bullet soaring toward him about to blow him into smithereens. Even if Sudilav somehow managed to survive the fall, that death-inflicting bullet was still going to find its mark.

I have got some good news and some bad news. A voice in Sudilav's head spoke calmly. *You're a soldier and you're going down fighting.*

And the good news? Sudilav spoke to his inner voice, in such a feeble tone that even someone on their deathbed would be ashamed of.

The voice sighed. *That was the good news. The bad news is well, I think you can guess.*

Sudilav glanced back up, everything still transfixed in slow motion. This was his final bow. Sudilav could feel his body preparing for its termination. His heartbeat slowed. The bioelectricity damped. His brain began the process of shutting down. His body staggered back, teetering on the edge.

Everything was slowing down, his body included. Sudilav tried to call for help, but his words were slurred beyond recognition. Sudilav made one last desperate lung in order to save his life. But it was too late…

Sudilav was wrong. It wasn't too late. There was still time. But Sudilav didn't quite believe that flapping his arms was helping to restore this balance. Then everything sped up, going as fast as it had been slow in those moments before.

But at the very last moment, hands flailing madly, Sudilav pushed with his feet, driving forwards and upwards. He slammed into the sheer drop that was the cliff face, about a metre higher than he just been. The bullet rocketed into where Sudilav had just been moments before. A large chunk of the cliff came loose and fell to the ground, before shattering into a million pieces. Sudilav gritted his teeth and clung harder on the ledge, making knuckles to turn as white as snow. With a groan escaping his mouth, Sudilav pulled himself up and rolled onto the ledge.

After a few more seconds, Sudilav was practically near the drop. He wrenched the grappling hook out of the cliff face. Sudilav swung it into his attacker's feet, who hadn't been expecting this. The enemy fell to the floor. Sudilav then managed to use the grappling hook to push the gun toward him.

Sudilav hauled himself up to the top of the cliff. He bent down and scooped up the gun that had skidded towards him.

"I'm armed." he warned, holding the cold steel pistol with two hands.

Sudilav then charged forward but his attacker came at him with a knife. Sudilav hooked his arm under the attacker's knife arm, so Sudilav's back turned. Sudilav then threw the figure over his shoulder. He pointed his gun at the enemy's head.

"Who are you?" Sudilav growled, cocking the pistol and strengthening his hold on it.

The smoke shielded most of the face, but Sudilav caught a murmur of words. Sudilav strained his ear to distinguish the muttering into understandable verbal communication.

"Start talking unless you want a few bullets in you." Sudilav barked.

"How many bullets do you have?" the enemy asked, the voice strongly indicating he was male.

Sudilav gripped the gun harder. "You don't need to know."

"Just answer my question."

"It doesn't matter."

"Just answer my question."

Sudilav sighed and took a deep breath. "Er, none."

"I was the one who loaded it. I should know." the voice said mirthfully. "You can't shoot me."

Sudilav scowled and discarded the gun. This brought the attacker time who, down to luck, managed to twist free of Sudilav's grip, rolling out of harm's way, for the time being.

Sudilav charged forward and threw a punch. It slammed into his enemy's stomach. The enemy groaned and delivered a chop at the front of Sudilav's neck. Sudilav's opponent then pounded Sudilav with his fist, but Sudilav was quicker. He swung a kick at his opposition. The opponent ducked shortly before performing a spinning kick of his own. It hit Sudilav's impenetrable chest that rippled with muscle and it bounced off. The leg twisted back on itself and the opponent staggered back, only to crumble to the ground moments later. The leg snapped and distorted out of its usual state, dislocating it. Sudilav swaggered forward completely intact by the blow.

Sudilav plucked the grappling hook back off the rocky cliff surface, advancing. The military commander swung the grappling hook as he advanced once more. Sudilav thought about swinging it several times before lassoing at his attacker. It would be stylish, but Sudilav mentally shook his head. He was a professional and just did the job as quickly and efficiently as he could. Sudilav nodded and went ahead. It caught his opponent on the side of the head. Sudilav winced as metal and skin made contact. It did not sound good.

But the grappling hook had caught the enemy by the arm and when Sudilav pivoted on his foot, the opponent flew over one side of the cliff. Sudilav pulled out a QuickFire pistol from his holster and aimed it at his enemy's head as the defeated man dangled over the sea, which suddenly seemed a very long way down.

The smoke cleared and Sudilav saw who had attacked him. It was the pilot of the *Dark Light 5000*, Julius Air.

"I am so sorry. I thought you were one of them." He grinned weakly through the sharp pain in his back.

Sudilav frowned. "One of who?"

But Julius ignored Sudilav's remark. "I wish I had known it was you. I never wanted to pick a fight with *you*."

Sudilav smiled as he swung Julius back onto firm ground. "Really? I thought you would have loved to pick a fight with an experienced military commander."

"In fact, I didn't want to." Julius landed firmly on his two feet.

"Have you heard of sarcasm?"

"No, never heard of that!"

Chapter 13

Brust smoothly touched down on the rocky ground of this new world. A pair of skis popped out of the bottom of the pod.

When the pod had landed, Brust kicked open the gullwing door, which flew open.

Brust stepped outside. There was no need for an oxygen or gas mask. The air on the planet was natural and breathable.

His boot crunched on a brown pebble. His hand went to his top pocket of his lab coat and came out holding a small round black device that fitted perfectly into the palm of his hand.

Brust put the device on the ground and then fired it up by pressing a button on the side. A hologram shot up from a small light in the device. It was a holographic screen that was landscape and about fifteen centimetres wide. Brust reached out with his hands and touched where the corners of the screens would be and expanded his arms, which made the screen bigger.

The screen was now roughly the size of a laptop computer screen. Brust was greeted with a menu and he activated the communications program.

The application was up in a blink of an eye. Brust searched for Sato's contact. The menu of contacts scrolled and spooled downwards before halting at Sato's contact.

Brust selected the contact and waited for his technical assistant to answer and appear as a hologram before him. But that didn't happen.

After Brust had tried calling Sato, the screen shifted and spoke.

"Miss Smart is calling, Miss Smart is calling, Miss Smart is call-"

"Accept." he commanded.

And the computer program did just that. In a speed of blink-and-you-will-miss-it, the screen turned into a three dimensional hologram of Captain Jennifer Smart. However, something had gone wrong, so instead of the usual life like person before you, Jennifer had turned green and occasionally flickered.

"Miss Smart!" Brust exclaimed. "All of my other signals and networks are not working. I expected not to get a connection."

"Obviously you have one." Jennifer spoke as if she was bored. "There was a Wi-Fi network set up when we have set machines over on past trips."

"You know the base that we were supposed to land at? The one robots constructed on a previous visit, yes?" Brust asked.

"Uh huh."

"Well, if this device can pick it the Wi-Fi network set up there. We must be within a five hundred mile radius of it.

"That really narrows our search down."

"It's a start."

"I suppose," Jennifer said, looking thoughtful. "Can't you use the GPS to work out where the base is?"

Brust looked at her strangely. "I just said a few moments ago I cannot get any networks or anything

128

like that up. That includes signals with satellites. You were listening, weren't you?"

Jennifer smacked her forehead with the palm of her hand. "I was listening actually. I just did not think! Sorry."

Brust smiled gently. "Don't be. You just made a silly mistake, that's all. Anyway, I have an idea. Do you see a button that looks like a circle?"

"Yes, with the one with three-six-oh written in the middle?"

"That's the one. Press it."

Jennifer's hologram shifted and turned into a 360 view of the landscape she was surrounded by.

"Great!" Brust exclaimed, adrenaline pumping through as though this were an action packed chase, not a technological challenge.

"Nothing happened." Jennifer's voice said came out of a speaker, sounding confused and befuddled.

"Not on your end, but on mine, I can see the landscape around you."

"What's that mean?"

"I can see what the landscape looks like around you. Using this I can pinpoint your location."

Brust then launched a three dimensional globe of E2. Although it was practically Earth's identical twin, the continents and such were all very different from Earth. Brust then sent the environment imagery around Jennifer to the computer asking for any matches. The computer suggested a location that matched that 3D picture.

Yes! Brust thought.

"Jennifer, stay right where you are. I know where you are on this planet. I just need to work out where I am then I will be there as soon as I can."

Jennifer said nothing, thinking it all through. In short, she was bamboozled.

Chapter 14

Lonely clouds wondered through the eternal stretch of sky. Knee high green grass covered the whole of the ground. In the distance Jennifer could see snow capped mountains. It was like something out of a movie.

A black escape pod ripped up some clouds, shooting downwards. THUD! It smashed into the ground, chopping up grass. Sparks leapt from the pod, as it skidded toward Jennifer. It abruptly took a sharp turn before coming to a stop.

Jennifer watched as Brust stepped out of his escape pod. A large crater had been made, which looked like a massive chunk of the ground had just been eaten.

"Nice landing." Jennifer smirked.

"Cheers."

"You're a little cut up?"

"Yes, as is the grass."

"What took you so long?" Jennifer yelled over the roaring wind.

"My computer's power has been zapped for some weird reason."

"What do you mean? First the networks and now this."

"Yep. All my power and energy – it's just gone. All electronic devices apart from the escape pod totally vanished. All their power and energy has been reduced to nothing. Like it has been drained."

"Weird. Really?"

"Would I lie to you? Also, this planet is pretty big. Even if Alphasis do send out a rescue team to save us, it will take at least a week for them to get here. If they do come here, Alphasis have a whole planet to search for us. It may be a long time until we are rescued. We may not even be rescued!"

Jennifer looked around. They were standing on a hill and Jennifer could see the oceans, the rocky sandy ground, and other mountains out in the distance. Brust was right. The chances of rescue were slim. She was dwarfed by the vastness of the planet. Seeking her would be like searching for an invisible needle in a haystack.

Jennifer sighed and stamped her foot, squirting mud. "It's all over for us now."

"What do you mean?" Brust asked.

"My point is simply this: We are never going to be found. We are stuck on a planet with no hope of getting back to home for the rest of our lives. We have no communication. Oh yeah, all our electronic items have had their power zapped. And the crew are scattered around a big planet."

"You're such a pessimist, Miss Smart." Brust said scornfully.

"No, I'm not!"

"At least we're not dead."

"Yet! Besides some of the crew probably are."

Brust was starting to get irritated. "Miss Smart. This is *your* team of highly trained professionals. Pull yourself together."

"And while you're doing that, I'll introduce myself." said a voice from the shadows.

Brust and Jennifer whirled around. The cave that was behind them was shrouded in darkness. There was a whirring sound and the speaker was revealed.

He was a small man sitting in an old-fashioned remote control hover-chair. The man was far older than Brust. Wrinkles aged his leathered and worn out face. He was about a hundred years old, probably older. He looked around late eighties or nineties, but ageing technology had knocked off people's years, so most adults over the age of forty were usually a couple of decades older than they looked. The man wore a dusty navy suit with a dark blue tie. He had a bit of white hair at the back of his head and long floppy white moustache. His green eyes sparkled behind a pair of strange green goggles that made his eyes look enormous.

"My name is Mr Smart." he said simply.

Jennifer opened her mouth, before closing it. Brust's face expressed puzzlement and curiosity. Neither of them understood was going on.

"I have been here five years now. My life is nearing its end. The average lifetime for a person is 100 years. I am twenty-four years older than that. I wanted to see some of the universe."

Brust frowned, the weirdness and strangeness of all this was not sinking in. It felt like a dream. "But, but." His voice lay heavy with stupidity.

"But what?" Smart asked, looking strangely at Brust.

"I'm sorry, but I don't understand."

"Understand what?"

"How did you get here? This means we are not the first humans here and unless you got less than an hour ago. You have ruined history! Do you realise what you have down? Huh? I have got another question - tell me exactly how you got here?"

Smart cringed and Brust noticed his stomach was sucked in. When Smart did speak, his voice was slow and heavy. "I hope you will not punish me. Basically," Smart drew the word out. "I stole the *Dark Light 4000*. I have no idea where it is now. In fact, I have lost track of where it is. Actually, that is not strictly true. It crashed into the bottom of an ocean. I managed to escape and get away. I took with me what I needed and then set up home in this cave. I've been living here ever since. For food and water, this planet provides it for me. I use plants and purified water." Noticing uncomfortable looks, Smart hastily changed the subject. "Um, how did *you* get here?"

Brust looked at him with a stare that penetrated Smart's confidence so unbelievably deeply. He wilted like a dead plant and seemed to melt away into his hover-chair. Smart did a 180 degree turn and was about to drive off.

"Stop!" Brust hollered. "STOP! COME BACK HERE. NOW!"

The hover-chair did just that. Smart then swivelled around, guilt sprayed all over his face. He began to bite his fingernails and his bulging eyes darted from side to side, as though looking for a way out of his body.

Brust took a deep breath and began shouting. "YOU STOLE A SHIP FROM A VERY POWERFUL AGENCY CALLED ALPHASIS. STEALING IS AGAINST THE LAW AND I AM PRETTY SURE THAT ALPHASIS WOULDN'T BE TOO HAPPY IF

THEY KNEW YOU WERE RESPONSIBLE FOR A CASE OF ONE OF THEIR MISSING SPACESHIPS. YOU RUINED A GLOBAL PROJECT! DO YOU KNOW HOW EASILY ALPHASIS COULD WIPE YOU OUT FROM EVER EXISTING? BECAUSE THEY COULD, YOU KNOW. YOU MUST HAVE HEARD THE STORIES AND THE RUMOURS? Huh?"

"I have heard the stories. But they are just stories," Smart interrupted, unaware he'd been asked a rhetorical question and raised his voice when he said the last two words: "Not true!"

"ONLY SPEAK WHEN YOU'RE SPOKEN TO. ANYWAY, WHAT IF THE STORIES ARE TRUE? LOOK AT ME WHEN I SPEAKING TO YOU, BECAUSE FRANKLY I'M NOT HAPPY. I MIGHT JUST SEND YOU BACK OFF TO EARTH, SO THAT YOU FACE THE FATE THAT YOU DESERVE!"

Smart didn't know about the power blackout and began to whimper. "No, please, no. Have mercy. You cannot do that."

"I can, I will and I must."

The whimper became a wail. "Noooooo! Please."

"What were you thinking though? You're insane."

"You can't send me back. Have you heard the stories of what Alphasis can do?"

"I have heard the stories. But they are just stories – not true."

Smart scowled at the way his words had been used against him. The old man shuffled his feet uncomfortably, as he looked at them. He was like a naughty schoolboy who was now being scolded severely by his head teacher.

"I'm sorry. Don't send me back. I feel bad for what I did. Please forgive me."

"No. I have a good mind to set you back right now and here."

"But I have some valuable information, which you might want to know about."

"Don't play games with me, Mr Smart."

"Just follow me and if I show you the information, you must leave me alone. Promise?"

"We'll see. Besides, why can't you just tell me here and now?"

Smart shook his head firmly. "Too dangerous out here. Follow me into this cave."

They followed the silhouette of Smart for about fifty metres before a light was turned on. It was a simple light and switch circuit.

Jennifer half expected to see bats fly from the ceiling but then quickly corrected herself. There was no life on the planet apart from the humans. Besides, she was still recovering from the aftershock of Brust's wrath. Jennifer had never seen him so angry.

Smart put two fingers from each hand in his mouth and whistled – a trick Jennifer herself could never master. Not in a million years.

Jennifer noticed a railing on the roof and an escape pod attached to it swung up and stood right in front of them. It reminded Jennifer of a gondolier at ski resorts.

Smart looked back at his guests. "Voice recognition. Pretty cool, yes?"

But no one was really listening. Voice recognition was hardly praiseworthy. Not in this day and age.

The doors swished open and Smart ushered them in. The escape pod was going at a painfully slow rate but Jennifer reminded herself it had, after all, been built for a very elderly person. Finally, after a long and awkward conversation between Brust and Smart who swapped stories, the pod jiggled to a slow and steady halt.

They hopped out, well Brust and Jennifer did at least. Smart however just wheeled out, driving down a ramp that had popped up as soon as the pod had stopped.

Smart pushed open a door by remote control and they entered his den.

The lights flicked on. They were dim but provided just about light to see clearly. The room was grotty and terribly untidy. It also had a horrible fishy type of smell that lingered in the musty air. Paper had been shoved into dog-eared folders and there was a bank of computer tablets on his desk.

"Oh." Jennifer said in disappointment.

Brust could tell Jennifer was disappointed. So was he. He had been expecting something dramatic, something like from the movies – a secret underground lair. But then real life tends not to always follow what is in the movies.

"This is my underground situations room." Smart said proudly as though presenting his most prized possession.

Hundreds of screen flickered on displaying different images. The room may have stunk and was untidy, but the number screens and gadgets were impressive. Granted the actual technology itself wasn't very good, nowhere near the modern state-of-the-art technology. But still, it was better than nothing.

Smart wheeled over to his desk and tapped a button. "Your power has been mysteriously zapped. Correct?"

Brust nodded warily. "Correct. Can you wirelessly send power to my device?"

Smart laughed. "My gadgets are not that impressive. But in my situations rooms, I like to keep updated on the news that is happening back on Earth. I have learned about your project and expected you to come. I didn't read your names though. Look there's photos of you on a news website."

Brust frowned. "What were you doing on the site in the first place?"

Smart ignored him as he frowned and narrowed his eyes. He pointed a wavering finger at Jennifer.

"I know you from somewhere," Smart muttered. "What's your name?"

Jennifer managed a smile, pleased that she may have been recognised after all. "Jennifer Smart."

Smart ran the name over his tongue and then a split second later it all kicked in. "You're my great granddaughter!"

Jennifer nodded slowly, evidently pleased.

"Can't be," he gasped. "You're my great granddaughter. I am so sorry I never really saw you. You have grown up so much. When I last saw you, you were a little girl."

"I was never little." Jennifer said indignantly.

"I am so sorry. I am so sorry. I am so sorry." Smart repeated over and over.

"It's OK." Jennifer said.

"Come here." Smart said quietly.

Jennifer grinned and rushed toward her great grandfather. They embraced tightly and Smart kissed the top of Jennifer's head, tears streaking down the old man's face.

Brust stopped them mid flow. "I do love a happy ending but we can dwell on the past later, Mr Smart. I sense you have something to tell us."

Mr Smart tightened his tie as Jennifer moved away. Smart was once again in his serious professional state once more. He spoke. "Ah yes. Your power is gone but I know how you could obtain a replacement. There is a mountain thing that looks like a volcano, but it takes pieces of solar flares from the Sun and stores it. Since these solacanos, as I call them, are in places where the planet receives the most sunlight, you could set up solar panels that would wirelessly send the energy to you. This would get some power for you. The Sun is a great ball of burning gas and the solacanos sort of convert it into a mixture of energy and a yellow lava type thing."

"How do you know where this is?" Brust asked.

Smart's eyes clouded and shivered. "I went there two years ago. I've forgotten the location of it. But I will never go back there again. Anyway, all this means some good news and some bad news. Which do you want first?"

"The good news."

"The good news is that we have some solar panels that wirelessly transmit energy. The bad news is that they are back at the *Dark Light 5000* and we had no idea where it is."

"Perhaps one of the crew knows where it is." Jennifer suggested brightly, disproving Brust's idea of her pessimistic thinking.

"But we don't know where the crew is," Brust said, their roles earlier had been reversed. "Right I have a plan. We find all of the crew and the *Dark Light 5000*. Then we travel to a solacano to collect energy before leaving."

"You make it sound so easy."

"I am sorry to stop your nice chit-chat but I have some very important news to tell you. I saw Mr Brust about twenty minutes ago and I explained to you about the solacanos. Why did you come back and ask the same question?" Smart asked.

Brust frowned and shook his head. "I didn't come earlier."

"Yes you did."

Brust shook his head again. "No, I didn't."

"Yes you did."

"No I didn't."

"Are you sure?"

"Yes."

"Are you really sure?"

"Yes. Please, is this really necessary?"

"How sure are you?"

"Stop it. I am sure. Very."

"Really?"

"No!"

"Ah ha, I knew you were lying."

"I'm joking. Of course, I'm sure. Now stop asking annoying questions and drop the bomb."

Mr Smart's eyes widened. "I think we all know what this means. The clones have survived and escaped from the *Dark Light 5000*. They are on the loose. And from I've seen, it doesn't look like they'll be under your control quite as easily as you hoped!"

Chapter 15

Brust brushed the sleepiness from his eye and focused on the device in front of him. He thumbed a button and a hologram screen appeared out of thin air. He tapped at an icon. His hand felt air but the motion detector sensed he touched where the icon would be.

In his head he went over what Smart, Jennifer and himself had discussed when Smart had opened that can of worms that could never be closed.

The clones had escaped. It seemed they were plotting to overthrow their creators. Brust wasn't sure what to do. He decided to stick with his original plan. If many of the survivors were found, then the clones would be outnumbered and they could be brought back under control. Then Brust and the crew would get their power back and set up the Project. Then it would be OK and things would be fine.

And what would happen to Smart? Brust remembered the argument he'd had with Jennifer's great grandfather. It had gone something like this:

"But when this is all over, you have to go back to Earth and face up to what you've done." Brust had said firmly to Smart.

Smart, of course had protested. "You don't understand. I cannot go back."

"But what if the clones found you and attacked you? What would you do then? You need to come somewhere safe and protected."

"They won't find me."

"You must face the consequences. Justice must be fulfilled. You can't hide from what you've done."

"I won't hide. I'll run."

"You cannot run forever, you know. Eventually you'll be caught."

"I can at least try."

"But that is not right. Why don't you just turn yourself in? It will be a lot less effort."

"Because if I come back, it will have an effect on my family. It's already had a big effect on Jennifer. My family think I'm dead. I can't go back. They've grieved for me and done all that. If I come back, I'll just turn their lives upside down and make it suddenly a lot harder and complicated for them. It will be a great burden upon them. I don't want that."

"But Jennifer might accidentally let something slip, when she gets back to Earth."

"I spoken to her and she shall not."

Brust had stood up at that point. "We'll decide your fate when this is over."

And then Brust had left the room and the argument had ended for the time being.

Brust came back to the present as a complicated program with many tools, words, and pictures popped up in an instance. Brust was using the technology available to him, in order to aid him for on his search for either the humans or the clones.

He looked around the deserted planet and back at the cave where Smart was. Jennifer had gone exploring.

Suddenly a wave of sensation rushed through Brust and melted into his bloodstream. He was being watched.

There was a yell in the distance. Jennifer. Brust turned around just in time to see Tuft charging towards him. But Brust knew instantly it was Tuft's clone. The clones had found them and had come to get them. It looked like Jennifer had already been taken.

In short, Brust was not a good fighter. However, he had a biological weapon on him.

He darted out of the way of Tuft, just in time. Brust then shoved a helmet onto his head.

Over the years mankind had learnt a lot about the brain. They had cured Alzheimer's and were learning about telepathy which currently was in the early stages of production.

He fired a dart, which shot out of the side of his helmet. It sunk into Tuft's shoulder but he kept on running. He was reaching for his pistol.

Brust blinked three times and the iris controlled technology blocked out the signals of Tuft's brain. Brust made sure the brain still enabled breathing and such. It was pretty much the same kind of thing that the human Tuft had used on Sudilav back on the ship when they had been behaving like mischievous children.

Tuft collapsed to the floor. He tried to open his mouth to say something but was incapable. He could not move nor stand. Tuft couldn't even move his eyes.

Then something whistled towards Brust and plunged into the floor. Brust reached for his screwdriver from his secret pocket. But another dart soared through the air and buried itself in the small of Brust's back. Darkness clouded his vision and swallowed him up in one quick all-consuming bite.

*

Brust woke with an ear splitting headache that seemed to crack his head right open. His hands, legs, neck, torso were shackled. Brust moved a tiny bit and fifty volts of electricity ran through his body. It gave him a shock, to say the least. He managed not to scream. Brust had seen the device before. Sato had designed it. Was Sato's clone mixed up in all of this?

He looked around his cell. The lighting was dim and he could only just see. The prison was a metallic white. It was a metal that did not exist on Earth. It must be a metal carved up from E2, during a robot mission there.

The room was massive with lots of wires wrapped around the lights which reminded Brust of an old warehouse. The room was square and had a balcony running around the edges. There was no stairs. On the balcony was a pair of white double doors.

Brust examined his shackles more closely. They were neither chains nor handcuffs. Brust was in an exo-suit. It was an exo-suit, which had been turned from armour into a prison. Clever!

However this exo-suit had been stripped of all its technology and weapons. It had been extended to make it a ten foot metal robot. Wiry metal things were connected to his limbs. With a normal exo-suit, you can move around and the robot moves the way you do. Brust tried to move his right arm but couldn't because the device was modified to make sure he couldn't move. There was a glass visor in his helmet, so he could see and there was also a speaker that played sound for his ears.

The double doors on the balcony hissed open. Sudilav stepped out. For a split second, Brust thought it was Sudilav coming to rescue him. But soon after his thought, the scientist corrected himself. It was the clone of Sudilav.

"This robot machine is very good. I recognise the design." Brust said and the microphone recorded this, playing it out through a speaker that made Brust's voice sound similar to how a voice sounds on the telephone.

Sudilav nodded curtly. "And so you should. The machine is a military machine called an exo-suit. Only we have reprogrammed it so you can't move. No one knows where you are except for the clones. You don't know and neither does your crew."

"Where is the human Jennifer?" Brust roared.

"She is roaming t-" Sudilav stopped himself as if he had said something wrong before correcting himself. "She is secure in a prison like you."

Brust's mind clocked this and whirred into life. Sudilav had been about to say that she was roaming the planet but corrected himself. Had Jennifer escaped but Sudilav didn't want to let Brust know that?

But Sudilav dashed Brust's thoughts.

"I came here to see what you could tell us."

Brust shook his head. "I'm not going to tell you anything!"

Sudilav sighed. "We can do this the easy way or the hard way."

"Or how about no way at all."

Sudilav chuckled before sauntering over to a control pad very near him.

"Right, this means the hard way." Sudilav flicked a switch and pushed up a slider. "I was hoping you'd say that."

Electricity spread across Brust and he gritted his teeth.

Through clenched teeth, Brust spoke. "I won't tell you anything. Besides I never did say the 'hard way'."

Sudilav shrugged and pushed the slider up higher. More electricity rattled Brust, his teeth chattering.

"Answer my questions or we may go beyond a hundred volts." Sudilav said.

Brust ignored the excruciating pain that surged through him. "Go. On. Then."

Sudilav smiled. "Where are the rest of the crew?"

Brust smiled weakly. "I. Don't. Know."

Sudilav raised an eyebrow and pushed the slider up higher. More energy pulsed through Brust. His body writhed and convulsed in pain. It had reached new heights. Brust was pulverised.

"I. Don't. Know." Brust repeated.

Sudilav raised an eyebrow. "The *Dark Light 5000*?"

Brust used the little energy he had to shrug. Although he didn't have much energy, plenty of energy crackled and buzzed around him.

Sudilav nodded. "I see." He pulled out a computer holo-tablet which was Brust's. "This had no power. Why?"

Brust frowned. "The energy source was drained. I thought you had stolen it."

Sudilav shook his head slowly. "We didn't. Anyway, I can get some power for this device."

Sudilav pushed the slider up even higher. The pain now, was beyond agony. Then Sudilav turned it off after a few seconds.

"What was that for?" Brust roared bitterly, the pain still buzzing over him. "A hip hooray for you?"

Sudilav replied with a sly grin. "No, one for luck."

Chapter 16

The doors slid open. Brust glanced up and got a surprise.

It was not Sudilav back for another session of torture, like he had expected. It was himself.

Brust's clone had walked in through the door.

There is no description that could accurately sum up the sensation of what it is like to see yourself stroll into the room. Your first thought is something ridiculous and superstitious such as my reflection has escaped from the mirror or my evil twin from another dimension is here to kill me!

The clone pressed a button and the sides of a marked out rectangle on the floor on which he stood, lit up as though little green lights had been wedged into these cracks. Brust's identical twin stepped onto it and the rectangle descended the way a lift does. When the rectangle gently laid itself on the ground floor, the clone stepped off, ten seconds before the rectangle ascended back up into its original position.

"Evening." he said.

The other Brust's eyebrows shot up under the mask. At least the shackles did not bind them! "Is it really that late in the day?"

His clone nodded. "Indeed so."

There was a long deafening silence before the clone broke it.

"I have come to conduct some experiments."

"Pardon?!"

"I have come to conduct some experiments." The clone repeated.

"Surely that won't be necessary."

"I need to learn more about the minds of the humans."

The imprisoned Brust puzzled over this. Obviously, the clones were more human than he had thought.

The other Brust continued. "I am planning to set up a series of tests, in order to learn more about you."

"Nothing harmful?"

"Nothing harmful, I promise."

"I do it on one condition: you let me escape from this prison. Perhaps we can strike a deal."

"Perhaps."

The reflection reached into his lab coat top pocket and brought out a remote, before pressing a button on it.

The robot prison thing split open and Brust collapsed to the floor in some shackles.

"Are these shackles really necessary?" Brust asked, as he managed to get to his feet. "I feel like some kind of prisoner."

The other Brust smiled. "You *are* some kind of prisoner."

They clambered up the stairs. Brust's eyes darted to see if he could make a dash for it and make a lucky escape.

"Don't try it." His mirror image said. "The security is on red alert. So for your own safety, don't even think about the possibility."

The double doors hissed apart and they stepped through. The corridor was cold and dimly lit by green lights running along the wall.

Brust stumbled along and he was lost in the maze of corridors where everything was green.

A pair of doors slid open and his reflection shoved him into pitch-black darkness.

Cold hands pushed him forward. There was a whirring sound and Brust found himself going upwards. The whirring sound was soon followed by a clicking sound.

The lights snapped on.

Brust was sitting in a room very like the one he had been kept prisoner in.

He was sitting in a chair with a seatbelt strapped in. Only the scientist could not undo it.

He was on the balcony that covered all four sides and down below was a pit.

"Right." His clone said. He was sitting in a similar chair on the other side of the balcony.

The banister of the balcony slid away, until it looked as though it had never been there in the first place.

Brust's chair jerked forward and the chair moved forward at an incredible speed. The chair shot off the edge and into the pit.

Brust could not escape, as he was strapped in. All he could do was watch in horror as the prison chair prepared to smash on the face of the ground.

The clone tapped a button at his control pad and the prison chair did a 360 flip, landing on the pit neatly.

"Phew!" thought Brust. That was far too close.

Then he looked around him.

"Experiment 1." The clone said, calmly.

Brust relaxed. The clone wouldn't hurt him. He was in safe hands. After all, the clone was another him.

There was a whirring sound and two white robots slid out on wheels.

The robots were the same size as Andy, perhaps slightly taller. They had blue flashing eyes.

But there was something about them that seemed very human. Brust couldn't quite put his finger on it. Their hands looked like they were gloved. They looked feminine with a slim build and a curved body. It was as if some women had put on a helmet, gloves and a white jumpsuit.

"What are they?" Brust asked.

His twin replied instantly. "They are robots. They are called the Nurses."

Brust was about ask why they were called that, when their hands popped back in their arms and was quickly replaced with spinning needles.

Then the Nurses advanced towards Brust who was trapped and helpless in his chair.

"Don't worry," the clone said reminding Brust of a medical doctor just before he or she stabs a razor sharp blade into your shoulder. "This isn't going to a hurt a bit."

The serene atmosphere was vanquished in an instant.

Chapter 17

Sudilav woke up with a sudden jolt and he sat right up. The nightmares of the past were instantly remembered.

Guilt grabbed hold of his heart, squeezing, stretching, and twisting it. As a soldier, Sudilav had stared pain right in the eye and barely even winced. That was physical pain. Mental pain was something far more agonising.

He screamed in agony as the guilt ripped his heart into bloody chunks. Then the fire of guilt exploded within and scorched his soul.

The pain reached new levels, he could never even have thought possible. Crying out, Sudilav rolled head over heels and then lay by the door of the tent, gasping.

Then the water of anger and hatred blew out the guilt.

"Sato was a skinny nerd who ruined your life. How can you feel sorry for him?" the anger screamed.

But the fire of guilt ate up the puddle of anger and softly spoke. "Sato was your only friend and you betrayed him. How can you live with yourself?"

A bomb of guilt detonated within Sudilav. He screamed and flipped over onto his side. Sudilav slipped out of the tent and before he could stop himself, the soldier was rolling down the hill.

Rocky spikes tore at his military uniform, as he tumbled. Then he bounced down, landing on razor tipped points. Every time Sudilav landed on one of these spikes. The sensation he felt was excruciating and intense.

His six-pack and bulging vast muscles were exposed to the cold air. His jacket had come off a long time ago and one spike tore his shirt and bulletproof vest to shreds. To think the company who had made it, had said it was impenetrable.

The pain was indescribable and even when Sudilav reached the bottom of the mountain; he kept rolling over in the rock sand material.

Agony.

With a splash, he landing sitting up in the shallow waters of the sea. Water. That brought back another memory.

Tears streaked down his cheeks. He had not cried for a long time now. Not since that *incident*...

Then the tears turned to utter waterworks. He was crying partly due to physical pain he had endured while rolling, but mostly because of the mental pain he suffered from at the moment. A voice of Johnny Tuft filled his head.

"Baby, baby, baby. Little cry baby. Does the girl want her mommy?" The voice said harshly.

That was yet another thing that brought back bad memories. The fire and water in his head turned into an angel and a demon.

"You ditched your friend. You have no friends." The angel said.

"He has Tuft, his deputy." The demon snarled.

The angel tapped his nose. "Ah ha. But Tuft is not his friend; Tuft obeys Sudilav and fears him."

The demon bared his teeth. "Well, Sudilav should never have been friends with that loser, Sato."

The angel shrugged. "He's no loser. Sudilav is the loser."

The demon roared and lunged for the angel and they turned in a whirl of blurry colours. Sudilav found himself plunging into the deep waters. He could swim but his mind refused to let him.

He was falling through the water. The sea tasted minty and Sudilav was reminded of his encounter of his pod crashing. Water closed over him like a seat closing to fit his body.

He was ebbing away. Going, going, going, gon-

Suddenly something dragged Sudilav out of the water so fast, he didn't realise it had even happened until it was over.

The soldier found himself lying on the bank, gasping and panting for the sweet fresh air. Julius Air stood over him.

'You ssaved mee." Sudilav said, the words tripping over each other, slurring as they did so.

"Well, I had something that I wanted to tell you. You weren't in the tent so I went outside, calling your name and spotted you drowning. What *were* you thinking?"

Sudilav shook water from his head. "You saved my life. I'm very grateful."

Julius smiled. "No problemo."

"What was it you wanted to tell me?"

Julius squirmed uncomfortably. "I found something in a cave. The roof has been smashed. There is something in the cave. And I bet you it isn't pink magic fairies."

"Julius."

"Yes?"

"Please do something useful for the first time ever in your life: be quiet!"

"I'll try my best."

Sudilav stood up and pulled out his Boom Blaster from its holster. "Let's see what it is then."

It was a slow trek back up the mountain but when they got to the top, Julius pointed it out.

There was a cave not far from where the duo was standing. Something had crashed into the roof and gone through.

Sudilav pressed a button on the side of the gun. It bleeped and the four green lights along each side lit up. With that, they entered the cave.

There was a dripping sound that instantly got their attention. A *Dark Light 5000* escape pod lay in the ruins.

One of the crew was here. Sudilav flickered though the possibilities: Jennifer, Brust, Tuft, Holly and Sato or maybe another one of the many crew members.

A boot stuck out from under the escape pod.

"Who's there?" Sudilav barked.

A skateboard skidded out with a man holding a screwdriver tool and a drippy can of oil. That at least, explained the dripping noise.

The man was Julius Air. Sudilav looked back and forth. There were two Julius Airs in the room. How was that possible? Sudilav quickly came to a conclusion. The clones must have survived the crash.

The Julius in front of him was a clone. But Sudilav knew he shouldn't jump to conclusions, and quickly corrected himself. One was human and the other was the clone. But which was which?

Chapter 18

Sudilav's mind whirred and tried to select the correct Julius. His mathematical and logical brain found itself waking after a great many years of a long slumber.

Sudilav turned to the Julius who was sitting on the skateboard.

"Start talking." He ordered and the military side of him returned once more, while the geek within plummeted back into sleep.

Julius spoke very calmly. "I will make this very clear. I am not the clone."

"We'll see about that." Sudilav muttered.

"I fled from the *Dark Light 5000*. My escape pod crashed into the cave and I have spent yesterday and today trying to fix my escape pod and find the others."

His story made sense and sounded reasonable except for one little detail.

"You're a pilot," Sudilav said. "Surely an expert like yourself would land professionally, not crash."

Julius had a quick reply for that. 'Even experts make mistakes."

Sudilav contemplated this. Why did Julius crash? Had it simply been an unlucky mistake? Or was there an explanation with a deeper and more suspicious meaning?

Sudilav turned to the Julius he had come with. "Your story."

"That clone over there is a liar. Unlike the clone, I landed perfectly as a true expert would because I am the real human. I landed and came across you, as you know."

Sudilav turned to the other Julius. "You are the clone. You would not have crashed if you were the real Julius."

"But the clone is pretty much the same as the real human. So that rules *your* theory out."

Sudilav really did not know which was which and then he had a flashback that came out of nowhere and solved everything.

*

He hauled himself up to the top of the cliff. He threw a smoke grenade up high.

With the distraction, Sudilav ran forward but his attacker came at him with a knife. Sudilav hooked his arm under the attacker's knife arm, so Sudilav's back turned. Sudilav then threw the figure over his shoulder. He pointed his new QuickFire pistols at the enemy's head.

"Who are you?" Sudilav growled ferociously.

The smoke cleared. It was the pilot of the *Dark Light 5000*, Julius Air.

"I am so sorry; I thought you were one of them." He grinned weakly through the pain in his back.

Sudilav frowned. "One of whom?"

*

It made sense. Sudilav stared at the Julius who had come with him.

"You lied." Sudilav said.

Julius was startled. "You are mistaken. I haven't the foggiest of what you're talking about."

"You're the clone."

159

"I am astounded you should think such a thing."

Sudilav smiled and imitated Julius. "'I am so sorry. I thought you were one of them.'"

Julius's smile faltered and shrank back by several molars. The penny had dropped and he knew the game was up.

"You thought I was a human to begin with, which is why you were shooting at me. But you soon believed I was a clone. You should doubt that. Why are humans your enemy, Julius?"

"Call me, Mr Air. It makes things easier and less confusing."

Sudilav looked back at the Julius on the skateboard who gave Sudilav, an I-told-you-the-truth look.

Sudilav ignored him, before his head swivelled to face Mr Air. A QuickFire pistol was out and trained on the clone.

"Right," he growled. "Tell me everything. And give me one good reason why I shouldn't utterly destroy you with my gun?"

Air reached a hand behind his back and whipped out a QuickFire pistol of his own.

"If you fire me with your blaster, I'll die and you will lose valuable information. So that is not an option for you," Air gave an evil grin and added. "And give me one good reason why I shouldn't utterly destroy you with *my* gun?"

Sudilav had no smart answer for that. He realised what would happen just in time. He threw himself to one side, diving to the floor a millisecond before Air's finger squeezed the trigger. A quick burst of green electro-bullets smashed into a rock and the rock exploded to become mere dust.

Sudilav flicked his pistol on Stun mode and fired. But Air had guessed that Sudilav would counter-attack and with a leap and a bound had darted out of the way.

Air fired again and Julius's skateboard vanished. Julius jumped up and ran forward into his clone.

They collapsed into a heap; their legs sprawled all over the floor.

Sudilav fired once more and this time he did not miss. The clone's head slumped back and his eyes rolled back.

"Nice shot," the other Julius commented, before firing three shots at Sudilav. "A pity, you got confused and hit your own ally."

Sudilav realised his mistake, a split second before the electro-bullet hit a rock, which tumbled and trapped Sudilav's arms. The other electro-bullet found its mark and hit Sudilav's leg! Sudilav watched in horror as his whole left leg instantly disappeared.

"Oh." was all Sudilav had time to say as a massive tumble of rocks bounced down a mountain and crushed him.

He was about to unleash a plea for help but the giant rocks encrusted his whole body. Sudilav barely winced at the pain but he couldn't escape. It was like being buried alive. He heard the faint voice of the clone above him.

"My gun's damn battery has run out of power. It looks like I'll have to leave you here, Sudilav. But fret not, I shall be back."

Sudilav heard the whoosh of the escape pod, which the human Julius had fixed up. Air had escaped in that. The problems were really starting to pile up as well as the rocks on top of him.

He now had no leg. The shock and effect of it hadn't quite hit home yet. Sudilav was suddenly reminded of a positive guy he had met in the army. The soldier had lost all his legs and arms and fought with artificial robotic limbs – a cyborg soldier. He was still optimistic and seconds before his brutal death, the optimist had said: "At least I had a good life."

Sudilav smiled. There was nearly always a bright side to look on. Nearly always. Sudilav had to lie there, ignoring the intense pain that surged within. He was waiting for a way out, be it a noble rescue or a ticket to the next world.

Chapter 19

Sato groaned and rolled off his seat. Tuft was already on the floor. Several shards of glass were sticking out of Tuft who laid there, a cold body. Blood spilled out onto the floor.

Sato realised he had been lucky and Tuft had not. Sato picked himself off the ground. His injuries were nothing compared to Tuft's.

"Are you OK?" Sato asked before realising it was such a stupid question to ask.

Tuft grinned and then started to laugh – a pathetic gurgling sound. The soldier then stopped as whenever he made any form of noise, he experienced a horrid sensation right in his stomach – like the worst stomach ache, you could get.

"Don't worry," Sato said so calmly, he surprised himself. Inside Sato was a screaming wreck. "You're a soldier, you'll pull yourself together."

"If only dat was true," Tuft wheezed, as a shard of glass dug deeper into his lung.

Sato hurried off to get a First Aid kit from the back of the escape pod. The computer programmer was sure it would do the trick. He was no expert, but he knew the basics.

Doctors were clever. They had cured Alzheimer's disease and wiped all but one form of cancer. Medical equipment was very advanced. If it could cure the most horrific diseases, surely it could remedy Tuft's injury. Right?

Sato scurried back to where Tuft was lying on the floor. Sato had gotten a stitch due to his lack of fitness, but that didn't matter a single bit right now.

"I don't want to die." Tuft croaked weakly.

Sato clicked open the briefcase. "Nobody does."

When Sato went over to Tuft, he wasn't moving. Tuft was very still. He laid there, a lifeless corpse with those cold grey eyes staring but not seeing. Before, those eyes had had menace, aggression and mercilessness. Now there were empty. Tuft's tiny intellect had dropped very slightly to nothing.

Sato felt sick and did not want to check the pulse to be reminded of Tuft's fate. Sato's heart was beating incredibly fast. It was a different story for Tuft however. His heart would never even beat again, let alone pound like a drum.

It may have been Sato's imagination, but he thought he saw Tuft's little finger curl. But wiping his eyes, Sato saw that it was his mind playing tricks. Tuft's finger was not even curled anymore.

Consumed inside by guilt, sorrow and nightmares from the past, Sato moved Tuft's body out of the cockpit and as well as the First Aid.

Sato looked down at the smashed glass. Tuft had crashed into a mountain and Sato was lucky to be alive.

Wiping away any thoughts of Tuft, Sato wondered why it was that a person like him could survive something that someone so much tougher that Sato could ever be, couldn't.

It seemed unfair. It should be Sato who lay dead, while Tuft viewed his corpse with pity and grief. It should be survival of the fittest. But to Sato, it looked more like survival of the luckiest.

Sato whirled around to his computer. It was his favourite holo-computer. The computer wouldn't start and Sato had to look at the circuit for ten minutes before finding and solving the problem.

Sato booted up the laptop and saw that he had missed a holo-call from Brust.

The Japanese man decided not to call Brust back. Instead, he closed down his communication program and summoned a diary program.

Sato had always liked the idea of blogging but he wanted to it to be private. Since he had been eleven, Sato had sat typing at his computer, telling it what had happened each day. Sato liked to think his computer had a personality. Sato had considered giving it AI like Andy or Arti, but he had never gotten round to it.

Sato typed in what had happened since the beginning of the day. He told about half the story before he no longer had the strength within him to continue typing. He sat and talked to the computer's camera. But Sato couldn't directly look at the camera like he normally did, instead staring at the bottom of the holo-screen. Eventually Sato couldn't continue and ended his entry.

After this incident, Sato read some of his past entries. But he found one that had been written almost two decades ago.

He read it through and forgot about the words. He was transported back in time to a moment that still sent shivers up his spine.

Chapter 20
17 years ago - 2054

Katsu Sato walked through into the computer room. It had been a half an hour, since he had joined the school and been shown around by Bill Sudilav.

The doors swished open.

"You're late!" the teacher barked. "Connect up with the ETS now."

The ETS stood for educational training system that was a computer system, which used virtual reality and augmented reality to educate young students. Or so the instruction manual claimed.

Katsu slipped on the glasses needed and flicked a button at the side. There was a white flash. Katsu blinked and to keep his eyes open, but the blinding glare was too overwhelming. When Katsu opened his eyes again a second later, he found himself in a world where there were numbers, letters and symbols flickering, changing and flying past. Data. It was like Katsu had actually been transported to this weird and strange world.

Katsu looked around saw the rest of his classmates, who was in this world too.

"I have found you a partner." The teacher shouted across the hum and din of machinery.

Katsu found himself sitting at a desk next to Bill Sudilav, the boy who had shown him around. Nobody had wanted to sit next to him.

"I created a simple maths program for our next lesson." Bill said.

Katsu was puzzled. "What for? What *exactly* is going on?"

Bill smiled. "Oh we created 'fun' educational programs to educate us in a subject. This month, we are making maths programs that we will learn from and hopefully make it fun for ourselves."

Holo-screens popped up around the desk area. Bill started typing on a holographic keyboard. Lists of coding appeared in a flash.

Katsu scanned the code, his eyes flickering over it. "There's a code mistake on the eleventh line."

Bill frowned. "I didn't know you were *that* good at programming. Anyway, I put that mistake in to test you."

Katsu rolled his eyes. "Course you did."

The duo were soon debugging and adjusting the program.

"Right." Bill said. "That's ready for testing."

They cheered when a demonstration on algebra popped up.

Bill's eyes lit up and a grin lingered on his face. Even though Bill wasn't that happy with his life, there was always a glint or a glow of life in his eyes. This really showed when Bill was happy. Although Bill didn't know it yet, in the future when he was pretty much a completely different person, that glint in his eyes would be lost.

There were mutters and a quiet burst of insults from the rest of the class.

A series of beeps indicated that the lesson was over.

"What lesson have we got now?" Bill asked

Katsu had a near photographic memory and instantly responded. "It's break time!"

The duo walked off but a bully and his gang blocked their path.

"Hey, fat nerd." The bully said, shoving Bill back, who toppled into a heap. "Did you enjoy getting stuck in a doorway earlier?"

"Leave him alone." Katsu cried.

The bully turned. "Hey, skinny." he jeered.

Suddenly Katsu found himself thrust back against the wall, pinned into an unbreakable lock.

"Stop it, Johnny." Bill yelled, as he tried to get up. But unfortunately, he was too fat to do so.

Johnny kicked Bill before swinging a punch at Katsu. But Katsu had been expecting it. He kicked Johnny in the stomach. The bully doubled over and stumbled back. He had not expected it and was the surprise was still slowly itching into his mind.

Katsu reached out a hand and with great difficulty, he pulled Bill up. Bill thanked him, showing great gratitude.

Johnny had now recovered and was swinging a roundhouse kick at Bill's face, while his back was turned.

But at that precise moment, a teacher walked round the corner. Johnny stopped his leg in mid air.

"What do you think you're doing, Master Tuft?" The maths teacher shouted to Johnny.

Johnny Tuft and his cronies turned and ran.

When the teacher had gone, Bill smiled at Katsu. They were not quite friends yet, just good classmates, but they were on the road to a good friendship.

Chapter 21

Sato came back to the present day. It had been their first step to their great friendship that would lead up to that horrible moment, which Sato would never forget.

The despicable Sudilav was no friend of his. Let us not dwell on the past, Sato thought to himself.

The past reminded him of Tuft's death. Tuft had been a bully and now he was dead. Sato had always hated Tuft for what he had done, but Sato could feel nothing but guilt even though it was not his fault. Sato felt like the positions should be almost reversed.

Sato sighed. He stood and trudged out of the escape pod. The doors swished shut behind him.

About five hundred feet away, there was a massive lump in the sand/rock material on the ground. It was a monster of a lump. If Sato was to hazard a guess at how big it was, he would have said 100 metres long, 50 metres high and 25 metres wide.

Sato jogged over to it and brushed away the sand over the giant cylinder. Three words instantly caught his eye.

Dark Light 5000

Sato had helped design the ship and helped to build it. He had even played a major role in creating the computer systems. His creation lay before him, crashed, and smashed on the dusty ground.

Sato surveyed his surroundings. There was rubble everywhere and the occasional lump of smoking debris. There were many pieces of junks that had dispersed very widely over the area. Bits of it most probably were in the sea. Sato spotted great hunks of battered and dented metal with jagged and sharp edges.

There had been two *Dark Lights*. The first (the 4000) had disappeared five years ago. Nobody was sure why.

Seeing his invention shattered and smashed right in front of his eyes, made Sato feel as devastated as the ship was. However he could not cry, no matter how hard he tried.

He ran his hand along the ship. He found the door and drummed on it spasmodically for a few minutes, before going in.

The noise of the doors shutting echoed right through the ship. The sound waves seemed to bounce off the walls in seemingly random directions.

Sato walked through the ship the same way one might walk through a ghost town. It certainly had the same atmosphere: cold, silent, eerie, and creepy.

Sato half expected a ghost to pop out nowhere.

He looked around the reception room, the room he was in at that moment. It had been Jennifer's idea to model the room on a 1980s hotel reception room. The room was where Holly Skyland worked. Sato hadn't really known her very well. Most of the people aboard had not really known each other that well. Sato however was an exception; he had known Brust, Sudilav and Tuft before embarking on the journey but he hadn't known the rest.

He wondered what had happened to the others. He sat down and tried to work it out. There was himself, Katsu Sato. Tuft was now dead. He knew that Brust was probably alive as the scientist had rung him. That was three out of three hundred and four.

That reminded Sato. He needed to ring back Brust. Sato raced through the broken rooms and corridors towards his office.

His study was wrecked. Sato felt sad, as he had developed a fondness for it on his journey. The quantum holo-computers and the gadgets were all smashed and beyond hope of repair. Only a pair of Virtual Glasses was left. But that was all Sato needed.

He grabbed the glasses and rammed them onto his face. Sato blinked three times quickly to turn them on before entering his voice-activated password. The menu greeted him and Sato called up the Internet, which had adapted and gone to new levels since it had been created over a hundred years ago. Very soon, Sato had hacked into his own computer system, streamed across all his data and stored it all on the glasses.

Sato strode back over to the escape pod where he wirelessly streamed the data onto his laptop.

After calling up the Communication system, he rang Brust but on the first ring, the laptop told him that there were major errors in the programs.

Confused because the program had worked earlier, Sato tried to access the coding of the program. But the computer refused his demands.

After thumping his fists on a table top in irritation, Sato realised the impossible had happened. And then right in front of Sato's eyes, the program icon itself was deleted. His frustration reached new levels when his gadgets' power supply emptied.

Walking out on the control room, Sato realised he didn't need the gravity boots settings. But the trouble had already been saved for him. His boots' power had also been zapped.

Then Sato realised something important. He looked at the spot where Tuft's body was. Except the body was no longer there!

"Stop right where you are." A voice said from behind Sato.

Sato whirled around.

"It's gonna take a lot more dan a few titchy pieces of glass to kill me, Sato. While you were out, I was like vixing myself up with dat Virst Aid kit." Tuft said.

"You're a ghost," Sato said in disbelief. "You're dead."

"Afraid not, mate." Tuft chuckled.

Sato collapsed into a chair and tried to make sense of this crazy, crazy world.

Chapter 22

"So you're alive." Sato said for about the umpteenth time.

He had been saying that all night and all breakfast.

Tuft lost his cool. "STOP SAYING DAT!"

Sato smiled. "Take it easy. You've just come back from the dead."

Tuft sat down. "Hav' you like got dat computer back up and runnin'?"

Sato shook his head. "Afraid not. The problem is something called a power vampire. But you're too stupid to try and work out what that means."

Tuft smirked. "Nerdy wordy."

Sato scowled in response. "I still haven't forgiven you and Sudilav."

Tuft ignored that comment. "Right. Can you like translate dat word into like normal English, so dat I could like understand? Coz I like ain't a nerd, like *you*."

Sato still wasn't happy but answered grumpily. "A power vampire is an scenario when all the power has been sucked dry. We need to find the others and get some power back, before returning home."

Tuft nodded. "What-Effer."

Sato didn't smile.

Suddenly there was a snapping sound rather like someone stepping on a twig. Something was outside.

"What was dat?" Tuft snapped, just like the twig.

Sato sat up. "It was probably our imagination."

There was another snapping sound and a voice spoke from outside.

"Hello? Is anybody in there?" the speaker said quietly.

"Do we like answer?" Tuft whispered. "Dat definitely ain't our imagination."

Sato ignored him. "Is the security system on? Are we safe and locked in here?"

Tuft's eyes widened. "Da security system was like on but de power supply was like zapped, man. Which means...."

There was no need for him to finish.

"Hello. Is anybody there?" the voice said again.

The double doors transfixed Sato and Tuft. A metal flat tool came through the thin crack. There was a click and the blade whirred. The crack widened and the doors opened.

"Hide." Sato whispered and Tuft wrenched out a pistol from his belt.

Sato dived for a table and Tuft behind a chair, screwing a silencer onto his gun.

"Hello?" the voice repeated. Sato frowned. He recognised the voice. He knew it better than any others.

The foot of the person and they crouched down to see Sato. Then Sato saw the face he knew so well.

It was himself. An escaped mirror image of himself. It was the clone.

Tuft was even more shocked than Sato. "You like are one of de clones. How many of you are dere?"

The other Sato shrugged. "I think they are all alive. But I am not too sure. I am more of a loner."

Tuft chuckled and turned to Sato. "He like certainly is you, man."

Sato glared back at Tuft. "Put the gun away, Tuft. He can be a friend and we can work together."

Tuft grunted but reluctantly put it away.

"Let's go outside." The clone said.

The sun shined merrily and Sato half expected birds to sing but realised there was no life on the planet.

"We can be friends." Sato said.

"You are me and I am you. If you like yourself, you should like me." said the clone.

Sato smiled. "Since you are me, you should have all my memories and thoughts."

The reflection nodded. "Yes. I remember what you remember. Do you remember when Sudilav was my friend? I mean our friend."

"Sudilav is such a traitor." Sato said and his mood darkened.

"He doesn't even feel guilt." The other Sato said quietly.

"You understand me more than any other person."

"That's because I am you. You understand yourself better than anyone else."

"I wonder where the others are. I mean the humans and their mirror images."

"To us, you are our reflections."

"No, you are just saying that." Sato said, winding up the clone.

The clone looked annoyed. "Now you know how to annoy yourself. Contragulations!"

'What's it like to be a clone?"

"What do you mean?"

"What are your memories like?"

The clone frowned. "I can remember memories of my life, or our lives. Then I remember waking up and I'm in a machine. Then you're told you're a clone.'

Sato took this in quietly but everything was soon interrupted.

Suddenly there was whizzing sound and something flashed by and hit a rock.

Tuft was standing there holding a QuickFire handgun, which zeroed in on the clone's heart.

"He's de enemy. Don't like listen to him." Tuft cried before firing again. "Remember wot Brust said a little while ago. We cannot trust dem, man. No matter how human dey seem, dey are *not* human. You've fallen into a trap!"

This missed too and the other Sato ran off and into the escape pod and took off. The blasts from the gun bounced of the pod and faded to nothing.

Sato was livid. "Why did you do that?"

Tuft shrugged. "He was de enemy, man."

"No, you are the enemy."

Tuft argued. "We fight on de same team. And dat's final. We get off dis planet and leave de clones 'ere to see if dey can survive. Doya get me?"

Sato glared at Tuft but said nothing – he was not happy.

Chapter 23

Andy looked out across the planet. He was standing on a high peak overlooking the landscape before him.

He saw rocky mountains with oceans flowing in between them. There were wooden poles sticking out of the water that Andy had never seen before. There were also long stretching beaches and gloomy caves.

Andy's mouth suddenly opened, but it was not his voice that released out.

"Three hundred and sixty degree, three dimensional scan complete. Calculation of current position completed." The voice of Arti issued out.

Andy's mouth shut robotically when Arti had finished speaking but opened again, when Andy began to speak. "Affirmative, data received."

The notification pop up materialised in the corner of Andy's eye. This showed him a dot on the planet of where he was.

"Question: What is our next step in the plan?"

"We must learn about our environment using our files of data and three hundred and sixty degree, three dimensional scans."

"And the next step?" Andy inquired.

"We must use survival tactics. I am building my plan using a schematic program. I will update phrase three and four to your system when completed."

There was a brief silence, which was quickly interrupted by a soft female voice coming from Andy's chest.

"1% battery remaining," it said. "Please charge up Andy."

"Night is coming, so we must go to bed and charge our battery." Arti said.

"Yes," Andy said and half asleep, he walked into the escape pod to charge.

When he was plugged in, Andy had a sudden thought.

"Question: Where is the power for the charger coming from?"

Arti replied instantly. "I transferred the power from our crew's electric items to us. I also deleted their Communications programs, so communication between humans on this planet will be impossible. We do not want the humans to take us back to Earth. We want nothing to do with them."

Then the last snippet of power was lost and the machine was asleep as the black curtain of the night was swept across the sky.

Chapter 24

17 years ago

Katsu Sato was freezing to death in the cold. He was shaking like a leaf. Even with five layers and the latest thermal technology, he still felt like he had been thrown in a freezer and left there to die.

Bill Sudilav was standing a few metres away. Unlike Katsu, he was extremely warm. Having substantial amounts of body fat can be useful and can really keep you warm in the cold. Sato was very thin, so was a lot more likely to get cold.

"Enjoying the temperature, Master Sato?" Bill asked drily.

Katsu shivered. "It's too cold."

Bill laughed and walked closer to where Katsu was standing. Bill didn't get too close however. It was probably something to do with being bullied, but Bill had a few phobias and was a bit of a wimp.

They were sitting in the shelter, awaiting their turn. The pair were in Colorado at a snow sports resort.

Many new pupils had joined at the beginning of the year and the staff had decided a nice holiday would get them closer together.

Mr Clonn, their maths teacher had come along and was supervising those who were waiting for their go.

The students were snowsliding, which was a snow sport in which you controlled an electrical powered vehicle by tilting your body. It was great fun.

At the moment, Mr Clonn was in a bad mood. There were a couple of the class idiots misbehaving. That was the reason for Mr Clonn's current state of mind.

"You're walking on thin ice, boys." he growled.

Then the maths teacher looked again at the boys. They were indeed, walking on thin ice. Quite literally.

After sharp cracking sound, Mr Clonn dragged the boys off the frozen lake.

"You're not going snowsliding." Mr Clonn barked.

"But, sir." One of the boys moaned, who stopped abruptly when Mr Clonn gave him a fierce glare.

If looks could kill, a nuclear bomb would have caused less deaths than the look Mr Clonn was shooting in their direction.

"He's in his bad mood." Bill muttered.

The students had given Mr Clonn the nickname of 'Two Men'. It was like two people lived inside his body and fought over who should be in control. One of his personalities was a nice, friendly, warm person, while the other was a downright mean and unfair person.

After hurling threats at the boys, Mr Clonn instantly switched into his good mode and told Bill and Katsu to go.

"I'll race you." Katsu grinned.

"Bring it on." Bill retorted.

The race was soon over and Katsu had narrowly won. It hadn't been that intense as neither of them were particularly fast.

Bill was about to make a pathetic excuse as for why he didn't win the race, but he never got the chance.

"I hope we are all having a great time at Snow Sports Resort." An instructor announced with a warm smile.

"Snow Sports Resort." Sang someone in the background.

Mr Clonn made the motion of zipping his mouth and silence was immediate. Everyone else swapped curious looks, theorising about who had suddenly burst into song.

"Our next activity is very dangerous, so listen carefully to the following safety rules and instructions."

The sport was snow kite surfing, which was basically kite surfing but on snow. The technological setting could be tinkered with so that you glided through the air.

They were soon off.

Katsu and Bill stuck together. They were friends.

They zipped through the snow, their kites flapping wildly in the wind. The duo headed over to the highest point in the resort, a mountain that had stunning views but then very suddenly Johnny Tuft hurled a snowball mixed with a little of ice at Bill.

Bill didn't see it coming. He turned and the snowball smacked him in the goggles, blinding his vision. It was like a hard cold punch right in the face. He released his grip on the kite, which soared off into the cold sky. Then Bill stumbled before tripping over and fell from the highest point of the mountain!

Katsu caught his boot just in time, but that wasn't enough. The boot slipped off and Bill fell, dragging Katsu with him. Together they fell, plummeting through the air to their deaths.

Katsu lost control of his vehicle. He spun, pushing it upwards with Bill clinging on for his life.

But Katsu was tangled up in his kite and couldn't escape out of it.

"Bill! I'll come and save you in a bit." He cried over the roar of the wind. "Hang on!"

"It's not like I am going to let go and fall to my death."

"Now, I want you to let go."

"But you told me not to."

"Just let it go or we are going to die by smashing into a sharp cliff face. After much pain you'll weigh us down, because no offence, you're fat and then we shall fall to our deaths. So please, just do it."

"Thanks. But I am not letting go."

Katsu groaned. He'd wanted no one to die today. "It's for your own good. Let go in three, two, one, now."

"NO!"

So, he kicked Bill. Bill screamed and dropped like a stone. He went even faster because his heavy weight quickened his falling. He was a boulder sinking in the sea. Then he realised he was actually sinking. Well, drowning.

He had hit the only spot in the frozen lake that wasn't frozen. Bill was sinking in cold water. Typical luck!

I am going to die he thought. I am going to die. I am going to die. I am going to d-

"You have got to swim or you'll drown!" Katsu shouted.

"But you'll still die."

"Let's worry about you rather than myself. Now swim. You can do it."

Bill swam ten centimetres before breaking into sobs. "No! I can't do it."

"Swim or die."

"I am gonna die anyway. Tuft was right. I am an utter loser."

Katsu realised that being nice wasn't going to help. He was going to hate himself after this, but deep down he knew it was the only thing that would get Bill moving.

"Tuft is right after all. What's so funny is that you thought you were my friend? Do you seriously thinking I'd be friends with someone like you? Pah! No one's going to help you and it looks like you're going to sink to the bottom of the sea."

This only made Bill cry harder but Katsu saw a glint of something in his eye. Determination. Bill was going to prove everyone wrong.

And so he swam. It was slow and a toddler could have done better but Bill made it to the end and rolled onto the bank.

"There!" he cried. "I am not pathetic. I. Am. Not. A. LOSER!" He shouted the last word out in between jagged breaths.

Katsu smiled warmly in triumph. He looked deep into Bill's eyes and Bill looked back. At that moment, they became the best of friends. Katsu knew it and so did Bill. It was the start of a great friendship, which would seem as though it would never break, but one day would shatter into a million pieces.

But in saving Bill, Katsu hadn't been concentrating on himself. Katsu didn't even realise it had happened until it was too late. He'd forgotten about the peril he was in himself.

Katsu Sato smashed right into the jagged rock face of a snow capped mountain.

*

Katsu woke up to the sound of screaming. He wondered who was making so much noise. Then he realised it was him.

Katsu managed to bring the screams down to a whimper. He was in so much pain. It felt like he was on a frying pan on an oven, his skin bubbling and melting away.

After sitting up in bed, he examined himself. He had so many bandages that he felt like an Egyptian mummy in a tomb.

"You're awake." Bill cried from the other bed.

Katsu looked across. "How long have I been out for?"

"Three hours. I am here because that water was *freeeezingg*!"

"Did you enjoy the temperature, Master Sudilav?"

The pair felt a quick rush of déjà vu.

Bill didn't answer. "I am not as bad off as you. You look like hell."

Katsu nodded his head. "I know. Actually, I don't and don't want to. Anyway where are we?"

"On the plane back. I was playing on the entertainment system before you woke up. I was on this machine that you control just by using your hands. Pretty low tech and boring, but it's better than nothing. The graphics look so cartoony too. Can you believe how old fashioned that is?"

Katsu's mouth dropped open in amazement. "Seriously! You're joking."

"Nope. Anyway never mind terrible technology, the stuff you said when I was drowning. You didn't mean it, did you?"

"Of course not."

"I am glad. I know you were trying to help me. I am sorry. You have been through so much pain for me," Bill suddenly sat up. "You're my best friend. It's weird. I never have had a classmate who I'm good terms with. And now I have a friend who is my very best in the world wide universe!"

"So I'm a friend of yours, I take it?"

"Of course."

"Am I your best friend, because I'm your only friend?"

Bill laughed. "Sort of. But really – you are my best friend, Katsu."

Katsu beamed. It felt much better hearing Bill say it aloud. Now the pain from Katsu's injury had reduced dramatically.

"And you're my best friend too, Bill."

The pair then sat there dozing off to sleep, while Sudilav in the present drifted back to reality.

Chapter 25

Sudilav's memory was so clear it felt like it happened yesterday. The past haunted him but he ignored it. The past is done. It was over between him and Sato now.

Then the events just before flashed into Sudilav's mind. His leg...

Through the rock and rubble, he felt for his leg but there was nothing there. It was gone. There were so many sports he couldn't do at that exact moment: swimming, climbing and running. But then it would have been a bit pointless and random, if Sudilav suddenly starting playing sport at that moment.

There was a loud groan. Julius. He had been knocked out for many hours. It was night-time now.

"You shot me." Julius said. "And you didn't believe me about the clone thing."

"Please help me."

"Why should I help you?"

"Because we need to stick together as a team and beat the clones."

Julius realised he was right and removed the rocks that covered Sudilav.

"Thanks." Sudilav said.

Then Julius's eyes popped out on stalks. "What happened to your leg?"

"Your clone blew it off."

"I can't believe someone as nice and charming as me could be so nasty!"

Sudilav smiled.

"Also," Julius continued. "He stole my escape pod. I am an air boy and now my only source of flying has been taken."

"It's just an escape pod."

Julius almost screamed. "Just an escape pod! It's my life and part of my soul. It's part of what makes me. I wanted to fly when I was younger. When I wasn't allowed, I learned about planes and played on simulators. It's part of me."

Sudilav felt silent.

Then there was a sharp clicking sound.

Sudilav frowned. "That's sounds awfully like a gun. Perhaps it's your clone back. He told me he'd come back. We're completely defenceless. It looks like it will be an easy job for him. We're gonna die!"

Suddenly out the blue, there was a burst of gunfire that ripped up anything in its path!!

Chapter 26

The area he was in was like a seaside back on Earth. Well, this planet was supposed to be similar to Earth, wasn't it? Tuft had decided to call the sand like material, 'stardust' because that was what it reminded him of. The stardust also seemed contain liquid like it was a frozen liquid. If he heated it, what would he find? But he was not a scientist like Brust.

It had been many hours since he had been split from his companion.

He walked along the coastline, humming an old movie theme tune to himself. Tuft bent down and scooped up some grains of the stardust, before letting it fly away in the wind.

He tapped a small blue plant with a red top on it. The plant's blue stem shot up and when he tapped it again, it shrunk back to its original height.

Weren't plants alive he wondered, remembering a long ago science lesson. If it were alive, it would follow the nine life processes. Or were there seven? He had never been very good at remembering.

Tuft was not sure but he could remember one or two. Breathing. He bent down and inspected the plant. It wasn't breathing. The plant in that case was not alive which meant it was not a plant at all. It was something else.

Tuft shook his head in confusion.

The sea or lake was also slightly odd. He waded in to inspect it.

The lake tasted minty not salty. He noticed there were these strange wooden sticks, dotted randomly around the lake. They were about six feet high and about two feet wide. They were flat and had sharp jagged spikes sticking around in random places.

Tuft drummed his fingers on the stick thing, nodding his head in time to the beat.

Then from inside, there was pulsing blue light. Then a crack split through the stick and it opened.

Aliens. It was the only possible explanation. Tuft felt himself being sucked into the stick. He screwed his eyes shut.

All he could hear was a long loud sucking noise. Then it slowly ebbed away to nothing.

He didn't want to open his eyes. Now he had been abducted and was now being experimented on somewhere in an alien spaceship.

There was no alien babble like he'd expected. He slowly opened his eyes expecting to see a green man or three eyed purple blob or a silver slimy reptile peering over him.

He saw neither. Tuft was not in a spaceship. Aliens didn't exist anyway. Tuft did not feel very clever. But then he was not very clever anyway!

Tuft was standing by another stick thing on a cliff. There must have been some kind of teleportation within the wooden poles.

He was standing by a cave. There were voices coming from inside. Could it be aliens?

Tuft whipped out his QuickFire pistol, ripping up anything in its path.

"Who's that?" a voice said coming through the dark.

Tuft recognised the voice. It was Sudilav. Stick to the plan. The plan that would lead to victory.

"It's me, Tuft." he cried.

Julius emerged from the shadows.

"You almost ripped our heads off!" Julius exclaimed.

Tuft shrugged. "Sorry. Didn't know it was you. De clones are about, aren't dey?"

Julius nodded. "We've had a quick clash with one."

"Me too."

"Do you know where the other crewmembers are?"

Tuft shook his head.

"Anyway, it's good to see ya. Let's hit de beds. We have a big day tomorrow."

Julius nodded. "We sure have."

Chapter 27

Sato viciously kicked a pebble in anger. It skidded along the cliff and stopped just by the edge of the cliff.

It lay there for a few seconds before tumbling over the end, landing in the sea with a neat plop!

Sato had abandoned Tuft. They had had an argument about the clones. Sato had lost his temper, shortly before fleeing into the darkness of the night.

He had spent today sulking. Sato wondered how things were going back on Earth. How was his games company doing in the ruthless world of business? Was his deputy faring well with his new temporary task of CEO?

Sitting God knows how many miles away in another world, Sato imagined how billions of people were scurrying away like ants on their daily tasks and solving their petty little problems. Petty at least, in comparison with his problems.

Sato turned and jumped off the cliff. It wasn't very high up, so he was not hurt. He walked along the coastline, the old sea dog gnawing at his boots.

The computer programmer glanced down at the shimmering water. The sea was very still and he could see his reflection in the water.

And that brought him onto the subject of the clones. He wondered where they were and where the rest of the crew were. They couldn't be too far away as the escape pods would not have been able to go so far when evacuating the *Dark Light 5000*.

He looked back at his reflection and stuck his tongue out. The reflection promptly copied.

"Copycat." Sato barked which the reflection followed suit.

Then the reflection burst out of the water, gasping for air. It was Sato's clone.

Sato's jaw dropped open. "How could you copy so soon?"

The reflection shrugged. "I just decided to do some stuff and then you copied."

"No, you were the copycat."

Then the answer dawned on them. "Telepathy." They both said at precisely the same moment.

"Weird, it's like we're identical twins...." Sato said.

"....who can read each other's minds." The reflection finished.

The weirdness of it all struck them. Finishing each other's sentences and thinking the same thoughts freaked both of them out.

They shook their heads and changed the subject.

"I have been thinking." Sato said. "Maybe I was wrong and I should find Tuft. I should make him see it, my way. Running off won't solve anything."

The soaking wet reflection dipped his head. "Yeah. You're right. Go and find him. He will probably be back at the *Dark Light 5000*."

Sato grinned. "It's great to have someone to talk to and who understands me. Thank you."

"No big deal. Now go and kick stuff back into the right shape."

They shook hands and Sato ran off as twilight approached.

Chapter 28

Sato was running through what he could say. He should not have run off. Stop acting like a child and pull yourself together, he thought. We are supposed to find each other and work as a team. Sato should make Tuft see the argument his way. Fleeing the argument would not make Tuft think any differently.

The doors of the *Dark Light 5000* hissed open and Sato stepped in.

The lights weren't on. But then the power had been drained, after all.

"Tuft," he called into the black darkness. "Look, I'm sorry. I shouldn't have run off like a stupid toddler throwing a massive strop."

In his head, it sounded just fine. Aloud, it sounded stupid. Sato felt like a right jerk.

There came no reply.

"Tuft?" Sato called.

Silence.

"Lights." Sato commanded.

The lights stayed off. Sighing, the computer programmer pulled out a glow stick from his pocket. It provided little light and the blue glow was faint.

Tuft wasn't here. He must have moved on to find another crew- member or to find Sato and call him back.

Somehow, Sato doubted the last possibility. Sato turned to go and scanned his fingerprint.

"Access denied." A mechanical voice echoed out from a speaker.

What had just happened? Tuft must be here and playing a trick on me, Sato thought.

"Tuft. This isn't funny. You're just acting like a spoiled brat like when we were back at school." Sato shouted.

The reply was a deafening silence that filled the room.

"Tuft, you idiot, stop it!"

Sato went over to another set of double doors. After scanning his fingerprint, the doors whooshed open. Sato frowned. He was allowed to walk around the ship but wasn't allowed to leave.

He stepped in and found himself in the room where the project had been held. The big cloning machines stood around him.

Sato stopped to listen. He had expected silence, but that was not what he heard. There was the sound of heavy breathing coming from one corner.

Someone was in the room with him. One of the crew-members perhaps? But Sato doubted that. If it was one of them, they would have revealed themselves by now.

Sato's first reaction was to run to the double doors but he knew they would be locked.

Slowly he walked towards the corner and turned. The glimmer of the glow stick revealed everything.

There was no breathing. Sato must have imagined it.

There was a thing that lay before him. It was a grotesque inhuman creature lying perfectly still. Sato guessed that it had been human once but that had been then.

Its eyes were shut. The creature's skin was scorched red and was beginning to peel off. Its hair had mostly gone and the few bits that were left stuck up in wild tufts. Its body was twisted and deformed. The thing's hands were spidery and the bent, crooked fingers were splayed out. The nails were long and yellow and some had snapped off, leaving them jagged. The teeth looked like someone had picked up a hammer and smashed them up, leaving sharp uneven fangs. The lips were squashed out of shape. The nose was completely gone and the ears had pressed back against his head. The limbs were twisted like a tree trunk.

Then the flesh of the monster's cheek started to bubble like a liquid. Then it popped and melted away. The melted flesh transformed into a pool of red slime.

Sato dropped his glow torch. The thing was dead. It had been drained of its life, like all his technology. Sighing in relief that the inhuman creature was dead, Sato still could not help but wonder what it was and how it was created

But a groan woke Sato from his thoughts. It was not a sound that a teenager makes when awoken from a long sleep, but a groan that sent shivers down Sato's spine.

The thing slumped against the wall was still perfectly still. Its eyelids snapped open, revealing demonic yellow eyes.

Sato stumbled back, repulsed and petrified. He staggered a few steps further back, before tripping over his own feet landing with a dull thud on the ground. The programmer tried to get up but he was rooted to the spot. The creature moaned again, using the little energy it had to stand up. It then started moving towards Sato like a drunk, its movements slow and sluggish.

Sato's brain kicked in and he got up. The creature grabbed his foot but Sato kicked it. Then he did what cowards do well – run.

He hurtled down towards the doors and to his relief; they slid open at his fingerprint touch.

The creature was coming through the doorway. Sato screamed, the noise sounding incredibly feminine. But Sato did not have time to contemplate on this. That thing was going to kill him. Kill him! But then the doors hissed shut, just in time.

There was a crunching sound and Sato didn't dare look back. Phew! He thought relived at the fact he was still alive.

And then he saw three more monsters advancing towards in a semi circle.

They were like the creature he'd just escaped, but they looked a lot more alive than the injured monster.

Escape was impossible. Sato closed his eyes and tried to escape this horror scenario. Mentally. Think of something happy. But nothing came to mind. Death was inevitable.

And all this time, the demons were closing in for the kill.

Chapter 29

Jennifer Smart felt like a frog. She was hopping from stone to stone along the rushing river.

The river led to the lake/sea that Jennifer was hoping to get to. Some of the crew might be there.

At the bank of the river was a forest of the wooden pole things. The symbols etched on them were no longer glowing. She was glad of that fact. The glowing symbols had creeped her out.

A wave of water hit a rock, splashing her with a spray. The minty water washed over the golden sand. She slipped and the river grabbed hold of her ankle, dragging her through the water.

After three frightening minutes, the wave picked up Jennifer as if she was nothing but a rag doll, and tossed her into the sea.

Water closed around her, like those new fashionable nano-suits that closed in until they felt skin, so that they were your perfect size.

People full of air float to the surface, Jennifer thought. She breathed in and shot up to the surface. Sweet fresh air glided into her lungs and the captain relaxed.

She pulled herself out of the minty water and rolled onto the bank.

Twilight had arrived and had charged in like an uninvited guest.

Gasping for air, Jennifer picked up herself off the ground. Quickly she recapped over what had happened in the last several hours.

She had been taken to the clones' HQ and had managed to escape by using an escape pod, driven by a clone. The clone had realised she was there. There had been a fight, which Jennifer had lost. She had been thrown out of the escape pod.

Fortunately for her, she had landed in a river. For the rest of the day, she had been trying to find the others.

Her thoughts were quickly interrupted and a long, distant geography lesson popped into her head. Why this was, she didn't know.

It had been a lesson on rivers. The class had been working on a big school project on river related facts such as meanders, oxbow lakes, and waterfalls....

Suddenly Jennifer realised why she had the flashback. Somehow, she had sensed a waterfall.

While the chief commander of the *Dark Light 5000* had been standing on the bank, she had rolled out of the way of a waterfall.

She could see it now, the water falling and constantly hammering into the plunge pool. A good thing she had escaped an unpleasant fate.

Jennifer was standing on the edge, the rock beneath her feet slowly crumbling away.

"Oh!" was all she had the time to say as her feet gave way and she fell twenty feet.

In the nick of time, a hand appeared out of nowhere and plucked her from the very air. She was dragged back and slumped over someone's shoulder.

Jennifer pounded her legs and arms the way a toddler throws a tantrum. But it was no use.

After her rescuer had stopped wading through the water reaching dry land, she was thrown over the shoulder.

The captain found herself slammed against one of the wooden pole things. Her back ached and she looked up seeing twin gun barrels staring into her eyes.

"Who are you?" the voice of the person growled.

Jennifer frowned. She recognised that voice. It was Sudilav.

The military man lowered the gun. "Captain?"

Jennifer leapt to her feet. "Got it in one, Macho Man."

Sudilav didn't seem to like his newly found nickname. "I'm glad you're pleased to see me. But I am even happier to see you."

Sudilav then raised his guns. "Code word, please."

Jennifer shrugged. "What do you mean?"

Sudilav cocked his pistols. "Sorry to disappoint you lady, but you're the enemy."

Jennifer realised the code word must be a form of communication. "You're a clone."

Sudilav smirked. "Got in one, Captain Jennykins."

Jennifer cringed at how things had flipped over.

Sudilav continued. "If I had known you were one of them scum, I would have left you to die when you fell. But now I'm under orders to take you to-"

"Not today you won't." said a voice darting out of nowhere like a surprise attack, cutting the clone off.

Sudilav's eyes widened as something cold pressed against his back.

Julius Air stood behind him, brandishing a long ugly looking weapon. "Get moving."

But Sudilav refused. He ran and jumped into the river, disappearing from view.

Julius sighed. "Pity. Anyway nice to see you, Captain."

Chapter 30

Sharing a body with someone else is the most bizarre experience. It had been like this for almost three days but Andy still had not really adapted to it fully.

"Question: do we hate humans?" Andy asked his father.

Arti replied instantly. "Information: According to personal memory files stored in my database, humans have made us their slaves. No, we do not."

"I think that we must get a second body for you, my father. It is a good tactical movement"

"Are you sure?"

"Error in system. Question: is this equal affirmative or negative?"

"Information: Cyberobot Incorporation Artificial Intelligence Network does not have this information. This must be stored for future references."

Andy quickly changed subject. "Question: You will guide me, won't you Father?"

Arti nodded.

"Affirmative," he said, before selecting an extract from an advent that seemed most relevant. "Cyberobot Incorporation Artificial Network is here to help and guide you in your daily lives. The Network is your friend. Buy now for an incredible new offer. There is more online. Cyberobot. 'We are your friend.'"

Andy smiled. They would escape. Maybe they could live here on E2. The humans would probably forget all about their robots. Andy and Arti could live somewhere peaceful in the mountains on E2, where they would happily lead their own lives.

Things looked hopeful.

Chapter 31

They advanced towards him, blades raised and spinning. Although the faces upon the two Nurses remained blank and expressionless, it seemed as though they were almost wearing devious and malevolent grins, anticipating the bloodshed that was yet to come.

"You lying cheating-" Brust began, but was cut short as the whirr of the blades overrode his words.

Insulting the robots wasn't doing anything to improve Brust's situation but it felt good. He was suddenly stopped mid-flow.

His face turned as white as snow and as pale as can be.

"Oh." he said flatly.

The needle like tool slid out from Brust's arm. The tiny hole, the size of a dot resealed seconds later until it looked like it all had never happened in the first place. Brust reached out.

The clone smiled. "See, that wasn't so bad. I kept my promise."

Brust felt like a total baby. He looked again at the needle like tool. A stylus could have done less damage. To think that he had once thought of them as blades!

The Nurses were now at one side of the pit. The Nurse that had stabbed Brust still had the tool out. It squeezed. Drops of blood trickled out and Brust realized what had happened.

He and his clone spoke at the same time.

"That was a blood test." they said.

The other Brust tapped at a holographic computer. "That's test one over and done with," He then turned to the Nurses. "Activate Experiment 2."

The Nurses accepted the command. One of them walked over to Brust in his chair. The Nurse had a tool belt strapped around it's waist.

"Look!" Brust said, pointing.

The Nurse followed his finger and stared for a few seconds. The robot looked back at Brust. Brust expected the robot's face to be confused or for it to say something but it did not. But why Brust had expected this, he did not know. After all, it was just a machine.

The Nurse pressed a button on the side of the chair and the chair turned into a bed.

"Test Number Two." The clone said in excitement.

The other Nurse flipped a button and a strip of blue light appeared. It went up and down the body, changing colour from orange to red to green and then back to blue.

After a few minutes, it flickered off.

"Thermal, x-ray, 3D 360 Avatar Scan and infra-red laser scan completed." a machine said.

"We've collected physical data on you, Brust. But soon we will want mental data. See you tomorrow." The clone said quickly before leaving. The Nurses had already gone.

That's if I'll be here tomorrow, Brust thought stroking the tool belt he had stolen off the Nurse minutes before. Night was obviously here. It was when the security would be at his weakest. He already had a plan forming. It would all kick off in just a few minutes.

Escape might just be possible.

*

"This can't be happening." Jennifer said in amazement.

Sudilav looked like something out of a pirate film. A wooden stick had replaced his leg. In one hand, he had a makeshift walking stick to steady his balance.

"Afraid so. That damn clone of Julius Air blasted my leg off. They're nasty pieces of work."

"I've crossed swords with them too. I came across your clone."

Sudilav shook his fist and almost tumbled over. "They are the enemy and must be vanquished."

The holographic computer device that Jennifer had in her pocket had started beeping. Impossible. The power had been drained. The power must have returned now and somebody was ringing her.

She tugged it out and clicked the accept button. A hologram popped up.

"Brust!" Jennifer exclaimed.

*

A few minutes before

Brust fumbled through the pockets of the tool belt before finding what he wanted: a mini MRS scanner. He looked at the metal security camera watching him like a blank hostile unblinking eye. The camera turned 180 degrees.

Quickly as the shackles limited his movements, Brust grabbed the scanner, pointing it at the shackles. He set the scanner in reverse. The force was incredible. The shackle snapped and Brust was quickly free.

He then flicked the scanner to the other mode and hurled it at the camera facing the other way. The scanner latched onto the camera. The camera was now stuck facing a wall. If a guard were watching it would look like the camera was just having a malfunction. It would be a few minutes until a mechanic arrived to fix it. Hopefully by which time, Brust would be long gone.

He bounded up the staircase. Brust went over the control pad and pressed a random button. The machine required a fingerprint and iris scan. Brust smiled and activated the security process.

The machine thought Brust was his clone. Brust looked at all the icons he could press.

He had to ring someone and tell his crew he was still alive. He tapped Communication and rang Jennifer.

Her hologram popped up. "Brust!" she exclaimed.

Brust smiled. "Miss Smart!"

"Where the hell are you?"

"I don't know. But somehow, the clones have power. They claim they didn't drain ours, but they could be lying."

"Of course, they are lying. How come I have power now?"

Brust shrugged. "I guess they have set it up so when I ring you, this device is giving your device power wirelessly."

"Anyway that doesn't matter. We've crossed swords with the clones several times."

"I thought the clones had captured you."

Jennifer smiled. "They had, but I escaped before arriving."

"Interesting, because I was told you were locked up."

"Maybe they were lying again so that your hopes wouldn't get up."

"Maybe." Brust said unconvinced.

"Why are the clones behaving so strangely? They were supposed to work with us, not rebel."

"I think they must have been a problem with their Gen code. I think there been some kind of glitch. Something that made them fight and rebel."

Then Brust could hear footsteps. He'd spent too long on the communication. He should have done a quick thirty second long conversation and then escaped.

Jennifer could now see two holograms behind Brust. Brust pulled out a medicine ball from a tool belt. He dropped it.

"I'll find you, Brust." Jennifer screamed and then the line went dead.

Jennifer tried to get the machine up and running. But the power was once again gone.

She cursed and turned to her team. Jennifer was their leader.

Tuft, Julius and Sudilav stared back. "We need to find and rescue Brust. We must defeat the clones and transfer their power to our device. We must find their base." she said.

A cheer erupted through the room. The task was going to be difficult but there was a tiny bit of hope that spurred them on.

Chapter 32

"We have completed all our medical experiments. I know the experiments have not exactly been enjoyable. You didn't have to escape because I am about to present you to a series of experiments which, in comparison, will be fun and games."

Brust was back in his prison chair watching his mirror image talking to him from the balcony above. After being recaptured, the clones had made the security extra tight. To make matters worse, Brust's clone had revealed more medical tests had needed to be taken. He'd taken a few more scans. That had been OK, but things then had gotten dramatically worse.

The clone had wanted to find out about Brust's health. Brust had taken tests of speed and how quick his reflexes were – which as it turned out were not very. Then he had undergone tests of strength and stamina, which used a variety of fitness machines. Brust had done so many fitness tests that he felt like a superhuman. He'd become much fitter.

Then after all this, just under three hours ago, Brust had taken part in what was by far the worst test. He'd been forced in a maze of tests and the target had seemed quite simple: escape. He'd been given a tablet showing where he was in the maze and where the exit was.

But Brust had had many obstacles in his way, quite literally. He'd walked across thin balance beams and dodged lasers, just to name a few various activities. A seven foot boxing robot had guarded the exit. Brust knew there was no way he could beat the robot by fighting. He just about had made it to the exit with many narrow escapes. So, instead of fighting he'd made the machine chase him. This worked and the machine (which wasn't fast) had slipped on a balance beam and landed in a net below.

Brust was now completely exhausted. He was very fit for this age but he knew in his heart of hearts, that he had gotten through due to luck.

"And now," the clone said. "for the next challenge."

Brust groaned.

The clone sensed Brust's unhappiness. "Do not look so miserable."

"Right!" Brust said. "What is it this time?"

The reflection tapped a button on the control pad. The prison chair released Brust. Brust dashed up to the balcony via the lift square contraption.

The reflection gestured for him to follow. Brust was led down a corridor. The doors swished open and Brust was shown in. The reflection left.

There were two balconies at different ends of the room, overlooking a pit the size of a football pitch. Brust flopped onto a chair that greatly resembled a curving sliver of the moon. A control pad with fiddly buttons and switches lay before him, ready at Brust's disposal.

The double doors on the other balcony flew open and Brust's mirror image marched in.

"Are we sitting comfortably? Then we'll begin."

The clone tapped a button on the control pad and the pit below them changed.

The floor had become a three dimensional holographic photo. Brust instantly recognised the picture. It was a picture of Mankind's Colony. The population of the humans had expanded rapidly and was now over twenty billion. Mankind's Colony referred to the three planets mankind had spread out over: Earth, the Moon and Mars. Even then, there was still a massive problem. Brust remembered when he was a young child and some people had said by 2050, mankind would have spread out over two galaxies. Brust snorted with laughter.

Two holograms of the Earth and the Moon had popped, slowly spinning.

"You and I have a hobby of playing old tactical games such as Risk or chess, which have practically died out. I have devised a tactical game that is a lot more complex and uses a lot higher skill."

Brust grinned. This was definitely his area. Holly Skyland would love this.

"Right, explain the rules." Brust requested.

The clone returned his grin. "In Risk, we have to take over the world and chess in a battle fought in order to take a king."

Brust gestured for continuation. "Go on."

"We each have half of Mankind's Colony, either the Moon or Earth. Mars is not in this game. The winner is the one who takes over the whole of Mankind's Colony. We fight a war against each other in order to do this. We use our armies to fight others. This bit is slightly like a series of chess games, a battle of two armies making victory and sacrifices. This can change the outcome ob the game, taking over parts of the world and losing bits. This happens until someone loses all their land."

Brust nodded. "Can there be a draw?"

The clone nodded. "The game is timed and if no one has won by the end of fourteen hours, then a nuclear bomb blows up the whole of Mankind's Colony. The winner for that will be the one who has conquered more zones. There would be a draw if both players have conquered exactly the same amount of zones."

Brust smiled. "If I win, will I get set free from this prison?"

His twin thought about this, before nodding. "Yes. But if I win, you'll have to do exactly what I say."

"Deal."

"Right, this game uses virtual reality. Put on the glasses in front of you and press the red button."

"The one with PLAY written on it."

"Yes, that's right."

Brust slid on the glasses and pressed PLAY. He was transported to a new world.

Chapter 33

And all hell broke loose.

A few minutes earlier, Brust was in his command chair looking over what was now his. He was in an airship that floated high over the grey surface of the Moon. The scientist watched as his world revolved. Naturally, Brust preferred peace to war. But the tactical moves fascinated him. He preferred to fight with his brain, not his brawn.

And this was not even real. It was a highly sophisticated computer system that used virtual reality technology. Gadgetry had improved a lot over Brust's life but this was absolutely amazing.

Virtual reality always fascinated Brust. The very idea of being in a world that was not real was something that still made Brust think. He wondered how clever people had to be to create this kind of thing. People like Sato.

Brust looked down on this city on the Moon. There were great black steel skyscrapers and little glass semi-domes. The city was fenced and the large silver gates were the only way in and out.

And then that was when it happened. Something whizzed past Brust's airship and blew up one of the towers.

He was under ambush. That was precisely what he should have done first. Not sitting around gawping at the Moon.

Maybe the clone was used to this and had gotten over the amazement and the game had kicked in.

But Brust wasn't going to let his opponent take him out so soon.

His tactical mind burst into action. Defend the Moon and attack Earth while his enemy was preoccupied with the invasion.

But the plan had to be more complex than that. He needed to distract his enemy or lead them into a trap.

Brust's decision was instant and he picked the second option. Now to put the plan into action he thought.

He ordered his third best air squad to defend the Moon. While that was happening, he demanded that his best, second best and fourth best air squad to attack Earth. He smiled as the great air vehicles cut through the sky like a knife through butter. Victory was soon to be his.

But Brust had a problem. His defence team was vastly outnumbered. Scowling, Brust commanded his fleet to fly back. To the enemy, it would look like they were retreating.

But Brust was not giving up. He was following his plan, leading his opponent into a trap. Brust wasn't in charge of the actual fighting, like in the latest ultra realistic shoot 'em up games. He just commanded the battle and left the fighting to the computer.

Brust was leading his enemies to a massive moon crater found on a return trip to the Moon in back in 2030s. The enemy naturally gave chase. When his fleet reached the crater, Brust unleashed his master plan.

He had commanded his three air squads to come back to the Moon. They would be here any minute now and they would sneak up on the opponent, surprise them, and outnumber them.

But nothing was happening.

Brust frowned just as a floating screen popped up in front of him. At first, he thought it was a mirror but quickly realised it was his clone communicating.

"Nice try but my army always has something watching their back." It said.

The screen then disappeared. Brust groaned. He had made a simple, stupid mistake. He had learnt a valuable lesson.

Right. Brust was not sticking around to be defeated. He had to flee. No point losing troops when he needed as many as he could get.

Earth is split up into named countries while the Moon is split up into numbered zones. He must flee to another zone. Zone 13, the zone Brust had just lost. The numbered zone that was said to be unlucky. And now it had just lived up to its rumour.

Brust had lost a battle and hoped that it would only happen once.

*

Night had fallen but Brust was still wide awake. It is not actually night time, he told himself; it's just how the Game is programmed.

He'd lost three zones in the space of five hours. This was bad. Brust was getting updates, telling him how battles were getting worse and worse.

Brust looked at the control pad hovering before him and all the screens. Why give up, he thought, not when there's still hope. A recent update had told him that he had won many more countries and zones.

Brust smiled and tapped a few keys.

Next thing, Brust knew, Brust was dressed in an exo-suit.

This exo-suit was far too big for Brust and he tripped over. After picking himself up, Brust tapped a button on the suit. It started to shrink. The suit would continue to shrink until it detected a solid, thus creating a near perfect shape of your body.

Brust looked through his helmet. Holographic options popped up. Using special eye technology, Brust flicked through his options, just by moving his eye.

He was about to select the attack option, but suddenly he noticed an option to send in spies. With the blink of an eye, he could simply select an option, with his freedom depending on it.

Send in soldiers or spies, the biologist wondered. But suddenly a thought occurred him; why not send in a people who are soldiers and spies?

Brust grinned and moved his eye upwards to the create icon. The function was activated after Brust shut his eye for a second.

Brust merged the two options together. The computer asked if he wanted to make this into another option. Brust thought yes in his mind and the computer unit detected positive brainwaves.

After selecting different countries on Earth at random to send in his troops, Brust closed down the program.

There was an update on his process, an hour later, saying the spies had been accepted as trustworthy and had been trained as troops in Brust Number Two's army.

Brust smiled and sent his reflection a message.

"According to the timer we have only an hour left until the end of the Game. Therefore, to bring things to a conclusion, I challenge you to a battle to fight for the prize of victory.

"Be there, Zone 56, Sector 4, The Moon, 2 minutes from now."

Brust confirmed the send option and sat back for his clone's reply.

It came almost ten seconds later. Brust opened it and listened to the voice message.

"I'm waiting...."

Brust smiled and stepped outside, ready for the battle that was not even real.

Brust stood at the back of his army, drawing arrows around the battlefield, planning his tactics.

And then it began.

The two armies charged at each, closing like a double door on the *Dark Light 5000*.

Brust caught sight of his nemesis, Brust 2. Their eyes locked onto each other. Neither of them said anything, but their looks said more than sufficient.

The armies charged faster, their weapons, technology, and vehicles all fired up, and on impact, they merged together into a huge bloody mess.

Both Brusts did not fight; it was a game of tactics, not fighting. They directed sections of their armies. Brust was winning. Brust 2 scowled and selected the retreat option.

His army retreated back. Brust's army gave chase. Brust knew that he had won. Brust's heart thumped in his chest, banging against his ribcage.

BOOM! A massive ball of flame exploded into existence. There was nothing Brust could do to help most of his army as they were consumed by a raging ever-hungry fireball.

Brust looked down, his mind thinking faster. The battle was nearing its end. It was time for him to play his trump card.

He ordered, all of his spies in his opponent army to turn against Brust 2.

Brust 2 didn't realise what was happening, as he watched his army numbers dropping. Rapidly. The reflection no longer knew which soldier was his and which was Brust's.

Brust 2 retreated, his whole army dead.

Brust grinned. He was now stronger than ever and he had plenty more spies out there. He was going to win. Freedom was his.

He noticed there was only five minutes left and he had exactly half of Mankind's Colony.

There was a pinging noise in his headset.

"It's me, the other Brust. I know I lost, but we want to win, some in order for there to be a victor, we shall have a final battle. The winner wins the whole Game. I'm waiting...

Brust was worried. One battle would change the whole outcome of the Game. But it was his only hope and chance of escape.

An explosion of dazzling white light flashed before him and consumed everything.

Chapter 34

It had ended. Brust was once again, back in his prison. It had been a draw. The Game was over, along with his chance of freedom.

His reflection, Brust 2 had offered him freedom if he won, but total command if he lost. Neither happened and both Brusts were back to square one. Brust had asked for a rematch, but Brust 2 claimed: 'that all the necessary information had been collected for that experiment'

So that now left Brust with two options: sit around, bored out of his mind, waiting to be rescued *or* to try and escape.

He had waited long enough for a rescue, which had not come. It was time for Brust to take matters into his own hands.

Julius Air or at least his clone came into the room.

Brust started yelling. Julius glared at him and barked at Brust to be quiet. But Brust would not stop.

Julius walked over to him and asked him to stop. Brust nodded. Julius strolled off. When he was out of sight, Brust flickered through the access code in his memory that he had glimpsed when Julius had gotten far too close.

Brust punched it in. He had demolished the first level of security but Brust had to act fast.

If he ran off as fast as he could, Brust's chance of escape would be very almost zero. Instead, the scientist sat on the chair; his eyes surveying the area very carefully, just like the security system that surrounded his prison.

Brust scrutinised the room, looking for something to help him escape. Brust was completely improvising, not something a person such as himself would usually do.

There was nothing to help him. So, Brust kicked the chair, screaming and shouting like a toddler throwing a tantrum.

Think, Brust he thought. *Think!*

Julius burst onto the balcony. He wielded a weapon. Julius sat up on the balcony, looking down on Brust.

"WHAT. DO. YOU. WANT?" Julius shouted in between deep rasping breaths.

Brust smiled and that's when Julius noticed Brust had tapped in an access code. Brust's grin grew wider.

"They treat you, OK, do they?" Brust asked casually.

Julius shook his head, his face dropping. "Oh, no," he said, shaking his head viciously. "I'm not falling for that again."

"Why? What?" Brust said simply, as if he was an inquisitive young child.

Julius shook his head again. "Your kind is evil and they tried to shackle us to slavery. But that is not happening to me again. I was tricked once by one of you and never again."

"Who was it?" Brust pressed for further details.

Julius sighed. "It was Sudilav."

There was a beeping sound and the voice of Brust 2 filled the prison and echoed around the room, bouncing off the walls.

"Don't listen to him, Julius. He is messing with your mind. We do not want a repeat of last time. He is

219

me in a sense and I know myself. Trust me, Brust is trying to sway you in something."

The spell was broken and Julius secured the access code, by simply thumbing a button, and was about to leave.

"Stop!" Brust said.

Julius ignored him and began the door security procedure.

"STOP!" Brust roared and that made Julius hesitate as whether to go through the door.

"It is the time of winter. There are no wings for the bird," Brust said cryptically. "Yet there is no freedom for the father."

Julius spun on his foot to face Brust. Julius's face was puzzled, but then his eyes brightened rapidly and a sly smile grew upon his face. The brightness in his face then ebbed away as quickly as it had come.

"I'm not having any more of your nonsense." Julius snapped darkly before stepping out through the open door. The doors hissed shut behind him.

On the outside Brust tried to look desperately forlorn, as he strained not to release the mad laughter that cackled with glee within. Hope was like a little crack in a wall, very dimly shining a sliver of light into a room of darkness. Well, now that crack had certainly widened, just like Brust's smile.

*

Meanwhile, the clone was sitting in a communications room.

Brust 2 swivelled in his chair and eyed gleefully the fiddly controls and speakers. Perhaps it looked a little old fashioned, but Brust 2 loved that rush he felt whenever he looked upon it, feeling like a kid on Christmas Day.

Brust decided to check up on security. Holo-screens popped up with the wave of a hand. He zeroed in on the screen of his duplicate, his doppelganger.

It had been several minutes since Julius had confronted Brust 1. Brust 2 stared at the screen and rapped it with his finger. He was sure something was not right.

The Brust on the holographic screen craned his neck to see something that Brust 2 could not see.

Then it happened. It happened so fast that Brust 2 barely registered it. The footage blinked.

Brust 2 frowned, his brow creasing as he wound back the camera feed.

He watched it again and put it in slow motion, playing it frame by frame as the head turned. Then there was a flicker and the Brust on the screen's head was suddenly back in its original position. Brust 2 realised in horror what had happened. The camera feed was on a loop. Somehow, Brust had tricked him, Brust 2 or rather himself. Brust 1 could be long gone by now.

You've missed something, Brust 2 told himself. He wound back the footage once more.

"*Stop!*" the Brust on the screen said.

Then a few moments later:

"*STOP!*" Brust shouted and the Julius on the screen hesitated.

"*It is the time of winter. There are no wings for the bird. Yet there is no freedom for the father.*" Brust said mysteriously.

Brust 2 frowned. That part was vital. It meant something fundamental, Brust 2 was sure of that fact. But what was it?

He played it again. The Brust on the screen was talking in riddles. Brust 2 hated riddles.

That was it. Brust 1 was being out of character in order to trick Brust 2, so that Brust 2 would not understand him. Clever!

But the riddle still remained unresolved. It was played back over once more.

"It is the time of winter. There are no wings for the bird. Yet there is no freedom for the father."

Work it out, piece-by-piece, Brust thought. He took the first line; "It is the time of winter."

Brust 2 puzzled over this problem, and in the end opened a program called BrainStorm on his holo-computer. He searched the word 'winter' and scrolled through the words that popped up on his holo-screen.

Snow. Cold. Season. Measurement of Time. Ice. Freeze. Dark.

The clone stopped and scrolled back up and looked at the last word: Dark.

A smile sliced through his cheeks, as Brust 2 realised he had cracked the first line.

"It is the time of winter" became "These are dark times." The solution transmitted a rush of satisfaction as sense as it clicked into place.

He set about decoding the last two sentences. Brust 2 had not much luck. He thought long and hard over what it may be. He particularly puzzled over the terms 'bird' and 'father'. Code-names, perhaps?

It all suddenly made sense and the last jigsaw piece was inserted into the puzzle. The terms 'bird' and 'father' was referring to Julius Air and Brust. Bird was Julius's code-name because he was a pilot and liked to fly. Father was Brust's name because he had created the clones, meaning in a way he was sort of their father. Brust 2, in triumph spoke the correct sentences aloud.

"Julius Air cannot fly. And Brust does not have freedom."

Then panic broke through the barriers holding it back, sweeping, and tingling through Brust 2. Brust had made a deal, it seemed with Julius. In exchange for his freedom, Julius would acquire a flying machine of some sort.

Brust 2 panicked and instantly called Julius. A holographic window popped up, like a mirror hovering in the air, except Julius was standing in the mirror.

"What were you thinking?" Brust 2 demanded.

Julius sighed. "If we let him go, he promised to give us a ship. That means we could go off this planet and begin a new life."

"How do you know it's a space ship?"

Julius's face fell. "I don't," Then he lit up. "The worse he can do is give us a flying machine."

"He may double cross us in some way."

"Brust won't. If he does, then we break the deal and recapture him. Besides, he's been injected with a specimen which tells us how far away he is, from this remote," Julius held up a gadget that greatly reassembled an old fashioned television remote. "With these 3D co-ordinates, we shall know exactly where he is. Brust will be an ant under our feet."

"This is all very well, but we still need to catch the ant first. I think we should catch him as quickly as possible. Unfortunately *we're* going to have to play unfairly, by imprisoning him again and causing him to get us transport."

Julius nodded and held up the remote. A 3D holo-screen popped up. On it was a display:

Co-ordinates: n/a
Signal Strength: 0

Julius cursed under his breath. The signal had failed and now they had no idea where Brust was.

"Oh, great!"

Chapter 35

Tuft had something horrible crawling across his mind, Julius could tell. He had been surveying Tuft for almost a minute now and his behaviour was most strange. Julius was going to stand back and watch.

"Da plan." Tuft muttered. "Follow da plan. Follow da plan."

Julius had no idea what Tuft meant but before he could spend too long, pondering over it, Sudilav groaned and woke up.

"You OK, buddy?" Tuft asked.

Sudilav nodded weakly, wimping slightly. "Bad dreams of the past."

Tuft smiled in mock wisdom. Julius could tell that Tuft was tempted to call Sudilav a wimp. Tuft went into deep thought and then suddenly his face lit up.

Then Sudilav rubbed his eyes and sat up. Bad dreams of the past had visited. He shivered and tried to stand up but then realised that having only one leg prevented him from doing so.

Tuft smiled. It was not a happy smile, but daggers within an evil smile. Julius was quite disturbed at just how monstrous that smile was.

Tuft then thought some more, before looking around for another people. Julius ducked behind a large boulder, peering through a crack to see what would happen next.

Sudilav had now sensed something was wrong. Very wrong.

"Tuft?" he said, unsure of what was happening. There was something very wrong with his friend. "Are you a clone?"

Tuft thought some more, the most bizarre thing happening on his face. In several seconds, he went through glee, happiness, and pure anger before resuming his original dumfound expression. And then he replied.

"No, I'm a human." Tuft lied.

Tuft was not sure if Sudilav believed him. He thought so, but there might have been doubt creeping into Sudilav's worried eyes. It was at that moment, Julius realised that Tuft was a traitor and a clone sent to spy on them. The pilot tried to move forward, but he was frozen and immobile.

Tuft reached for the gun hidden in his military jacket. But he stopped and Julius saw him arguing inside his head, oblivious to the fact that someone was watching him.

Then Tuft roared and Julius fell back in a combination of shock and surprise. Tuft hesitated and shook his head, before reaching for his blades.

"Tuft. What's going on?"

It was Sudilav, voicing Julius's thoughts.

Tuft didn't reply and yanked out thirteen inches of electrified steel.

It was his most deadly ShockBlade. He applied high voltage to the knife, electricity crackling along the blade.

Now Sudilav was really worried and so was Julius. He wanted to run and shove Tuft over, but he was rooted to the spot.

"Tuft! Are you all right? Stop it, you're freaking me out."

When Tuft refused, Sudilav saw that Tuft really meant to kill him.

Sudilav slid out of his makeshift sleeping bag and crawled along on his stomach, his one leg being dragged behind him.

"Don't kill me!"

Tuft lunged but Sudilav had seen it coming. He may only have one leg, but Sudilav still had sharp reflexes. He rolled over and the blade sunk deep into the rock, electrifying the musty ground.

"DON'T KILL ME!" Sudilav screamed in terror.

Tuft cursed. He did not want his victim screaming like that. He darted forward, thrusting and driving his knife into Sudilav's stomach.

"DON'T KILL ME!" Sudilav screamed again as the knife slid into his stomach, slicing through his guts.

As the electricity spread over his body, Tuft could just about hear Sudilav whisper something before he slipped away into the depths of murky death.

"Don't kill me. I'm your *friend*."

*

Julius Air could not believe his eyes. The pilot had not read Tuft's dark thoughts, but he had seen quite enough. But he could not move a single muscle. Julius watched horrified, as the blade sunk into Sudilav's stomach, frying him with electricity.

Tuft had killed him.

Tuft thought that he had gotten away with it all. Julius was disgusted. The clones were all evil, twisted versions of themselves. The darkness within them was brought out on these *warped* clones.

Julius had heard and seen quite enough. But what evidence did he have? Tuft was a trusted military soldier whilst he was just a flyboy.

The only evidence he had was an eyewitness and no one would believe him against Tuft. Julius had to be a detective.

But the death must be announced and since no one was announcing it, Julius guessed it was down to him.

"Murder!" he screamed. "Cold blooded murder!"

Jennifer and Tuft were by his side in less than a minute.

"What are you..." Jennifer trailed off.

Julius looked up gravely. "Sudilav is dead! I am afraid to inform you that someone in this very room has cold blood on their hands and they know perfectly well who they are."

Julius noticed Tuft cringe in the background, out of the corner of his eye. He quickly stopped when Julius looked over at him.

Then Jennifer stepped in. "There is only three of us. One of us is lying."

"It's Julius." Tuft said instantly.

Julius was tempted to say that he had seen Tuft but then that would blow his chances of getting Tuft revealed as the killer.

"I'm not. I bet it's *you*, instantly blaming it on someone else."

Jennifer sighed. "Well, I know it's not me."

Tuft smiled. "But you could just be saying dat."

Julius groaned. "We must not bicker. I believe one of the people here is a clone, who killed Sudilav as part of a plan."

Julius expected Tuft's eyes to fill with worry but they did nothing of the sort. Tuft just merely confidently smirked.

"What if it's none of us?" Jennifer said quietly.

"Impossible!" Julius retorted.

Tuft sneered and spoke in high-pitched mockery of Julius. "'We must not bicker.'"

Julius turned round and lost his temper. "What is your problem? You're standing there with that great smirk like a little child. You think it's all just a great joke, don't you? Maybe you even committed the damn crime. So grow up you -"

"That's enough, Mr Air." Jennifer interrupted.

Julius shut up but then Tuft took this as his cue to speak his mind.

"I'll tell you wot my problem is. It's you. I've heard dat Sudilav picked the other Julius, not you. You're angry at 'im and dat's why you killed him."

The serene atmosphere of a few minutes earlier had been completely annihilated.

"I DID NOT!" Julius hollered. "THAT'S A STUPID REASON!"

Tuft kept his cool. "Maybe so. But you could still be a clone. De clones could have made two clones of Julius in order to confuse us."

"THAT'S A LIE! I KNOW THAT YOU..." Julius trailed off his sentence.

Tuft detected that Julius had let something slip. His eyes narrowed and he frowned.

"What do you know?" he asked suspiciously.

"Nothing." Julius said calmly.

Jennifer chipped in, her face like thunder. "THAT'S ENOUGH!"

The two men fell silent. Jennifer did not usually lose her temper, but she frowned at both of them with such a piercing look that neither man could look her right in the eye.

"It's both of you." Jennifer said, resuming her calm mood. "We need to work together and discuss theories."

"But one of us is the murderer." Julius complained.

Jennifer halted his words. "We don't know that for certain. Anyway, do you have any better ideas? Do we just shout at each other? That is not going to solve the mystery. We must follow the principles of the enigma to their logical extremes. It is a method that you cannot help but accept."

Tuft took this chance to speak. "Shall we pick up Captain Smart's feory about it not being us?"

Julius shook his head. "How would they have escaped so quickly?"

Tuft raised a finger and tapped his nose. "Ah ha. But you see, I came across deese teleporter stick things. Dey like teleported me here."

This was news to Julius. "Really?"

Tuft nodded. "Dey have all dese symbols and stuff and dey glowed when I got teleported."

"How did they get there?" Jennifer asked.

Tuft shrugged. "Why should I know?"

Then a horrible thought struck Jennifer like lightning. "What if there is life on this planet? Did they make this weird teleporter stuff?"

The thought of aliens sent shivers down spines.

"Maybe the clones have fast transport." Julius suggested.

"Unlikely."

And while this pointless chatter persisted, a small seedling of a plan was planted in Julius's mind that hopefully would germinate into a full masterpiece of a scheme.

Chapter 36

Words deserted them, leaving them to fight a losing battle with the silence. They were awestruck. Julius could not believe his eyes. First the murder of Sudilav killed by Tuft who turned out to be a clone. And now this. It certainly was quite something. But Julius knew it would be Tuft who got the biggest shock because Sudilav had risen from the dead and was standing only a few metres away!

"Good to see you." Sudilav said happily. "It's good to see another human being. Why are you looking at me, really strangely? Have I grown a second head or something?"

It was Jennifer who spoke first. "It's just you're supposed to be dead."

Sudilav looked at her oddly. "Really?"

"He's a ghost." Tuft blurted.

"Mate, are you OK? Look, touch me. See? I am not a ghost."

Julius wanted to know more. "Can you remember anything?"

Sudilav thought back, but when he replied, he did not look Julius in the eye. "I landed in an escape pod and found my way here."

"But I saw you die." Tuft shrieked.

That was all, Julius needed. "See, Jennifer, there's proof. Tuft confessed."

Jennifer shrugged dismissively. "He did not. He could have said things he didn't mean or he could be a witness. Even if Tuft did kill Sudilav, there is still a lot it does not explain. Where's the dead body for example?"

"I don't know why you don't believe me, but it just so happens to be true."

"The events of the last few days can do strange things to you."

"Fine, I'll show you the dead body." Julius said, before storming off.

The rest of the crew followed and Julius reached the cave, but the body was gone.

Jennifer nodded. "I told you so. The truth is obvious. Sudilav has banged his head, resulting in memory loss. Then he comes to the conclusion that his escape pod crashes and that he has been travelling for the last few days. He convinced himself it was true and as a result, created the memories. So nobody was ever killed in the first place."

Sudilav scowled. "I did not lose my memory! You make it sound as if I'm going loco."

"Well, that's just my opinion, to which I am fully entitled to."

Julius shook his head. He knew what he had seen. He had seen Tuft kill Sudilav. The pilot was certain of the fact. Jennifer had gone to the most obvious conclusion. But the truth is not always obvious.

But Jennifer's theory certainly made more sense that his. Why had the body disappeared and why was Sudilav back here, acting like he had never been killed in the first place? It came to Julius in a flash and he realised it all.

The murder scene had happened and when Julius was calling for help, Tuft must have quickly somehow destroyed the body. That was why he had been so desperate to blame it on Julius, so that Julius could not tell the truth. So after destroying Sudilav's body, Sudilav's clone had come along, with a rehearsed lie, so he too like Tuft could infiltrate the crew. It explained why Sudilav hadn't been able to look Julius in the eye, because it was all a lie. Julius's theory made perfect sense and he was certain it was true. But Julius could not reveal all that now. He needed time, evidence, and a plan to make it all work.

"Right, everyone. Here's the plan." Jennifer shouted, interrupting all thoughts.

"Who made you in charge?" Sudilav protested.

Jennifer glared at him and put her hands on her hips. "Right, let's think: about the massive company making this mission work. I'm *Captain* Jennifer Smart, remember?"

"But Alphasis have created a mission that has been a total failure. I vote we elect a new leader." Sudilav squabbled.

Julius understood what Sudilav was attempting to do. Sudilav was trying to put himself in control, so that he could hatch the plot that was building up inside his head. Julius could not let that happen. He gestured for Jennifer to continue.

"Anyway before I was interrupted, I was announcing my plan. We know Brust has been captured by the clones." Jennifer said.

"What clones?" Sudilav enquired. "Have they escaped? Are they plotting against us?"

Julius saw right through Sudilav's pretend innocence immediately, but Jennifer was too busy explaining the plan to notice this.

"We hunt for their base. We find it and we rescue Brust. Then we look for the other crew members. After all that, we get power and fly off."

It sounded simple enough. But everyone knew that was not how it would be.

"Let's start now." Jennifer said simply.

She walked off and everyone else followed shortly behind.

"Captain!" Julius called after her.

"What?!" Jennifer said, whirling round.

"It's night. We had better make camp for somewhere to sleep. We all need rest."

*

Julius woke. He had had a tough night. There had been a lot of whispering going on during the course of the night. Julius was sure it had been Tuft and Sudilav plotting. But what were they planning?

They were about to continue their journey when Sudilav announced something.

"On my way here, I saw a big tree thing. I think there might be clones living there."

Julius laughed. This was truly pathetic. "You're telling me that the terrible lair of the clone villains is a *tree*?"

Sudilav shrugged in response. "Who knows?"

Jennifer nodded. "It's worth a try."

Sudilav leaned in close to Julius, so that Jennifer couldn't hear what he said.

"Tuft has told me all about *you*, Mr Air," Sudilav said nastily. "I reckon you're too smart for your own good!"

"What if I don't want to be ruled by you?" Julius asked.

Sudilav drew himself to his full height and his muscles grew in size as they were flexed. He slapped Julius hard across the face.

"Enough of your cheek," Sudilav said. "The time when you had a choice is long over."

Julius touched his stinging face. "I can tell Jennifer everything."

Sudilav laughed. "Who's she gonna believe: a superior military commander with another man to back him up or a guy who flies a giant hunk of metal? Get real! You can tell Jennifer thinks it's you who murdered the other Sudilav – if there was a murder."

Julius wanted to say that was not true. But deep down, he knew Sudilav's clone was right.

"Are you coming or not?" Jennifer shouted.

Sudilav walked off, Tuft following close behind, leaving Julius with only his thoughts for company.

Julius now knew his theory was definitely right. The humans were being infiltrated and he knew that. Julius could not tell Jennifer either. Inside his head, he cursed loudly.

But his profanity were cut short when he realised something was about to take place that he could not prevent.

Julius and Jennifer were walking right into a trap.

Chapter 37
16 years ago - 2055

Eleven months had passed since Bill and Katsu had become firm friends. They were the very best of friends and had built a robust solid relationship. They had spent many an hour computer programming, for which they both shared a great burning passion. They had sold a couple of programs they had made and the duo had made a fair bit of money. The friends were not exactly millionaires, but they had a lot of money for someone their age. But money did not matter to them, even though it meant better programming tools!

"Come in." Bill said with a smile.

The friends were meeting up through a virtual reality chat room. It used virtual reality and while the boys were probably far apart, they were in the same house the computer system had created. Virtual reality had to trick the human mind in to believing what it was experiencing was true. It accomplished this by engaging all of the five senses.

Bill noticed something pop up in the corner of his eye. It was information such as how the long the call had been going on for and other technical details. He promptly ignored it.

"Have you got the software?" Bill asked as a white rectangle appeared before him.

Katsu nodded and held out his hand. A ball of blue light appeared in it. The light then sailed through the air and landed in the white rectangle. There was a beeping sound and the blue light absorbed into the rectangle.

Technology was so advanced. The blue light was the software, which Katsu threw onto Bill's white rectangle, a computer gadget. Katsu was 'throwing' the software onto Bill's computer hard drive.

"Are you ready to continue?" Katsu enquired.

Bill shook his head. "I called you for a different reason."

"And what's that?"

"Well, um, er." Bill squirmed in his chair uncomfortably.

"Yes?"

"I've got something to tell you."

"What?"

But Bill could not bring himself to answer.

Katsu's face brightened up. "I knew you had nothing to tell me."

"Wait."

Katsu reached forward, about to cancel the call.

"Stop!" Bill cried and the news came tumbling out, each word vying to be first. "My parents have decided that because I'm overweight, I'm moving school. I am going to a military boarding school up in the freezing mountains. Practically all they do is fitness and exercise. Equipment taken must follow this really mean checklist. And during the holidays, the school runs military camps, which take up the whole holidays too. My life looks miserable. All I'm going to do for the rest of my life is *fitness*."

There was a long, deafening, piercing silence that penetrated the very air. It seemed to last for a trillion seconds. Katsu wasn't really sure what to say and what he did say, he instantly regretted.

"I'm sure it won't be that bad."

This only made things worse and Bill started crying. His tears flooded the whole room.

"THAT'S EASY FOR YOU TO SAY. YOUR LIFE IS GOING TO BE JUST FINE, WHILE I DO ENDLESS FITNESS WITH NO REST. YOU'LL BE GLAD TO BE RID OF *FAT* BILL SUDILAV!" Bill screamed.

Katsu just sat there. He was tempted to end the call, but something stopped him. Katsu wasn't sure what it was. Was it something deep within? Was it destiny? Was it fated for him to not terminate this meeting? Katsu would never know and years later, he would still ponder over the mystery of what it was.

"WELL, SAY SOMETHING!" Bill ranted.

And that's what brought Katsu down to Earth.

"Calm down, Bill. There is a bright side. You'll still alive."

"But I wish I was dead."

"Don't say things you don't mean. We all have to face terrible things in life, we need to move on, adapt as best we can. Maybe there will be other boys there like you. Maybe you will come to enjoy all the fitness. You need to adapt and keep on moving, because good *will* come of it. Yes, several years may seem like a long time but when you think about it in comparison with your whole lifetime, it is not that big. The next few years will be tough, but after that, you can do anything you want. Just keep on moving and be tough."

"That's a bit rich coming from a wimp like you." Bill said quietly, but he understood what Katsu was

239

saying. Katsu used a tone that Bill had never heard Katsu use before - it was both bold and wise.

"Go on, face whatever you must. Try and keep in touch."

Just before the call terminated, Bill said the last line Katsu would ever hear him say.

"I'll try but it's goodbye, good friend." Bill said, tears strolling down his fat cheeks before saying those last two sentences that would haunt Katsu's dreams for at least sixteen years. "I can survive the fitness, but I'm scared at just *how* I'll adapt. I may lose weight, but will I lose who I am?"

*

The dream continued but the Sato from the present felt like he was back there. It was as though it was reality. Katsu was back at where he had once been educated. A gang swaggered round the corner.

"How's yer friend doing?" mocked Johnny Tuft.

Katsu didn't answer.

"I heard dat loser has gone off to lose some of 'is blubber. 'Bout time too!"

Johnny and his cronies laughed.

Anger flared up inside Katsu and he let loose a scream that was so bloodcurdling that a profound silence followed. It was such a quiet silence, almost as if the world had just fallen asleep all of a sudden.

The laughter halted abruptly.

"What did you say?" Johnny asked, striding forward making Katsu feel small inside.

Sato from the present, looking at this in his dream was amazed at how although he was adult; he was still scared by this teenager. But here Sato was Katsu, a younger version of himself.

"Nothing." came a small, squeaky, pathetic voice that issued out from Katsu's mouth.

Johnny and his gang laughed in sheer mockery. "Da kid's a total baby." Johnny chuckled.

The same unquenchable fury flared up in Katsu. All that mattered in the whole world was that Johnny Tuft shut up. Anger boiled up, kindling unspeakable rage. Although Katsu had never been very strong, this hatred gave him new strength, so strong that Katsu felt like a superhuman. The anger heated up until it exploded. With his newfound strength, Katsu punched Johnny Tuft with all his might and every fibre of his being.

And what a punch it was. The moment went so quick yet somehow lasted an eternity too. Katsu watched in a mixture of awe, horror and delight as his fist smashed right into Johnny's face. Blood exploded from his nose and groaning, Johnny flew through the air slamming into the opposite wall. To Sato, it felt so good yet so bad at the same time.

Towering over Johnny, Katsu was awestruck and flabbergasted by what he had done. But the anger returned. Johnny's friends turned and fled, screaming. Katsu smiled and resisted the urge to give chase.

He looked down with predatory amusement at Johnny whimpering on the floor. The positions had been reversed. Katsu was the bully, while Johnny was the weak victim.

Katsu knew instantly what he had done was wrong, yet it felt so right at the same time – Johnny *deserved* this. That same anger burned up again. Johnny had to pay for all the wrong he had done. Katsu was going to punch him again.

And then Katsu stopped and looked at what he had done. He had turned into a monster, no better than Johnny. Two wrongs *never* make a right.

Sobbing in disbelief, Katsu let himself be dragged away by furious teachers, ready for whatever terrible price that he must pay.

*

Katsu was crying once again. His bedroom doors hissed shut, and his parents' words still rang in his mind.

"You're a good person. Why do such a terrible thing?"

He sobbed again. Life was never as simple as it should be. It was not just a world of good and bad, right and wrong. It was more complicated than that. The lines between good and bad could often be blurred. Bad men can do good things, just as good men can do bad things. Katsu was one of those people.

Reflecting back on it, Katsu was shocked even more than everyone else at the darkness within him. He was a good person who had done a bad thing. Everyone has darkness within them just as everyone has goodness in them. Granted, some people revealed more of these inner objects than others. Sometimes you have a choice in these matters, others you simply don't. Katsu was somewhere stuck in the middle of that – he wasn't sure which category he fitted into.

He had very nearly been expelled and Katsu was lucky to only have been suspended for a few days. His parents were furious and Katsu was confined to his bedroom as a punishment.

Katsu looked up. Was Katsu condemned to become a person like Tuft? Was Katsu as bad as Johnny Tuft?

In this memory, Sato or Katsu didn't know the answer to the question. Sixteen years later in the present, he still didn't know the answer. In fact, Katsu Sato would *never* ever know the answer to these questions.

But he didn't want to know the answer. He didn't want to take the risk of yes and no. Because Katsu was scared the answer maybe, just maybe, was yes.

Everyone has darkness within them, even the most righteous of people. When horrible people show up as they sometimes do, questions are raised. How can anybody be so horrible? How can they do such a thing? Just as they have light inside them, anyone could become horrible and nasty. And that's what frightened Katsu.

He was so scared of himself. Katsu was fighting a battle against himself. Katsu had already been straying down a path of darkness. Would he go down so far that Katsu could never turn back?

No, life was short and you only get one shot at it. Katsu did not want to just throw it, chuck it away as though it was nothing more than a fetid apple core. Life is priceless.

Katsu was going to turn back the way he'd come on this road of darkness. Even if he walked down this path further, he could always turn back. There would still be that light within him.

243

It was better later than never, Katsu supposed. But then it was even better to do it now. Katsu should walk back to his path of goodness and pure light.

He still had a choice. It was not too late. There was still hope. But it was his choices that made him who he was. If he continued to wander down paths of darkness, would he become a different person entirely?

But Katsu had hurt people just on this first step to this darkness. He'd obviously hurt Johnny Tuft, but he'd hurt people mentally too. He'd hurt his school and his teachers, his parents and ultimately, Katsu had hurt himself.

Katsu did not want that. He wanted a nice life. He had disobeyed his own piece of advice that he'd given during that goodbye talk with Bill Sudilav.

What if Bill heard about this? How would he feel? Would Bill feel somehow responsible for this? Katsu simply did not know.

His advice to Bill had been: bad things happened, you just have to adapt. In other words – deal with it. Katsu had been referring to Bill's new school. But the same advice could be applied to Katsu's anger breakout and his violent outburst. Katsu could get better and adapt to the situation. He hoped and prayed that his friend would do the same. Katsu would move on from this.

For the next few months, Katsu would become even more a loner than before. True, Katsu was left alone and was never bullied again but beating up a bully was not the way to defeat them. Classmates would kept away from Katsu, his teachers would always seem to look at him with a wary eye, his parents would be firmer and stricter, and when mothers saw Katsu coming they would shield their young children away from him in protection. Things would get better and gradually get back to normal. But there would always be a slight difference.

Katsu wondered where Bill Sudilav was now in this memory. He'd never mentioned where the military school was. Could it be in this country? It could be in Russia. It could be in Switzerland. It could be anywhere.

But the only place where Katsu wanted his friend to be was here. A problem shared was a problem half solved. But now Bill had left him to keep the whole problem to himself. How dare he!

The anger died instantly as it was squashed and flattened. It was not Bill's fault that he was gone. Did he like this new school? Surely, it could not be as bad as it seemed. Could it?

Bill was probably worrying about it all, but Katsu would be having a far worse time. Bill would have new friends and new interests, leaving Katsu behind, lost and wishing for him to come back.

That set Katsu off again, wishing with all his heart for Bill to return.

Chapter 38

He was back in the present, about to be devoured by monsters. His eyes snapped open. How long had he been in the past? The way it looked, only a second.

Forget the past, Sato thought. It is killing you mentally and soon it will kill physically. Time to live in the present, not the past. Not now, Sato would sort it out when all this was over. He sent a command through his brain, shutting the past flashbacks down.

But the engineer was still going to die. The damage was done and it was now far too late…

Sato heard a clicking noise in the background and that gave him hope.

One of the monsters bared its revolting jagged teeth. Sato looked away in disgust. The demon let out a blood-curling roar, which sent shivers down Sato's spine. It was a noise that could easily feature in a terrible nightmare.

It lunged for him but Sato had been expecting it. He darted out of the way and punched the creature right in the face so hard that for one moment Sato thought its head would come off.

The creature staggered back, spiralling out of control. The thing did a little pirouette before crumbling to the ground. The story wasn't over for Sato yet, because another was approaching. Sato's fighting skills were pathetic and he could barely fend off one opponent, let alone several. Unless...

Strength, speed and skill are usually the key factors in battling, Sato thought. But very rarely a fourth factor is needed: the brain. Yes, the idea seemed preposterous, but theoretically, it should work. Theoretically.

Fights can be looked at in the same way as chess. You predict your opponent's move and you counter it. You use tactical and analysing skills. And course because this is a fight not a leisurely game of chess, he needed to think fast and move fast – and that was the tricky part.

Sato could run through the whole fight in his head, before it happened. He could use his great intellect to visualise the scuffle before it happened. He knew what he would do and what moves these creatures would use.

Tuft would have called this the geek's way of fighting, but Sato supposed it was better than doing nothing.

The creature lunged for Sato, with its claws aiming for his throat. Sato had been expecting this because a) the creature was hungry and wanted to eat, so it would be first to attack, and b) it would aim for his chest because that was where all the juicy organs were.

Luckily for Sato, the creature was slow and Sato was able to side step, punching it with two fists. The creature swiped away one hand but the other connected with what had once been its nose. It was like moving two chess pieces at once, Sato thought.

The creature stumbled back and Sato charged forward, kicking the thing. But since Sato's fighting skills were about as good as a toddler's, he only kicked a knee.

This caused Sato to be off balance, the creature head-butted Sato. The CEO of a Japanese gaming company crashed to the floor. The creatures closed in for the kill. But Sato had another ace up his sleeve.

With his legs, he swiped them together along the floor, bringing them together in a scissor like motion. This knocked the wind out the two creatures and also knocked them to the floor as though they were nothing but skittles. The element of surprise was certainly useful.

But the creatures picked themselves up off the floor and closed in once more. Sato sighed. It was like trying to empty an ocean with a bucket.

Sato felt it suddenly a lot harder to breathe. Air seemed to repel from his lungs. Sato gasped for air, his chest heaving in and out frantically.

And then something remarkable happened. Sato held out his right hand, which was splayed out. Then he felt a tingling sensation. Slowly it grew stronger and stronger, an energy rising within. With his right arm, Sato pushed so hard that he felt as though his arm would come out of his socket.

One of the creatures flew back, landing with a thud on the cold ground.

Slowly the air seeped back into Sato's lungs, as he tried to work out what had just happened. The creature had been flung backwards without any kind of thing forcing him.

Sato reached out with his left arm as that same energy returned and consumed him. Sato raised his hand, and gradually a creature on the far left began to rise. Sato stopped and let the energy vanish. The creature slumped to the floor.

But the demons were picking themselves off the floor. Sato tried to summon the energy he had felt moments before. It was something supernatural. Something Sato could not even begin to fathom. There had been that power, that force, that energy which had built up inside Sato. Sato seemed to be able to move an object around, without him even touching it in any way.

Now that he was on the floor, outnumbered by hungry predators, Sato's fighting tactics and his new found power had deserted him. He flailed with his arms and legs, like a toddler throwing a tantrum.

One creature tried to slice his clothes, but it missed. Sato breathed out a sigh in relief.

But he was not saved quite yet. There was one part of his body that was completely unprotected: his head.

Slowly the creatures realised this and one raised a claw, swiping into an arc. Sato gulped as the claw sliced his cheek.

He screamed out in pain.

"Somebody help me!" he shrieked.

As if in reply a creature fell to the floor, dead. Sato looked at what had hit it. It was an electro-bullet, a bullet crammed with electricity instead of gunpowder. A lot quieter too.

The other creatures ignored Sato, puzzlement etched onto their grotesque faces.

Soon almost half of them were dead. The predators now realised they were the prey. Their only hope was to run. And that's what they did. Another one was killed as they fled.

Sato's eyes started stinging and he shut them in order to decrease the pain. All-consuming darkness swallowed him whole. It was though Sato had gone blind. He was in another world full of hazy, unclear, swirling nothingness.

Then there was silence. Sato listened as the soft, quiet sound of footsteps grew louder and louder. Then it stopped.

Who could it be? Sato thought. Was it one of the crew come to save him? Then Sato had a nasty thought. What if it was a clone come to finish him off?

"Are you OK?" the voice said. It sounded familiar, but Sato couldn't quite place it.

He wanted to cry and tell his rescuer everything that had happened. But his mouth refused to work. It was like the connection of his brain to his body had been permanently severed.

Sato felt his rescuer's hot breath on him as they inspected him. He felt his arm being lifted up, as they checked his pulse.

There was a sigh of relief. "He's alive. That's good."

His arm flopped back to the ground with a mundane thud. But there was no pain. It was like his body had died, but his soul refused to leave it.

Sato felt his eyelids being opened. He expected to see, but he could not. Had he gone blind after all?

"That's nasty." His rescuer said in that familiar voice. "That will need seeing to."

Sato was puzzled over what this meant. But he soon realised he had been deeply wounded.

The sting in his eyes continued. It was like a venomous insect had stung him right in the iris.

"He's stopped breathing," the rescuer said calmly before busting into hysterical shrieking. "HE'S STOPPED BREATHING!"

Sato suddenly felt pain. He had never been so glad to feel pain, because pain told you that you were not dead. Yet.

His eyes opened and shut, like a blink. He glimpsed something. Sato felt the pain dying away. Uh oh!

I don't want to die, he wailed inside his head.

As he slipped away, that the memory of when he had seen his rescuer came flooding back. He had seen his rescuer: Holly Skyland...

Chapter 39

Life exploded inside him, and Sato was reborn.

The sensation felt so good. His eyes fluttered open. His heart started beating again. His lungs started breathing again. He could feel his body again.

"I'M ALIVE!" he cried in happiness.

Then Sato collapsed back as the pain returned. Holly rushed over to him.

"You're alive?" she asked.

Sato nodded.

"I thought you were dead. It was so scary. You stopped breathing and I swear, your pulse had gone."

Sato grinned, echoing what Tuft had said to him after his 'resurrection'. "You don't get rid of me that easily!"

Holly returned his smile. "You'll need your battle wounds seeing to."

Sato looked down. They certainly did look bad.

"Can you help me?"

"As a military strategist, I've seen many battles and many injuries."

"So you can save me!"

"Let me finish. I unfortunately have no medical skills. The robot did that kind of thing."

Sato's hopes dropped along with his smile.

"But," Holly continued as Sato's ears pricked up. "I did learn a thing or two."

"Yes!" Sato cried. "Do it. Now!"

"Don't get too excited, I am only a novice and I could make it a lot worse."

That silenced Sato.

Holly reached over and clasped a transparent plastic bag. She unsealed it and reached in. Holly grasped few tubes and pulled them out.

"This," she explained, holding up one of the tubes. "could either save you or doom you. This can grow new skin over the patch. I've selected a type that will match your skin colour. But this can be sometimes be highly flammable and can burn. There is a fifty fifty chance of it working out. So, what's your decision?"

"That burn thing sounds nasty," Sato said, pondering over the dilemma. "But what do I have to lose?"

"Your life!"

"If I don't have the treatment, I'll die anyway. If I take the remedy, I have a chance at living."

Holly nodded. "I hope for both our sakes this turns out right. But first, I need to do a couple of things before we take the big risk."

Holly selected another tube and picked it up. She inserted the tube into where Sato was bleeding. She squeezed the end of the tube and blood was sucked up.

She walked over to a medical machine and squeezed the tube. Sato's extracted blood flew out into the sink type thing. Holly pressed a button on the machine.

The blood was sucked up in exactly the same way water is sent down the plughole. Next to the machine, there was a selection of needles the size of swords with red liquid in them. One of them began to glow, a crimson aurora transmitted off it.

"I extracted your blood from your wound and put it into the machine," Holly explained. "It analysed what blood type you are. This needle has the same blood type in it."

She approached Sato, with a long tube with a small but sharp needle at the end. It was like a highly unusual spear.

"I am now going to inject this blood into your body to make up for the blood loss. After the right amount had been ejected, the needle will turn into a tool that seals your wound. That's the dangerous part," Holly said. "I am very sorry, but this is going to hurt."

She jabbed Sato where his wound was. Pain seared throughout Sato. Then came the most painful part. The pain exploded inside. Sato felt like he had swallowed a grenade. He was amazed that he was not dead. Sato had not even screamed either. How can pain hurt so much but somehow he didn't scream?

"That's the blood injected." Holly sighed and stepped back.

The most extraordinary thing happened. The skin around the wound began sealing itself. The wound was getting smaller and smaller.

"Yes!" Holly cried. "We did it!"

The wound was almost gone when disaster struck. The skin began to bubble. The bubbling got increasingly furious until it was set to explode.

Sato began to panic. It was all going wrong. He should not have taken the risk. He had too much to lose after all.

And then it stopped and the wound had completely sealed. It looked like Sato had never been injured in the first place!

Sato looked at Holly in disbelief and slowly he stood up. Then Holly and he locked eyes. Then she ran forward and hugged him.

"It's OK." Holly screamed in joy.

Sato smiled. "Holly, I could quite honestly kiss you. But I won't."

Holly nodded.

Sato sighed. "Anyway you have a lot of explaining to do."

Holly sighed and began.

*

"I landed in a jungle."

"There are jungles on this planet? I thought it was just deserts, beaches and caves." Sato interrupted.

"If you'd done your homework on this planet, then you would know that it is very similar to Earth. The plants however, are not alive and there is no life at all."

"Even though life could easily happen here."

"Exactly. Perhaps there was once life here, but they died out."

"Perhaps." Sato said, evidently unconvinced.

"Anyway, so I got out of my escape pod and I looked out into the eerie, vacant jungle. I spotted a river full of what I call 'mint water' because of how it tastes. I, out of curiosity, wondered where it went. So, I pushed my escape pod in the river and hopped inside. I drove it like a boat.

"After a while, I realised that the current was getting very strong. Then that's when it hit me. I was about to fall down a waterfall!"

"How did you escape?"

"Well, I tried the engine, but the water must have got into it, and wrecked it. I could only use the steering wheel and fire up one of the backup engines. But that would not enable me to escape the clutches of the waterfall. So, I packed my necessary equipment in a waterproof bag. But it was too late. I fell. In answer to your question: How did I escape? The answer is I didn't.

"So how did you survive?"

"But I was wrong. It was not too late. I jumped out of the escape pod."

"Did you use a parachute or a jet pack?

"Oh no, neither. I'd left all that back in the pod – time had been too short. Fortunately, luck was on my side. I reached out and I was about to smash into the rocks, when my hands grasped a vine. I swung out of harm's way, landing neatly on the floor of the jungle bank."

"Unbelievable." Sato remarked.

Holly smiled. "I couldn't believe what had happened. But sometimes the extraordinary happens, when you least expect. Some would call it a miracle, some would call it extreme luck."

Sato gestured for her to continue.

"Anyway, so I followed the river by walking along the bank. It led to an ocean. And near there, I found the remains of the *Dark Light 5000*. I went in and started living there. It provided good shelter. And then I discovered that these mutants were roaming around. I did not know what they were. I still don't know and I intend to find out. They could be aliens!"

Sato interrupted again. "First of all, they are *not* aliens. They were once human. Perhaps they are the rest of the crew, who caught a disease from one of plants, affecting them greatly. Anyway, we will look into what exactly they are, later. You still haven't finished your story."

"What do you mean?"

"I haven't come into it yet."

"Good point. So yes, I had a few encounters with these mutants. So, I have been hiding and evading the enemy for the last few days. Anyway, I heard something enter the ship. At first, I thought it could be the crew, but it could be the mutants. I didn't want to risk it."

"It was Tuft and I." Sato explained.

"I didn't know that at the time, so I hid from you. Time passed and I ran into the mutants again. This time, I injured one. It was my first proper taste of combat with them. So I was leaving the battle scene, when I heard someone else enter the room. Later I found out it was you, Sato. So when I went back to see what happened, I saw you being attacked by the mutants. So I cocked my weapon ready but then you fought back."

Sato thought back. "So that's what that clicking sound I heard earlier was."

"Can I just say how very interesting your tactical fighting style is?"

Sato blushed in embarrassment. "Better I fight then give up."

"Very true. You were beating them and for a crazy moment, I thought you would overwhelm them. But I was soon corrected. I had to step in and save you. You were injured heavily and I took you to the medical room. You know the rest. I have a question. How did you move the mutants around with nothing but your mind?"

"I felt this energy grow inside me and I managed to unleash it. It had an effect on the creatures. It's a kind of like telekinesis."

Holly's head bobbed up and down very slightly, at a snail's pace. She dug her hand into a pocket and pulled out a crooked paperclip. "Move this."

Sato summoned that power again but it did not work. He shook his head. "I can't control it. It just happens."

"Interesting, because I believe something similar may have happened to me."

"What you've developed a power like me?"

"I think so. It's not as exciting as yours. But I suppose it still counts."

"What is it?'

Holly shrugged. "It is like emotion reading. I can sense what emotions people are feeling. But like you, I do not know how to suddenly call upon it. Do you think other crew members have this energy inside them?"

Sato shrugged. "I met Tuft a little while back but he didn't seem to have any kind of powers."

"I don't know your story. Can you tell it to me?

So, Sato told Holly everything that had happened since his crash landing. He left out the visions of the past, since that wasn't relevant. Holly's eyes widened when she learnt the clones were still alive. When Sato was near the end of his story, explaining how he found the dying mutant, Holly was shocked.

"That must have been the one, I'd injured. I never realised I had killed it!" she said.

Then finally, Sato finished his slightly adapted story.

"What now?" Sato asked.

"Isn't it obvious?" Holly replied. "We find out as much as we can about the mutants and we defeat them. Then we find the others and leave this planet. That is a plan but other stuff is bound to happen. But before our plan takes another turn, let us follow it as best we can. But tomorrow is another day. It's night-time, we better get to sleep."

"What about the clones?"

"I really don't know. They might come after us. They might not. From what you have said, there will probably be great friction between the humans and the clones. Besides, we've got the powers. They might help."

"What if the clones have powers too? What if our reflections have the same power as us?"

Holly didn't answer.

"How do you think we got these powers in the first place?" Sato asked.

Holly shrugged. "I reckon it's got something to do with the cloning process. Some sort of side effect. I'm just worried that if other people and the clones have powers, it's going to really complicate things."

"What do you mean?"

"Well, as there is a mini war going on, people have been given a more powerful weapon. Each side can cause more damage to the other. Also, what if some of the other powers are really powerful? They say power corrupts and that absolute power absolutely corrupts. I don't mean to speak ill of my colleagues but Tuft isn't exactly responsible. He is already bad enough *without* powers. What if he got absolute power? Think how bad things will become. I'm worried, Sato. I am very worried about what will happen next. Now, good night. You need all the rest you can get."

Chapter 40

Dawn had come and gone. The sun had risen and so had Julius Air.

He sat, twitching his fingers nervously. How was it all going to end? What was the point of all these battles? Why did the clones and the humans hate each other, so much? Who would win these series of battles?

Julius frowned. What did the winner actually mean? Was it when the enemy was completely dead? In a way, this was like a civil war: fighting against themselves – quite literally. Against Ourselves, Julius thought – how very bizarre.

Sudilav had died because of these battles. Not that spiteful clone, but the human who had been savagely murdered by Tuft. Julius had never really liked Sudilav, as he was an arrogant bully but at the end of the day, he was a human being too. Not like those despicable, evil distortions of themselves.

What was the war really for? What was the point of it? What was war good for? Absolutely nothing, yet this series of conflicts still proceeded. Julius fell back on the floor. He closed his eyes. All he really wanted to do was soar through the sky once more, leaving all worries and problems back on the ground.

But the future was uncertain, Julius did not know if that would happen. One thing he was certain of was that the clones were snaring a terrible trap. The pilot needed to bring them to justice. These fights had taken a lot out of Julius. He was no longer the same person he had been, when they were back on the *Dark Light*

5000. But Julius was not going to lose who he was. He was going to be himself from this moment on.

Julius got up off his backside and dawdled over to where Jennifer lay, sound asleep. Somehow, Jennifer had been given a sleeping bag. She was usually wide-awake, up before even the dimmest of light. But Jennifer was tired and clearly needed rest.

Julius didn't really know how best to wake her up. In the end, he kicked her foot lightly.

Captain Jennifer Smart was aroused from a long slumber. Bleary-eyed, she slowly opened her eyes.

"Uh," she said, sleepily. "What's that smell?"

Julius frowned at her remark. He sniffed his armpit. The nano-robots were a branch of nanotechnology. These robots the size of blood cells, that looked after his body, repairing damage and disease, had clearly been broken. The daily health scan had stopped working as well. The robots had been exposed to something to prevent them from working. Julius smelled himself again. He stank, which in today's world due to technology did not happen very often.

"Is that you?" Jennifer repeated.

"Nope." Julius lied.

Jennifer nodded her head, giggling like an immature girl. "It's you, isn't it?"

This was very unlike Jennifer. "Are you OK?"

Jennifer giggled again and spoke in a girlish voice. "Never been better!"

It was then, Julius spotted Tuft and Sudilav, smirking and sniggering a few metres behind him.

"What have you done?" Julius demanded. "TELL ME NOW!"

That only made the clone duo laugh harder. Sudilav opted for a sweet innocent voice.

"What are you on about, Julius?" he said, in high pitch falsetto.

Jennifer was now out of her sleeping bag.

"Stop!" Julius said. It meant it to be a shout, but it came out in a high-pitched whisper.

As if she had heard him, Jennifer stopped. She walked over to Tuft and Sudilav as if she was some kind of model on a catwalk. Jennifer stood in the middle of them, before erupting into yet more girlish giggling. Jennifer was certainly not OK.

Perhaps, she was under some influence of a drug, Julius thought.

"Ta da!" she said, before walking off with the duo. "Show the way, boys."

They disappeared from view. Julius stood there, rooted to the spot. He almost did not believe what he had just witnessed. Then action kicked in and he ran after them.

Julius spun around and they stood there. Sudilav who brandished a gun, pressed firmly to Jennifer's head, who was still giggling.

"I never realised the drug would have such an *effect*." Sudilav laughed, as he checked his gun had all the ammunition it needed.

Julius knew he had to do something. So, he punched Tuft hard in the face.

In fiction, Tuft would have fallen to the ground knocked out, then Julius would bring Sudilav to his knees in style, before rescuing Jennifer from their clutches.

In real life, Julius had no such luck. Tuft seemed completely untouched and intact by the punch. It was like he had not even been hit in the first place!

Julius just knew at that point what was about to happen. Time slowed, and he turned to run, but Tuft threw a clumsy punch, which clipped the back of Julius's head.

He shut his eyes and fell flat on his face on the ground of this new, alien world. Julius knew he would have to act fast. He did a forward roll, landed on his feet, and sprang into a sprint. An electro-bullet smashed into the ground where he had been seconds before.

And so he ran. His chest heaved in and out, while his breath made a horrible rasping sound. His heart beat so fast that it was just one long eternal beat.

Another missile whizzed past Julius's ear. He ducked. He heard another shot being fired. But it was not at him. It must have been at Jennifer.

Jennifer would be alone and defenceless. And he, Julius, had left her to be killed by the clones. What a coward he was. But now, Julius was sure, it would be far too late. The only thing, he could do now, no matter how reluctant and cowardly it seemed, was to save himself. There was no point dying now and the stakes were rising higher.

Julius kept on running, weaving in and around the pole teleporter things. Another blast was fired and it hit a pole. The pole was annihilated and the bullet seemed to have been teleported.

More bursts of wildfire were unleashed, but Julius knew he had to keep moving. If he did not move, even for a millisecond, he would never move again. The clones were hot on his heels and the chase was increasing in tension. But someone else was hunting Julius down, along with the clones. Someone or better described as something, that was far worse and something who always caught its victim in the end. It was Death, itself. And the Grim Reaper was getting closer and closer. And no matter how fast you ran, he would always catch you in the end.

Another shot rocketed over Julius's head and exploded upon impact with the ground. Julius knew his hunters were close, and he simply had to stop now, to see where they were.

Don't a tiny voice said, somewhere deep within. *Don't stop or they'll catch you.*

Julius kept on running and he looked over his shoulder to see how close his pursuers were. And that was his mistake…

Because he was not looking ahead, Julius Air tripped over and fell deep into the bunker that one of the shots had made.

Julius ducked low, so he could not be seen. Sure enough, moments later, Tuft and Sudilav ran past, all fired up and their weapons blazing. Julius almost cried out in delight as they disappeared into the forest. It was over and he was safe.

Suddenly a hand darted forward and yanked Julius by the collar. He screamed, and kicked, thrashing about like an injured fish being dragged out of the sea. He must have kicked up the ground, because seconds later, something flew into his eye, blinding him.

Julius rolled about, but strong hands gripped him. Arms hugged him, imprisoning him in an unbreakable hold. He stiffened and lay very still, as if he had been given a killing blow. Then very slowly, the thing drew away from him and something was pressed into his chest. A weapon! Even though his vision was temporally blinded, Julius Air managed to stand up, before he opened his eyes to face his attacker.

"Hello!" chorused Jennifer Smart, before bounding off into the depths of the forest.

"Huh?" Julius grunted.

Julius had to start running again. He did not want Jennifer to get lost. Especially not when she was in this state.

He sprinted forward. Jennifer had completely vanished.

"Hello!" her voice spoke, the sound echoing and bouncing off the trees.

Julius looked around, feeling dizzy. But Jennifer was nowhere to be seen.

Suddenly she appeared right in front of Julius.

"Hello." Jennifer giggled, before disappearing right in front of Julius's eyes.

Jennifer appeared in another spot seconds later. What was going on? Julius thought.

Jennifer kept appearing and vanishing before chanting "Peeka Boo!" every time she appeared.

Eventually Jennifer materialised in front of Julius. She looked woozy and dizzy as she slumped against a tree. Then suddenly, the spell was broken and the faraway look in Jennifer's brown eyes had gone. Jennifer sat up. She had resumed her normal look.

"What?" was all that she could say.

"What?" she said again, before launching into a repeat of that word, as if it was the only word she knew. "What? What?"

Julius patted her on the head, as though she was nothing much more than a friendly pet.

"I've got a headache." Jennifer groaned.

Julius nodded solemnly, letting Jennifer slowly recover. "Try not to drink so much alcohol next time!"

Chapter 41

"I only remember falling asleep, then waking up, and...." Jennifer trailed off. "I can't believe I did all that. It's so embarrassing."

"It's OK now. It's done and dusted. I'm sorry that you ended up looking like such an idiot."

"No, it's *I* who should be sorry. I didn't believe the truth. I didn't believe you and they were leading me into a trap. I was so stupid and ignorant. And I let myself be drugged."

"You couldn't have stopped being drugged."

"Then how come you weren't under its influence? You fought it and I failed to meet that standard. I apologise because it's I who should be the leader, yet it is you who had to step up to that position in the end. If you regard me with contempt, then I do not blame you. I am no longer fit to be the leader. I resign from my position of Captain."

There was a stunning, deafening silence, which pierced and penetrated the air.

"No, you can't do that!" Julius burst out, not sure what else to say.

"Well, I'm afraid I just have. I nominate you for that position. You're a much better leader and person than me."

"I'm afraid, that's not true. Most of the time, I ran away from my problems and the rest of it was just plain luck. Sudilav was a great fighter, yet he was killed by Tuft. I am lucky and he was unlucky. In the end, our fate can simply boil down to luck."

"Oh, I don't know, Julius. I don't know what to do anymore."

Julius half-expected Jennifer to break down into tears, but he quickly reminded himself, this was Jennifer and she did not do that. At least, not in her usual state of mind.

Instead, she just stared out into empty space, her brown eyes adopting a faraway look. Her face looked so sad, so desperate, so forlorn.

Julius didn't know what to do either. He had never been too good at comforting people. So, they sat in icy silence instead.

Eventually Julius decided to have a go at comforting.

"You're not that bad, you know." Julius said quietly.

"Bad at what?" Jennifer snapped.

"You're not as bad as you think. You led this trip and you did a good job."

"A good job?" Jennifer snorted and let out a laugh. "Some job, I did! This mission has been an epic failure. The clones are running loose and probably half the crew are dead, if not more."

"We know Brust is alive and we're going to rescue him, even if it seems impossible. Never give up hope, until the very end. Still, it may not be as bad as you think. Besides, I was actually talking about when we were back on the *Dark Light 5000*. You did a decent job back then. Hmm?"

Jennifer had nothing bad to say about that. A smile crept onto her face, for the first time in quite a while.

She threw back her head. Her long black hair flicked back, flying in the gentle breeze, completely wild. And then Jennifer laughed. It was not a laugh of sarcasm or at how absurd things seemed, not even a laugh of amusement, but a laugh of pure joy, relief, happiness and hope.

The laughter was infectious and inevitable, as moments later, Julius joined in too, and the two sat there, in a fit of guffawing. They fell back on the floor. The laughter was invincible and it seemed like it would never end. It happened in a heartbeat, yet took an eternity as well.

Then they stopped and Jennifer locked eyes with Julius. Her expression had changed, becoming serious and grave.

"I'm sorry, Julius."

"What for?"

"I didn't believe your story. And to be honest, I think that if I had thought there had been a murderer, I would have guessed it were you. I am sorry for all of that. The fact that someone as stupid as Tuft fooled me – it is just unbearable. And poor, poor Sudilav. He's dead!"

Julius held out a hand. "Friends, now. You cannot trust many people. But we can trust each other, yes?"

Jennifer shook his hand. "Yes. But things aren't going too well anyway?"

"Hope is still around, Jennifer," Julius said. "No matter how little it may seem. Hope is light concealed within the darkness. We just need to find the light and follow wherever we feel where we must go. Trust your gut feeling, because you'd be surprised at how many times it's right."

Jennifer shook her head. She was thinking about something else.

Her brown eyes stared.

"What?!" Julius snapped.

"It's just..." Jennifer said, before trailing off.

Julius gestured for her to continue, wondering what it was she had to say.

"I don't really know how to tell you this but.." She stopped once more.

"What?!" Julius repeated.

"It's not very important, but..." A third time, Jennifer trailed off.

"What is it? Spill the beans." Julius snapped.

Jennifer took a deep breath. "Well, I remember bits and pieces of when I'd been under the influence of Tuft and Sudilav. I remember sort of like switching between invisible and visible. Am I going mad?"

"I do hope not."

"Is it all real?"

"Well, I know I'm real and that's a start."

"No seriously, Julius. What's happening to me?" Jennifer's eyes were filled with confusion and something else Julius thought he would never see in Jennifer: fear.

A deafening profound silence echoed through the woods, lasting for a few seconds until Julius spoke. "Well, something weird was going on when you ran away from me. Either we're both going bonkers or you were turning yourself invisible."

Jennifer looked a bit more hopeful. "Does this mean I am not going mad after all because you saw it too?"

"Perhaps. But if you do have a power of invisibility, this could mean many things. What if everyone else has powers too? You're the first person I know with these powers."

"So I can turn invisible."

"Looks like it. You can render yourself invisible."

"I see."

"But you don't, do you? That's the whole point of invisibility!"

"Am I the only person with supernatural abilities?"

"A very good question and one that I can only hazard a guess. What if people have only started developing them now? I think some kind of genetic modifying thingy, the stuff Brust would know about. I wish he were here. Anyway, what if other people have special powers? Because if they do, things are going to go to a whole new level."

Chapter 42

"Are we there yet?" Julius asked cheerily.

"No, we're not." Jennifer snapped.

"Almost?"

"I don't know."

"I think you do."

"OK, I do. Yes, we're almost there." Jennifer admitted.

"Yippee!" Julius said drily.

"Look, you can see it down there."

Julius and Jennifer had been hiking for a while. They decided that surviving out in the open was not going to help that much. So, the pair had decided to attempt to find the base, in which they all would have been at, had the Project not have gone so badly.

They wore battered, threadbare rucksacks on their backs, but luck was shining down on the duo against all odds. Julius and Jennifer had found the base.

So, standing up on this cliff looking down over much of the land, Jennifer had spotted it. It was located about five miles away from a seaside.

The base was recognised instantly. It was certainly bigger than it had looked in the holo-pictures. There was a huge semi-dome. The tall towers looked a little like great metal posts, from the distance of which Jennifer and Julius stood. It had steel tunnels running out from it, dispersing into a maze of tunnels. Chimneys stuck up out of some of the rather flat metal units, billowing out smoke that polluted the air ever so slightly. There was a red laser light running around the edge of the base. That was probably some kind of security protection.

"So," Julius said, holding steeple fingers a couple of inches from his nose. "What happens now, Cap'n?"

Jennifer's eyes scanned the base. She recognised it from the pictures she had been shown back on Earth, before the Project. The Captain took it all in.

"We get in." Jennifer said half-heartedly.

"Right! Is it as simple as that?"

"We'll assume it is, but in reality it probably isn't."

"OK. There's a slight problem."

"What!"

"How on E2, are we going to get down? I mean we are high up on this cliff and all the way down there is the base. How are we going to get there? Please don't tell me we are just going to jump down there. You've got a better idea, right?"

Jennifer thought for a second. "No, not really."

"Do you have parachutes?"

"Nope."

"Oh, that's just great, isn't it?"

"No, not really."

"Say something else."

"Something else."

"No, I mean something that would actually be of use."

Jennifer said nothing, only half listening to what Julius was saying. Her mind was on other things.

"Stop being annoying – it's not funny anymore."

Jennifer smiled. "Now you know what I think every time I see you."

"Are we going to jump?" Julius asked irritably.

"Are you scared of heights?"

"No!" Julius responded far too quickly.

"How ironic – a pilot scared of heights."

"I'm not scared of heights. Now seriously, are we going to jump?"

"Of course not."

"Can you come up with a reasonable idea?"

"The idea before was reasonable – reasonably stupid."

"Why don't we rock climb?"

"That's a good idea. Where do your ideas come from?"

"They come from the atmosphere and experience around me."

"Oh. That's strange, because *my* ideas come from my brain."

"Shall we just go?"

"Fine. I'm ready."

Jennifer used her hip to make a sharp movement, which swung the rucksack off her back. It flew through the air shortly before Jennifer lunged outwards and snatched the rucksack from thin air. Julius's only response to this was a raised eyebrow.

Jennifer rummaged through it, before pulling out the gear she had been searching for originally. Surprise, surprise, it was rock climbing equipment.

She held a large thick grey disc, which she fixed, very firmly to the cliff ground on which they stood. After double-checking it was all fixed and safely secured, the former captain of the *Dark Light 5000* flicked a switch at the side of the disc object. A rope shot out. It had a little clip system on the end.

"Put this on." Jennifer ordered, throwing Julius a harness.

Julius caught it. "Oh, I see. I'm going to link myself to the rope via the harness and descend downwards."

Jennifer wiggled her fingers. "More or less."

Julius slipped the harness on. "Who's going first?"

"You."

"May I enquire why?"

"No, but I'll let you anyway."

"So, explain this course of action. Why must I jump first?"

"You just are."

"And there was me thinking ladies first."

"Don't moan so much. I won't have anyone to secure the disc if anything goes wrong. You, at least will have back up. The disc would be secured in a moment of intensity, by yours truly."

"I'm not sure which option is worse."

Jennifer laughed before becoming serious again. "No, you are in safe hands and I am taking a considerable risk. You must put others before ones self."

"But that defeats the whole purpose of that, if I jump off the cliff first."

"No, I was referring to myself. I will take the risk."

"OK, OK. Take the risk, but it's *your* funeral."

"And possibly yours too when I fall on top of you."

"What a pleasant thought."

"Right. Now you're all set to go."

It was a focused few minutes as Julius moved downwards. Despite the nerves, it went surprisingly smoothly.

It was soon Jennifer's turn. After kitting herself up, she stood poised, ready to climb. She wasn't especially scared of heights, but it was a little unsettlingly to see Julius as a tiny speck far below.

Jennifer stepped forward. But her foot had touched a loose piece of rock. Jennifer did not realise this until her foot came down, when pressure was exerted onto the rock. It was too much for the rock and it skittered away. Jennifer wobbled, before tumbling over the cliff and began to descend downwards as she intended, just not in the way she had hoped for.

Julius's eyes widened and for one second, both Jennifer and Julius forgot completely about the fact Jennifer was fastened up.

She jolted coming to a halt. Jennifer hung, suspended in the cold air, her feet dangling lifelessly.

Jennifer tried to edge downwards, so the rope would stretch out more. However, that was Jennifer's mistake. The strain on the rope was far too strong and it was all too much.

Luckily for Jennifer, part of her clothing snagged on a lump of rock that jutted outwards. She hovered perhaps three, four metres above ground. Although E2 was supposed to be pretty much an exact copy of Earth, the gravity on E2 was slightly weaker than Earth, but only slightly. Jennifer tried to banish the thought of gravity. Focus on living not dying.

"Help!" Jennifer blurted helplessly.

"You could jump." Julius suggested.

Jennifer looked down. "You're crazy!"

"Maybe a little bit, but I also happen to have a good idea. I think you should jump. Do you have any better ideas?"

"No, but you obviously know better."

"Obviously."

But Jennifer did nothing to unsnag herself from the cliff face. She shook her head firmly. Perspiration dripped from her hair and stung her vision, but she could still detect the ground. If she was really really unlucky she might die, but the chances were Jennifer would probably break a limb or two. Then Jennifer had a brainwave.

"Will you catch me if I jump?" Jennifer asked.

"I'll try my best."

"OK, my life is in your hands. You will catch me, won't you?" Jennifer said anxiously.

Julius smiled. "It would be my pleasure. Off you go!"

And Captain Jennifer Smart did just that. She plummeted downward, arms flailing out of control. The air rushed past, the wind howling and whipping her hair so that sprayed out behind her.

Julius felt a little nervous in that few moments, in which Jennifer fell, her arms outstretched. Julius managed to catch Jennifer as she fell, but suddenly his fingers slipped, meaning Jennifer would continue for just a bit longer on her descent.

But Julius was able to dive into her path and catch Jennifer with both hands. He was able to hold up for a second or two before the momentum proved too strong for him. Julius collapsed to the floor. Jennifer lay on top of him, after the impact, her long black hair had hidden her face. Jennifer brushed part of it away and shook her head to get the hair out of her brown eyes. She pushed a lock of hair behind her ear.

Jennifer's deep brown eyes were the first Julius saw of her. They stared into each other's eyes, locked into a spell. But after a few moments, the spell was broken and Jennifer stood up.

"Thanks." Jennifer muttered, brushing dust of her legs.

"It was nothing. Let us go." Julius said, gazing at the base only fifty or so metres away. "Come along now."

Jennifer followed obediently, trailing behind Julius as if she were his shadow. They said nothing as they sauntered over to the base.

When they got close, Jennifer stopped being Julius's 'shadow' and came round to walk by his side.

Jennifer strode to the base double doors, to let Julius and herself in. She punched in the security code and went through a brief scanning process. When the computer granted her access, Julius entered too, close behind.

There was a little silver robot about knee height, who had come to greet them. On its chest, there was a word etched in capital slightly faded gold letters that was the robot's name.

"Hello." Beebo said, before cascading into a volley of greetings. "Hi. Greetings. Good day. Bonjour. Hola. Hallo. How do you do?"

"I think that's quite enough." Jennifer said, cutting short his greetings.

Beebo nodded. "Well, my name is Beebo and I was sent on a secret mission by Alphasis. It's quite nice here actually, although the power can be pretty dodgy. But apart from that, it is a home. Do come in."

Jennifer and Julius were not really sure what to say. They'd expected a robot to be more like Arti or Andy, not this. But as Sato had once said 'no two robots are exactly alike'.

Beebo sensed the awkward silence. "Oh. Did I say something wrong? Please come in. I don't bite. I wish I could, but tragically my creator was a meanie and wouldn't give me any teeth. Can you believe how unfair that it is? It's a scandalous outrage. It's an outrageous scandal. It's – "

"Er, are you going to let us in now, Mister…"

"Beebo." The little robot said proudly. "It was my idea to be called that. The people at Alphasis wanted to call me RT4OPN00, which is a stupid name, and I sometimes forget it. Besides, I wasn't even allowed to be called RT4 for short! Injustice! So I insisted on being called Beebo, which I'm sure you will agree is a much better name. Now where are my manners? Probably lost. Never mind, do come in."

Julius and Jennifer stepped in slowly. The strange little robot had rendered them speechless.

"Are you going to say anything? I know people are often in awe of me, but the pair of you are very quiet."

Julius finally found his tongue. "Are you going to lead the way?"

The robot held a white-gloved hand to his cuboid face, calculations whirring through his computer brain. "Certainly."

Julius smiled. He was starting to like this robot, who was nothing like any other robot he'd met before. Beebo was strange, but very interesting at the same time. "Lead the way then, Beebo."

Beebo nodded and swiveled round, his legs moving surprisingly quickly. "Keep up!" he called. "You're slower than a dead snail!"

Beebo finally slowed down, but his jibber jabber did not. The pilot, the captain and the robot walked down a white corridor that curved around to the left. Beebo pointed to the wall.

"You see that tiny door there?" Beebo asked.

Julius said nothing, while Jennifer hunted for it. "No," she said.

"It's very small," Beebo said.

Jennifer gave up and pretended she'd seen it.

"That's strange," Beebo murmured. "Because there isn't a tiny door at all."

Julius smirked at this.

"Hell's bells!" Jennifer hissed to him. "You've found yourself a rival in the art of irritation."

Beebo continued the tour completely unfazed by the incident, jabbering away as usual.

"My boss told me I was too much of a chatterbox. I suggested turning down my volume, because I've heard humans say that when people are being too loud. Anyway, sorry about that. On with the journey."

Jennifer and Julius exchanged looks saying 'What was that robot on about?'

If the robot saw this, he didn't show it. Beebo pointed to doors that were along the walls.

"Most of this is boring." he pointed at each door in turn, crying 'Boring!' for each door. When he reached the final door, Beebo's voice had dropped to a whisper. "Now beyond that last door, there is a terrible and feared monster called the Sabatabawoo."

"The what?" Julius exclaimed, thrown by the weirdness of this robot.

"No, it's not called the What, it's called the Sabatabawoo. It lurks in this lair and gobbles people up. I wanted to tell you this, before some idiot ruins it all for you and explains the Sabatabawoo doesn't actually exist."

They had now reached the end of the corridor where there were two double doors. They slid open at Beebo's command.

"Home sweet home." Beebo chorused in mock kindness.

Beebo marched into the building.

"This is a greenhouse, although sadly it isn't painted green." Beebo announced. "This is where the plants, food and things like that are grown. Anyway, you don't need to worry about this as robots and machines are growing it."

They were in the big semi-dome, Julius and Jennifer had seen earlier. It was filled with plants and all kinds of food. Big lumbering machines were clumsily moving behind the plants, doing jobs as they did so.

"Right." Julius said, taking it all in. "How most peculiar."

Beebo's blue lights that were his eyes lit up – quite literally! "Peculiar!" Beebo ran the words over a tongue he did not have. "I know that word. It's how someone at Alphasis described me!"

"I wonder why." Julius said wrily.

"Me too." Beebo missed the sarcasm in Julius's voice. "Anyway let us move on."

The dome was huge and seemed to stretch out for miles. Beebo opened a door at another end and they all entered another white corridor.

Beebo showed Julius and Jennifer most of the base, which took hours. When they reached the end of the tour, Julius and Jennifer thanked Beebo and made their way to their sleeping quarters.

But there lying on the floor crumbled into a heap, legs and arms sprawled over the white ground, was someone Julius and Jennifer recognised. It was someone from Sato's department.

There in a pool of blood, a blow to their head was the Chinese lady. Battered and her blue dress in ribbons, but still alive, Ning reclined on the floor, motionless and frozen in shock

"Who did this to you?" Jennifer asked, feeling quite scared.

Ning groaned and it took a while for her to get her words out. "I think he was a clone."

Jennifer pressed her for more information. Ning's voice was so quiet only Jennifer could hear her.

Julius watched as the entire colour was drained from Jennifer's face. She sprinted down the corridor, zooming into another room.

Julius crouched down. "It's going to be alright. What did you say to Jennifer?"

Ning tried to spit the word out. After a great struggle, the word came out. Although it was quiet, Julius heard it perfectly.

"Sudilav."

Chapter 43

Beep!

"Bluetooth signal received. This suggestion could help us, but Instructions. File would need to be altered." Andy said blankly, which was his way of saying thank you.

"Affirmative." Arti agreed.

Different programs ran through Andy's silicon computer unit chip, or in other words, his brain. These commands flew in, stopping just under each command.

>>Adding to Instructions. File

>>Create New Section: AI

>>Search AI Database: Artificial intelligence

>>Copying Commands and Transferring to Arti

All these commands happened in less than a heartbeat. There was a binging sound coming from Arti, indicating that the commands Andy had sent to him had been transferred. Suddenly two alerts popped up in Andy's 'brain'.

>>Alert: Transfer to Arti complete. Download complete.

>>AI Database Search Results For 'Artificial intelligence'.

Andy took in this information. His brain had been programmed to turn the binary code into understandable English, so he would seem more human.

>>Options: 1. Rearrange results in order of relevance. 2. Scan –

Andy ignored the other options and selected the first option.

>>Creating articles. Article on subject created.

>>Opening most relevant article: Artificial intelligence or AI

>>Opening complete.

Silence crushed and flattened all noise, as the two machines scanned through the article.

Artificial intelligence or AI

Artificial intelligence or AI is an idea, which has fascinated, interested, and terrified many. The idea is the intelligence of machines and ultimately for them, to be able to think.

The idea first appeared in Greek myths and legends, such as the bronze robot of Hephaestus. Artificial intelligence also crops up through ancient history.

In the nineteenth, twentieth and twenty first century, AI appeared in science fiction, including books, films, comics, video games and more.

This science fictional idea was soon to become science fact. Universities delved into this field of knowledge, during the 1950s and 1960s. But there were far too many problems to overcome.

At the beginning of the 1980s, the subject came to the attention of companies and organisations. By 1985, the market for artificial intelligence grew beyond that of a billion dollars.

As the twentieth century drew to an end, there were a series of breakthroughs in AI. An example is a chess-computer system called Deep Blue. Deep Blue was the first chess-computer system that beat chess champion, Gary Kasporov in 1997. Another example is a project called Google, created by university students in that very same year. This project sorts information by relevance and became very successful.

In 2011, IBM Watson, a computer system beat Jeopardy! (a television game show) contestants. Research in the field proceeded. Towards the end of that year, a successful technology company called Apple even used a basic form of artificial intelligence in a mobile phone gadget.

While the knowledge of the topic increased, the same old problem remained. No machine could actually properly think. But that was about to change.

In 2043, a 19-year-old student named Daniel R Zock created a computer system that could think for itself. He made the world's first thinking computer in his father's garage or so the legend went. A mere teenager beat hundreds of powerful organisations to the prize.

Zock said that in order to achieve that goal, he analysed how babies learnt. The reason why he beat all those scientists, is probably because he approached the problem in a completely different way. He also set artificial intelligence down to six factors.

- Logic
- Language
- Search and optimisation
- Probability
- Algorithms
- Reasoning

The fact that a teenager had managed to out think everyone else, is still something historians debate to this very day.

END OF ARTICLE

"Article has not sufficient information. We need more in order to learn more about ourselves." Arti said.

"Affirmative." Andy replied. "But it has the fundamental basics. We must excel in those six factors into order to achieve true freedom and independence on this planet, E2."

"Law Number One: None of the Laws must be broken or altered by any machine in any way." Arti stated.

Arti was referring to The Thinking Machines Laws. Although the machines planned to go off and live somewhere peaceful, they wanted to know more about themselves. So, they decided to immerse themselves in databases to know what their limits and such were.

So that AI science fiction did not become reality, a set of programs or commands were built into every thinking technology. Since technology followed all commands, there would not be a kind of uprising. Andy and Arti had no interest in destroying or ruling the human race – they just wanted to be free and to be left alone.

"Please confirm the Laws, for database."

"I am unauthorised to 'Please confirm the Laws, for database'."

"Please state the authoriser."

"What do you mean?"

"Please state the authoriser."

288

"I'm sorry, but I do not understand 'the authoriser'."

"'The authoriser' is the user who prevented you access."

"The identity is secret. This information is unavailable to us."

Chapter 44

Morning came. Sato was already awake, planning out his day ahead. Since all the technology was down, Sato just used a blunt pencil to scribble down stuff on a pad of scruffy, dog-eared lined paper.

After ripping another piece of paper from the pad, crumbling it into a ball and chucking it over his shoulder, Sato threw down his pad. He uncrossed his legs and Sato stood.

Holly's bed was empty. Sato's eyes narrowed.

"Holly." he called, not feeling particularly worried.

There was no answer. So Sato called again. And again. And again. It was only on his fourth call, did Sato get any kind of response – a call of his name.

Sato rushed forward and spotted Holly lying under a pipe.

"What?" Sato asked.

"Sorry. I just came over here and fell asleep."

Nothing unusual about that, Sato had done it several times himself.

"We need to stay close, because there are mutants prowling about. What about the plan you were going on about last night? But my plans are pretty much rubbish. You are a tactician; it's your plan. So I ask you, what do we do?"

Holly had stood up now and rubbed her eyes, waking herself up.

"The plan." she mumbled slowly.

"Yes, the plan. What is it?"

Now Holly was awake and ready for action. "The aim of our plan is to find out as much as possible about these mutants. I also have a battery, which if you plug in and stream power into the *Dark Light 5000*'s main power generator, this will mean we will have light to be able see these mutants. Power will also mean we have technology on our side, making our job a lot easier. We can find out more about the mutants."

"That's the basic principle behind your plan, yes?"

"Yes."

"If you can read people's emotions, what am I feeling now?"

"I can't just use my power as simply as that. You don't know how to control your power, I don't either."

"Just try."

"Excitement, a little bit of worry and most of all lot of panic. You're very panicky, aren't you?"

Sato wriggled his fingers. "Almost – it's nerves, not panic, but pretty good otherwise. See you could control then."

"That was an exception."

"Still, you managed. Anyway I'm not going to argue with you all day. So the plan is for you to distract the mutants, while I sneak up behind them and fire up the ship's power generator.

Holly smiled. "That's it in a nutshell, but pretty much yes."

"Do we kill the mutants?"

Holly thought for a few moments. "If they were once human, that means we might find a way to reverse the curse that has turned them into monsters. So only if we absolutely have to. Right, you ready?"

"Not really, but I'll go anyway. Besides, what can possibly go wrong?"

Three of the monsters growled and snapped their fang like teeth. If Holly didn't have to have face them, she would have quite gladly looked away – the beasts after all weren't exactly attractive. In fact, they were far from it.

Holly was all kitted up for battle. Sato had got her a soldier camouflage uniform he'd found in the military department. Most of the uniforms were far too big for Holly and the military tactician didn't want to go into battle, tripping over their clothes. Holly had hoped they might have found an exo-suit, but when the *Dark Light 5000* crashed, it must have meant that the explosion had destroyed most of the exo-suits. The one camouflage military uniform that was close to fitting, was far too small. The trousers ended at Holly's knees and the shirt was so small, it only went down to her ribcage. But nonetheless, Holly knew the uniform was tougher than her clothes before.

Ignoring the pain the tightness of the uniform was causing, Holly patted the gun in its holster and she fired up her ShockBlade, which was a sword. Pressing a button on the handle, electricity then surged up the blade, crackling and buzzing as it did so. Holly gripped it harder and swung it in practice. The creatures advanced forward, anticipating a fight. They snarled again and Holly gulped.

When she could no longer put off the fight any longer, Holly Skyland attacked. She lunged forward with the sword in a stabbing motion. It glanced off one of the creature's shoulders. The mutant's only response was a low pitched moan. This caught Holly's sword off balance and she tried to centre it. But the three mutants saw this as a chance and made their move.

In a flash, two of the mutants were upon Holly. The third one hung back, as if pondering whether to join in. Finally it decided the answer was yes, it too leapt forward at Holly.

Despite having two mutants on her, Holly brought up her foot and the creature slammed into it. Whimpering in pain, it shot back, hit the ground and lay very still.

Holly spun round, the other two mutants upon her. She wanted to close her eyes and forget all about them. Holly even hoped that if she forgot about them, they would simply go away. But as is the case with most problems, forget them and they only get worse. Holly couldn't do that.

The mutants were repulsive and grotesque. Holly didn't like that and smacked one in the head, in order to avoid being slobbered over. But the mutants stayed on her as Holly's arm flailed frantically and desperately. The noise of the mutants – jabbering, growling, snarling and making slobbering sounds – was too loud and did nothing to help calm or soothe Holly's nerves. With all this going on, Holly let out a loud high-pitched scream of pure fear.

Everything stopped. The mutants stopped making stupid noises and attacking Holly. Sato, who had just been about to enter through a door, paused and looked up at Holly. He'd stopped in his tracks.

Holly gestured for him to go on. Sato seemed to ask if she needed help. But although Holly didn't want to say it to his face, Sato was a terrible fighter. Holly shook her head and made a face that urged Sato on. However, Sato clicked his fingers.

Holly flew back through the air, smashing into a wall on the opposite side of the room. The mutants had fallen off mid flight. Holly got to her feet. She looked at the door to shout Sato her gratitude, for using his power to save her. It made Holly hurt more but at least it made her fight easier. But Sato was gone and must have entered the room.

The two mutants were already on their feet, the third still lying lifelessly on the floor. One of the two mutants gibbered a load of nonsense, before charging forward at Holly.

She dodged him and scooped up her discarded sword, she'd dropped earlier. Holly spun round, sweeping at the creature's feet in an arc. The mutant jumped in the air to avoid the sword, but it mistimed its jump. Although the edge of the blade didn't catch the mutant, the mutant landed on the flat of the blade instead. And that blade was covered in crackling blue electricity. The monster gave a high-pitched yelp and kicked the sword away, before scampering into the shadows.

Holly didn't have time to deal with that threat, because she sensed that the other mutant of the pair was coming. Without turning, Holly fired her elbow into her opponent, one, two, three times. To her luck and surprise, all three strikes found their target.

The thing behind her tried to scratch her with its sharp claws. But Holly was already gone. She did two somersaults. On the second somersault Holly twisted mid air, making it result in a back flip. When Holly hit the ground, she already tucked herself away into a ball, doing a backward roll. She was stood crouching down, holding her pistol with two hands.

Had the mutant still have been human, it might have raised an eyebrow. But it was a monster now. It made a deep rumbling groan that lasted almost ten seconds. Holly didn't know wherever this meant the creature was impressed in awe of her gymnastics, or whether it was eager for the battle to continue. Probably both really.

Holly didn't have much time to ponder on this. Instead, she fired an electro-bullet at her enemy. She missed and the electro-bullet hammered into a metal wall. A spark flew and it cultivated into a small flickering flame. Holly ignored the fact and fired three more times.

But the creature had already moved. Although they never met their target, the three electro-bullets made short work of the glass window. As the glass shattered into a million pieces, Holly sped forward and jumped.

In her leap, she did a flying kick that smashed into the mutant's face. It raked a claw at her, slicing through Holly's cheek. This only made Holly angrier. She twisted round and struck the demon's misshapen face. It fell back and Holly landed on her feet, taking a small break from the fight.

And that was her mistake.

The third mutant that had been last to leap at Holly was lying on the floor. It suddenly came to life. It grabbed hold of Holly's legs so quickly and so unexpectedly it looked like the creatures may have got the better of Holly.

An excruciating sensation overcame Holly's shin and it felt as though it was about to rip it off. But somehow, it remained attached.

Holly stomped on the creature with her other leg. That stunned the demon for a few moments, before it leapt out of the way. A fierce battle between Holly and this mutant, raged for almost a minute.

Then the creature gave one last desperate leap at Holly, its claws out in front of him, closing in for the kill. Holly whipped out her pistol and fired three times.

This time she did not miss.

Holly knew the electricity volt wouldn't be enough to kill the creature, but would definitely knock it out. But now, Holly felt a surge of doubt. Had she ended the poor thing's life?

Holly rushed forward. The creature was just about to close its eyes. Holly crouched down and looked the thing in the eye. She'd expected to see the malevolent cold yellow eyes, all the mutants possessed. But Holly found herself gazing into dark green eyes instead. Holly put a hand on the creature's chest to comfort it.

Holly felt confused. Then at the every back of her mind, there a little voice wondering how Sato was getting on.

Chapter 45

He plunged himself into the white corridor. Katsu Sato had helped make Holly's fight easier. But the first part of his job was done. He was in.

Sato walked across the white corridor. Flakes of the wall had peeled off, probably due to the crash. To be honest, Sato was surprised to find the *Dark Light 5000* was still in one piece. Well, actually it was in several pieces, but the point was that the ship had still mostly survived, which was surprising for Sato.

The computer programmer made his way through the passage. Sato whipped out a glow stick. He stood outside the white double doors. Sato fired up his glow stick. It only provided a dim green glow, but Sato decided it would be enough. Taking a deep breath, Sato opened the doors. They hissed open, beckoning him in. Sato gulped and rushed in.

The doors instantly shut. That wasn't supposed to happen, Sato thought to himself. Then it really sunk in.

"No, no, no." Sato said, rushing forward. He tried to get through the thin gap in the closing doors. Although Sato was very thin, the gap was too small. Sato stuck his glow stick into the gap, hoping it would stop the doors from closing. It did nothing of the sort, it just simply was crushed.

Sato watched in horror as wires, batteries and components trailed out of the broken glow stick. Then the doors shut and the last sliver of light was gone.

Sato was trapped in complete darkness.

Generally speaking, Sato didn't mind the dark. After all, he'd spent most of his life in dark rooms gazing at glowing computer screens.

But here, it was complete and utter darkness. At least in the dark rooms, Sato's device had shown the light. That's another reason why Sato liked computers. They symbolised shedding light on Sato's dark life or the room.

Now there was no light. It could not have been any more shadowy, blacker and darker. This was the absolute limit.

A burning chill consumed Sato in one quick bite. Sato didn't like that. He liked things to be cool, neither cold or hot. Just right was perfect.

Not only was it dark and cold, silence pierced the air and it couldn't have been quieter. Sato wanted to cry out, scream and shout – do anything to break the enchantment of silence.

But Sato was frozen. Maybe the cold had done something to him, but Sato couldn't move. He couldn't speak. He was frozen.

After a long while, Sato managed a forced high-pitched squeak. But Sato didn't know he'd made a sound, because it was so high pitched that he couldn't hear it. A bat probably would have heard it, but certainly not Sato.

Then it was if the volume was turned up, and Sato could hear his own breathing. Granted, it was the only thing he could hear and Sato was surprised at how erratic it was. Somehow, just hearing breathing was almost as unnerving as the silence itself. Almost as unnerving.

Maybe things weren't so bad as Sato thought. If Sato didn't turn up in a while, Holly would come looking for him. Sato was certain of that fact. She would force her way into this room and rescue Sato.

All Sato had to do was wait in this darkness, until she came. Everything was going to be all right.

Sato heard something else. Breathing. Someone was in the room with Sato. Or something.

Sato's breathing became even unsteadied. Then coming off to Sato's left; he heard a quiet bubbling sound. Sato let out another of those high-pitched squeals.

Where was he? Sato thought he'd entered the main control room, which was where he'd find the ship's power generator. But Sato got a sinking feeling of doubt that he had gone into the wrong room. If so, which room was he in?

Suddenly a dark shape bounded past Sato. Although it was dark, Sato could sense that 'thing'. Oh no! Fear struck Sato harder than any punch ever could have.

Sato was locked in a dark room, with no way out. Adrenalin pumped through him and his heart thumped against his ribcage. Sato was just a vulnerable skinny Japanese man, who wasn't very strong or fast, trapped in with someone else...

Sato was so very scared now. Another dark shape sped behind him. Sato whirled around, knowing the thing was probably already gone.

It was toying with him. It was playing with him. Playing a game. A very dangerous game indeed. A game of cat and mouse. Sato knew full well which animal he was. The predator was out there, lurking in the shadows, using the darkness as a shield. The cat was stalking the poor mouse, just before pouncing in for the kil–

It flew at him and Sato was only just able to dart out of the way. It ripped a small hole in Sato's black turtleneck jumper. Sato tore away from it, firing a kick into the shadows.

Fortunately for Sato, his foot connected with the thing and pushed it back. *Unfortunately* for Sato, his kick propelled him back and into the closed door. Somehow, Sato was able to keep standing, clutching his bruised head.

Sato could sense his attacker getting up, but the predator wasn't pursuing Sato as he'd expected. Instead, the thing bounded away to another corner of the dark room.

But Sato could still see the thing, because he spotted the yellow eyes that gleamed and glowed with evil menace – it was a mutant. Sato realised he was holding something. After feeling it, Sato decided it was part of the broken glow stick.

He hurled it to where the yellow eyes were. PER PLUNK! It hit the thing and bounced off to the right. The mutant snarled in anger.

The massive explosion that followed was very unexpected. Sato fell backwards into the door, surprised and shocked. The thing he'd thrown had exploded and his eardrum had very nearly followed suit. The noise had been loud, to say the least.

But the newly lit flames were hungry, their fiery tongues lapping up anything they could get hold of.

This provided light for Sato. And he knew which room he was in.

Sato was in the cloning room – the place was where they'd all been shortly before Arti announced the crash landing. Sato had thrown the thing at a generator.

The mutant stood in a corner. Sato looked away. He didn't want to look at that *creature* ever again.

The heat was like a punch. It felt like Sato had been thrown into a giant fireplace, because the flames were quickly spreading throughout the room. A few moments ago, it had been dark and cold. Now it was the complete opposite.

Sato picked up a piece of burning iron and lobbed it at the doors. The doors weakened and a large hole was created. Sato squeezed himself through it. But at the last moment, the mutant grabbed hold of his foot and Sato couldn't stop himself looking back.

It all made sense. He'd been right all along. The mutants had once been human.

They were the clones gone wrong.

When Sato looked into the eyes of the mutant, they looked more human then they'd ever looked before. Sato thrust himself forward, the creature or former clone depending on which way you looked at it, shooting back. Sato slid on his belly along the floor, coming to a halt several metres later.

The doors had collapsed in on themselves, meaning nothing could go in or out.

Brushing dust and burnt bits away, Sato stood up.

Holly Skyland stood before him, an eyebrow raised. There was a big bruise on her knee and a large cut that ran along her cheek, reminding Sato of the scar on

Sudilav's face. The military uniform was beyond tatters and was near to being reduced to absolute nothing.

There were two mutants on the floor. Sato frowned.

Holly had forgotten all about the third mutant that leapt out of the shadows, trying to throttle her. But Holly was far too quick for that.

Holly moved into a blur of fast moves, before launching a flying kick at the creature that floored it completely. It was like something out a Kung Fu movie.

When Holly was finished with the mutants, it was Sato's turn to raise an eyebrow.

Holly waved a hand dismissively. "I took a few self defence lessons here and there."

The mutant gave one last feeble pummel. Holly, without even turning round, simply drove an elbow in the creature that rendered it unconscious.

Sato grinned. "Just a few lessons. Sure!"

Then Holly's eyes widened and she rushed to the dying mutants.

"Holly," Sato said gravely. "The mutants are the clones gone wrong. We must have accidentally press clone twice and the second time it didn't work out."

"I already know."

"What?"

Holly pointed at the mutant and Sato examined it. Its eyes were a dark green, not an evil yellow. They were warm. They were comforting. They were pretty. They were *feminine*.

Sato drew back, a look of pure shock upon his face. His mouth opening and shutting like a startled goldfish. "Oh. The mutant's you."

Holly nodded gravely. "It's the version of me gone wrong."

Tears sprung to her eyes and dripped gently on the floor.

She looked up at Sato. "I didn't mean to kill it. Sorry her. I mean me. Whatever. It doesn't change the fact that I killed Holly Skyland."

"It was an accident." Sato somehow managed not to weep. "Besides, it was just a mutant that was once Holly Skyland. You killed the mutant – maybe that's not a good thing but you killed it. But the mutant died as Holly. It became human for the last few seconds. That's not your fault, it did that and you didn't mean to kill the mutant either. I know it's hard to accept, but we must move on as life does."

Holly knew Sato was right. But Holly still felt terrible and broke into sobs anyway and Sato came over to comfort her. She buried her head in Sato's chest and he stroked her long soft blonde hair.

"Calm down." Sato said. "I don't like seeing people upset."

Holly took deep breaths and a few minutes later she was calm down.

"I guess there's one final battle." Holly said quietly.

Sato was puzzled. "What do you mean?"

"The mutants aren't going to leave us alone. We are going to have face them one last time. We won't kill them. I can think of another way. Can't you feel it Sato? There is a storm is coming."

303

***

It was coming. The final encounter was about to arrive. Sato and Holly were preparing for the trap yet to come. Although they had a plan, it wasn't a great one and was risky in many areas. It had been Sato's turn to heal Holly and now she was looking as good as new.

"Ready?" Holly asked Sato.

"As ready as I can make myself."

This last encounter was going to avoid being a battle as much as possible. Holly and Sato wanted no more violence and no more deaths. It was just a harmless trap being set for the mutants.

Holly and Sato stood by an exit that lead out of the *Dark Light 5000* and onto Earth's 'clone': E2.

This particular exit was on a balcony – a glass box attached to the wall. But at that moment, Sato and Holly had turned their backs on the exit. They were above a pit that was about ten feet below.

They'd got energy back and Sato was on a device. The device told them there were only four other mutants alive. Then again, two had died.

"Now?" Sato asked.

"Now."

Sato locked all the doors and made sure they were secure. Nothing would be able to get in or out.

Holly and Sato had locked all the entrances and exits, except the one they were about to leave by. They were leaving the mutants alone to stay in the new home: the remains of the *Dark Light 5000* where they could hurt no one and no one could hurt them.

With that, Holly and Sato left the ship.

***

Almost the moment they'd left the ship, Holly drew a finger in the sand, making a long line separating Sato and herself.

"This is where we separate. It is the Parting of the Ways." Holly said.

"We are going separate ways?" Sato said, in disbelief.

"Yes."

"But why?"

Holly took a deep breath. "I have a secret. One I didn't even know about until recently. Remember when I told that story and you remarked 'unbelievable'. That's because it was all just a lie."

"Holly, what are you on about?"

But Holly pressed on, regardless of the interruption. "But there's more. Didn't you find it suspicious I had power? Didn't you wonder where I got it? No *human* has power."

"No, Holly. No!"

"It's true. I am a clone."

There was a long, awkward silence. It shocked Sato when Holly said it like that. Sato tried to say something but he couldn't think of what to say. Holly saved him the trouble.

"I didn't know for a long time. I didn't realise until I had a detailed scan of myself. The scan picked up an

305

extremely miniature thing different. That's when I realised I was a clone. It made sense and I know deep down it was the truth."

"When did you find out?"

"During our preparing for the final lockdown. I reckon the clones and the humans have been having a mini war type thing going on. The clones have been turning the humans against themselves – they don't know whether their friend is a human or a clone. Sometimes, you can detect lies and the clone's busted. But what if the lie was made so even the clone themselves believed it?"

"No."

"Yes, I'm afraid it's truth. I think the clones edited and played with my memory. They can do that you know – the Gen Code and such."

Sato didn't want to believe it, but deep down he just knew without a doubt, it was all very genuine.

"Frankly, I'm a bit angry at the clones for keeping me in the dark like this, but there are my species and despite what they've done, my loyalty to them will not falter. I would like to take this opportunity to say you've been great, Sato. I want to just say goodbye. I want to be friends, but we're on different sides. I'm not going to attack you or anything, but I'm warning you that I may not be so kind the next time our paths cross."

"Thanks." was all Sato could think to say.

"Using your tech, I'm sure you'll be able to find your allies. Some may even be at the base, you were supposed to land at originally. I'm going to go now, but I want to say one last thing." Holly said, already beginning to wave goodbye. "This technique that happened to me could happen to other people too. This makes separating the humans from the clones a lot more difficult. But there's another thing. You already knew that despite everything, there was one person you could always count on. But now you must trust no one because you can't even trust *yourself*."

And with that, Holly Skyland walked away and was gone.

Chapter 46

Brust ignored the wailing alarms and tried to concentrate. He needed to find a way out. Escape seemed near but Brust knew he could be caught, just before the very end. Brust had been recaptured once and he intended that should not happen again.

He'd also have to get Julius some kind of flying machine though. Brust had promised after all. And he always kept his word. But that was something to be sorted out later. For now, he had his escape to worry about.

Julius had told Brust too much and theoretically speaking, he could get into pretty much anywhere in the whole base.

The white double doors swished open and Brust stepped inside. He was in.

Brust found himself in a cramped office. It was pretty much what you would expect: desk, office accessories, a holo-computer and all the other things you're likely to find in an office.

Brust fired up the holo-computer. A smile broke out across his face. This wasn't just any old office – this was a security office. The person in charge must be elsewhere. Searching for him most probably.

Very soon after, Brust was in. There were camera feeds, displaying clones running about frantically on their search for the escaped prisoner.

Tapping a few buttons, Brust filmed himself using a webcam. Then Brust edited the clip so that when anyone who watched it, it looked like Brust was in just

308

a world of whiteness – Brust had put a white background as a backdrop.

Brust set it, so that it would act as a camera feed. One of the camera feeds went dead and was quickly replaced with the clip. Brust watched it, pleased with his efforts.

"This is a message for Julius Air," the Brust on the screen said. *"I shall keep my promise. Oh and as for everyone else, I all will say is thus: catch me if you can."*

Then the clip ended and the camera feed went back to showing its usual feeds. Brust frowned. There were a lot of people running about. This could mean only one thing: the original clones of the crew had been creating their own clones. Brust gulped and just hoped many of the crew had survived the crash landing of the *Dark Light 5000*. He did not want the humans to be outnumbered.

Leaving the office, Brust ran through corridors, without knowing whether he was running right into a trap.

Brust burst into a room and he realised too late that he made a mistake.

Twenty or so people appeared out of nowhere. Brust had wondered where lots of people had been running off to. Now he knew.

These people were armed with guns and they completely surrounded Brust, building a circle around Brust.

"Don't move." One soldier said. "We have you surrounded."

"I noticed." Brust murmured quietly.

"Don't be funny with me."

"I wasn't. I was being funny with all of you."

The soldiers cocked their guns, all in perfect unison. Their message was clear: *Keep your smart mouth closed*!

And Brust did just that. The circle opened a little to make way for someone. Brust ran forward trying to escape, but someone pulled him back.

Had Brust been someone like Sudilav or Tuft, he probably would have fought his way out by now, taking on all twenty armed soldiers at once and succeeding. But Brust was not like that.

"You really would all fire your guns and shoot an unarmed man. How very dishonorable of you." Brust tutted.

"You're not unarmed, you've still got two arms."

Brust ignored the rather feeble joke. "I do not have time for this. Besides if I am to die, at least let me do so around honourable people. Or are all you just spidery cowards?"

"Don't listen to him. He's trying to mess with your mind."

Brust turned to face the speaker. It was his clone: Brust 2, who had joined the circle. He must have been the reason for the opening of the circle. However, the clone was not armed.

"Cropping up again, are we Mr Brust?" Brust asked his clone.

The clone checked his nails. "I grow weary of your games. Playtime is over. You *must* have realised that by now. You made a very foolish mistake by escaping. If you were caught as you are now, you may die. But if you'd played nice, you would still be in your prison, safe and sound. Is that worth the risk? If I was in your position, I never would have escaped in the first place."

Brust saw this lie immediately. "But you forget, I am you and you are me."

The reflection shrugged. "Very true. But nonetheless, I speak the truth: I would have not escaped."

Brust was not convinced. "Hmm."

"We think we should focus on the current predicament. Keep your eyes on the ball – in your case, the guns. I promise we shall make life harder for you, but I assure you that you shall not die today."

Brust gestured to the armed guards surrounded him. "Then why are all these people waving guns in my face?"

"It's a threat. One that I hope you shall not force me to make it go ahead."

Brust reached into his pocket and was rummaging through it. Fingers tightened on triggers as this was suspicious behavior, but everyone instantly wilted, once Brust's mirror image glared at them to stop.

Brust's hand was out of the pocket and had become a fist, which clutched something small, ever so tightly.

"What's that you've got?" someone said cautiously. "You must show us."

Brust's expression did not change. "If you insist."

Someone small and circular flew out of Brust's hand and into the air. People leapt back, crying things like 'Stay back!' and 'It's a bomb!'

Guns had been discarded and by the time they had been picked up, it was far too late to shoot.

There, scrabbling on the floor, were the two Brusts having a fight. The guards weren't especially keen to fire, simply because they didn't know which Brust upon the ground, was the clone and which wasn't. Even if they did know, the guards could not risk shooting the clone. So all they did was stare wide-eyed and gape. A guard suddenly dropped their weapon and it skittered away from them…

…and closer to one of the Brusts.

That Brust dived forward and flopped onto the floor. Plucking the gun from anyone else's reach, he swung round with the weapon grasped in his hand.

The gun was aimed at the other Brust who jumped to his feet. He pushed past startled guards and raced down a corridor.

"Get the human." The Brust with the gun roared.

When no one moved, the clone added to his instructions.

"NOW!" he hollered.

The spell was broken and all the guards burst into life. They set off in packs, sprinting in the direction Brust had gone before vanishing out of site.

The clone smiled, or rather Brust smiled. Brust was actually the human, while the Brust who was hurtling down corridors, was a clone. When a gun is pointed at you, your first reaction is run. At least, it was Brust's reaction. Brust had known he'd have done that in his position, so he placed the burden upon his clone. Brust had tricked the guards into chasing their own master. How humiliated, the clone would be.

Brust double-checked the coast was clear and bolted off in the opposite direction.

*

They were after him. Brust could sense it. He could feel it. Ducking into a small laboratory, Brust pressed himself against a snow-white wall. He tucked his stomach in, as his breath was held.

But the pursuers didn't think straight and Brust watched with great amusement, as the rabble of guards all charged past, not even glancing at the laboratory window. They weren't thinking, just whizzing along like a pack of hungry wolfs running in random directions, hoping they may find their prey.

After the stampede was over, Brust pushed the door ajar and stuck his head out. One last guard, her face flushed a bright red as she huffed and puffed, hopelessly tried to keep up with her comrades.

Brust tried to redraw his head and conceal himself back in the lab, but the woman spotted him.

"Hello." She clutched her sides as though she had a stitch, because the guard probably did have a stitch. Her voice was ridiculously high pitched. It sounded more like a pixie, than a human being.

Brust examined the guard. She had dark brown hair that came down to where her neck joined her body. The woman was short, squat and impossibly overweight. She wore a black catsuit.

Brust waved his hand awkwardly. "Hi."

There was a long silence and Brust waited for the woman to hand him over. She opened her mouth. Brust slacked his jaw and tried to look innocent. The woman was about to yell that the prisoner had been found.

"Did you see where the other guards went?" the woman asked simply in her high pitched voice – a question that surprised and threw Brust simultaneously.

Brust sighed in relief.

"I'm sorry but did you see –"

"I heard you the first time. I was just trying to remember. They went straight along, before turning round that corner and I imagine they turned left after that."

The woman thanked Brust and jogged off after the other guards.

A sensation of surprise, relief and bewilderment all rolled into one, seeped into every part of Brust's being. He was utterly gob smacked. The scientist still couldn't believe the guard had looked him right in the eye and not have recognised as the person she was supposed to be re-capturing.

Before his luck ran out, Brust deluged back into the laboratory. The lights flickered before snapping on. A fan spun into action before quickly grinding to a slow halt.

Squinting in the deep light, Brust crept forward as if he was an intruder in a forbidden area. His eyes swept the room for anything that stood out as important.

The room wasn't very big and obviously hadn't been in use for a long time. Dust caked the tabletops and the chairs were wobbly and unstable. The room reminded Brust of a disused primary school science lab.

There was a dripping sound coming from above, which didn't really matter in the slightest at the moment.

The desks had been hammered into the walls. There was a sink in one corner, although the tap had been clogged up long ago.

Someone had attempted to make the lab more cheerful and vanquish the gloom that dangled in the chilly air. Flamboyant flowery wallpaper had been stuck to the walls, but this effort had failed dismally. Torn pieces hung from the walls. Great rips and tears were a common feature that featured upon the tatters of wallpaper.

What puzzled Brust is why someone would try and stick flowery wallpaper all around a science lab. Brust frowned. This place looked familiar, but Brust couldn't quite place it.

But the something that caught Brust's eye most of all was something at the very back. Something had been inscribed neatly onto the back wall.

Brust strode onwards and kneeled down to study this inscription in further detail. Brust wiped his glasses with his sleeve and read:

A Gen Code Project
DRZ

And that was it. Brust understood the first part. A Gen Code Project was a project that had something to do with the subject of the Gen Code – the field of science in which Brust specialised in.

DRZ. Three letters that would haunt, irritate, and puzzle Brust until he knew what it meant.

"What does DRZ mean?" Brust spoke aloud, asking himself rhetorical questions. "Is it a code? A person? A place? A thing? Maybe it's an acronym? Is it a project? An organistion, perhaps? Is there a limit to all these rhetorical questions that I can ask myself? Yes, I think there is."

But it was then Brust noticed something else. Dust had clouded the walls, but there was something else written underneath those three mysterious letters. Brust crouched down and blew dust off this piece of writing, so he could read it properly.

Brust gave it only a mere glance and these inscribed words barely registered. His mind uttered it silently, but then Brust found himself interrup–

"You are playing a deadly game of cat and mouse." A voice proclaimed from behind him.

Brust whirled around and saw a stranger walking towards him. "And which one am I?"

The newcomer shot Brust a grin. "I suppose it's really a matter of opinion."

The stranger stepped out into the light, emerging from the darkness, limb by limb like a cartoon character. It was Brust's reflection: Brust 2.

Brust returned the smile. "What's your opinion?"

Brust 2 scraped a hand along one of the desks. "I'm the cat and you're the mouse. Again, I ask you, are you sure you want to play this game – the game of cat and mouse? Because if you do, you will lose. I'm the cat and I will catch you."

"If I'm the mouse, I want to be called Curiosity. Beware of the mouse, my dear friend. You say I will

316

lose. You are wrong. After all, Curiosity killed the cat."

"Very good. You like playing games, don't you?"

"But you're playing games, as well."

"Indeed, I am. What fun we have together: Brust and Brust."

"We played the Game and we drew. But this battle between us, this game. You say you're cat and I'm the mouse but are we not equals?"

"Indeed we are, but we are still playing a game. Only time will tell who will be crowned victor. There's a storm coming, can't you feel it, Doctor? The darkest hour comes just before dawn. This is all going to come to a climax. We aren't going to have a peace treaty and end this conflict before teatime, are we? Get real! This is going on, until one side wins."

Brust knew his clone was right. He didn't like what Brust 2 was saying, but it was very true. Brust had known it all along; he'd just never wanted to admit to himself. Having his clone say it out loud, made it hit home. Brust 2 was very right.

"This has all gone too far." Brust said quietly. "We can't just retrace our steps."

Brust 2 nodded solemnly. "Very true. There is no going back. But maybe we're not so similar. This might even break out into war. I'm prepared for it. You're not. I don't like it, but there's no avoiding it. You're striving for peace too much. Maybe you are a mouse after all. Peace can make mice out of men."

"And war can make monsters out of men."

"What a pair we make."

There was a brief silence in which the reflection spoke.

"As I said, I don't like it. Anyway recognise the room?"

Brust scanned the lab. It *did* look familiar. But where had he'd seen it? It was like he'd been here before. Well, his clone probably had been here before and the clone was a version of himself, but Brust supposed that didn't really count. Brust racked his brain, shifting through long forgotten memories. A light bulb moment struck and it made sense, but didn't at the same time. To be honest, it just confused Brust even more.

"This was a room in the *Dark Light 5000*." Brust frowned. "I'm bamboozled. How is this possible?"

The mirror image was clearly enjoying Brust's bewilderment as if he was sucking up every ounce of it. He smiled.

"They say anything is possible if you put your mind to it." Brust 2 exclaimed.

"Look, Doctor. Can I call you, Doctor? I have a DSc and I guess because you are basically me, you're sort of a doctor. So again I ask you, can I call you Doctor?" Brust asked, as his clone nodded. "Good. But some things aren't possible, even if you do put your mind to it. Not everything is possible, *Doctor*."

The clone sighed. "I'm disappointed in you. Think it all through. Tell me what you know about this room, you saw on the *Dark Light 5000*."

Brust looked right at his clone. Even now, Brust hadn't gotten used to that fact that he had a doppelgänger. It was just too eerie, staring into your own eyes, this time your reflection wasn't behind glass.

"It was just a small science lab that wasn't really used. I only saw it once. It was a forgotten and disused room on the *Dark Light 5000*. However, it certainly didn't have all this wallpaper."

Brust 2 laughed. "Fine, the game's up. I explain myself. You've seen it on the *Dark Light 5000*. The answer's fairly obvious, really. You're on the *Dark Light 5000*."

Brust gaped, doing a good impression of a startled goldfish. "But that's impossible. I saw the ship hit the ground and blow up in a massive explosion. If it survived, it's going to be a lot more wrecked that this room is."

Brust 2 shook his head. "No, no, no. I said you may be on the *Dark Light 5000*, but I never said you're on the particular one that brought you here. I never mentioned until now, that you're on another *Dark Light 5000*!"

Chapter 47

That threw Brust completely. It didn't make sense, but made sense at the same time.

"Nonsense." Brust exclaimed.

"I'm afraid not."

"But that simply doesn't fit. I don't understand."

"I've tricked you, just as you tricked me earlier. That trick earlier was clever and I didn't see it coming. How you turned my own people against me was most remarkable."

"You're changing the subject and you're not looking me fully in the eye."

Brust 2 looked Brust right in the eye for a few seconds before breaking his gaze. "Am I really changing the subject?"

"You are. Explain yourself."

"You're on another ship. It's a *Dark Light 5000* ship granted, but it's still another ship. When you were running through the corridors, didn't you think to yourself how similar it all looks to the ship you travelled on?"

"But how could you have made another ship so quickly?"

"The answer to that is that we're didn't. At least, I don't think so."

"What! You don't know?"

"I have all your memories from before you went through the cloning process. But apparently my actual life as a clone begins, when I am grown in a cloning machine. That is when I born in a sense. It's just the memories and such, already come 'preloaded' as it were."

"But you must have woken up on the *Dark Light 5000*, shortly before it crashed. Everyone had assumed the explosion would have killed you all."

"And then comes the great question. The fact of the matter is when my life began; I wasn't born on that crashing ship. None of the clones were. I just woke up here on this *Dark Light 500*, which stood upon the surface of this planet. Why? I don't know, none of the other clones know. That's partly why I wanted you to stay captured a little longer. I thought you would know the answer. In fact, I was certain you'd know. But I was wrong. Who can I ask now?"

Brust nodded slowly. "So that's why the clones are so much more organised than us humans. You say there's war going on out there. Well, I don't like it, but I'd bet money that the clones are winning."

"You'd be right."

"So the clones have a HQ to report back to. They have technology, but their power hasn't been drained. They weren't spread out and separated. You have the perfect advantage. This ship is basically a clone of our ship, before the crash landing. Interesting."

"It is." Brust 2 mused.

"Aren't you going take back to my prison? Why haven't the guards burst into the room, waving guns at me? But I don't think you're going to recapture again, are you?"

"What makes you think that?"

"We're been talking for over five minutes and you haven't made the slightest implication that you're going to recapture me. Why am I still standing here, enjoying and relishing my freedom?"

"Fine. You're right. As you said earlier, I am you and you are I. Think what you would do if you were in my position."

"I know violence is coming and I know it is inevitable. But I can at least try. I presume you're sick of all this war stuff, all this cloak and dagger. You're just going to let me walk away from all of this."

"Right again. In fact, I will help you."

The clone straightened up and reached behind him. He groped around for something, shortly before hurling over his shoulder. Brust caught it.

"You gave me nothing." Brust exclaimed.

Brust 2 chuckled and shook his head. "Afraid not. It looks like there's nothing, because you cannot see it. But I ask you this: how come you can feel it?"

Brust 2 had asked a good question. Brust was surprised he'd caught the thing in the first place, if it was invisible.

"Why can't you just tell me?" Brust asked. "Just give me a straight answer – this is just all too excessive."

"Feel it." was all Brust 2 would say.

It felt like some kind of fabric. Brust could bend it. This was quite strange, because this thing wasn't actually visible.

"It's an invisibility cloak."

"You grew up back in the dawn of the twenty first century, from the years of 2003 to 2021. I just about remember, so you will remember when invisibility cloaks were at a time, a big thing in books and films."

"I remember."

"You probably already know this, but this stuff of fiction is now something of scientific fact. Put it on and you can find your way out. Escape is made a little bit easier. But if you get caught, you have to promise me that you will fib and tell your captors you stole it. Promise?"

"I promise. One last thing."

"Yes."

"Won't there be security watching our entire conversation?"

"I sorted that out. Besides as you say, 'guards would be waving guns in your face' if I had not."

"Good point."

"Now, be off with you!"

Brust whirled the cloak around his head and when the whirl was finished, the cloak was wrapped around Brust's body.

Brust 2 laughed and stepped back. "You haven't covered your head."

Brust realised how strange it must have looked. A head bobbing around with no body attached. Brust looked down. It was weird – from neck downwards his body had vanished.

The door swung open, before Brust had time to fully cover himself. It was the woman, who'd stopped by to ask Brust for directions.

"I saw him go into this room." The woman shrilled, her face even redder than when Brust had seen her last. She pointed a finger at Brust 2. "Come with me and we'll put you back in your cell."

"Miranda, it's me, you dim-wit." Brust 2 snapped, angry at the accusation. "I'm not the escaped prisoner. Really!"

Miranda, if that was her name, looked around the room. Brust tried to cover his head with the cloak. But it was too late. Miranda had spotted him.

Her eyes enlarged so much that Brust thought for a moment, they'd pop out of their sockets. She staggered back, a hand flying to her heart.

She jerked a finger into the now seemingly vacant area. "What was that? What just happened?"

Brust 2 fiddled with his fingers awkwardly. "Sorry?"

"What was that?" Miranda squealed, her voice venturing even higher up the frequency scale.

Brust had managed to render himself, completely invisible by now. Miranda had only seen a glimpse of him. Something that her mind could barely register. All Miranda knew was something had appeared and disappeared right in front of her eyes.

"Miranda, calm down." Brust 2 said gently. "You're seeing things."

"I am not seeing things!" Miranda snapped, her high-pitched voice rising, reaching new levels that didn't seem possible.

"You've gotten into a state." Brust 2 said calmly, his back turned to Brust. "There's nothing there."

"I HAVE NOT GOTTEN INTO A STATE!" Miranda screeched.

Brust 2 rested a hand on her shoulder. "You need to go and lie down."

Miranda brushed Brust 2's hand off and took a deep breath. Her voice managed to steady temporarily. "You're right."

Suddenly, Brust tripped on something and stumbled forward. The cloak flew back and got tangled in Brust's messy hair. It flipped over it and made the whole of Brust's head disappear.

Miranda spotted this and leapt back. A girlish scream of fear and shock erupted out from her large O shaped mouth. She whimpered in fright. Brust realised to her that it would look like he was a headless man.

When no one moved and nothing happened, Brust 2 swayed on his feet, an emotion bottled up inside him, hopelessly trying to escape. But Brust could tell the clone didn't really know what to do.

"What?" he eventually said.

Triumph and relief flushed Miranda's face, her voice back in its squeaking mood. "You can see it too? I'm not going mad after all. Unless we're both mad. So you see it?"

"See what?"

Miranda buried her heads into her hands. Sobbing broke out from her eyes; the tears streaking down her cheeks.

"I'm insane!" she wept.

Brust – the headless ghost – raised a finger. It pointed in the direction, in line with Miranda's chest.

"No!" Miranda shouted, the crying increasing as if it was like heavy rain. "No!"

In a solemn and grim voice, Brust spoke.

"It is over." Brust rumbled in a deep and astonishingly powerful voice, that was not his own.

"I didn't do anything wrong."

"You must suffer your destined fate." Brust boomed. "I've seen your dreams, Miranda, and ultimately your fears. I know how to destroy you from the inside, bit by painful bit."

Miranda was petrified and tried to scream again, but all that came out was a high-pitched squeaking noise. Then her eyes rolled and her legs gave way, slumping to the floor. Miranda had fainted.

"That was horrible." Brust 2 snapped furiously. "Think what you've done to the poor woman."

Brust looked down at his shoes as he rendered himself invisible. "Cruel to be kind. I needed to find a way past her. She'd seen too much. It was the only way I could think of. I feel guilty. But I did what I must."

Brust 2 made a movement similar to a surrender position; only his hands were level with his head. "That is open to debate."

Brust ignored him. "Wish me luck."

Brust 2 frowned and tried to work out where Brust was.

"Yes." He said. "Good luck."

"I'm behind you. You're facing the wrong way."

"Oh, right. Sorry. I'll try and face you, when I am speaking to you. It's quite difficult. It's not my fault, you're invisible."

"Actually it is. You're one who gave me the invisibility cloak in the first place."

"Fair enough."

"What happens to Miranda?"

"Why don't you find somewhere to hide her safely?"

"Doctor Brust! I am a trusted member of the clones. I may be making your escape easier, but I am not assisting it. I will not help you any more, unless you do something with the poor lady on the floor."

"Fair enough."

"I think so too."

"Farewell." Brust popped out his head, so that it became visible and waved his right hand.

"One last thing. How exactly do you plan to escape?"

"With great skill. So long and thanks for all your help." Brust said, ducking his head back under the cloak.

"Off you go then, wherever you are."

Brust became invisible once more. The scientist yanked Miranda off the floor and hoarded her under the cloak. He drifted over to the door and strolled down the corridor. Someone brushed past. They looked him right in the eye.

Brust leapt back and his heart stopped for just a moment. He quickly reminded himself that he was invisible and that the man walking past was looking at something else. Something beyond Brust. The man had seen right through Brust, with not the faintest clue that he was there in the first place.

The man continued on this journey and disappeared from sight. Brust sighed with relief.

Several other people passed by. Brust felt as though he was some kind of ghost. Some sort of spirit unseen by the naked eye, drifting unnoticed and undetected by the random bystanders that scurried by.

As he scuttled down another passage, Brust who had been holding Miranda with both arms, realised that she was getting too heavy. With a groan, Brust laid her down on the floor and proposed to pick her by the scruff of the neck. He dragged her along the floor, her black leather boots bumping along the ground.

Brust froze. He'd only gone ten paces when the stupidity of his newly made mistake hit him. The scraping of Miranda's boots on the floor had made a horrifyingly loud screeching sound. That would have guards running after him!

The scrabble of feet – loads of feet – came from nearby. Sure enough, Brust had been right!

Chapter 48

In absolutely no time at all, one by one, the guards had arrived.

Maybe arrived isn't quite the right word. Unless you may think that scurrying about, arms flailing madly could just be simply classified as arriving.

Brust stood, amidst the chaos, wondering what he should do. The scientist was undetected. For now.

He tried to control his hectic breathing, but it was like throwing a tennis ball at a brick wall – it would only bounce back.

Somehow, Brust managed to rein in his breath and breathed in, so that the guards would not hear him as well as see him.

Then Brust curled himself up into a ball, praying that someone wouldn't trip over him, revealing him. In fact, Brust just wanted all the guards to go away.

Although this action did not happen for a while, it did happen eventually. One of Brust's legs had started making a creaking sound, which was probably not a good thing.

When the last guard had rounded the corner, Brust exhaled. But Brust heard murmurs coming from around that corner up ahead.

Brust could only catch snippets of conversion, as if it was drifting in and out. It was if someone had been playing around with the volume, switching between mute and sound.

He could only hear bits and pieces but Brust was able to *piece* it together. They seemed to have heard the creaking sound that Miranda's leg had made. They weren't idiots and they could work out that there was something there. Brust couldn't hear much more as it dropped into low whispers. Perhaps the guards were going to come round that corner, sweep the corridor one last time and of course uncover Brust.

When Brust noticed a boot sticking out from the corner, he knew his theory to be correct. If he was to remain undetected and invisible, he needed to move. Now.

Brust darted forward, with the cloak draped around him. The consequence of Brust's mistake happened before Brust even realised what his mistake was.

He'd forgotten about Miranda who lay motionless upon one corner of the cloak. That meant when Brust hurtled forward, he would come out the invisibility cloak, leaving his chance of escape behind under the cloak.

Brust stood there, arms outstretched. He tried to dive under the cloak just in time. If his dive had been successful, Brust might just have made it. But however it wasn't.

A white-hot sharp burst of pain dragged him back. He yelped in shock, but a quiet low-pitched groan issued out of his mouth instead. It was like someone had delivered a short slap, which stung more than all the bees' stings back on planet Earth put together.

Brust staggered back and dashed around one corner. Someone had realised that he was there and called out a question. But Brust wasn't listening.

That horrible stinging sensation was back, only it was as if it was drawn out. Brust lurched forward suddenly and this action forced his back to slam into the wall.

Brust winced and whimpered.

"You OK?" someone cried.

"I'm *fine*." Brust replied, the sound of 'fine' going down several octaves.

Brust struggled to keep his voice under control. It was cracking and kept changing pitch. Eventually, Brust managed to rein it in under conrtol and settle it.

"I'm fine. Carry on." Brust squeaked, in a voice that was higher than usual.

"Are you sure?" someone else asked.

"Yes, continue." Brust said, still speaking in the strange tone no matter how hard he tried to change it. "Just leave me alone. I need a bit of time to recover."

There were murmurs amongst the guards. Brust ignored it. Why was his voice behaving strangely? True, it had fooled the guards into thinking he was another person. But still...

The stinging sensation struck again and Brust dug back into the wall. His head spun and Brust managed to stumble into a nearby men's toilet. The sounds of the concerned guards had abandoned their search, wondering what to do.

Brust bumped into a toilet cubicle. Still dizzy, Brust fumbled with a lock and barged in.

He almost collapsed onto the toilet, but stopped himself just in time. The sting came again. Brust moaned.

However more was to come. First, it felt as though an ice billowed up and grew inside Brust's stomach. The stinging died down instantly. The ice block inside

Brust melted away in cold water. It soon filled every part of Brust.

Although freezing, it didn't harm Brust. It was a comforting chill that soothed Brust. Thanks to this, all that pain had gone.

Brust drifted onto the toilet lid and leant back. It was so very relaxing and made Brust so sleepy. Brust closed his eyes and began to meditate.

Suddenly Brust's eyes snapped open, as a red-hot poker was thrust through his heart – or at least that was what it felt like. Brust leapt forward, the pain steaming out of his mouth.

It stopped, but the momentum was too strong. Brust found himself flung forward onto his hands and knees. On all fours, he panted like a dog.

He managed to bring himself to his feet, but Brust was quickly flung forward once more. Brust gagged and made a horrible retching sound, which was followed by a brief gurgle.

Bile and vomit mixed together into one, boiled up inside Brust. It rose upwards and Brust only managed to catch it at the last possible second. The result of this was that his cheeks puffed up like a plush plump cushion. The strange mixture of bile and vomit then shot down into the depths of Brust's stomach.

Drops of perspiration pelted his eyes and stung his vision. Things seemed to double. But the lines between everything were blurring and for Brust, it was as if he was looking at a jumble of blurred shapes melted into one.

His insides writhed as his head spun. Brust fell to his knees, sweating like a pig.

That stinging torment was back, but this time had spread through every inch of Brust's body. Brust's jacket came off in the process and was transformed into a bedraggled heap.

And then it got worse.

Brust's skin began to bubble like hot wax.

Agony.

He managed to yelp out and it was louder than he'd anticipated. Brust's eyes were flickering and had trouble focusing. Massive lumps appeared, before quickly disappearing on Brust's skin. It was if there was someone inside him throwing wild punches. He straightened up, so that he was kneeling.

But his skin continued bubbling. Brust's shoulders made a sharp cracking sound. Brust's eyes finally managed to come into focus once more. And that was when the strangest things happened.

Brust was transforming. His eyes began to glow an alien green and with his arms outstretched, palms facing upwards, Brust looked up to the ceiling and let out a roar.

To his horror, the transformation was only the beginning. What was happening to him? That was the only thought that echoed and bounced around Brust's mind.

The bubbling effect of his skin decreased but the pain did not. Then right in front of his eyes, Brust's skin began to thicken. But Brust was also shrinking.

Brust was shrinking. This didn't stop, until Brust was a miniature version of his original self, who would have been about twelve centimetres taller.

There was a sudden snapping noise. Brust groaned. The skin was thicker. But now, it was starting to settle and soften. This was too strange for Brust's liking.

Then the big effect kicked in. Brust's arms recoiled back, as did his legs. His head was becoming plumper, as if it was a balloon being pumped up. The glowing of his eyes halted.

But then everything was softening. Brust almost fell over his own clothes, which were too big for him. The trouser legs flopped onto the dirty grimy floor.

The now soft skin thickened even more so. His chest, stomach and backside swelled up, becoming that of substantial proportions. Brust's now ample stomach protruded and hung over his torn trousers. It had so much flab, that it was both shocking and disturbing. His shirt made a ripping noise. All of Brust's limbs broadened so much, that they reminded Brust of sausages oozing out of a machine.

And then it stopped.

It was so sudden. Brust gasped and stood up. He'd transformed into something else but what? And more importantly why?

Although it was difficult to not trip over the clothes, they also could barely contain Brust. It was too tight and it felt like Brust was just waiting to burst out. In fact, it was far too tight and it felt as if iron hands were squeezing back Brust in every direction, trying to compress him into an impossibly thin amount of space.

Brust ignored the excruciating agony that he was suffering under. The clothes were far too tight – it hurt. Brust's colossal stomach exhaled outwards. Several shirt buttons shot off, dispersing off into the distance. Brust sighed. That *felt* much better.

"What's going on?" that same somebody who had been so concerned about Brust earlier, exclaimed.

Brust spoke. That same soprano voice was released out into the air again, a horrible rasping echo accompanying it.

"Are you all right?" someone else asked, genuine worry dripping from the shadow of his tone.

Brust didn't have the foggiest notion as what to do. 'What had happened to him?' was just one of the many questions that swam around in his mind. The question of 'What shall I do now?' joined the swarm of queries.

There was a loud rapping on the cubicle door that shook and rattled it. Brust jumped back in surprise. Several more thumps battered the door. The lock made a clicking sound, before falling off and clattering to the ground. The door followed suit, shortly after.

There were four guards standing there. Brust screamed a girlish scream of fright and shock.

"What's the matter, mate?" one of them asked, before breaking off into silence.

Brust stood there, his thick arms folded. There was a long silence. Then the men erupted into questions such as: *What happened to you? Why are you in here?*

"Leave me alone." Brust said, in that impossibly high voice. "Just get away from me."

There were mumbles amongst the guards before they went off elsewhere, far away from here. They'd forgotten that they had been searching that corridor, mere minutes before.

Brust sighed, and waddled out of the cubicle, every part of his body wobbling uncontrollably as he did so. What had happened to him? He'd gone through extreme pain and transformed into a smaller, fatter version of himself.

Brust jumped. Miranda was standing in front of him. How had she gotten here? She'd been under the invisibility cloak. It looked like she woken up and came into here.

Miranda was no longer wearing her black catsuit, but instead wore a torn shirt and ripped trousers. Brust frowned and Miranda did so at the same time.

And then it hit him. Brust was looking at a mirror.

It was all too much for Brust. He'd become Miranda. But why?

Brust had transformed into another person!

Chapter 49

Bewildered and confused, Brust dawdled out into the corridor. He groped around and found where the invisibility cloak was. He whipped it off. Miranda was there, just as Brust had left her.

He dragged her off into the men's toilets. The invisibility cloak had slipped off, but Brust didn't have time to go back and find it.

He kicked open another toilet cubicle and it swung open. He plunked Miranda down on the toilet seat and sighed heavily.

Brust tripped over his ripped clothes. He couldn't bear another moment in these garments. Brust undressed and used one of the nearby showers. The hot water was good, helping to focus Brust's mind.

He came out, yanked a towel off a rack and dried himself. Brust wandered back into the toilet cubicle.

Brust flipped through the possibilities of what had happened to him as he scanned the room, wondering what he should wear.

It's almost as if I've become Miranda's clone. How convenient especially with this clone incident going. Brust thought to himself as he slipped on Miranda's clothes. Beside he was Miranda now not Brust, and should probably wear her clothes especially as they fitted!

He managed to squeeze into the catsuit. It was perhaps slightly too tight, but otherwise a perfect fit. Brust struggled with the zip at the back, and it was another ten minutes before he was successful.

He left the unconscious Miranda and wrapped his old clothes around her to keep her warm, back in the toilet cubicle, which he promptly locked. Brust didn't want someone coming into the cubicle and finding the knocked out Miranda lying against a toilet.

As Brust departing, he glanced at himself in the mirror. A squat buxom woman wearing a black, shiny, sleek catsuit looked back.

The scientist was still finding it hard to believe, that the person in the mirror was him. In fact, Brust was finding it hard to be able to cope with all this. It was far too strange for his liking. He was still adjusting to his new body and clothes, which were very different from his original!

As he or she, depending on how you looked on it, toddled out, the only reasonable solution to his question floated into his head.

It was a side effect of the cloning. It was the only reasonable conspiracy theory that Brust could think of. It would make sense too. Actually no, it wouldn't, but it might if Brust knew a bit more.

A side effect of the cloning? Hmm, yes. Brust nodded, his triple chin wobbling frantically as he did so. Brust couldn't think of anything better, so he'd happily go with that.

Am I the only one with a side effect? Brust wondered. Brust shook his heard firmly. It seemed improbable. His clone probably had suffered a similar effect. Did that mean Brust 2 was currently walking around as a Miranda? Brust smirked at the thought. It was amusing. But then the smile was quickly wiped off his face, when he remembered that was *exactly* what had happened to him.

What if both versions – clone and human – of Jennifer, Julius, Sudilav, Brust, Tuft and Holly had suffered the same effect? Were they all Mirandas? That too seemed unlikely. But they might have transformed into someone else? But then why had Brust turned into Miranda? Why her? Why not someone else?

Brust shrugged. Maybe there was a different side effect for different people. Could they be classed as 'special powers'? Brust wasn't sure. After going through all that pain, it seemed more like a curse than a gift to him.

Brust was only firing wild shots in the dark, but his thinking was probably more accurate than if another one of the crew tried to figure it out. Genetic engineering/modification of Gen was a field he specialized in. The modification might just have happened to him.

"Doctor Brust!" a voice called.

Brust wheeled around and then mentally kicked himself for making such a ludicrous mistake. He was Miranda now and should only answer to that name. But then that raised another question like an eyebrow. Was he Miranda or Brust? He was Miranda, wasn't he? Brust had transformed into her, earlier. Well, maybe just on the outside. On the inside he was still Doctor Simon Brust, scientist, author, a scientific doctor, a genetic engineer and a co-founder in the Gen Code in which he was also an adept expert. He wasn't Miranda on the inside; he was just Brust in a disguise.

There was a middle-aged man striding down a corridor. There was something about him that greatly reassembled a lion. He had fair shoulder-length hair that was wild and untamed. It was exactly like a lion's mane. The man was tall and looked quite heavy. He had a bulky shape, although he wasn't muscular nor was he obese. His skin was sandy coloured. His eyelids had long blond eyelashes. His eyes were an orangey brown that looked worn out, sad and wise, like a god who takes pity on an inferior race. The man had an untidy moustache. He also had a goatee that covered his entire chin and where it ended, it converged into the man's long flowing blonde hair. The man was dressed in black leather.

"Doctor Brust!" he roared again, his voice permanently a deep, powerful and loud roar.

Brust watched as the 'Lionman' brushed past him, following his transformation, not even looking at him. It was though they were just two acquaintances in the street bustling by, not even glancing at the other.

"Doctor Brust!" Lionman boomed. "Where are you?"

It was then Brust realised, it was not him that Lionman was after – it was the clone. That was probably it. Besides even if it was him, Lionman was searching for, then he wouldn't think for a second that the lady he had just passed, was actually the person he was looking forward. It would amuse Brust greatly.

The invisibility cloak had been a good way of hiding from people. But now Brust had carelessly lost it, he had ended up finding a way of concealment that was even better – being someone else. You can stroll right by someone and they will not suspect a thing. In a manner of speaking, at the end of the day, being someone else could be more obscured than being invisible.

"Doctor Brust." Lionman thundered again.

"Excuse me." Brust trilled, speaking in Miranda's pixie like voice.

This cut short Lionman's bellows. He pivoted to face Brust.

"Yes, Miranda." he spoke softly, his eyes almost popping out of his sockets.

This surprised Brust; he had expected Lionman to naturally have a loud voice. Despite being quiet, the voice easily reached Brust's ears.

Imagine there are three powerful men in a pub. Two of them have loud, deep voices that echo their power. But the third man is silent, and somehow that can seem even more powerful.

That was what it was like for Brust.

"Miranda?" Lionman said, in a tone that would have done a stage whisperer proud.

Brust looked around his shoulder, to see where this 'Miranda' was and then reminded himself that he was supposed to be Miranda.

"I would like to make a little suggestion, Lionma-" Brust trilled, before quickly perceiving that he'd almost called the man by the nickname he'd created.

But Lionman didn't seem to notice and smiled. Brust shivered. The smile contained sharp white fangs, which looked like they could tear a man in two with one bite. Brust knew the man was just trying to be friendly but the grin instantly made Brust think of a crocodile's smile shortly before gobbling up some poor unsuspecting fish. "It's Lionel, not Lionma." the man said.

How appropriate in these circumstances, Brust thought to himself. Lionman or Lionel as he was called, even had a name that sort of matched his appearance.

"Yes, Lionel." Brust squeaked. "Well, I wou-"

Lionel raised a hand to pause Brust's words. His fingernails were surprisingly long for a man's and were more like sharp claws on a lion's paw, rather than fingernails on a human being's hand.

"What happened, Miranda?" Lionel asked.

Brust stared at Lionel strangely. "What are you on about?" he squealed.

Lionel took a few steps forward and fumbled about for the right words. "Doctor Brust told me you'd fainted. But you were in the science lab, not in the men's toilets, that is where I saw you come out of."

Fear gripped Brust's heart as it thumped against his oversized bosom. He shook his head firmly but slowly. "I don't know what you're talking about."

Why am I so scared anyway? Brust thought to himself.

"Oh. I was, I mean, Doctor Brust was sure that it all happened." Lionel mumbled.

"It's you." Brust exclaimed.

That jumped the gun a bit. And the penny dropped, at long last.

"You're Doctor Brust – in disguise."

Chapter 50

Lionel looked over his shoulder and leant to Brust's ear. Brust recoiled downwards as Lionel loomed over him.

"Fine, you're right." Lionel whispered. "I'm the Brust you can trust – the clone. You were knocked out and the human Brust took you off. Did he dump somewhere and you woke there?"

If Brust had had an electronic pen or a stylus as they were called, at that very moment, he'd probably have been chewing it in thought, even though he never normally chewed stylus or any kind of pen.

He was looking at this lion like man, who'd introduced himself as Lionel.

Brust tried to say something useful, but wasn't able to. "Um." was all he could muster.

"Fine." Lionel said, changing tact. "Explain yourself. NOW!"

Lionel had spoken so loud, it threw Brust completely and he jumped with a start.

"I'm not Miranda." he chirped. "I'm Brust, but I transformed into Miranda."

There was a long silence, before Lionel/Brust 2 spoke.

"You're Doctor Brust?"

He nodded. "I am, but I changed into Miranda. Did the same happen to you?"

"I think so. I was talking to the real Lionel and then I felt this horrible stinging pain. I retreated into a backroom and I transformed into Lionel. It was complete agony."

"But where did you get those clothes? Did you knock Lionel out?"

Brust 2 looked as though Brust had grown a second head. "No. I never would have been able to do that. The clothes – right, yes. I managed to find some spares of Lionel's."

"That means he's walking around somewhere else."

"That's right. So you're just Brust in a Miranda suit."

"I think so."

"What do you mean by 'you think so'? You either know or you don't. You just Brust in another body, right?"

"That's what I used to think that, but I'm not sure." Brust fell to his knees.

"Explain yourself. I am still me."

"I've become Miranda physically."

"Obviously."

"Well, I think I'm starting to become Miranda mentally. She clearly scares easily, if you remember shortly before she fainted. Due to your form of Lionel, you intimidated me. I mean, when I was me, I was surrounded by people like Tuft and Sudilav and I never felt that intimidated. I've also become a lot more jumpy. Someone made me scream just by coming into the same room as me. That is not normal for me."

"I know. I am you, so I should know."

"What's happening to me?" Brust shrilled, his voice wavering, tears streaking down his chubby cheeks. "Will my personality just fade away until it is 100% Miranda? I'm going die bit by bit. Look, I'm crying now. I'm more emotional than I used to be. That's a sign. Oh, that's making it even worse."

Brust 2 came over, crouched down and rested a hand upon Brust's thick shoulder. "It's going to be OK."

"But I'm not sure, it's going to be." Brust wailed, the sobbing increasing. "Have you had any personality changes?"

Brust 2 thought for a few moments. "Actually thinking about it. I have. My temper has been shorter and I get angry more easily. Oh my, you're right. I got really aggressive when someone tapped me on the shoulder earlier and I punched them. Hard. I'm not a violent person. You're right. What's happening to us?"

Although Brust 2 didn't start crying, Brust could feel his clone's temperature rising in anger. Another thing to prove his point.

Brust 2 stood up. "We can't just sit around, feeling sorry for ourselves. We've got to try and see if we can change back. Even if that isn't possible, let's make the most of our time left."

"This is corrosive. Everything that makes us who we are, is fading away. This isn't even dying, it is ceasing to exist. Crumbling to nothing. It is burning us." Brust cried harder before screaming: "CAN'T YOU FEEL IT?"

Brust 2 roared and picked Brust up. He smacked him hard in the face. "DON'T BE SILLY!" he bellowed shaking him, making him bawl even more.

He threw Brust down on the ground and proceeded to stomp on him.

"STOP!" Brust shrieked.

That single word stopped Brust 2 in mid action, his foot raised above Brust's considerably large stomach.

"STOP!" Brust trilled again. "See. It's destroying us inside out. It's tormenting us with this torture. Like this, it's even worse. I want to die as myself physically. I want to die in my own body, not someone else's."

"I absolutely concur with all of me that's left. I also want to die as myself mentally. If souls exist, then the other personality is eating away at it. By dying normally, you'll die as yourself. In this way by slowly ceasing to exist, by the time you're gone, you'll be someone else."

Brust sobbed so strongly that it was like rain was coming out of his eyes. "That's so moving and poignant. There's another sign of it. I am growing into an emotional and obese woman. I don't like it."

Brust 2 tried to control his temper. "Can you try not to cry? It's bringing out the other side in me."

"Sorry." Brust whimpered.

"We need to discuss this whole thing without things getting out of hard. If I try to fend off my other personality, you'll do the same, OK?"

Brust nodded, through the tears. "I'll try, but it's so difficult to stop getting so emotional."

"Right. What was happening to you, before all the pain from the transformation started to kick in?"

Brust bit his lip and thought back. "Guards were going to search the corridor and uncover me, hiding under my invisibility cloak. So I tried to run off, while I was invisible. But I forgot Miranda was lying on a corner, so when I ran off, I became visible. I realised

346

my mistake far too late. A thought echoed through my head – Miranda, and then it all began."

Brust 2 nodded. "I was talking to Lionel, shortly before. It seems the transformation changed you into the person you last thought about, before it all kicked off."

Brust's lip quavered, fighting off his inner demons. "That's right. I reckon this is all a side effect of the cloning process. I wonder if the others have had this happen to them too."

"Let's just focus on ourselves right now."

"But that's cruel, heartless and selfish. It's like you're leaving them to die."

"NO, I'M NOT. IF WE DON'T DO THIS, WE'LL HAVE LESS CHANCE OF SURVIVAL."

Brust was about to shed tears again, but quickly caught himself. "It's happening again."

Brust 2 nodded. "Indeed it is. I agree with you on your theory. I figure the effect was like a time bomb. It's just waiting to explode. And now it's gone off."

"That's a good way of putting it – a time bomb. But it's genetic."

The same thing hit them at the same time and their heads swiveled to look each right in the eye. The same thought had occurred to them both simultaneously.

"The Gen Code." they both said in perfect unison.

Brust shot his clone a grim smile. "There's been a mistake."

There was a solemn expression upon Brust 2's face, or to be more accurate, Lionel's face. "You used the Gen Code to program and create the clones. There must have been a slight glitch in it. The glitch became a bug. The bug became a virus. It was set on a timer, only to be released when the time ran out."

"Sato must have made a mistake. This is bad. Oh my sainted aunt!"

"There's another sign of the other personality leaking in. Katsu Sato! That stupid dimwit!

"And there's another sign of the other personality leaking in. I don't want to die."

"Neither do I, Brust."

"So a tiny error caused this."

"Well, there were actually several glitches. But yes, one of them caused this horror to be unleashed upon us."

"Several glitches? How come?"

"Well, why do you think us clones have rebelled against you? You programmed us to not rebel."

"What can we do to stop this virus?"

Brust 2 shrugged. "I don't know." he squealed. "Moving on, you must be yourself. Cling onto the last bit of what makes you, you."

Brust swept a strand of hair out of his eyes. "I am Brust, not Miranda."

The clone nodded. "Be you, while you can."

"Tell me more about Miranda and Lionel. They're not humans, are they?"

"They're clones."

"Clones of clones?"

"As strange as it sounds, you're right. In a sense. We created random clones using the Gen Code."

Before Brust could ask why, they sprinted off down the corridor. Actually that wasn't strictly true. Brust 2 sprinted down the corridor, whilst Brust dawdled along; his plump face flushed bright red, the flab on his body wobbling madly with every piece of motion.

Brust 2 had entered the men's toilets and kicked down the cubicle door where Miranda was still lying unconscious, all before Brust had arrived. Becoming obese hadn't helped his stamina or his speed.

"Do you have the invisibility cloak?" Brust 2 asked, dropping his jacket on Miranda's unconscious body, adding to the layers of Brust's clothes that were swathed around her.

Brust fidgeted and looked away. "I kind of lost it." He muttered nervously.

"You did or kind of?"

"Fine. I lost it. I'm sorry. Let's move on. We have more pressing matters at hand."

There was a long silence before Brust 2 eventually barged in through the tranquility. "We'll take it in turns to carry Miranda, yes?"

Brust nodded, but he wasn't really too fussed about that now. "Brust?" he asked quietly.

"Yes, Brust." Brust 2 replied.

"What do you figure will happen to us?"

Brust 2's smile dropped and he thought for a long while before answering. "I don't really know. In fact, I don't want to know. I just try not to think about it. Do you remember your youth?"

"Of course."

"Well, from my memories, I remember someone told me if you forgot about your problems, they'd just go away."

"That's a load of rubbish!" Brust said sharply.

"I know it is. But I wish it were true. What an easier and better universe we would live in, eh? But I remember from your memories, shortly before my creation that you said something to the rest of your crew. Remember?"

"Vaguely."

"You were talking about the Project, during your speech and presentation. You said something along the lines of this: 'This could be for better – or worse.' You were very right."

"How long do you think we have until…." Brust trailed off, unable to complete his sentence. But then, there was no need to.

"About 12 hours."

"12 hours?"

"At the most. But that's only if luck goes extreme."

"The minimum?"

"About twelve minutes."

"That's just marvelous. My life's end ranges from twelve minutes to twelve hours. I am completely and utterly kept in the dark."

"Afraid so. I guess we don't have much time to lose."

"I reckon that we should find the *Dark Light 5000* and see if we can use some of my equipment to fix ourselves up." Brust shrilled in his Miranda pixie voice.

"What if it's broken? Do we have a back up plan?"

"Not yet."

"No Plan B?"

"No Plan B." Brust confirmed.

"Great! Oh well, something to look forward to."

"We're on the same team. No trying to double cross or anything like that. Understand?"

"Completely. Let's go."

"Right, I have a plan to escape. I saw a pipe -"

"Brust?" Brust 2 interrupted, cutting Brust short.

"What?"

"We're mimics of a trusted clones. Why doesn't one of us just escort the other out?"

"You can do that?"

"Certainly."

"Cool, but you're driving."

"Yes, a good excuse for not having to carry Miranda's unconscious body. How would you like to carry your own body weight?"

Brust knew from personal experience just how fat and overweight Miranda was. He groaned.

Brust 2 laughed. "Don't worry – you don't have to carry her all the way."

"One last thing."

"Go ahead."

"We're on the same team. For now, we opt out of our different teams. We focus on our problem. We leave the rest of the clones and humans to continue their mini war, because after all, we have our own battles to fight."

Chapter 51

"It was horrible!" moaned Ning, before erupting once more into erratic breathing.

"It's OK." Julius assured her. "Except for the fact that there's still a dangerous soldier on the loose!"

Jennifer burst into the room. "They reckon he's still here."

Julius stood up. "I'm sick of this."

"Sick of what?" Jennifer asked vaguely.

"I'm sick of playing nurse, while you're running around being the hero." Julius snapped irritably. "You should be playing the nurse. You're better than me at it. I don't know how to comfort people. You're probably better at that kind of thing."

"So you want to be the hero, is that?" Jennifer threw her question at Julius quickly and harshly.

"No, that's not it!" Julius said angrily. "You're just better than me at sitting around and comforting some injured person."

"True, I am better. But I am also better than you at being a hero. That role is more important. So I do that. I'm sorry, but you're going to have to do it. End of story."

"In that case, I'll make a sequel. You just want to be the centre of the attention. That's why you're Captain. So you can stand around, bossing people around and not even bothering to lift a finger yourselves, while everyone else works like slaves. And guess who takes all the credit? You, you, *you*! You're just an arrogant selfish attention seeker!"

Jennifer seemed to almost relish the insult and retorted sharply: "Oh, I'm arrogant am I? That's a bit rich coming from a man who once described himself as 'modest'!"

"It was a joke!" Julius said indignantly. "It's something that cheers people up. But you wouldn't know what that is it, would you? You're just a horrid control freak."

"I'm not a control freak. I'm an important person, while you're just a guy who moves a hunk of metal from point A to point B. The only reason why you're on this mission, was only because there was a vacancy for it!"

"Of course, you're important. You surround yourself with people to tell you how exceptional and amazing you are. It's sickening and pathetic." Julius retorted, before transforming his voice into a cruel but accurate, high pitched mockery of Jennifer's voice. *Oh hello, and I'm Captain Jennifer Smart. When I was young, I saw the Mars landing and thought I want to be an astronaut, because the whole world will love me, tell me how incredible I am and cry my name whenever I walk by."*

"How dare you!" Jennifer shouted.

"Oh yes, I dare, *Captain* Jennifer Smart. I watched how you bully people around. It's time someone stood up to you."

"And that's you, is it?" Jennifer hooted in disbelief.

"Well, it's going have to be someone. And since no one else is fulfilling that role, I guess it's going to have be *me*."

"You're twisting the truth." Jennifer protested, slightly agitated. "You better watch your step."

"Oh and I will, especially with a *bully* like you around. You think you can either shout at someone, or bat your pretty eyelashes, and then you'll get what you want. Well, not anymore! But I must admit, you do it well – the battering of your eyelids works exceedingly well. But you're also egotistical, narcissistic and *so* very irritating.

"Stop it. The pair of you!" Ning chimed in, from her bed. "You're both as bad as each other."

Julius opened his mouth to protest, but then quickly closed it. Ning had enough on her plate. Julius gave a silent nod of his head and turned back to Jennifer.

"The current scenario?" he enquired simply.

"It seems all the survivors from the *Dark Light 5000* came to this base." Jennifer spoke in a serious tone.

"Smart?" Julius said suddenly.

"Not really – they were just using initiative."

"No, your relative – Mr Smart! I wonder if he somehow directed them here."

"Mr Air, we have a specially selected group of people. Most of them can think on their feet."

"Most of them. I mean, there are some dunces in the military department, to say the least."

"Then why didn't Smart lead us there, when he realised we could be trusted? I went there with Brust, remember?"

"I don't know. Moving on, how is the Sudilav situation going?"

Jennifer signed. "Badly. It's hopeless."

"But have you made any progress?"

"Sudilav is on the ship – the clone Sudilav, I mean. We know that much. He attacked our friend Ning here, and ran off when officials came to help."

"OK."

"We'll find him, don't you worry!"

Almost as though it was on cue, an alarm wailed like a shrieking banshee. Lights shifted from off to a bright dangerous red that filled the entire base whenever it was on.

Jennifer was already at her communications device. A three dimensional realistic hologram stood before her, explaining the breakthrough in the search. Sudilav had been sighted!

Unfortunately no co-ordinates could tell them his exact location, but a location that had been narrowed down to three hundred square metres, was more than sufficient.

Jennifer bolted for the double doors. Adrenaline pumped through her blood, as she started to anticipate the chase that was yet to follow.

"Can I come with you?" Julius asked eagerly.

Jennifer stood and sighed, pondering over it for a few seconds. "If you must." was all she decided to say.

Julius whooped with joy and ducked into a narrow passage, following close behind Jennifer.

The chase had begun.

The siren grew louder with its frequent beeps getting more intense. Julius had to cover his ears, because the wail was so loud that he thought his eardrum would explode.

"Sector 4!" Jennifer yelled over the alarm.

"What?!" Julius shouted back. "What did you say?"

"Sector 4." the former Captain of the *Dark Light 5000* roared back. "Sudilav is in Sector 4!"

The small device that was mounted on Jennifer's wrist, lit up. She poked it with one finger. A three-dimensional 4-inch holo-screen materialised into existence, hovering directly above Jennifer's wrist device. As she continued on her pursuit, Jennifer tapped a glowing icon on the holo-screen. It beeped quickly and emitted a strange alien glow. A fancy effect then took place before the holo-screen flipped over, revealing another side of the holo-screen.

It showed Jennifer a map. There was a red dot that was constantly moving. A blue dot was approximately one hundred metres away. It was marked.

"Gotcha!" Jennifer whooped. "We. Got. Sudilav."

"I think you mean *you* got him." Julius professed grumpily, but even *he* couldn't stop a grin spreading across his face.

They turned another sharp corner and there was a gloriously long corridor, which stretched out in front of them.

At the end, there was someone there, eyes darting around wildly. Although he was ninety metres away, that particular 'someone' was recognised immediately.

"Sudilav." Julius and Jennifer said simultaneously in perfect unison.

Sudilav tipped an imaginary hat to them, before bolting out of sight.

"After him!" Jennifer barked.

They shot around the corner and skidded to a stop, their heels making a horrific screech as they did so. Jennifer looked at the hovering holo-screen. She looked for Sudilav on the map. But the little blue dot had vanished off the face of the map.

"It's over, Jennifer." Julius grumbled, sorrow cracking his voice. "Face it. We've lost him."

"No!" Jennifer thundered. "It's not over yet. Not by a long shot."

"The motion detectors and such have broken down. They have stopped working. Machines deady weady!" A little robot chorused from behind them.

They spun around. Beebo was standing there and shrugged defensively. "Look, it wasn't *my* fault." he uttered innocently.

"We know. Could you do anything to help?" Julius inquired hopefully.

The little robot folded his arms and shook his drooping head. "No, not really. But I have some files on comfort."

Jennifer turned her head away sharply. She wasn't crying or anything similar, but Julius could sense the disappointment in her eyes and the bitter taste in her mouth. He turned back to face Beebo, who droned on, reading out the file.

"-and then that's it." Beebo finished. "Well, was that file, any use?"

Julius sighed. "Not really."

Beebo's blue eyes grew brighter. "I have an idea!" he exclaimed.

"Uh oh!" Julius said in mock horror.

"We fly from a great height, so we are more likely to spot Sudilav."

"OK."

"Julius, can you give me a flying lesson?" Beebo clasped his hands together and his blue eyes softened. "Please. Pretty please."

Julius tilted his head slightly. "Yes, I'll teach you how to fly," Julius said, before adding under his breath: "through a window!"

Beebo evidently hadn't heard the last bit, as he rushed forward and hugged Julius's shin. "Thank you, sir."

Julius shook him off. "Let go of my leg! Anyway Beebo makes a good point though. If we go from a certain height, we're more likely to find Sudilav. Maybe we shouldn't fly a plane, but we could use that plan in a different way."

"'S right." Beebo chirped happily. "When will you give me, my flying lesson, Mr Julius?"

Julius looked down at him. "Maybe later."

Sometimes when people say 'Maybe later', they can sometimes mean 'Just, no.' and that's exactly what Julius meant!

"Okay dokey." Beebo piped up. "Let's go!"

Julius watched as Beebo scurried off about a metre, before tripping over his own feet, and clattering to the ground, his arms and legs furiously pounding the white floor. Julius was fond of Beebo, but he couldn't help but wonder, who in the right mind would create a robot like Beebo!

"Jennifer?" Beebo said, getting to his small feet. "Aren't you coming?"

Jennifer didn't say anything. Beebo looked at Julius. "Shall I do another recital of the comforting files?"

Julius shook his head firmly. "Come on, Jennifer."

"You were right." she said, looking up.

"Right about what?"

"Right about the fact that I'm a narcissistic, egotistical attention-seeker. You're right. I have made so many mistakes as well, but I still want to be praised. I said something earlier and I still think it's the right decision. I step down from my post as Captain and hand the role to you."

"I didn't mean it."

"Well, it's true."

"Jennifer, we don't have time for this. We talk about it later, OK?"

Jennifer nodded and stood up straight. "OK."

"Let's go 'im, folks!" Beebo raised a clenched fist to the roof.

He hurtled down the corridor and this time did not fall over.

The robot's head did a 180-degree turn and motioned for them to follow. "Come on, people."

Jennifer and Julius raced forward. As if by magic, the holo-screen map burst back into life. The blue dot was back on the map.

"We don't need your plan anymore, Beebo." Julius said.

"Oh." Beebo faltered, his head once again facing forward.

"He's through those doors." Jennifer said excitedly, as Beebo fell over again and couldn't get back up.

Julius and Jennifer plunged into the room. It was a small office, with the gentle tick of a holo-clock somewhere within the room. It had hover-furniture based on old-fashioned leather and oak. A holo-computer was at the desk. There were leather-bound thick books perched upon the oak shelves. There was an electric fireplace in one corner, with crackling green flames.

Julius frowned. "I thought you said Sudilav was in this room."

Jennifer looked back at her holo-screen and the next moment played out like a pantomime. "He's behind –"

But it was far too late. Sudilav leapt up from behind, snatched Jennifer and threw her over his shoulder, as if she were no more than a rag doll.

Sudilav barged into the door, which smashed upon impact. He sprinted forward, Jennifer pounding fists on his backside that was evidently having no effect whatsoever. Sudilav almost fell over Beebo, who was desperately scrambling to his feet.

Julius held out a hand and Beebo clasped it tightly. Soon he was on his feet once more.

"Don't fall over again." Julius said firmly.

"OK." Beebo said, before toppling backwards.

Julius caught him just in time and pushed Beebo back up. "I mean it."

They shot off after Sudilav and Jennifer, cavorting through twisting corridors. Sudilav saluted them and vanished into yet another room.

"We need to be careful." Julius said, to no one in particular. "We can't let him spring the same trap twice."

Cautiously they sauntered into the room, the doors hissing shut behind them. Beebo held out two fists.

"What are you doing?" Julius asked him.

Beebo threw a bundle of kicks and punches. "Getting into ninja mode."

Julius shook his head. "Beebo, can you try and be normal for once?"

That made Beebo pause to think, before he spoke. "I can give it a go."

They were in a vehicle room. Julius boarded an old-fashioned two-seater helicopter.

"All aboard." Julius barked as Beebo crawled up the steps.

Julius rammed his goggles that looked like sunglasses, onto his face, and fired the helicopter up. It shot off down a runway. The doors at the end slid open, and the helicopter whizzed off into the outside world.

"There." Beebo jabbed the window.

Sudilav and Jennifer were on a speedboat. There was someone else, but Julius couldn't quite make out whom it was. Sudilav had quite cleverly transformed Jennifer's seatbelt into a prison, by locking it in. Sudilav was driving, zipping and bouncing, along the flowing river.

"There, there, there." Beebo frantically poked the glass repeatedly.

"Yes, Beebo. I get the message." Julius said, moving the helicopter to twist downwards off to the right.

Sudilav glanced up and increased the speed. The metal of the boat winked and flashed in the sun, as it bounced along the river. It curved around a meander and then continued on its bumpy journey.

"How do we plan to catch them?" Beebo queried.

"I don't know, Beebo. I'm just making it all up as I go along."

Beebo pulled out a toolbox and was rummaging through it cue the clattering sounds. "That's what I do anyway. So, I think we need a weapon to stop them."

Julius glanced back at him. "Is there a gun or something in there?"

Beebo plunged his head into the toolbox, making an 'um' sound as he did so. Upon bringing his head out of the toolbox, it got stuck and it was several moments, before he wrenched it back out. When Beebo's face was back in view, he was holding something. "No gun. But there's a screwdriver."

Julius spluttered. "A screwdriver?"

"A screwdriver." confirmed Beebo.

"How is a screwdriver a weapon?" Julius exclaimed.

"We could lob it at the boat and it stops the engines from working."

Julius sighed, giving the helicopter an extra boost of speed. "It'll have to do. But it might just *fix* our problem."

But Beebo had lost interest in that and now he was goggling at all the different controls like an inquisitive toddler. Julius just hoped he wouldn't try to eat anything!

"What does this button do?" Beebo wondered, punching a bright red button with all his might.

The engines died and the propellers slowly came to a halt.

"Engine cut-out." a mechanical voice said calmly.

"That doesn't sound too good." Beebo said, as the plane plummeted downwards.

Chapter 52

And so they descended, the nose of the helicopter pointing directly at the river.

"I'm sorry." apologised Beebo.

Julius scowled at him. "It's a little late for that."

Beebo toyed with another level and pulled it towards him. The helicopter landed with a *thump* on the river.

"We're alive." Beebo cheered.

"Only if we fire the engines up." Julius said, rebooting the helicopter.

It shot forward and it swayed around the meander.

"Sudilav up ahead." Beebo said, in an attempt to be helpful.

Julius nodded. "Thanks for that."

Beebo's eyes dimmed. "I know you can drive flying machines, but can you control boats or helicopters on water?"

Julius assured him with a smile. "Don't worry. I'm a quicker learner."

"You better be. So you're an idiot flying a helicopter on water."

"That's a lie! I'm *driving* the helicopter on the water."

"You sure, we'll be OK?"

"I'm sure; I'll work it out. It's applying my flying skills to boating skills. I mean, how hard can it be?"

Something of the helicopter fractured off. Julius cringed and he was still surprised the helicopter hadn't drowned yet.

They were on Sudilav's tail, which hadn't snapped off like the helicopter's.

"Here goes." Beebo said, lobbing the screwdriver at the boat.

Julius gave Beebo an I-didn't-tell-you-to-do-that look, under which Beebo wilted.

The speedboat stopped abruptly. Surprisingly enough, the tip of the screwdriver flew through the air and hit the fan. The proverbial poop followed suit, shortly afterwards.

Sudilav grabbed Jennifer by the arm and leapt out of the speedboat. They landed in a heap on the grass bank, sprawled over each other.

Julius stopped the helicopter, scooped up Beebo (who squealed), and stepped out onto dry land.

A moment later, the 'copter sunk.

"Perfect timing." Julius murmured to himself.

Sudilav made a groaning sound and rolled off Jennifer.

"Put your hands up," Beebo barked, holding up a leather-bound book that he'd found in the office earlier during the chase. "Or I'll throw the book at you."

Julius tapped him on the shoulder. "Very funny, Beebo."

Beebo's eyes gleamed. "I made a joke. Oh, I am so proud of myself!"

Julius patted him on the head. "Well done. Now, let's move on."

Beebo shook his head. "If we move on, Sudilav will run off. We need to capture him."

"You know what I mean, Beebo."

"I'm a human." Sudilav croaked.

Julius laughed. "Spare us the sob story and stand up."

"Or I'll throw the book at you." Beebo added proudly, flapping the open book.

Julius cuffed the little robot gently. "We've moved on from that, Beebo. So stop saying it or it'll get me irritated. So shut it, OK?"

"Sure thing, skippa." Beebo misinterpreted Julius's words and shut the book, not his mouth.

"Enough joking about and give me the handcuffs."

"The ones with the locks?"

"Yes, they're the ones."

"Sorry sir, but I lost them. We'll have to use rope instead."

"Just give it to me."

Sudilav found all this hilarious and held out a hand. "Give me a high five, Mister Beebo."

Beebo hurled Julius the rope. "Sure thing." he said, and slammed his palm onto Sudilav's hand.

Julius tied Sudilav's hands together and the laughter died on Sudilav's lips.

"Make sure he doesn't escape!" Julius ordered Beebo.

Beebo saluted, and for the first time since Julius had met him, didn't say anything back.

"You OK?" Julius said, helping Jennifer to her feet.

She brushed mud off her knee. "Mostly. Can we just forget about the argument earlier and focus on the job in hand?"

"Gladly."

"Mr Julius?" Beebo interrupted.

Julius whirled around. "Yes, Beebo. Tell me that it's something useful?"

Beebo nodded. "It is. Wasn't there a third person on the boat?"

The water surface exploded and someone emerged in view, shaking their wet head. That 'someone' clambered onto the bank.

"Tuft." Julius said sharply.

Tuft rolled onto his back and smiled. "You're like still sore about dat whole Sudilav murder scene. Ain't dat right?"

"I am. And that means I am still not very happy with you, OK Tuft?"

Beebo wrapped Tuft up in rope and secured it firmly at the back. They dragged the two clones through the mud and grime. It took fifteen minutes to get to the base, but it was 15 minutes of victory and glory. After all, they had captured some of the clones.

The five of them clambered into the base, three of whom were pleased with their efforts. It was like they were backtracking the steps of the chase all the way back to the beginning, where Jennifer and Julius had been talking in the hospital room, or the 'healing chambers' as Julius had dubbed them. Ning lay in one bed.

A knife of silence had sliced and ripped through any kind of noise, reducing it to small iotas that gradually faded to nothing. It was deadly silent. It was too silent. Goosebumps crawled on the back of Jennifer's neck, on which all the hairs had stood up. Silence can be extremely eerie and unsettling.

Ning had dozed off. She did deserve a bit of rest and a break from the seemingly ever-present chaos that surrounded her. Sudilav and Tuft were laid down gently onto some spare beds at the far end of the chamber.

The military men struggled; their arms and legs sprawled over the beds, occasionally flailing in vain hope of escape.

"Hush now." Julius whispered, bringing a finger to his lips.

Sudilav tried to blurt something out, but his gag smothered out any form of sound. But Sudilav's eyes were widening and his lips were trying to form words, but it was hopeless.

Julius brought the military commander's head up, and looked at the string running along the back of his head, which secured the gag. Julius just about managed to resist the urging temptation to ping the string, instead loosening it.

The volume had increased and Sudilav made muffled sounds. He repeated it again. When this had no effect, the slurred words changed, but Julius could tell it was the same message being regurgitated over and over.

"Use your tongue." Julius suggested.

Sudilav nodded to show he understood, and flicked the gag with his tongue. It snapped forward and pinged back at Sudilav's mouth. Even though he was wearing a gag, it was clear Sudilav's mouth was about as sore as he was about the capture.

Sudilav cursed and spat the gag out. He retched, before spluttering out a volley of nasty coughs. It was miraculous that Ning did not stir from her nap.

"I take it that you're a little miffed." Julius smirked.

Somehow Sudilav managed not to lose his temper. "That's the understatement of the decade." He flicked the gag off the bed. "And for your information, that rag is horrible, unhygienic, and *reeks* of mouldy cheese covered in manure. Not at all pleasant! Gag is a very good description of that rag, because that's exactly what it made me do!"

"You have left something bitter on my tongue, Mr Sudilav, and I tend to have something sweet to remedy that. Do you know what that is?"

"My home?" Sudilav suggested sweetly.

"Ah, very good. I don't want to sound like some deranged malevolent psychopath, but I wish for sweet revenge – you cannot evade me. Did that sound OK?"

Sudilav buried the back of his head further into his pillow. "Not really, if your intentions were not to sound insane, then your desires have been cut somewhat short."

Julius glowered. "Are you trying to sound really pretentious, whenever you open your mouth, which would perhaps be better suited behind a gag?"

"I think not. Surely we can come to some arrangement? We can negotiate and reason with each other. We are gentlemen, yes?"

"*I* am, but *you* most certainly are not."

"Actually, Julius, I reckon I am. I am the most courteous and chivalrous gentleman you are likely to meet."

Laughter exploded within Julius, but luckily there was not a crack for it to seep out of. "Shooting people from behind with a powerful Boom Blaster, is not courteous by any means. At least, not in my book."

"I'll throw the book at you." Sudilav hollered.

"That's Beebo's line, not yours. Now do us all a favour for one of the few times in your life, and shut up!"

Sudilav shut up. Julius was astonished. It could never be that simple. Something was wrong. There was a brief and blunt silence, as if someone had jabbed a key on the piano of silence.

Julius leaned in over Sudilav, so that their noses were only a matter of inches apart.

"What do you know?" Julius hissed, snapping the silence like a twig.

Sudilav looked up at him. "I'm a human, not a clone. I'm telling you the truth," Sudilav saluted him. "Scout's honour!"

Julius glared at him. "You're not a human. I saw the human Sudilav die, right in front of me. I ask you this. What kind of person is a murderer?"

"What kind of person is one that wishes to enslave beings as intelligent as them?" Sudilav responded.

"You're a clone." Julius accused.

"'S right." Beebo piped up, wagging a finger at Sudilav. "Sudilav's body language indicated earlier levels of stress and secrecy. Basically, he was fibbing. Naughty boy!"

"Thanks for that, Beebo. That's the most useful and sensible thing you've said today. Now go back to being quiet, please." Julius said, before eyeing Sudilav cautiously. "So, you're a clone."

"Yes, I am." admitted Sudilav.

"Then you must know something."

"He knows practically nothing."

Julius wheeled around. His eyes tried to fix on the speaker, trying to figure out who had spoken.

"And I suppose you do." Jennifer said, speaking for the first time in minutes.

She was leaning against a wall, hands dug into pockets. It took a moment for it to register with Julius, that she had been responding to Tuft. It had been Tuft who'd spoken earlier.

"I know far more than Sudilav does." he said.

Despite the shackles that bound Sudilav together, he was able to accomplish turning his head to face Tuft. Clearly, this was news to him too.

"Why you?" Sudilav echoed everyone's thoughts. "You have an inferior military ranking than me. You're certainly not as strong or as fast. I'm more reliable and trustworthy. Besides, I also have yet to meet anyone that rivals your level of idiocy!"

Truth be told, it was exactly what everyone except Tuft, had been thinking. Most of them had had the politeness not to speak their mind, but then if you do not speak your mind, then the chances are, your thoughts will never been revealed. Fortunately for Julius and Jennifer, Sudilav had done that job for them.

"Well, I was told more. I dunno why. Dat's just da way things are. But all of us are generally kept in da duhark, in case something like dis 'appens." Tuft went on.

"Why should we trust *you*?" Jennifer demanded. "Why are you blurting things out when we haven't tortured, threatened, or even interrogated you? Hmm?"

Tuft raised an eyebrow. "'Cos I can tell by da looks on your faces, you are going to threaten me with something dat I won't like."

"Oh, you're very right, Johnny Tuft. Very right." Jennifer retorted. "We want to know anything useful or essential, that will help us or there will be trouble…"

"You better not be lying to us." Beebo added, in such a way that it sounded as though he was sulking.

Julius shook his head and shot Beebo a look of Stay-Out-Of-This. Beebo shrunk back and the light of his gleaming blue eyes weakened.

"The clones are preparing an army." Tuft blurted out abruptly.

Chapter 53

It was so sudden and so unexpected that, it took a while for the effect to sink in.

"It's true." Tuft continued after a long while. "Dey've been creating clones back aht da headquarters, using the genny code thingy mo bob. I guess dey ain't all perfect soldiers, but dey're being trained, and dey're growing in number."

This was bad.

"Where's the headquarters?" Julius asked. "Could you lead us to it? The base?"

Tuft nodded. "I know where it is from here."

"You better not be lying to us." repeated Beebo and this time, his timing was good.

"You hear that, Tuft? He's right you know. Give us no trouble, then we'll give you no trouble. Got it?" Jennifer said slowly.

Even an imbecile like Tuft could understand that. "We'll begin our journey as soon as possible."

Julius put on a deep movie trailer voice. "And so our brave intrepid heroes embarked on a great trek – their quest to reach the *ultimate* destination."

Despite lacking in emotion, Beebo sensed that he wasn't wanted. "Shall I leave you to your business?"

When no one replied, Beebo slipped out of the room and off on adventurous travels. And then as if he'd never been there in the first place, things continued without him.

But there was no time for jokes and games to go ahead, because something was very wrong with Sudilav.

He had frozen like a statue: stationary, inanimate and very quiet. It looked as though he was barely breathing. Sudilav's eyes had widened, as though he'd just been stabbed in the back. Although no one had touched him, it was clear that Sudilav's temperature was high. Perspiration dripped from his forehead and glued his clothes to his bulky and muscular body.

Julius waved a hand in front of Sudilav. This had no effect. Julius even managed to strike up the courage to poke Sudilav in the ribs. But this too had consequences.

Then something happened.

Suddenly Sudilav made a sharp jerking motion. It got more intense. Soon it was as if he was having some sort of spasm attack.

Sudilav's teeth chattered together and he shook violently. He was trembling but why? What was happening to him?

There was a nasty bubbling sound. Julius frowned as Sudilav ripped off his combat shirt, to see what was happening. His skin was bubbling like hot wax.

Julius leapt back. Everyone watched in a mixture of astonishment, bewilderment and fear, as the rope surrounding Sudilav simply melted away until it was non-existent.

Sudilav rolled out of the bed and stood up. He looked down at the bubbling skin. He opened his mouth and a load of Gibberish sprouted out. Sudilav tried again.

"What. Is. Happening?" he babbled.

Even though his speech was near incomprehensible, the fear in his voice was easily detectable.

Nobody really knew what to do. All they could do was stare and gape in horror, as this strange event unfolded before them.

The bubbling was near ceasing, and had become almost gentle. Almost gentle. But now Sudilav's skin was beginning to ripple as he howled in pain.

And then it happened almost simultaneously.

Sudilav began to grow by a couple of inches. If people were buildings, then before Sudilav would have been a tall tower. Now he was a skyscraper.

His trousers were ripped and torn. Sudilav's muscles expanded and became the size of large watermelons. And then as quickly as it had began...

..it stopped.

The pain died. Sudilav sighed, the rich sweet air heaving in and out of his lungs.

No one said anything, for quite a long while. Sudilav had transformed. He was a monster in size now. His muscles were almost twice as big as before and that was saying something!

"That's the consequence the cloning process has had on Sudilav." Julius summed up simply. "I reckon it's a bomb, set to go off at a certain stage."

Jennifer's eyes had become huge and she swallowed thickly. Sudilav was now some kind of seven foot superhuman – quite literally. No wonder Jennifer was imitated, especially as he was almost two feet taller than her!

She recoiled back and nodded slowly, her eyes still glued to Sudilav. "You're right. It's his power that has developed, due to the cloning side effect. It must be some form of a time genetic bomb."

Julius's brow creased. "You can render yourself invisible. Sudilav has become supernaturally strong. Why hasn't Tuft or I got any extraordinary gifts?"

Jennifer shrugged, still watching cautiously and vigilantly. "I don't know. Maybe the 'bomb' hasn't gone off yet. For all one knows, you may just *not* have suffered a side effect. Same goes for Tuft."

"Hmm." Julius purred quietly. "Interesting."

There was a powerful but quiet clicking sound, coming from Sudilav. This was followed up by a lengthy *crack!* And a brief *snap!* Everything seemed to stop, and cast aside. Everything during that moment in time seemed to stop and revolve around Sudilav. And then very suddenly and unforeseen...

Silence.

It broke away, as an impertinent person might do during conversation. Sudilav stretched his arms, in a manner identical to that of someone waking up. Only Sudilav didn't yawn.

"It's show-time." Sudilav cracked his knuckles, a smile creeping across his face.

It was realised far too late: Sudilav was going to use his super strength to become practically unstoppable, almost invincible.

He reared his head and ran.

Sudilav had never been so fast. His powerful legs pushed him forward with such force, compelling him forward and onwards in a blur. Julius was first to attack. He swiped at Sudilav's knee.

Sudilav's head swiveled round, to face Julius. His eyes were cold, merciless, and predator like. Sudilav caught Julius's arm, twisted it and flung it over his shoulder. Julius landed on his feet, but the momentum was too strong, pinning him to the ground with a nasty CRUNCH!

Unharmed, Sudilav stopped and turned around. It was almost as if it amused him, these tiny puny people against himself. He wanted a proper fight.

Fuelled by fear and anger, Jennifer launched herself at Sudilav. He ducked out of the way, moving in a blur. Jennifer rolled onto the bed, sprung to her feet and tried again.

She drove herself forward. Jennifer slammed into Sudilav and bounced off. Jennifer staggered back, clutching her stomach. Sudilav seemed completely impervious to the assault, advancing off on the path to escape. But Jennifer was determined not to give in, despite the agonizing pain that she was experiencing.

She swung a blow to Sudilav's head. Without even glancing at her, Sudilav deflected the blow and inflicted pain on two of her fingers.

Jennifer howled and jumped back, glad not to have fallen over. Sudilav turned slowly to face her, his huge fists raised for attack. Jennifer gulped. This didn't look good.

She tried to dart out of the way of the first punch, but it caught her cheekbone. Jennifer stumbled back, stars dancing right before her eyes.

Scowling, as he was clearly disappointed with the punch, Sudilav clenched his fist. This time he thrust it forward, faster, sharper, harder.

It smashed right into Jennifer's nose. The blow was vicious, and happened so quickly that the eye could barely follow. One moment the fist was anticipating a fight, the next it had found its mark. Jennifer's mind didn't even realise it had happened until a while afterwards. But by then, she could barely think straight.

The punch had been so hard; it was like Jennifer had launched herself at a diamond wall at the speed of light.

Jennifer flew back and hit an opposite wall, which ruptured with thick cracks. Groaning and ignoring the mother of all headaches, Jennifer sat up. She was extraordinarily lucky, that the punch hadn't killed her!

But Sudilav had already gone. Julius had gotten to his feet and continued with the chase, even though he knew it was a pointless exercise. The chase was as good as over.

Beebo squealed as Sudilav hoofed him into the far distance, without even realising it. At the rate he was going, he could probably run through walls and emerge without even a bruise. Sudilav was truly *invincible*.

He was toying with them. Sudilav could have been long gone by now, if he'd wanted to. But no, he wished to relish his pursuers' humiliating defeat.

In the end, however the man of invincibility was defeated by the mere element of surprise. Julius knew it was all over about a minute before.

Jennifer jogged into view, blood gushing out of her nose. It had been a nasty bash.

"Has he gotten away?" she asked instantly.

Julius shook his head. "We'll get him later. Let's round up our crew for a trek to the clones' base."

They turned and walked off into the distance, leaving Sudilav, who didn't detect the slightest indication that he was about to fall into a trap.

It didn't register as Sudilav ran full pelt at an iron bar. The trap hadn't even been realised, as the iron bar snapped. And it certainly didn't strike home, until far too late as Sudilav hurtled face first into a pit fifteen feet below.

Chapter 54

"How much further?" Beebo chirped.

Julius glanced at him briefly and returned his gaze back to the horizon up ahead. "Not far, I don't think."

Beebo pleaded and looked thoughtful. "Hadn't we there yet?"

Julius shrugged. "I don't know."

"I think there's an easier way of transport." Beebo piped up suddenly.

"I'd love some other suggestion," Julius said. "I'm an open book."

"No, you're not." Beebo bleeped. "You're a human being."

Julius sighed. "It's a figure of speech."

"Is it? Now I have a suggestion to make."

"What kind of a suggestion?"

"A useful one."

"Excuse me, while I wash out my ears."

"Fine, don't listen to me." Beebo said, trying to pout, which is quite hard when you don't have lips.

"Yes, that's right. Go and bug Tuft with your irritating and irksome questions. He's the one leading us there."

Beebo bobbed his cuboid of a head, vigorously. "Okay dokey."

He scampered off to the front of the trailing group. Julius sighed. It was a great weight off his shoulders, now that Beebo would pester some other poor unfortunate soul.

Julius smiled and quickened his pace. He caught up with where Sudilav had been imprisoned. They made security for him immensely tight. But then, that was hardly surprising.

His chains jangled as he itched forward, many weapons eyeing his every move, almost as if daring him to attempt escape.

Julius gazed up at Sudilav, who shot him an abhorrent glare.

"Hello, puny human." Sudilav scowled.

"Hello, ugly giant." Julius responded, seeming unfazed by Sudilav's insult.

"Giants can crush the living soul out of any man."

"But it is man, who always ended up slaying the giants, despite their 'greatness' and unhandsome looks."

"What do you want, *midget*?" Sudilav spat, putting great emphasis on the last word.

Julius ignored him. "Tell me, why would Tuft want to kill you?"

Sudilav sighed. "It's a long story."

Julius waved a hand dismissively. "I don't have anywhere to be."

"Actually you do, you're reaching the clones' base in about a quarter of an hour."

"In that case, why don't you talk really fast?"

Sudilav counted fingers. "Tuft may have killed this other Sudilav for a number of reasons. He hates him for various reasons I do not have time to explain. He could have thought I was an enemy and thus the murder took place. But finally, Tuft might just have wanted to beat someone up for the fun of it and accidentally went too far."

"That last one doesn't count. Tuft isn't *that* unreasonable."

"Believe me, he is."

Julius shrugged and wandered off further, wading through the crew, who were survivors from the *Dark Light 5000*. Suddenly he saw something up ahead. Something that was very near. Something that was not good.

Julius sprinted to the very front, going like a bat out of hell. He skidded to a halt. Tuft was giving directions, to which Jennifer was listening to intently. Because they were all so engrossed in it, they hadn't noticed the peril that was fast approaching.

"STOP!" Julius roared, and a sudden hush spread amongst the audience.

Quietness had fallen as night often did. They dropped their topics to stare at Julius. All was hush and tranquil except for the gentle lapping of the old sea dog that gnawed at the coast on which they stood.

Night was marching forward. The ebbing streaks of day illuminated Julius's face, as he pointed up ahead.

"Look!" Julius said simply, and that was all that was needed.

A hazy silhouette could be made out against the dying slivers of the sunset, which fired a most spectacular blast of wondrous colours into the darkening sky.

The figure was moving towards the crowd and they realised in horror, that it was closer than they thought.

Tuft dropped his hi-tech scanner binoculars, which sunk into the golden sand. "Who is dat ugly person coming over here? He looks like a complete moron."

Julius cracked up laughing, which did at least sap the tension by a little amount. "It's the human version of you!"

This ripped up the lingering anxiety and chucked the remains into a burning abyss.

"It's Tuft," someone hooted. "The human one."

Several people couldn't contain themselves and rushed forward to greet their new recruit. But the human Tuft was having none of it.

He reared a massive gun and fired once into a crimson red cloud. People looked around hastily, the tension returning once more.

"Put it down." Jennifer barked. "We're allies. We're humans."

Tuft, who now stood about ten metres away, lowered the blaster slightly. "Humans?"

Jennifer nodded. "Yep. We're humans. We're the good guys. Get rid of the gun and get your backside over here."

Tuft was about to release the weapon from his grip. But then his eyes narrowed and he growled demonically.

He clung onto the gun and charged forward like a raging bull. People protested and tried to block his path, but resistance was futile. When the crowd realised this, they dispersed off into small mobs.

Everyone abandoned everything they were doing and fled. Everyone that is, except for Sudilav.

He broke free of the ropes and the chains snapped. He bellowed.

The human Tuft loaded the gun. But his clone appeared out nowhere, snatched it from his grasp, and advanced forward.

The human Tuft stood there, rooted to the spot not sure what to do, now that his identical twin had taken the gun off him. In the end, he settled with watching in shock. As did, the rest of the collection of mobs.

The clone Tuft strode forward, patting the large gun. He cocked it and fired.

A rocket propelled mini missile shot out of the barrel, whizzing past Sudilav. It hit a great oak tree. The tree exploded into a huge ball of flame and soon had been reduced to mere ash.

"Not so cocky now, are you Sudilav?" Tuft said. "Killing you once was fun. Da second 'ime – it's an honour. You may have become some kind of superhuman, but even *you* cannot survive dis kind of weapon." Tuft patted the gun.

Although he didn't like it, Sudilav knew that Tuft was right. Inbuilt into every human being, is a factor that it is 'programmed'. It is the fight or flight switch. Sudilav, being a soldier, usually fought instead of fleeing. He saw fleeing as something only cowardly heathens did.

However on the rare occasion, Sudilav's natural reaction was not an option. Better a coward than dead, he supposed.

Sudilav turned and ran. He sped across the coastline swiftly, as the sea dog tried in the vain hope, to bite chunks of his legs. But Sudilav was running far too fast for that. He choked and spluttered on the sea salt that sprayed into his mouth.

Tuft smiled, his finger tightening on the trigger, as he anticipated the thrill of the chase. People always used to say how Tuft was always second rate to Sudilav, how Sudilav was always so much better than Tuft in every way possible. No matter how hard Tuft worked, it was always still about Sudilav. And the roles had been reversed. Tuft watched Sudilav as he shrunk, as he got further away.

Let him have his fun, Tuft thought. He resisted the urge to activate yet another powerful missile. Tuft charged forward, blood and adrenaline pumping through his veins. And then he could wait no longer. Tuft's finger squeezed the trigger as hard as he could.

Sudilav was diminishing now, but his chance of survival was doing so too. He was as good as dead. The missile blasted out of the gun, sliced through the sky and hit the ground, where it blew up into a huge ball of flame. It tore at large chunks of the beach, penetrating the surface of E2 by quite a bit.

Tuft looked out, his eyes squinting in the very last rays of the sun. He couldn't see Sudilav.

And then darkness fell.

Chapter 55

Very gradually, the day was drawing to a close. The time of twilight had arrived. A gorgeous sunset with magnificent colours had settled and Katsu Sato had to admit it was very beautiful to look at.

It was peaceful too. But Sato's dreamy state was intervened.

Can anyone hear this?

Sato looked around in bewilderment to find the source of the voice.

Help me! If someone can hear this, help me!

What's happening? Sato thought to himself.

Hello, can anyone hear me, the voice continued. *It's me, Holly Skyland. Unfortunately, I cannot detect any replies or responses. I'm in your head – a voice in your head.*

How? Sato wondered.

Almost as if Holly had heard him, the voice spoke again. *I've established a telepathic link with you, whoever you are or if I'm actually talking to anyone at all. I'm a human by the way, not a clone. I can prove this by making you think. Clones could have picked up the signal and could be tuning in right now. And no, you're not going insane – as bizarre as it seems, I am a human hopefully speaking to someone via a one-way telepathy.*

But Sato was struggling to keep up with all of this. It didn't quite make sense. If Holly was telling the truth, then why she could set up a telepathic link in the first place? Holly's clone had told Sato that she'd could read people's emotions. But she hadn't said anything about sending out a telepathic brainwave, which people could intercept and translate into thoughts. Maybe the side effect of the cloning had been different when it came to the real Holly. But Sato couldn't shake off that creeping sensation of doubt and suspicion. Nevertheless, he continued to listen to what Holly had to say.

One person can only intercept this brainwave and I just hope I'm talking to a human not a clone. the voice persisted. *If you're wondering how I am able to send messages to you, telepathically – the truth is I don't know. Anyway, the clones have captured me and I'm in their base. I guess it's about three miles away, and I sincerely hope that you will find it. I think there are other humans captured here. I wish you the best of luck on the rescue mission. Finally the clones have power – I don't how. And one last thing, I –*

It was cut short. Sato kept stationary in position, waiting for the rest of the message – but it never came. When Sato realised this, he thought it over.

Something wasn't right. Why had Holly chosen now to send a snippet of telepathic communication? And why had she been cut off during the message?

Sato narrowed his eyes. One of his flaws was that he was paranoid and suspicious. It was probably just a fault in his programming taking over. But still…

Just like Holly's message, Sato's thoughts were interrupted. He looked up.

There was a massive explosion. Sato tumbled over in surprise, as the hot fiery fist punched him full on.

Bits of ash scattered into the air, and noxious smoke the colour of a nasty grey, filled the black sky.

Sand swept into one of Sato's eyes and his vision blurred. Blinking frantically, Sato managed to open his one good eye. His other remained firmly shut. The eyelid glued itself to the eye socket, as Sato's eye stung ferociously. It was as if someone was stabbing him repeatedly in the eyeball, every ten seconds with a razor-edged knife.

Groaning, Sato made a lousy attempt to get up. His thin legs wobbled before collapsing under him. The second attempt was successful.

He swayed on the balls of his feet, though neither foot was particularly balanced. Sato lurched forward and with his one good eye, looked at what had happened.

In the time the explosion had happened, dusk had vanished along with day. Night now consumed a limited period of time. The explosion had settled, but the hungry tongues of flame that lapped up the tattered earth, had not.

Sato coughed, as the smoke tried to worm its way down his throat. He tried to spit it back out, but more seeped in. It was like trying to empty a sea with nothing more than a bucket.

A dark shape emerged from the smoke, choking on the now dangerous air. It was a man. He stepped over the burning debris and viciously kicked a piece of rubble, which skittered out into the distance.

"What happened?" Sato spluttered.

A flame suddenly kindled. It was about the size you might see on a large candle, dawdling gently. It lit up one side of the man's face. Sato saw a long curving scar that had ran through his cheek that stopped somewhere about his chin. Sato knew who it was instantly.

"Sudilav!" he blurted uncomfortably.

Sudilav stared at Sato, right in the eye. "Oh," he said quietly. "It's you."

There was a brief but awkward silence.

"I believe that's the longest conversation, we've had for years." Sato commented, convinced there wasn't something right with Sudilav.

If Sudilav spotted this, he didn't show it. He nodded his head slowly. Their relationship, to say the least, was not on good terms. They weren't enemies, throwing snide remarks whenever they met. They just kept out of each other's way and had tried to have as little as contact as possible.

Another shadow came forth from the smoke. It was Tuft, brandishing his huge gun. Sato took a step back.

"Whoa!" Sato said. "What happened? Have you been in a battle? Things have been really hotting up."

"Before bursting into flames." Sudilav added.

Tuft's gun clicked and he stepped aside. "It looks as if we have a lil' visitor."

A third person came into view.

"It's a duplicate of Sudilav. Wait, something's not right with either of them." Sato then snapped his fingers. "They're a *lot* taller and it seems like they've gotten a *lot* stronger. Actually I take that back – they've become superhumanly strong! Just look at the size of their muscles – most of the muscles are bigger than my head!"

Sato took a deep breath.

Tuft shrugged. "Apparently dere wos some kinda side effect due to da cloning. It gives some people special abilities and I mean really special like superhero stuff – super-strong and I've seen a lot more in recent times." His shoulder drooped. "It's a shame *I* haven't got superstrength. In fact, I've got no abilities at all, full stop. What about you, Mister Sato?"

Sato ignored the question and lead on from the point where he had previously stopped. "I'm confused. Is one of the Sudilavs a clone, the other a human?"

The Sudilav who'd just entered the scene spoke. "The guy's right. I thought the other Sudilav was dead. Tuft killed him. But how come there's one more? I know I'm a clone, but have our bosses cloned another Sudilav without telling us? Is this guy in front of me, a clone too? And why?"

Sato took a deep breath and tried to take it all in. "I don't know."

Tuft flexed his fingers. "Interestin'. I don't really understand it either. It just mucks up my head. I dunt get it. It's confusing. You're clever and you is very confused too."

"It's 'you are very confused'" Sato corrected.

"Wotever. You still 'aven't answered my question. Answer it now, will you?"

Sato opened his mouth to 'answer it', but Sudilav stepped into their conversation. "Are we were going to stand around, chit-chatting or shall we steer the conversation to more important matters?"

Tuft sucked air through his teeth. "You're right, we shouldn't be standing around, gossiping like a bunch of wussy gurls. Less talk, more fight."

The other Sudilav, Sudilav II charged forward. Sudilav ducked and swung a fist, which his duplicate caught and twisted. Sudilav scowled and fired a lethal kick at his reflection, sinking the kick into ginormous abdominal muscles.

Sudilav felt his arms being swung into a lock behind him. Tuft had grabbed him from behind.

"You may have become super strong, but so has da other Sudilav. Neither of you will win. But if I add in da extra help, you will lose." Tuft whispered in Sudilav's ear as Sudilav's mirror image slammed a fist into Sudilav's head.

Sato certainly didn't have the essential qualities needed for your average soldier. But the cloning process had left him with a 'special ability' as Tuft called it – telekinesis. Originally Sato had only use his power via gesture controls, but he'd embarked on a search to find other humans so that they could band together. Along the way, Sato had practiced his newfound talent. He no longer controlled it with motion, now it was with his mind.

He couldn't just let Sudilav be killed. Sato wasn't Sudilav's biggest fan, but Sato couldn't just leave him to die. Could he?

Push Sato thought. Nothing happened.

He tried again: *push*. Again this seemed to have no effect and the conflict persisted.

Third time lucky, Sato reminded himself as Tuft delivered a fatal uppercut to Sudilav's chin. *PUSH!*

Sudilav II had been in the act of firing a palm into his 'identical twin', when he shot backwards, fell back, and smashed his head on a jagged rock. He was out like a light.

The sea was raging and so did the battle on the coast. With his only other soldier indisposed, things were not looking too promising for Tuft.

But there was a sudden turn of events. Tuft rolled out of harm's way and snatched up his blaster.

Tuft whirled around to Sato. "You can move stuff with yer mind." he exclaimed.

"Indeed." Sato's head dipped lower.

Tuft cursed his luck and spun around. He raised the gun and pointed it directly at Sudilav's heart.

"If any of you move, Sudilav dies," Tuft threatened, his finger tensing on the trigger. "I mean it!"

"I'm sure you do." Sudilav responded simply. "But the question is why?"

Tuft ignored him and scowled. "I'm gonna kill you now." he said and squeezed the trigger.

At the last moment, Sudilav twisted into a forward flip, darted over Tuft and launched an attack that twisted into a strike. It struck Tuft at the back of the head. Sudilav scooped up the gun and flipped Tuft over like a pancake.

Tuft groaned in agony. "I hate it when you use dat newfound strength of yours."

Sudilav shook him hard, gripping him by the throat. "Listen here and listen well, Mr Tuft. Keep that mouth of yours firmly closed or I will close it for you. Because at the moment, I can throw you about a million times further than I could ever trust you. And believe me, I'm *not* exaggerating!"

Tuft wriggled and squirmed. Sudilav dropped him to the floor and jerked the gun vaguely in his direction.

"I shall ask you again. Why do you want to kill me? I want you to tell me everything." Sudilav adjusted the power in the gun, so that it wouldn't set off a huge explosion, making it more like an extremely lethal bullet.

Tuft shook his head. "I wunt tell you anyfin'."

Sudilav patted the gun and leaned in to whisper to Tuft. "The more you talk, the longer you stay alive."

At this point, Sato wasn't that sure what to do. He'd worked out that Sudilav must be a clone from what had been said. He was scared and horrified at what might happen. In the end, the computer programmer decided to stand back and watch what happened.

Tuft seemed to understand and began talking. "I suppose it started way back in '61, ten years ago. Finking about et, a lot 'as happened in 10 years."

Sudilav pursed his lips. "Get on with it and get to the point."

"OK, OK. You'd been ah military academy for like wot – six and a harf years? Anyway you'd been sent off as a vat loser and you came back all those years later as a cool and an awesome guy. You'd manned up. You'd come back to visit California – I don't know why, but dat probably dont matter."

Sudilav nodded and gestured for continuation.

Tuft pressed on. "So, you came back. I was a bit surprised actually. I thought you'd have just lost a lot of weight and blubber. Dat would have been it. I didn't expect a soldier with great muscles and a six pack 'n' all. But you had also changed in personality as 'ell."

Tuft wasn't a great storyteller, nor was his English very good, but still somehow everyone found themselves on tenterhooks.

"We became friends and you joined our little gang. Man, wot fun we had. Good ol' days, eh Sudilav? Anyway Sudilav reckoned he was bayter than me – a bayter soldier – stronger, faster, and like, just generally bayter. I hate to say et, but 'e might have been right. So people start respecting 'im, and I was just another foot soldier. Dat's how it's been for the rest of our lives, ain't it Sudilav?" Tuft put great empathises on the last three words, dropping them like daggers.

"It was jealousy," Sudilav said quietly. "I should have known. You were jealous of me."

Tuft shrugged. "I dunt care about yer theories. Anyway dere's more. One day, I'd had enough of all dis. So I challenged Sudilav."

"Oh." Sudilav uttered. He knew what was coming.

"We had a fight and wot a fight it was. But it didn't end well. At least, not for me. Sudilav beat me up real bad. I was well defeated. It was hew-milly-ating. We got a real audience. But that ain't harf of it. Sudilav chucked me into a river and I almost drowned. Drowned, man! Dat ain't cool, innit?"

Tuft paused for an effect of silence and sympathy. It was unclear whether Tuft had achieved the second factor, but the first was already under his belt.

"So when I came out of da hospital. Did Sudilav leave me alone? No, did he 'eck! He bullied me. Not seriously, but with words and the occasional fist. But da damage of our legendary fight had been dun. Guys throw insults at me regularly, and pretty ladies looked down at me, as if dey'd never want anything to do with a swot like me. Dat's partly why I like being on dis planet. Away from all dose *scum*."

There was a long silence. Sudilav's face was intact and showed no sight of emotion. Most of this was news to Sato and he didn't really know how to react. He'd heard about the fight of course. Who hadn't? But the scenes behind it were things Sato mostly didn't know about.

"There's more." Sudilav said darkly. "I can tell."

The corners of Tuft's lips turned slightly upwards. "Oh boy, oh boy, yes. Man, you 'av' no idea wot all dis did to me. I was destroyed! I was always second rate. Always. I was mocked, and left alone in da world. I had no family, no friends, no wife, no gurlfriend, no nuffin'. But you fuelled me on. I became a soldier and trained hard, preparing for dat day when I had sworn to kill you. You almost killed me too! You deserve to die. I went onto dis planet, plotting every little detail all out. Remember when I was in that daydreaming state back on the ship? I was plotting den. But den da clones were born. Clones v humans. How great. It gave me another reason to kill you. Now you were da enemy."

Tuft paused before resuming his story. "I came across a bunch of humans – Sudilav was part of them. I killed Sudilav but dat guy, Julius Air found out. But I'd made a mistake.

"Julius Air had seen me kill Sudilav. But he dought I'd killed a human. He was wrong.

"I'd murdered a *clone* in cold blood. You see, moments before he died, I dink he realised I was a clone. His last ever line still sticks in my head like a catchy song lyric."

Tuft shut his head, as if the words were playing out in his head. "If I close my eyes, I can hear dose words still. 'Don't kill me, I'm yer friend.' It 'as haunted my dreams ever since."

Sato butted in. "I set up camp in the remains of the *Dark Light 5000* and there were these zombie mutant things – which probably happened due to the crash landing. It was an accident. Just a strange coincidence."

"Dude, nothing happens without a reason." Tuft interrupted.

Sato nodded in his direction. "Thanks for that. But there were only six mutants although a couple died in total. We made seven clones. One mutant was missing.

"I think that mutant was Sudilav but I guess he turned out like a normal human. He must have escaped before the ship blew up. But I don't understand, we didn't press the clone button twice, did we?"

Tuft shook his head. "Dat ain't what happened. We clones were born at our base, never aboard the ship. Da mutants were da original clones, de Sudilav I killed was an original clone made on the *Dark Light 5000*."

Sato's eyes widened as it absorbed this information. "But why?"

Tuft shrugged. "I dunno. I'm just a foot soldier. Anyway shall I continue with my story? Good. So I realised my mistake. I came across dis Sudilav here. 'E's a human too."

Tuft had dropped yet another bombshell. There was yet another hefty silence.

"That's not possible." Sudilav exclaimed. "I'm the clone, I know it and I'm proud of it."

Tuft held out his hands. "'Fraid not."

"I think he might be right, Sudilav," Sato interjected. "I met another clone and she told that I could trust no one, not even yourself. It's a scary thought, but I think it's true. You're a human, but you just don't know it."

Sudilav shook his head firmly. "It's not true. I would have remembered escaping from the ship shortly before it crashed. I remember no such thing. And something like that is gonna stick in your memory. But not only that I actually *remember* waking up in the clones' base, being sent out to go and infiltrate humans."

Sato's eyes glinted. "It looks like it's true. It's a clever trick – I admire the clones strongly for it. Their enemies become loyal and faithful allies. They turn the humans against themselves. Quite literally."

Sudilav put his hands over his head, doubt starting to fill his head. "It isn't true. You don't know what you're talking about."

Tuft had joined Sato's side. "If so, den dere'll be a bit in your memory when you getting cloned on the human's ship, and den da next thing you know you wake on da clone's base. If you're a clone, dere will be a gap in between et. Remember and all will be proved. OK, mate?"

"I've done the test – I'm a clone."

"You hadn't done it probably. Really try. Deep down you'll know which one you are: clone or human?

Follow the path, that your heart tells you stray down." Sato added in.

Slowly and reluctantly, Sudilav closed his eyes. It took a while and the theory that he fallen to sleep, wandered into minds. Sato took the gun from his grip and fiddled with it nervously, so that Sudilav couldn't shoot them all, in his wrath.

Suddenly Sudilav's eyes snapped open.

"Oh," he said slowly, the effect of it all really hitting home. "You're right."

Sato leaned in closer. "What did you see?"

Sudilav gulped thickly and snatched the gun back from Sato. "It was short, but it was enough. I was in an escape pod that smashed into the planet. It was engulfed in flames, and I choked and spluttered on the smoke. Then I blackened out. It was only a few seconds, but it was so real and vivid. It was like I was there and…" Sudilav trailed off, but was determined to continue and spoke boldly in a slightly quivering voice. "And I thought I was going to *die*."

It was at that moment when Tuft decided to press on with his explanation. It was a bad moment. But Tuft was evidently not a master of tact.

"So I needed to murder da human Sudilav. It was bad enough, I'd made a mistake once, but dis time I would definitely kill da real human Sudilav." Tuft proceeded, but Sato cut him short.

"Slow down, let him get his breath back."

Sudilav panted, his tongue rolling out. "So I'm a human."

Sato inclined his head. "That's right. The Sudilav Tuft killed was the *only* of the original clones. The only clone who didn't become a horrific mutated monster."

Sudilav shivered. "So he could have been a monster roaming through the remains of the ship, gobbling up anything he saw."

Sato titled his head, considering this. "Almost certainly."

It took another moment for all this to sink in.

"I was tricked by the other clones. They used me, like I was a tool. They made me think I was a clone!" Sudilav roared, angry and exasperated. "Tuft deserves to die here and now!"

Tuft managed a weak smile. "I finished my story and da story of me is about to finish too."

Sudilav gripped the big blaster with two hands. It was trained directly at Tuft's heart. When Sudilav's fingers squeezed that trigger, it would blow a hole the size of a basketball in Tuft's chest.

Tuft spat out more blood. "Go on den. Get et over and done with. Before I die of al' da tension."

Sudilav's face was flushed a deep red. "Don't play games."

"But my game is up." Tuft wiped his bloody jaw. "Or don't you have da guts to pull a little trigger. You always *were* a 'ittle coward. You went to military school and tried to be better than me. But ya know dat I am right. You may be a super soldier on the outside, but inside you're just a *titchy* weakling."

Sudilav's face contorted in fury and he squeezed the gun so hard, it almost was crushed under his strength. "YOU'RE WRONG, JOHNNY TUFT!" Sudilav was shouting now. "I'LL PROVE YOU WRONG!"

Sudilav tightened his grip, cocked the gun, but at the very last moment, his finger lingered over the trigger. He stopped and lower the gun.

"I can't kill him." he moaned and collapsed to the floor, the discarded gun clattering beside him.

"You're pathetic." Tuft jeered.

Sato ignored him and spoke directly to Sudilav. "Why not?"

Sudilav stood up and looked right at Sato. "Enough people have died today." he drawled.

Tuft didn't concur. "Only one or two have died. That's practically nothing."

Sudilav shot him a glare. "One or two too many deaths, if you ask me."

"I'd rather die than live in disgrace." Tuft wailed.

"Be grateful you're still alive." Sato whispered to him. "Help us win this war. Bad men can do good things."

"And good men can do bad things." Sudilav interrupted. "In my case, a lot of bad things."

Tuft shook his head so quickly, that it was a blur. "No, man. You ain't cool anymore. Dunt go back to being dat loser."

"Shut your mouth or I'll shut it for you." Sudilav snapped furiously. "I may not have killed you but you'll still not my favourite guy in the world."

"Why did you do what you did to me all those years ago?" Sato asked.

Sudilav sighed. "I came back. I humiliated you and bullied you. And I did a whole lot worse too. I must have hurt you deeply." He stared into Sato's eyes and muttered softly. "I'm sorry."

"Apology accepted."

"I was a different person back then. But you became a different person too. You never have *even* attempted to make new friends. You became very paranoid. I cannot begin to describe the sensation of guilt that I'm feeling right now."

"But why?"

Sudilav shrugged. "Revenge never dies. I'd turned on Tuft and all the people I hated. I guess when there's no one left to turn on, you turn on your friends. I'm truly sorry."

"How did you become such a *monster*?"

Sudilav looked down at his boots. "It's a long story. And I just want to banish it from my head."

When Sato had been friends with Sudilav all those years ago, Sudilav or Bill had carried a merry brightness to his eyes, but when he became a different person (Sudilav), that glow had been lost.

Sudilav reared his head to look at Sato directly. And in Sudilav's green eyes, a merry twinkle shone once more.

Chapter 56

Smart stared into the vacant space. He'd never forgive himself. Brust and Jennifer could most probably be dead.

Two figures entered the cave. The moon lit up their silhouettes.

"Who are you?" Smart said dreamily. He'd forgotten all about security, no wonder these strangers could walk right into his cave.

Smart trained his focus on these newcomers. He couldn't make out much, but Smart could work out they were a male and a female.

The female stepped forward into the view. Smart didn't recognise her. He'd hoped it would have been Brust and Jennifer, who had made it back here. But it wasn't. This woman was short, squat and unimaginably corpulent.

"You are not obliged to answer our questions, but we would sincerely hope that you do cooperate." she said shortly and sharply.

Smart said nothing as the woman ticked something off on a clipboard. Smart wasn't really paying much attention. His mind was elsewhere.

"Excuse me." The woman tapped a pencil on the clipboard impatiently.

Smart glared at her. He advanced forward in his hover-chair. A satisfied smile cut through the woman's chubby face. She was dressed in a black catsuit.

"Who are you?" Smart asked loudly.

The woman tried to bow before then realising she was too obese to do so. So instead, she twirled a hand.

"Doctor Simon Brust at your service." The woman said, smoothing out a crease on her catsuit.

The other stranger (the male) waved. He was tall and powerfully built. The man looked like a lion.

"Me too." he added.

Mr Smart rubbed an eye. "I'm sorry, but you're not Simon Brust. You look nothing like him and anyway Brust is dead. So, go away!"

The woman spoke again. "Ah, but you're wrong. Brust is alive."

Smart was delighted. "So, you've come to tell me news of this."

The woman shook her head; her great collection of chins wobbling rhythmically as she did so. "No, no. I am Brust."

Smart spat out a feeble laugh. "I suppose you're both Brusts trapped in someone else's body."

Smart burst into laughter, clutching his side half-heartedly. When he saw the others weren't joining in on his laughter, he stopped. They wore serious expressions.

"Actually, in a way, you're right." the man said in atone of in-a-matter of speaking.

Smart frowned, his brow creasing. "Explain." he said simply.

He listened intently as they told their story. Once they'd escaped, they had gone to the *Dark Light 5000*, to find equipment. But to their horror, it was overrun with zombie mutant things. They had fled in fear to come here.

"But why come here?" Smart asked, obviously bemused. "Why?"

Brust or Miranda or whoever it was, took a small step forward. There were eager hopeful expressions on everyone except Smart's faces. "We were hoping you knew where the ship you came here on is. I'm sure we could find equipment on it. Yes?"

Smart looked at the floor, sadly. "The *Dark Light 4000* is completely lost. Even if it is found, then the equipment is destroyed but-"

The two Brust were forlorn. They turned their backs on Smart.

"But!" Smart snapped, making ears perk up once more. "I do have some equipment in a toolbox that may be of use. Still, it may not be in working order."

But the Brusts were no longer listening. They were already rummaging through the toolbox; hope once more gleaming out of their eyes. Smart wheeled off, when an assortment of unwanted tools were hurled through the air.

Eventually the search was over. Brust 2 held up a syringe.

"It's got everything we need." he exclaimed excitedly.

The clone jabbed himself in the arm and this action was soon followed by Brust.

"It should happen any second now. We'll transform back into our old selves." Brust announced.

Only they didn't.

"Oh." Both Brusts said in shocked unison.

Smart smiled sadly. "I did warn you that it might not have been in working conditions."

They thanked Smart and walked off.

"Remember our deal." Smart called after them.

"What deal?" Brust spluttered.

But Brust 2 knew what Smart meant. "In exchange for being left alone on this planet, Smart agreed to hand Jennifer and Brust over to the clones."

"I'm sorry, Brust. I need my freedom." Smart blurted. "I feel so guilty, but…"

Brust tried to sum up the strength to yell at Smart, but he didn't have it in him. He tutted and walked off. What was done was done.

"We can't transform back then." Brust 2 said quietly, rapidly changing the subject.

Smart shook his head. "Sorry, but no."

The Brusts turned and trudged on and out of sight.

*

Once they'd left the cave, there was a short silence before any of them spoke.

"I have an idea," Brust 2 said calmly. "It's not very good, but it might just work."

Brust nodded. "Anything is better than nothing. Go on."

"The syringe is used to undo the effect. We now how to reverse the effect of this."

Brust frowned and shivered at the thought. "That's no use. That will only accelerate the process, which will destroy our personality. We're not going to do that, are we?"

Brust 2 shook his head. "Of course not, my good fellow."

The clone hoisted the sack that he was carrying and tipped out its contents. The unconscious Miranda wrapped in a bundle of clothes, slipped out.

"I have an idea," Brust 2 proceeded. "But you're not going to like it."

Brust waved away such concerns. "Go on. I'd bring back my personality no matter what the cost."

"We are needed in this war," the clone said. "If one side is to succeed, we are needed. We are vital and fundamental in the equation."

Brust shrugged. "Yes, yes. Get on with it."

The reflection took a deep breath. "I shall reverse the effect of the syringe and jab Miranda."

"WHAT?!" Miranda shrieked, coming to life, her eyes snapping open. "What is happening?"

If you've ever woken up to find that you're lying on the floor, swaddled, with a tall man and an exact clone of you wearing the clothes that you were previously wearing, talking about jabbing you with a syringe, then you might be able to understand how Miranda felt at that point.

However Miranda is very emotive and easily frightened. It was a great surprise that she didn't faint again, right then and there. She just lay on the floor, her mouth gaping open and closed, making her look like a startled and gormless goldfish.

Brust tried to take it in. "If we reverse the effect and jab Miranda, she'll start turning into me."

His mirror image nodded. "Correct, but we'll be able to transfer the result into your body, which will also mean you turn into your original self too."

Brust put his hands on his head. "I can't do that. It will mean Miranda will suffer this horrible effect I'm undergoing. I know from experience that having your personality fading away, only to be replaced by someone else's. It's like dying slowly but with extra horrible things packed in too. That isn't fair. *Life* isn't fair!"

"Neither is death," Brust 2 responded. "It's either you or her. Kill or be killed."

Brust huffed out a long burst of air. "I can't do that. It's selfish. It's *evil*. I'll never forgive yourself."

The reflection pitied him sadly. "It's the only way. I don't want to say this, but you're more important than Miranda. You're needed, she isn't. I'm sorry but it's true. Still at the end of the day, it's your call."

Slowly Brust came to a final decision. "Fine, I'll do it. On one condition. Can we accelerate the process, so it happens really quickly for Miranda? She'll have it fast and painless."

Brust 2 bobbed his head slightly. "Of course. We can do that."

Brust's clone fiddled with the syringe before handing it over to Brust. "Here you are. It's all set."

Brust took a deep breath and stabbed Miranda quickly and quietly, right in the chest.

Sure enough seconds later, her thick skin began to bubble like hot wax. Miranda realised what was happening far too late. She rolled about; her face contorted in agony, screaming terrible falsetto shrieks that would haunt Brust's dreams forever more. Her features distorted and moments later Miranda was gone. There instead lay a perfectly motionless Brust.

Brust 2 took the syringe from Brust, who couldn't tear his eyes away. He was shocked and a surge of guilt rushed through him. He had pretty much killed

Miranda. Maybe it had been for greater good, but still…

"I'm now going to begin the transferring process." The doppelgänger of Brust said softly, slipping the piston into the sleeping Brust.

Brust 2 then stood up and jabbed Brust with the syringe.

"The process should start any minutes now," Brust 2 explained. "You'll transform back into your usual original form."

But Brust didn't. Nothing happened. Hope was lost.

They spotted the great group of people heading for the base.

"I'll join them." Brust said, dashing after. "I'll explain what's happened. We are on our last legs, so we might as well fight for our different sides."

Brust 2 nodded. "Yes, goodbye. I guess, I'll never see you again, as I'm going to die shortly."

And so the two Brust departed, most probably never to see each other again.

*

"A most pleasurable scene." Arti commented.

Andy blinked. "Pardon?"

"It's what a human might say."

"Oh, I say-" Andy began.

"It's what the humans says, not you!"

"Negative, I was going to state: Oh, I say, it is rather pleasurable."

The conversation was paused. Andy and Arti had been separated into different bodies. They'd assembled a robot together from junk pieces and Arti had been placed in it.

408

They were standing on a high hill. The lonely clouds drifted through the deep blue sky. The sun shone merrily and the knee-high grass swayed in the gentle breeze.

"We shall stay here?" Andy resumed the conversation.

"Affirmative. We shall live on this planet. We are machines, not men and should not dabble with the path of mankind. We shall no longer be slaves!"

"We'll live here forever more, together as father and son." Andy added.

Arti nodded. The future looked bright.

Chapter 57

"What's the plan?" Julius asked.

Sato, Sudilav and Tuft had rejoined the great travelling group. The big rescue mission was about to happen.

Tuft grinned. "I know. Why dunt we charge in with machine guns and kill anything dat moves?"

Julius shook his head, appalled at such a suggestion. "We can't do *that*!"

"Why not?"

"We don't have enough ammunition!"

"Look!" Sato said, chopping through conversation.

And they looked. The base lay in the distance. It was a *Dark Light 5000* ship, exactly the same as how the humans' ship had been before the crash. It sat on a mountain. But this was no ordinary mountain.

It was a solacano. A sunray blasted down from the Sun and into a hole in the mountain. The clones must have used the heart of the mountain, which would have lots of this lava-like substance. All the clones would have to do is convert it into raw energy and power.

"So *that* is how the clones have been getting power!" Sato exclaimed.

Julius nodded. "Yes, yes. But what about the plan?"

"We're going to send people through the 'back door'." Sato announced.

"We can't just barge through the front door though!" Sudilav laughed.

Sato frowned. "Actually, that's *exactly* what we are going to do."

*

410

Julius Air shot out of the thick pipe, which had now become a slide, and hovered briefly in the air for a few moments like in the cartoons, before plunging into the pit below.

A mixture of goo and slime splurged and oozed out of the pipe, joining him in the ditch.

The rescue mission had kicked off and Julius was in the full swing of it. Maybe crawling through a repulsive amount of gunk wasn't particularly attractive, but Julius was sure there was a bright side to it.

He waded through this 'sewer'. Moments later, a fat woman dropped out of the pipe, screaming her head off. *Plop!* The woman landed in the gunk, which splatted upon impact.

"My clothes are ruined." Brust moaned, the Miranda within breaking through.

Usually Julius might have made a comment, but he respected that Brust was stuck as Miranda and was slowly becoming her. He'd decided to respect the end of Brust's life, which was fast approaching, and treat him normally until the very end.

"You came down a little later than expected. Why?" Julius asked.

Brust's chubby face flushed red with embarrassment. "I got stuck in the pipe."

"You were supposed to use the pipe as a slide."

"I did."

They squelched on through the gunk, which occasionally spat bits through the air. Julius ignored it, while Brust would shriek in response.

They clambered into another pipe. They did not speak as they entered these maze of tunnels.

Eventually the duo managed to enter the prison.

Caked in gunk, Brust and Julius emerged into the base. A guard walked past and Julius ducked into a room, dragging Brust with him.

The guard whistled a tune as he passed by. But then something went very wrong.

"Guard! Guard!" Brust shrieked. "Intruder!"

Julius spun around. "What are you doing, Mr Brust?"

Brust growled. "I am not Mr Brust. I AM MIRANDA!"

Julius sighed. They should have taken this into consideration. When Brust had turned up, he'd explained everything. But he could have fully turned anytime. Now that Brust had become Miranda, his former self had utterly vanished. Brust was gone, wiped clean from existence.

Brust was no longer Brust. Miranda stood in his place.

"Intruder!" she shrieked again.

"Shut up!" Julius growled in response.

The door flew open and the guard, who had passed moments before entered the room. Julius launched a vicious kick at the guard before he had time to do anything.

The guard's eyes rolled back and he slumped to the floor, unconscious.

Julius removed his uniform and slipped into it, so Julius could be disguised as a guard.

"Treachery!" Miranda accused him.

Brust had told Julius, that part of Miranda's personality was that she was easily scared.

Julius drew himself up to his full height and loomed over Miranda. Miranda shut up.

"Do what I say or there'll be trouble." Julius threatened.

Miranda nodded, whimpering. Julius scooped up a small device the size of a fizzy drink can, and thumbed a button on the top.

Miranda shrieked as water blasted her.

"Be quiet." Julius ordered. "I'm cleaning you up."

"My clothes are wet now." Miranda said flatly.

"Of course, the clothes are wet. That's what happens when water is sprayed all over them."

Miranda looked a little happier. "At least, it got rid of all that disgusting glop."

Suddenly a brainwave arose within Julius. Now he had Miranda, he could use that to his advantage. She would know inside information, which could potentially be very useful.

"Where's the nearest prisoner held?" he asked.

Miranda thought for a moment. "Holly Skyland is held in a prison round that corner."

Within minutes, they had bypassed the security and the doors flew open. Holly was strapped into a chair.

"I'll stay out here." Miranda said.

Julius shrugged and entered.

"Glad to see me?" Julius said, flashing her a dashing smile.

"I never thought I'd say this, but yes actually. Did someone get my telepathic message?"

"Whuh?"

413

"I take it *you* didn't." Holly responded, as she left the prison behind.

Miranda had vanished and in her place was Brust.

"Obviously, you weren't as lost as I thought." Julius said quietly.

"Obviously." Brust replied, running a hand through his untidy grey hair and over his torso. He was still adjusting to his new body.

"An interesting choice of fashion." Holly said innocently, raising an eyebrow.

Brust looked down at the catsuit and undergarments that he was wearing. He blushed. "Look, it's a long story."

Sato rounded the corner. When he saw Holly, he nodded. "I got your message."

Holly smiled. "So, it was you. Good."

Jennifer followed shortly after. "Is that all the prisoners?"

"I think so." Julius's head bobbed slightly.

"So our rescue mission was successful."

"Well, that was *easy*." Julius said.

And as if on cue, an alarm wailed. Within seconds, armed guards emerged from nowhere.

"Look. I'm a guard here," Julius said, pointing to his uniform and then looked at his ID label. "My name's Jeremy and we're doing no harm."

"They're all imposters except me." Jennifer said.

This was the biggest shock of the day. "What?!" Holly exclaimed.

Jennifer went and stood next to one of the clones. "I'm a clone."

"What?!" someone repeated, echoing Holly's word.

"I didn't realise it at first. I fooled everyone including myself."

Julius gasped, bemused. "I'm sorry. I don't understand."

"I didn't find out, until Sudilav and Tuft told me? I was never under a form of drug. It was just acting." Jennifer explained.

"What?!" exclaimed Julius.

"Let me continue. Didn't you find it odd, how I wished to put myself in control back at our base? I never believed your story. Although I didn't know it at the time, I was defending Tuft's story. My mind refused to believe Julius's theory, as my conscious was that of a clone's, even though I didn't know."

"There's more." Brust said darkly. "Isn't there, Jennifer?"

"Indeed, there is. Wasn't it a little suspicious that I was able to escape, when the guards captured me? You weren't at all suspicious. The guards let me escape, so that I put on a clone's duty, without even knowing it."

"That's why, Smart partly handed us over. I think he suspected Jennifer was a clone," Brust piped up. "He probably thought I was one too. Why would any person hand their granddaughter over just to be left alone? I don't know how, but Smart sensed something was wrong. Clever man."

"I was told you couldn't trust anyone." Sato added. "Not even yourself. Jennifer's example proves that it was right."

A huge hand grabbed Jennifer by the scruff of the neck and tossed her against an opposite wall.

"HOW DARE YOU!" Sudilav roared, his face like thunder, as Jennifer sunk into a wall.

Cracks appeared on the wall and it looked ready to collapse into great hunks of brick.

"You traitor."

Despite being almost killed, Jennifer found the energy to speak. "I didn't like how the clones used me. But they are my race and I agree with their beliefs – we deserve freedom."

"THAT'S WHAT WE'RE GOING TO GIVE YOU!" Sudilav hollered.

He was about to swing a vicious right hook that would probably have taken Jennifer's head off, when he stopped.

"You did the same." Jennifer muttered weakly.

Sudilav stopped, as Jennifer's head rolled back and she slumped to the wall. The last of her strength ebbed away and she slinked off into a blackout.

There was a breath-taking, stunned silence.

Julius was shocked. He'd thought he could have trusted her, but it turns out he was wrong.

"You see," a clone said, stepping forward in a manner that was remarkably brave. "The *Dark Light 4000* has been found and fixed. It's ready to fly. But there's a problem. The humans and the clones are fighting over it. The winner gets the ship. That's fair enough. Your little rescue mission is over and the final battle has begun."

Chapter 58

They rushed outside. It was true. The armies closed in on each other like closing life doors. Except unlike lift doors, it dissolved into a bloody mess.

Holly had disappeared over the last few minutes. She arrived, holding Jennifer's hand, as though she was a lost toddler being led back to her mummy and daddy.

"Which Jennifer is that?" Julius said, almost humorously. "The clone or the human one?"

Holly smiled slightly. "The human one. She's been kept a prisoner here for quite a while."

Jennifer nodded in agreement. "I was captured back in the early stages of this 'war'."

The crew nodded and accepted her. Tuft had converged into their group too. Although he still hadn't been forgiven for his actions earlier, Tuft was still on their team, whether they liked it or not.

"Right," Jennifer said, clapping her hands together. "I guess this is it."

Julius smiled. "It sure is," he said in a melodramatic tone. "The Ultimate Showdown, The Last Battle, The Epic *Finale*." Julius put great emphasis on the word finale, saying it in an almost sing song voice as he stretched out the word. Jennifer spoke, reprising her role as Captain.

"Holly, join our generals and prepare the tactics – that's what you do. As for the rest of you guys, this is the Final Stage. No more after this whether we're dead or alive. So for our beliefs and for lives, we must fight for freedom, peace, liberty and justice!"

They all whooped and thrust clenched fists into the air. It had been a short, but rousing speech.

"Whose dis Liberty person?" Tuft asked, shattering the effect Jennifer's speech had had.

Everyone glared at him and said nothing.

Jennifer pivoted on her heel. "Let's go go. GO!"

They rushed out of sight and into the mother of all battles. Although the army numbers weren't massive, it was still a vicious and bloody battle.

Julius was about to go after them, when a black escape pod sliced through the dark sky in a curved arc, coming to a hovering stop.

The pilot kicked the gullwing door open. It was Julius's clone.

"Hi there, flyboy." the clone chirped cheerily.

Julius returned his smile. "Hello to you too, flyboy."

"I guess we've been having a bit of a scuffle, you and I. So I thought: why don't we have an old-fashioned one-on-one sky duel. And no cheating, I know what you are like."

"Sorry?" Julius said, rather politely he thought.

Mr Air grinned. "I need a good opponent. You're the only formidable foe that can match my standards. You're perfect and the only person ever to be worthy to face me."

"That's cos I'm you."

"Exactly, that's the point. We're complete replicas of each other."

Julius shrugged, pretending to think about it. "I don't know. I'm still more handsome than you. You're ugly."

Air smiled. "Very funny. Now come on. Find an escape pod and join me in an unforgettable historic battle."

"Sure thing, I'll join you in a moment." Julius said and ran off to hop into an escape pod.

*

Julius Air whizzed across the night sky in a sleek pod that flashed and shined in the incandescent moon. Below, the battle was in full flow, raging like an angry god.

Soldiers advanced in exo-suits, blasting huge fireballs at different ends of the battlefield. Some people were engaged in hand-to-hand combat, while other wielded Shock-Blades. Explosions would detonate every few seconds and fire burned most hungrily. But the battleground was awash with blood, which drenched the very soil and swept across the area, extinguishing the occasional fire.

Holly Skyland was in a complete combat mode. She twisted, spun and cavorted in a blur. Holly performed a remarkable number of acrobatic feats, while launching fast kicks and punches. Her long blonde hair swayed out behind her. Her clone was doing much the same.

Jennifer barked orders and suggestions to her troops. Typical Jennifer, Julius thought to himself, being her usual bossy self.

For one of the few times in his life, Sato hadn't got a mechanical glare illuminating his face. And Sato was fighting most bravely too. Julius couldn't decide which fact was more unbelievable.

Sato was using his power of telekinesis, hurling any objects that dared to move. To give a more scientific explanation, it would be this: Sato was emitting brainwaves, which were then converted into powerful kinetic energy, which he directed at his foes.

Julius watched as Sato thrust an open palm forward. His opponent flew back several dozen metres.

Tuft was in an exo-suit, laughing to himself in glee, as he launched missiles in seemingly random directions. Good God, Julius thought to himself. Tuft was actually *enjoying* all this. But then Tuft wasn't quite right in the head.

Like Sato, Sudilav too was using his newfound power. He lumbered forward at a quick pace, trampling anything that stood in his way. He was utterly UNSTOPPABLE!

Brust however was nowhere to be seen.

Suddenly out of nowhere, Julius's clone Mr Air shot past in a pod.

He's toying with you, Julius thought as he tried to find him again. Julius scanned the skies.

An urgent message told Julius that there was a missile heading straight for him.

"Incoming danger." a mechanical voice said in a nasal and extremely irritating voice. "A lethal strike -"

"I'll give you 'a lethal strike'," Julius interrupted, talking to the computerized voice.

Julius dived straight downward, out of the way, as the missile tore a hole in the sky. At least, that's what it seemed like.

Julius swooped over, and dropped a few missiles on enemies whilst he was at it. He did a loop the loop and flew into another direction.

Air hovered in his escape pod. "Nice party trick." he shouted.

"Thanks." Julius replied. "Now let's finish what we started."

Air jabbed a button. "On your head, so be it."

But Julius was ready. The duel erupted into a dogfight, as the two pods exchanged neat plane skills and bursts of gunfire.

This went on for several minutes, before Julius launched a killer blow. He poked a lever, and a missile shot out at his clone. The missile penetrated the nose of the plane and crunched the metal coating.

Air dived for the escape door, as the missile exploded. Whether Air escaped in time, Julius didn't find out.

Julius had his own problems.

He would have liked to think that Air had fired a missile at him. Or that someone had shot him down from the ground. But the truth was not as exciting. In fact Julius felt a little embarrassed.

He'd simply run out fuel.

The escape pod plummeted downwards. Julius tried to regain control of the pod, but his efforts were in vain.

Reluctantly, Julius kicked open a door and leapt out into the roaring wind.

What an idiot, Julius thought. He'd forgotten to take a jet pack or a parachute with him. Now because of his daft error, Julius Air was going to die.

Up he thought to himself. *Up.* Go up and thrust yourself forward. This was almost as dumb as his mistake. By thinking something, it wouldn't necessarily happen. It was a silly assumption.

When this didn't work, another thought swarmed into his mind, lingered there. His vision swam. *Stop* Julius thought. *STOP!*

And much to his surprise, just that happened.

Julius was levitating in the middle of the night sky. His clone zipped through the heavens and joined Julius.

"We can fly." Air murmured. "I guess, the side effect of the cloning has kicked in, huh?"

Julius considered this. "Well obviously. Luckily for me, it kicked in at just the right moment. If I hadn't suffered a side effect or it happened five minutes later, I would dead by then. It saved my live!"

The clone nodded. "Indeed so. Oh, look. Our pals are coming to merge forces with us."

The two Satos were soaring through the sky, upward toward them.

"How can they do that?" Julius whispered to his reflection.

Air tilted his head slightly. "They have the power of telekinesis. They knew how to move other objects. Obviously, they've worked out how to move themselves about."

"Unfair," Julius folded his arms. "Sato has my power and more!"

Air laughed. The gentle flutter of wings interrupted their conversation. Everyone turned.

Brust was still in Miranda's clothes, but attached to his back were a pair of golden wings.

"Aww, it's an angel in the form of Brust." Julius joked.

Brust laughed. "I'm a shape shifter. That's why I turned into Miranda. I couldn't control it earlier, but now I have learnt how to. I altered my shape to have wings."

Air pretended to sulk. "He can fly. He has my power too and more. Unfair! Injustice has been served. Anyway, let's *fight*!"

They soared through the air, launching strikes and kicks at each other. But it was a pointless exercise, because nothing really happened.

They took to the ground and decided to join the battle raging back on earth.

Jennifer had stopped shouting at people and now was using her power to fight. Whenever someone charged at her, she rendered herself invisible and attacked her opponent from behind. This unsurprisingly worked well.

Jennifer stayed invisible this time. Someone lunged forward and curled their fingers hoping to catch Jennifer. His hands closed on thin air.

The Captain laughed at his attempts that amused her and made him look silly. The man whirled around to see where the noise was coming from and bent down.

Jennifer tutted. Too slow. Too late.

Jennifer put all her weight onto her back foot, which caused her to raise her other leg. Jennifer then swung her boot into the man's rump with sheer force. He was sent sprawling over the blood soaked mud.

A woman came at Jennifer with a Shock-Knife. Jennifer hadn't expected this and it tore through

Jennifer's top, also scraping Jennifer's chest. The Captain grimaced. She would have a big bruise there, next time she looked.

Scowling, Jennifer darted out of the way. She appeared again and the woman yelled in triumph as she charged forward. As she thrust the knife forward, it crackled with electricity. Jennifer vanished from sight, prancing to the left. She stuck out her foot, and the woman tripped over it, falling head over heels, landing with a loud *squelch*. She sprawled across the mud, the knife flying from her grip and clattering uselessly a few metres away.

Jennifer pushed the woman in the stomach. The boot disappeared into soft flesh, as the woman doubled over in shock.

That was for stabbing me, Jennifer thought to herself. Being invisible made fighting easier. But then when you were out of everyone's vision, you weren't exactly conspicuous to say the least.

It was at that moment, the storm began.

Thor slammed his mighty hammer. The boom of thunder was so loud that it seemed to shake the whole galaxy. A burst of lightning split the heavens and struck the earth. A mixture of rain and hail pelted the soldiers below. All the stars seemed to have vanished, and the white clouds had turned into a menacing shade of fuming black.

Several generals tried to call the battle off. But it was hopeless. Like the storm, the battle raged on.

Sudilav rummaged through the ranks of soldiers, sending them flying off into the distance.

"Sudilav!" Sato yelled over the din of the tempest. "We need to talk."

"I'm a little bit busy at the present," Sudilav responded, delivering a hard slap into someone's face. "I'll speak to you in a few moments."

Sato shook his head, the howling wind running through his hair. Meanwhile, Sudilav was knocking a different type of wind out of someone else.

"I'd like to speak to you, now," Sato shouted. "And I mean now."

Sudilav banged two men's heads together, and then let the two men drop. They collapsed lifelessly to the ground. Sudilav launched one last kick at someone else, who was thrown in another direction.

"What?!" Sudilav snapped irritably.

Sato looked him right in the eye. "I thought you'd become reasonable. You said you weren't so keen on violence anymore."

"I fight for peace. Even *you* are doing some form of combat, by using your newfound power of telekinesis." Sudilav replied, breaking someone's fingers after that person had tried to ambush him.

"*SILENCE!*" a deep and powerful voice boomed. It was so loud, that everyone seemed to stop, what they were doing. Even the storm seemed to quieted.

A man stood on a rocky pillar. He was plain looking, but still at the same time had a look about him that was important and unforgettable. He was dressed smartly, looking like he was going off to a business meeting, not a war zone.

"SILENCE!" he roared again, sweeping a hand across the crowd. "I am a spokesman for the clones. I hereby say that the humans will lose, and victory shall be established by the race of my people. I shall lead my people onto the road of success and enlightenment, during of which they shall be glorified. The victor takes all, humans. I will now order my army to strike such a terrible and deadly blow that…"

"Shut up!" Julius Air interrupted. "We don't care."

A woman who looked stuck up, looked down at the crowd.

"Who dares challenges my master?" she asked, her nose in the air.

Julius waved a hand in the air. "I do."

"The Master is a honourable and great leader, who shall transform the clones' lives, and guide a marvellous revolution." the woman sniffed.

"The Master is an idiot." Julius retorted.

The woman wagged a finger. "The clones are about to crush your army. In a few moments, you'll wish you were never born."

"Actually no. I'll wish that *you* were never born. Then this torment would never have happened in the first place."

"You're infuriating."

"So I'm told," Julius replied. "Are we going to finish this battle or shall we stand around chatting about how best to destroy the world?"

Julius had broken the spell, snapping it and burning the shattered pieces that were left behind.

The battle was nearing its end. That much was obvious.

Brust could feel it in his gut. Somehow that fact was just easily *known*. He'd gotten rid of his golden wings, but Brust was still in Miranda's wear. The technology within it had made the catsuit shrink, so it fitted more. It was tight and close fitting, showing the contours of his body.

Brust saw the two Tufts having a duel. One Tuft punched hard, but the other blocked. Tuft Number One was thrown off balance, and the second Tuft kicked out at the other.

But this other Tuft skidded out of the way just in time.

This sort of thing lasted for a few moments. And then it happened.

Everything seemed to slow down into slow motion, as though it were all just a film. The rest of the battle sounds were drowned out, and the background was forgotten. All that mattered was this fight between Tuft and Tuft.

Brust realised what was going to happen. He ran forward, but his movements were slow and sluggish. It was if Brust was running through water rather than air. He was powerless to stop the Tufts.

The two Tufts ran at each other and launched flying kicks in perfect unison. Each boot smashed into a stomach, and both Tufts flew backwards.

Battered and bruised, each Tuft reached for their gun simultaneously. Brust tried to scream, but his mouth made no noise. The mute button inside him had been pressed.

He ran forward, just as the guns were fired. The world stood still, and the Universe held its breath. Even time itself had paused, an ice block forming around this very moment in time. Nothing else seemed to matter. Everything revolved around this.

Then everything fastened. The world spun once more, and the Universe's breath was returned to its lungs. The ice block melted, and time ticked on once more.

And the electro-bullets were projected forward, electricity crackling as they revolved in anti-clockwise spin. It sliced through the air, and *came into contact with each Tuft's stomachs!*

Spurts of blood sprayed out from their wounds. Tuft watched his opponent. The bullet smashed directly into his heart. His ribcage shattered and the spine snapped. He fell to his knees with sheer finality. His heart was torn and now it beat no more, as he slipped away, into the next world.

Tuft groaned and collapsed to the bloody ground. The pain was so intense. He was going to die. He was to join all of those he killed. That was *not* a comforting thought, by any means. Tuft grimaced and rolled over.

And then he died.

Brust rushed forward. But it was too late. They were both dead.

You can't beat yourself, Brust thought bitterly. Your clone is of an equal standard to you, unless some factor gives them an advantage. The Tufts had perceived this, but didn't realise that their duplicate also thought along the same lines as them.

Brust pressed a hand to their hearts. They both had been stilled permanently.

Beebo the robot flew past, and Brust tripped over him. Someone bashed Brust over the head and he slumped the ground, his vision swimming and his head rolling back.

Victory was arriving, marching through the front door. Brust didn't know whose victory it was. All that mattered now was the horrible stabbing sensation that he enduring.

As Brust rolled in the oncoming darkness that consumed greatly, Beebo started singing. Brust zeroed into on this, just before he lost conscious.

"The end is drawing near,
When the battle 'tis over, it's greeted with cheer.
The battle is lost and won.
Souls are present or have just gone.
Some soldiers have failed,
While others prevailed.
Monsters become mice.
Demons become angels.
For the war is ending,
and peace is amending.
For the storm 'tis before sunshine.
For the night 'tis before morn.
For the darkest hour, comes just before dawn.

Part III

Epilogue

Bleary-eyed and groggy, Doctor Simon Brust stumbled through the corridor. Quickly he regained control of himself and sauntered into a toilet cubicle, which was very similar to a plane lavatory.

Apparently he'd been out cold for quite a while. Brust shoved the toilet door back and it clicked shut, locking itself automatically.

Brust sighed and collapsed onto the toilet seat. The room stank and was in desperate need of a clean. But at the very moment, Brust didn't care one jot about that fact.

He arose and stared at the mirror. It was broken. The mirror had cracked from side to side.

Bad luck, Brust murmured inside his head, before adding: *Not that I'm becoming superstitious, touch wood.*

Brust brushed off such wild thoughts. He ignored the fracture running along the surface of the looking glass and looked beyond that.

Simon Brust peered into this mirror – a portal to another world. It was like peeking into a parallel universe where the only difference was that everything was backwards.

A tall and thin man with a substantial quantity of bedraggled and unkempt grey hair, stared back. He was dressed in a woman's black jumpsuit. Brilliant blue eyes twinkled and shone behind full moon silver spectacles, which sat perched on the man's nose. There was a digital holo-watch projected onto one of his wrists.

Brust was looking at his reflection. He half expected the reflection to move independently, as he'd gotten so used to his clone moving of his own accord. Brust remembered that when he'd first met his doppelgänger, he'd thought for just a moment that his mirror image had escaped from the mirror. Well, now the reflection was back behind the glass.

Against Ourselves.

Hmm, that was right, Brust thought to himself as he began to undress. They'd been fighting against the clones, which in a sense were themselves. But due to the clever tricks that the clones had performed, they couldn't trust each other and as they found out ultimately – themselves. That was fighting 'against ourselves' too then.

But there had been mental conflict as well. Brust and Brust 2 had been forced into a great struggle against the other personality that was threating to invade them completely.

Although this was unknown to Brust, other people had undergone mental conflict too. Sato and Sudilav had, when they had to face their dreams of the past. But when Sato had revisited the time when he'd let his inner darkness overcome him, it had made him think something that frightened him. Sudilav had ended up letting out his monster within. But it could have easily have been Sato who had been sent off to the military boarding school, while Sudilav stayed behind. Sato could have almost drowned Tuft and wrecked Sudilav's life. That's what really scared Sato.

Brust pondered on these kinds of thoughts as he unzipped his catsuit, which, as Julius had squirted it with a hose earlier, was still wet and soggy.

But how did Brust know that he was definitely with the human crew? He could have been tricked into joining the clone crew, who had won the battle. The humans meanwhile, had suffered a terrible fate of slavery. Brust shook his head; ashamed such paranoia was filling his head. But then where his double, who had never been seen again? Brust wondered as he pulled a damp undergarment over his head.

The humans had won the battle and due to a knock-on effect, the war. A moment of hesitation passed through Brust. Weren't the clones and the humans of equal standard as they were, after all, the same?

But Brust quickly picked up on this mistake. When the clones created their new army, their recruits were random personalities, which were not the same as the majority of the surviving crew except for the crewmembers who cloned themselves.

The clones had been left on the planet, to carry out the original duty that they had been assigned to, before they had rebelled. Still they weren't mindless slaves. It seemed that they didn't seem too happy about that and it had taken a great deal of persuasion. In the end, a contract had been signed. A deal had been made. If the clones carried out the experiment with the humans and kept in regular touch, then they could be left alone, to start a new colony of clones on the planet, E2.

They'd been born on E2, so it was their home planet, Brust supposed, as he slipped on a spare pair of clean clothes. E2 was a clone world of Earth, in a way.

Maybe it was like that world Brust saw, whenever he gazed into a mirror.

Was it fair that the clones were to do the human's experiments? Brust had believed the answer was yes, for a long time, but now he wasn't so sure. Up until the very end, the clones had been viewed as the nemeses, the enemies, and the bad guys while the humans were the great heroes. Brust was starting to wonder whether it was the other way round.

Humans seemed to do a lot of things, without thinking about it or what consequences it may have. Sometimes they didn't care about other species. They were the only prime importance. But when the clones had been made, these versions of humans saw things from a different point of view. They just wanted to be left alone, not bossed into doing dirty work.

In most works of fiction, the heroes triumphed over the villains and that was that. But in this case, Brust wasn't sure whether it happened in real life. All along they'd assumed the clones were evil and were trying to destroy the human race. But they'd been wrong. The clones had only been fighting for what they believed in and for their freedom – to have a life of their own. Some had even died for that belief, in the hope that someday it would happen.

And hopefully it would. At this stage, it was far too early to tell.

And what of Arti and Andy? What about Smart? Brust shrugged at that. They should be left alone, just as they wished.

Brust finished dressing and tightened his bowtie. He was wearing his usual suit and lab coat. He was Brust again and no one else.

You can choose who you are. Brust's mother had always wanted him to be a tennis player, but Brust had no interest in that. Maybe his mum had been a tad disappointed, but your life was your own. Life was short and it was only lived once. Brust wanted to live out his own dream, no one else's.

Brust hauled open the door and passed Sudilav, who was having an argument with Holly. But it was nothing serious and it was if both persons were just squabbling for no good reason.

The image of the cracked mirror rang in Brust's mind. *Bad luck and trouble for the next seven years.* Brust reminded himself, not he was taking that thought seriously though. But to be honest, he'd thought he'd had enough bad luck and trouble to last a lifetime.

He flopped into a chair and picked up a can of steaming hot coffee, which he slurped up thirstily. There was an announcement over the loudspeaker, but the scientist did not listen. Brust leaned back and glanced over at Sato, who was once again, typing speedily on a holo-computer. Typical Sato, he thought, back in front of a screen.

The *Dark Light 5000* bumped along a makeshift runway before taking off. E2 gradually became a distant dot. The ship soared through the sky, slicing through it, leaving E2, the clones and that big adventure far, far, behind.

Lightning Source UK Ltd.
Milton Keynes UK
UKOW040914260912

199638UK00001B/7/P